D0507625

TERRIBLE LIZARD

DISCARD

TERRIBLE LIZARD

WRITTEN BY:
CULLEN BUNN

ILLUSTRATED BY:
DREW MOSS

COLORED BY:
RYAN HILL

LETTERED BY:
CRANK!

EDITED BY:
CHARLIE CHU

BOOK DESIGNED BY:
HILARY THOMPSON

LOGO DESIGNED BY:
JASON STOREY

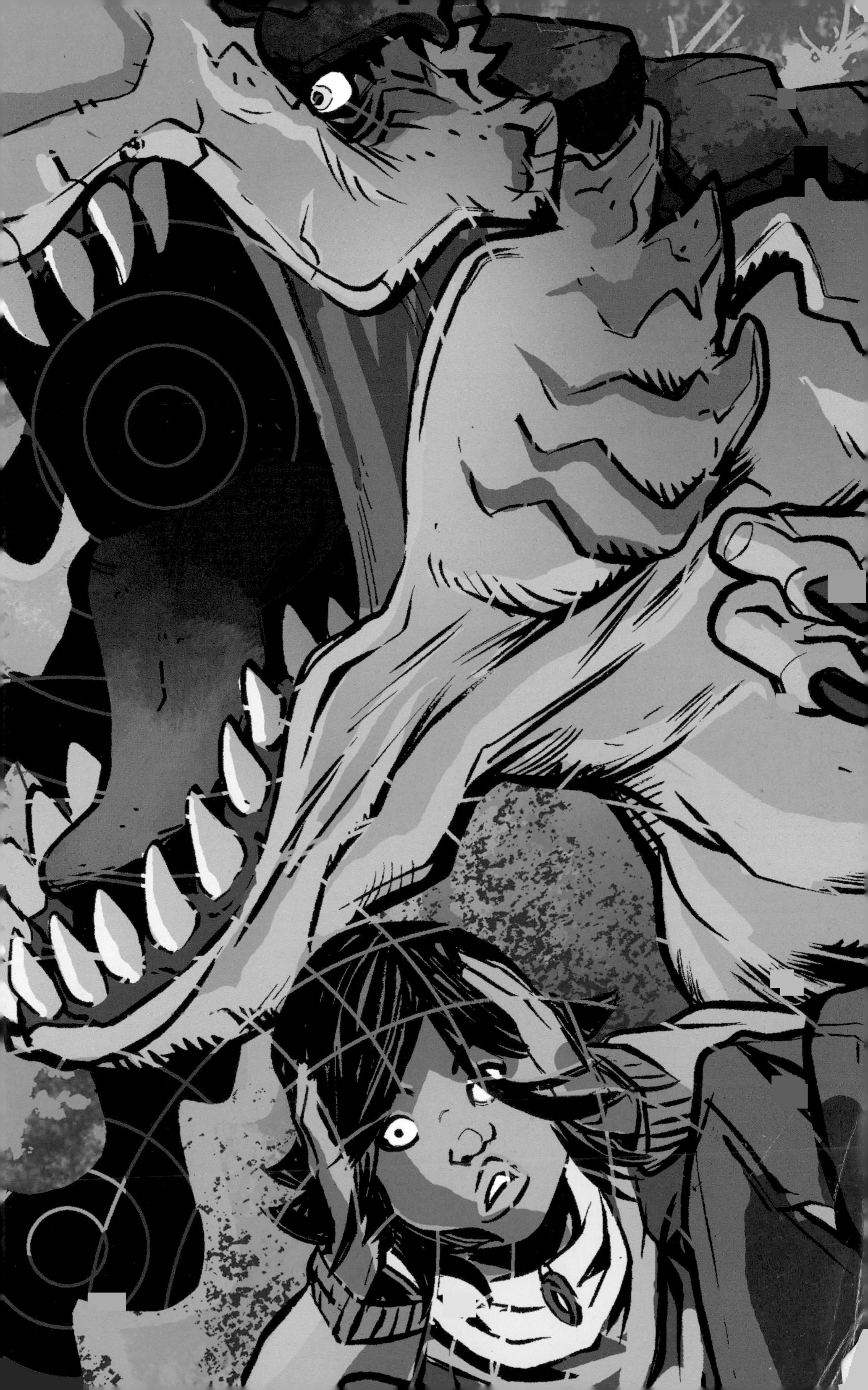

PUBLISHED BY ONI PRESS, INC.

JOE NOZEMACK, PUBLISHER

JAMES LUCAS JONES, EDITOR IN CHIEF

TIM WIESCH, VP OF BUSINESS DEVELOPMENT

CHEYENNE ALLOTT, DIRECTOR OF SALES

TROY LOOK, PRODUCTION MANAGER

HILARY THOMPSON, GRAPHIC DESIGNER

CHARLIE CHU, EDITOR

ROBIN HERRERA, ASSOCIATE EDITOR

BRAD ROOKS, INVENTORY COORDINATOR

ARI YARWOOD, ADMINISTRATIVE ASSISTANT

JUNG LEE, OFFICE ASSISTANT

JARED JONES, PRODUCTION ASSISTANT

ONI PRESS, INC.
1305 SE MARTIN LUTHER KING JR BLVD
SUITE A
PORTLAND, OR 97214

ONIPRESS.COM
FACEBOOK.COM/ONIPRESS
TWITTER.COM/ONIPRESS
ONIPRESS.TUMBLR.COM

CULLENBUNN.COM
@CULLENBUNN
FACEBOOK.COM/DREWERDMOSS
@DREW_MOSS

@JOSEPHRYANHILL

@CCRANK

Originally published as issues 1-5 of the Oni Press comic series *Terrible Lizard*.

First edition: April 2015
ISBN 978-1-62010-236-7
eISBN 978-1-62010-237-4

Library of Congress Control Number: 2014953579

10 8 6 4 2 1 3 5 7 9

Terrible Lizard. April 2015. Published by Oni Press, Inc. 1305 SE Martin Luther King, Jr. Blvd., Suite A, Portland, OR 97214. Terrible Lizard is ™ & © 2015 Cullen Bunn & Drew Moss. All rights reserved. Oni Press logo and icon ™ & © 2015 Oni Press, Inc. Oni Press logo and icon artwork created by Keith A. Wood. The events, institutions, and characters presented in this book are fictional. Any resemblance to actual persons, living or dead, is purely coincidental. No portion of this publication may be reproduced, by any means, without the express written permission of the copyright holders. Printed in china.

CHAPTER ONE

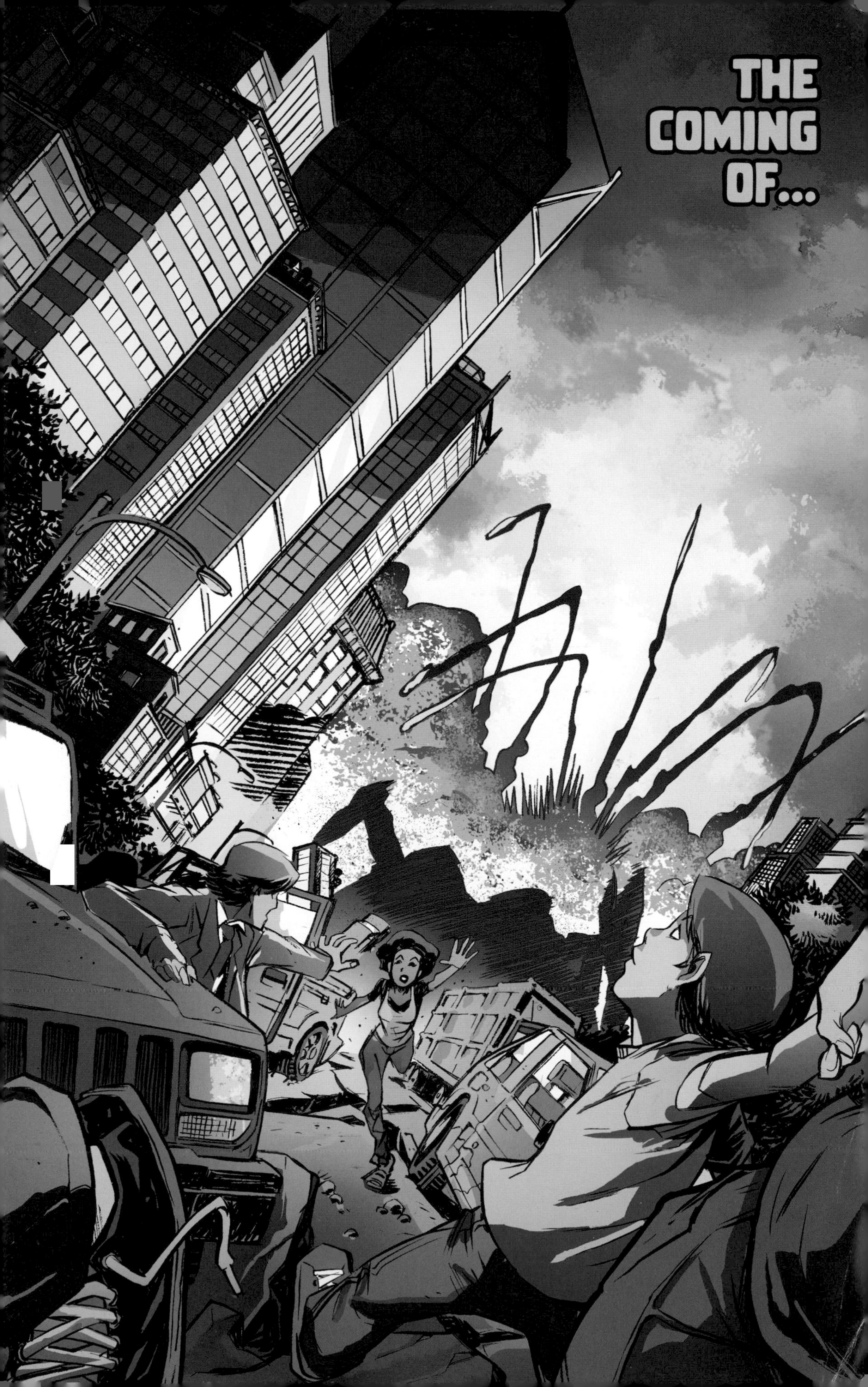
THE COMING OF...

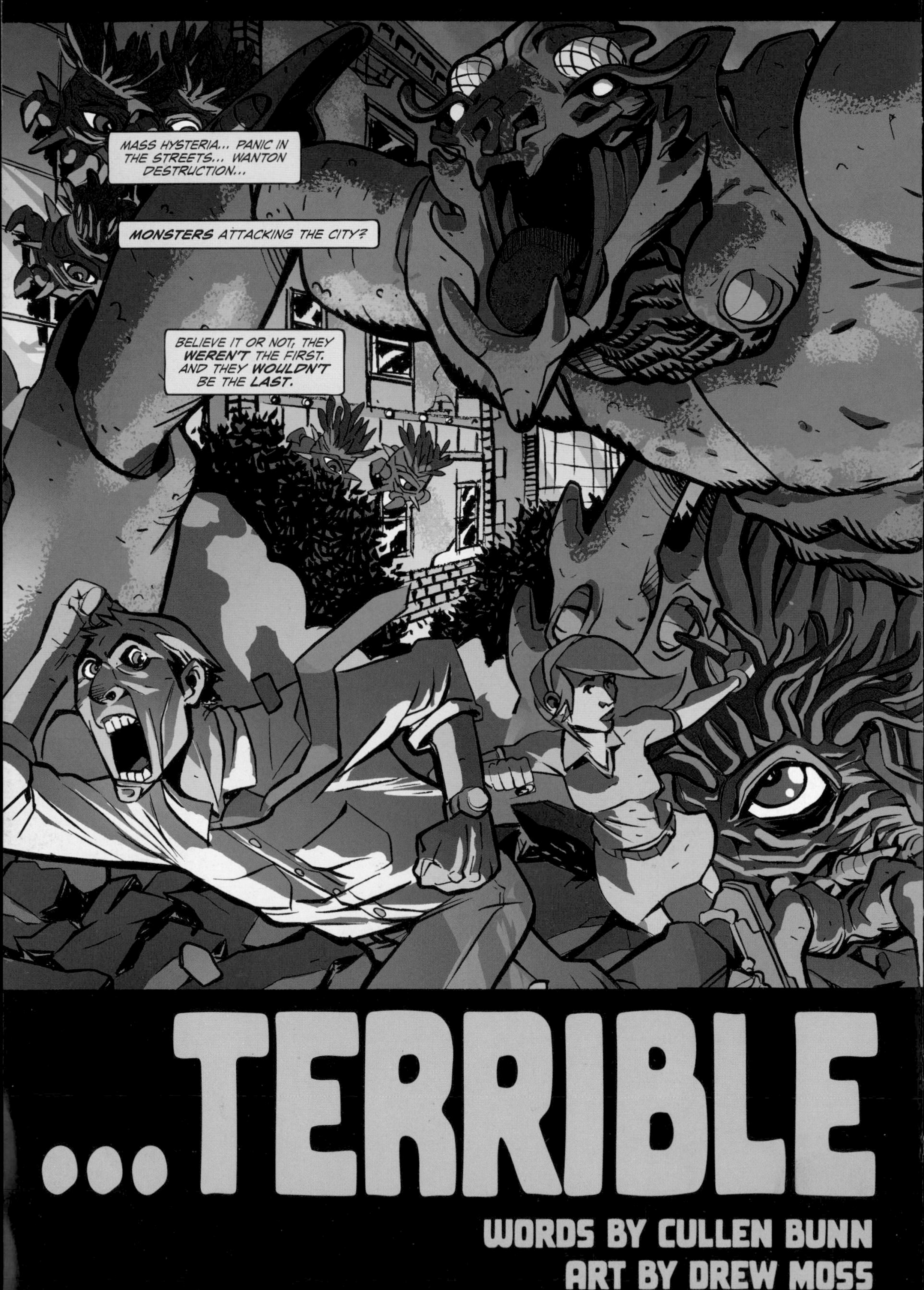
MASS HYSTERIA... PANIC IN THE STREETS... WANTON DESTRUCTION...
MONSTERS ATTACKING THE CITY?
BELIEVE IT OR NOT, THEY WEREN'T THE FIRST. AND THEY WOULDN'T BE THE LAST.

...TERRIBLE

WORDS BY CULLEN BUNN
ART BY DREW MOSS

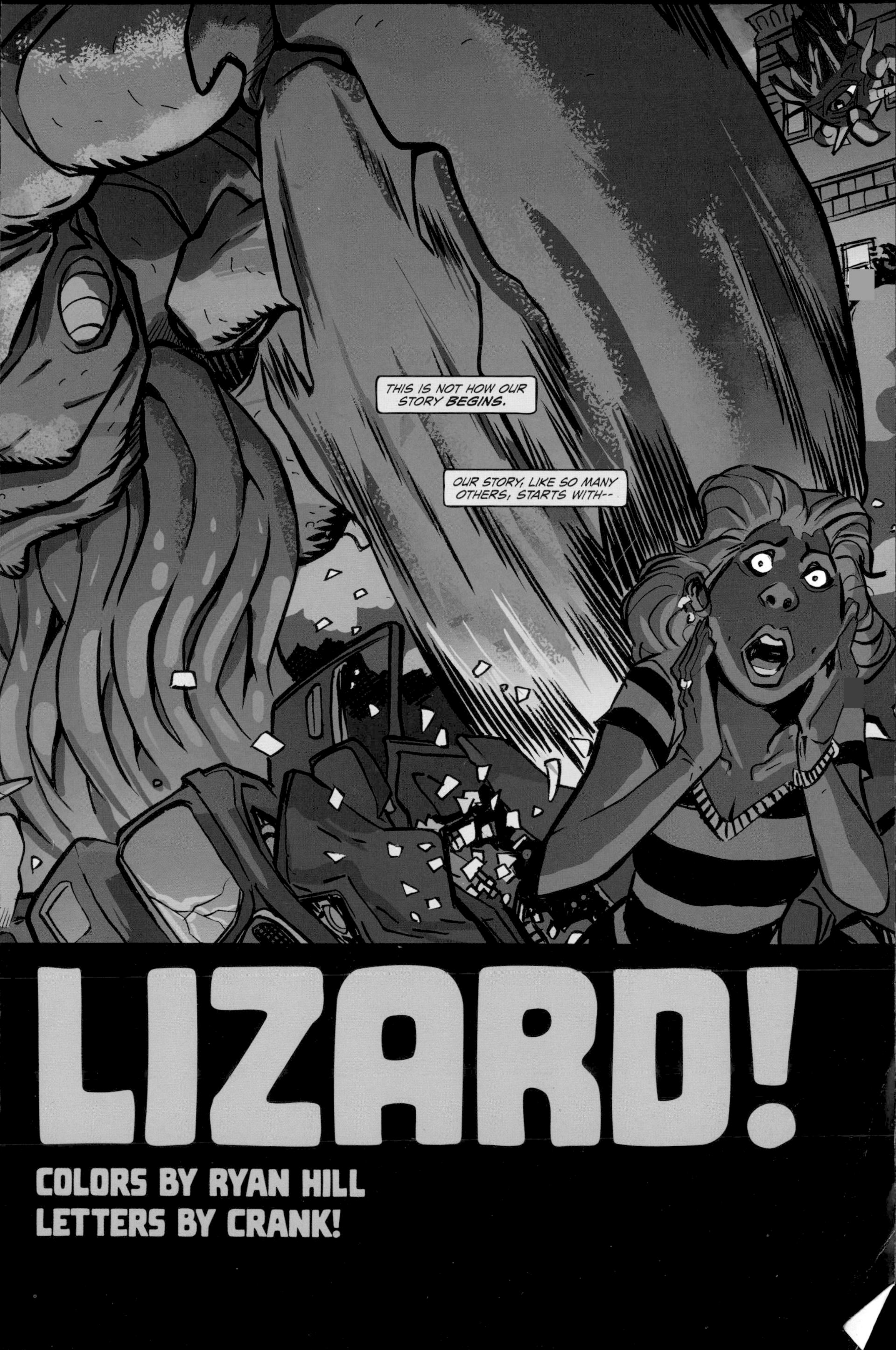
THIS IS NOT HOW OUR STORY BEGINS.
OUR STORY, LIKE SO MANY OTHERS, STARTS WITH--

LIZARD!

COLORS BY RYAN HILL
LETTERS BY CRANK!

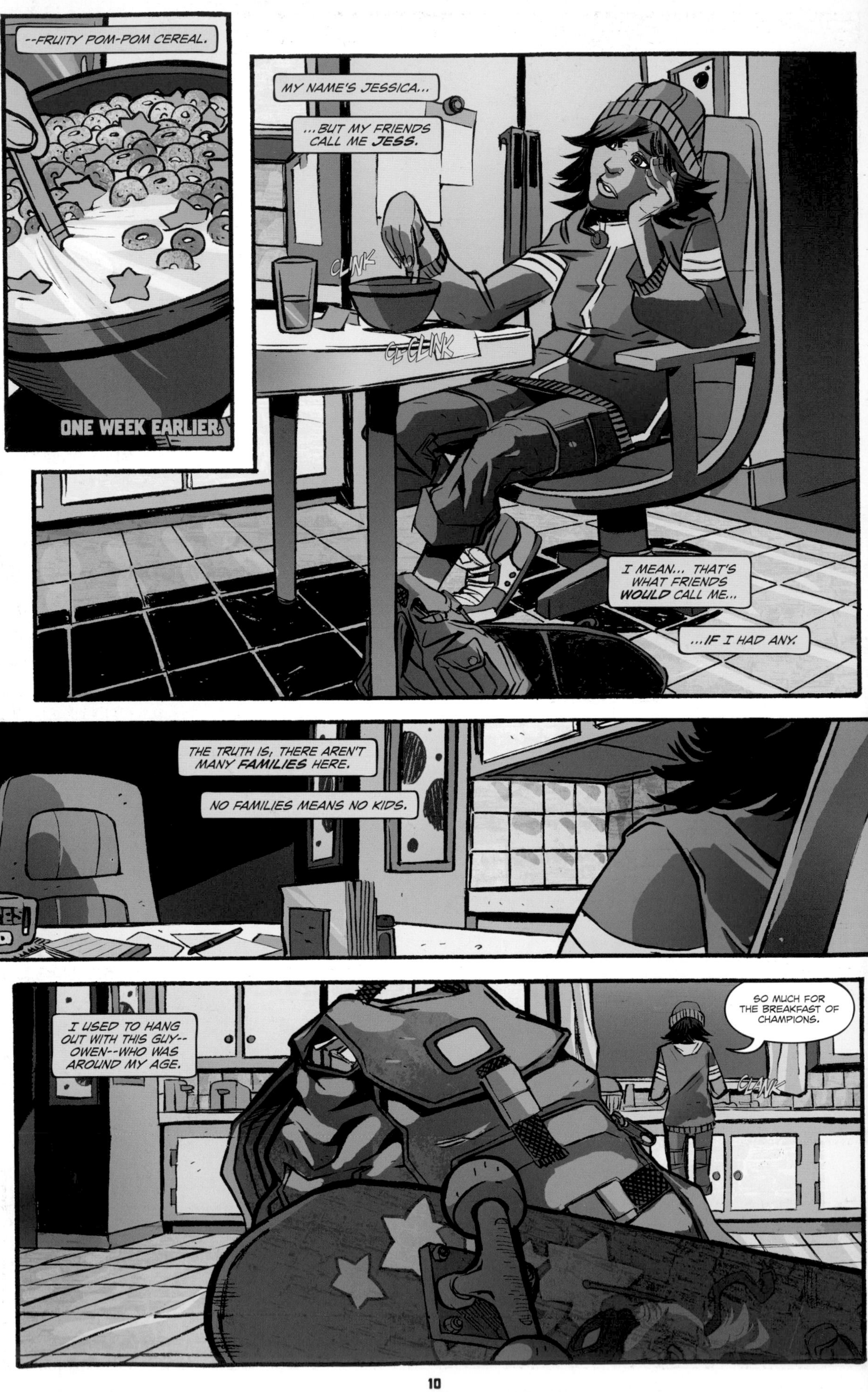

--FRUITY POM-POM CEREAL.
ONE WEEK EARLIER.
MY NAME'S JESSICA...
...BUT MY FRIENDS CALL ME JESS.
CLINK
CL-CLINK
I MEAN... THAT'S WHAT FRIENDS WOULD CALL ME...
...IF I HAD ANY.
THE TRUTH IS, THERE AREN'T MANY FAMILIES HERE.
NO FAMILIES MEANS NO KIDS.
I USED TO HANG OUT WITH THIS GUY--OWEN--WHO WAS AROUND MY AGE.
SO MUCH FOR THE BREAKFAST OF CHAMPIONS.
CLANK

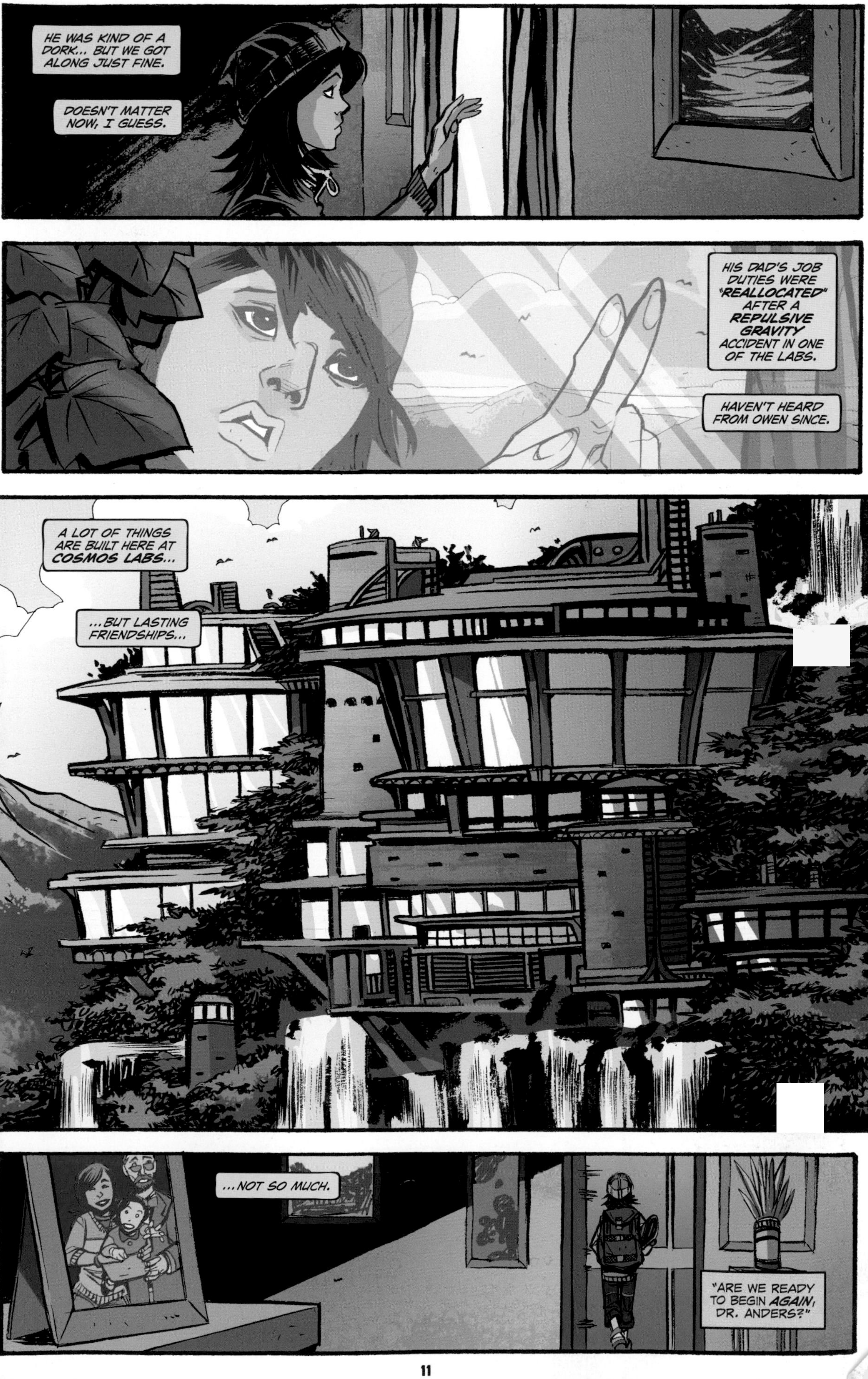
HE WAS KIND OF A DORK... BUT WE GOT ALONG JUST FINE.
DOESN'T MATTER NOW, I GUESS.
HIS DAD'S JOB DUTIES WERE "REALLOCATED" AFTER A REPULSIVE GRAVITY ACCIDENT IN ONE OF THE LABS.
HAVEN'T HEARD FROM OWEN SINCE.
A LOT OF THINGS ARE BUILT HERE AT COSMOS LABS...
...BUT LASTING FRIENDSHIPS...
...NOT SO MUCH.
"ARE WE READY TO BEGIN AGAIN, DR. ANDERS?"

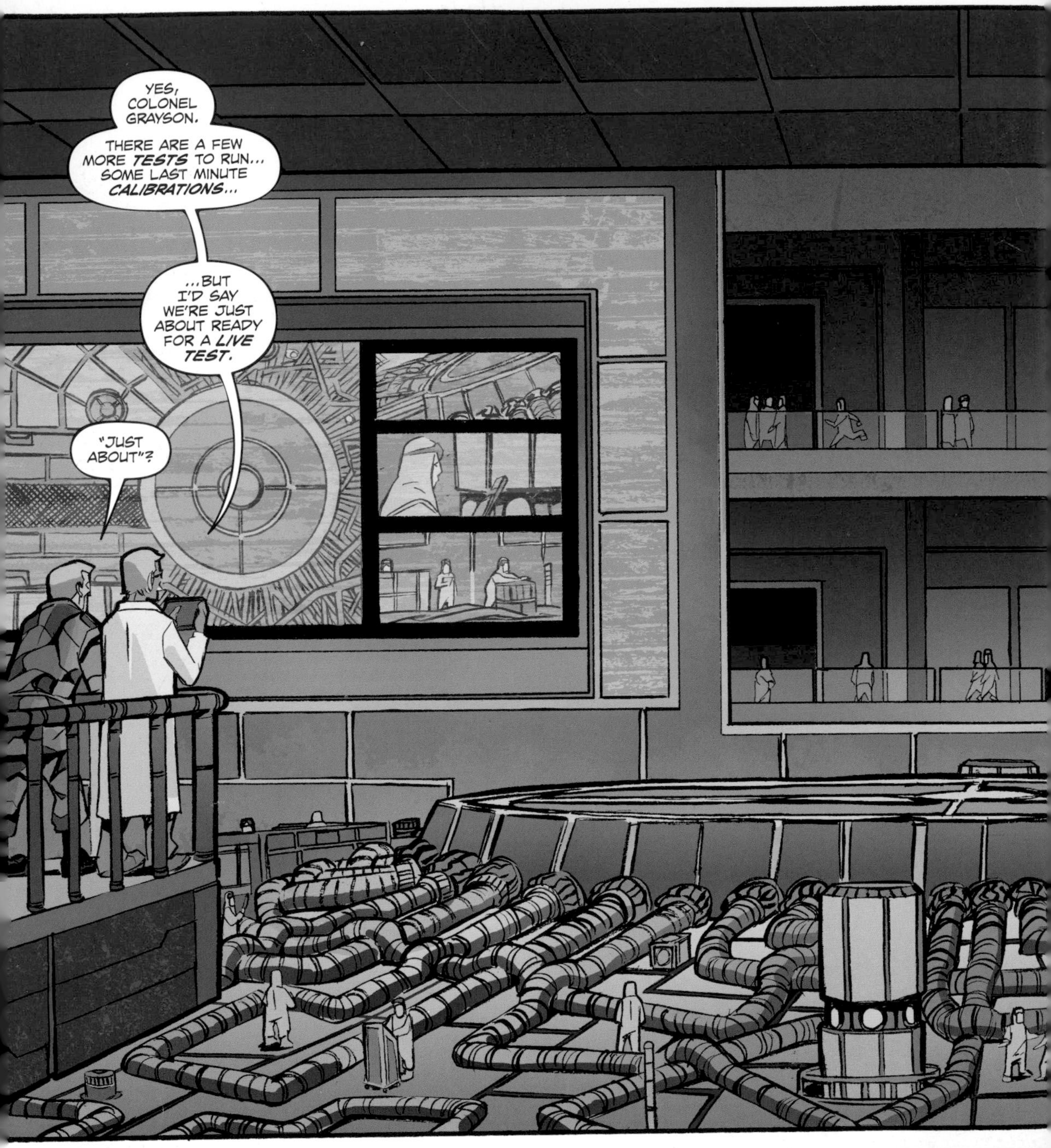
YES, COLONEL GRAYSON.
THERE ARE A FEW MORE TESTS TO RUN... SOME LAST MINUTE CALIBRATIONS...
...BUT I'D SAY WE'RE JUST ABOUT READY FOR A LIVE TEST.
"JUST ABOUT"?

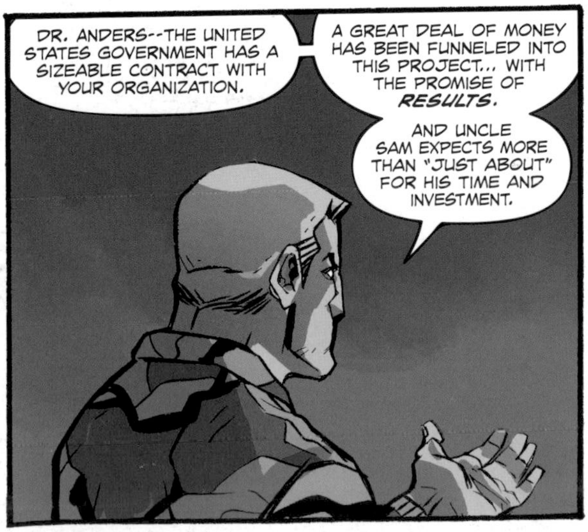
DR. ANDERS--THE UNITED STATES GOVERNMENT HAS A SIZEABLE CONTRACT WITH YOUR ORGANIZATION.
A GREAT DEAL OF MONEY HAS BEEN FUNNELED INTO THIS PROJECT... WITH THE PROMISE OF RESULTS.
AND UNCLE SAM EXPECTS MORE THAN "JUST ABOUT" FOR HIS TIME AND INVESTMENT.

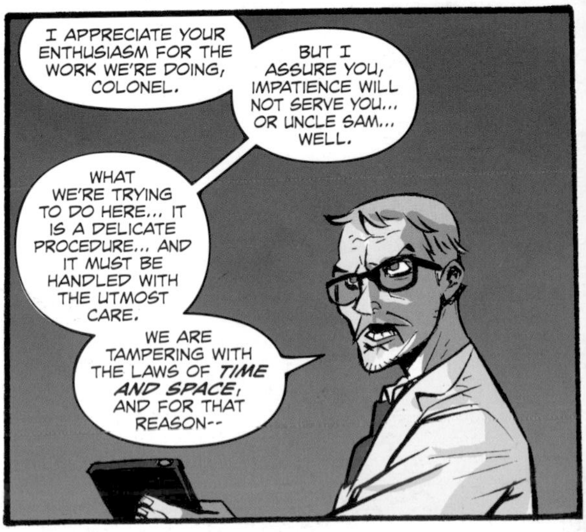
I APPRECIATE YOUR ENTHUSIASM FOR THE WORK WE'RE DOING, COLONEL.
BUT I ASSURE YOU, IMPATIENCE WILL NOT SERVE YOU... OR UNCLE SAM... WELL.
WHAT WE'RE TRYING TO DO HERE... IT IS A DELICATE PROCEDURE... AND IT MUST BE HANDLED WITH THE UTMOST CARE.
WE ARE TAMPERING WITH THE LAWS OF TIME AND SPACE, AND FOR THAT REASON--

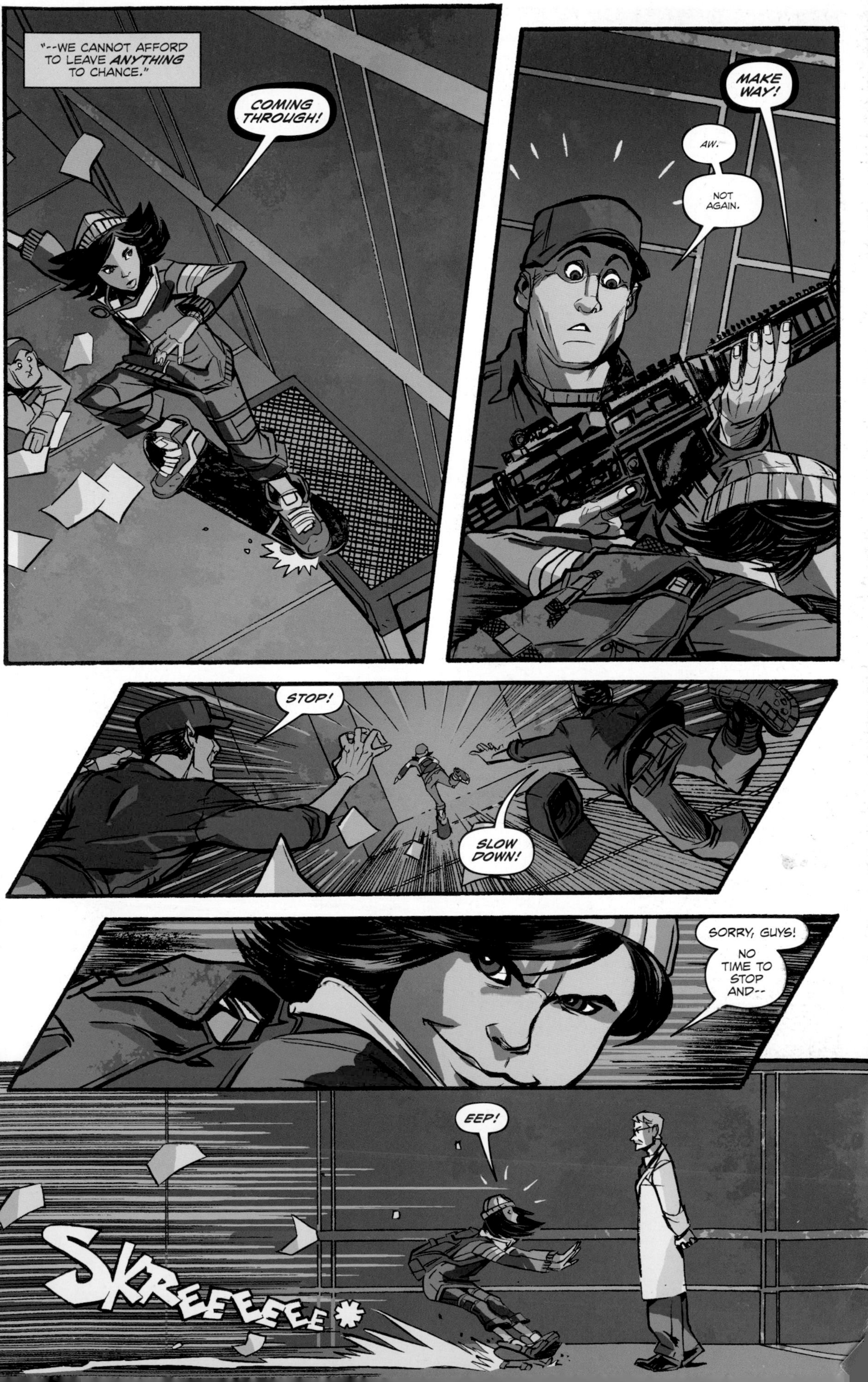
"--WE CANNOT AFFORD TO LEAVE *ANYTHING* TO CHANCE."
COMING THROUGH!
MAKE WAY!
AW.
NOT AGAIN.
STOP!
SLOW DOWN!
SORRY, GUYS!
NO TIME TO STOP AND--
EEP!
SKREEEEEEE*

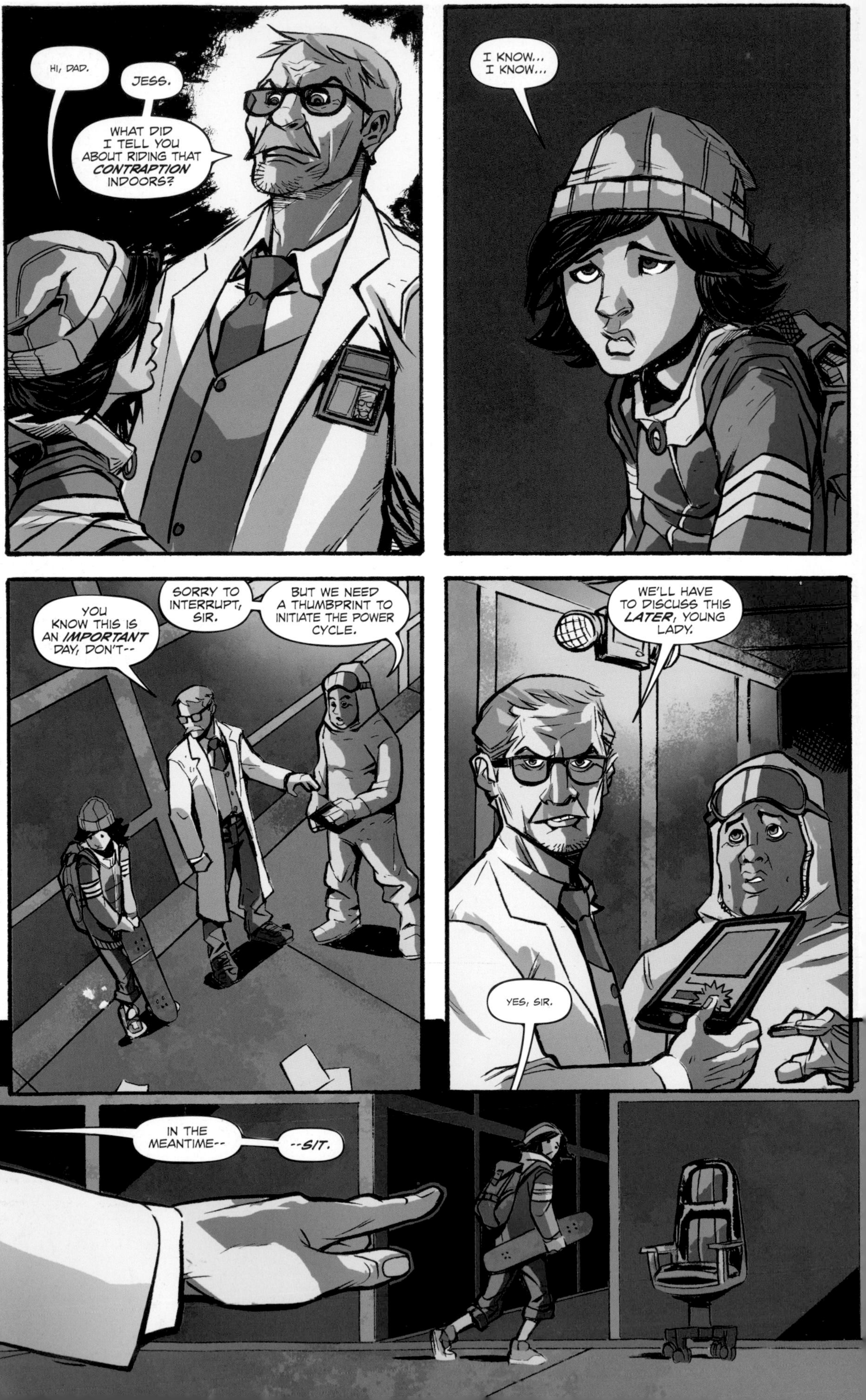
HI, DAD.
JESS.
WHAT DID I TELL YOU ABOUT RIDING THAT *CONTRAPTION* INDOORS?
I KNOW... I KNOW...
YOU KNOW THIS IS AN *IMPORTANT* DAY, DON'T--
SORRY TO INTERRUPT, SIR.
BUT WE NEED A THUMBPRINT TO INITIATE THE POWER CYCLE.
WE'LL HAVE TO DISCUSS THIS *LATER*, YOUNG LADY.
YES, SIR.
IN THE MEANTIME--
--*SIT*.

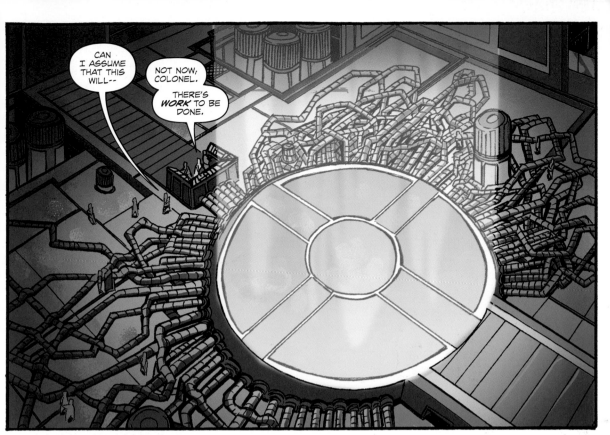

CAN I ASSUME THAT THIS WILL--

NOT NOW, COLONEL. THERE'S **WORK** TO BE DONE.

THAT'S MY DAD-- DR. JEFFERSON ANDERS.

HE RUNS THE **CHRONO-SCIENCES** DEPARTMENT HERE AT COSMOS LABS.

HE'S BEEN BUSY LATELY--**VERY** BUSY--ON SOME NEW PROJECT.

WE'LL OPEN THE WINDOW FOR TEN SECONDS.

SOMETHING TO DO WITH **TEMPORAL DISPLACEMENT,** WHATEVER **THAT** MEANS.

DAD DOESN'T TALK ABOUT HIS WORK ALL THAT MUCH.

TEN SECONDS. NO MORE.

WHO AM I KIDDING? HE DOESN'T TALK ABOUT **ANYTHING,** REALLY... BUT THERE'S SOMETHING ABOUT HIS WORK...

...SOMETIMES I THINK IT **SCARES** HIM.

SEQUENCE INITIATED. SEQUENCE INITIATED. SEQUENCE INITIATED.

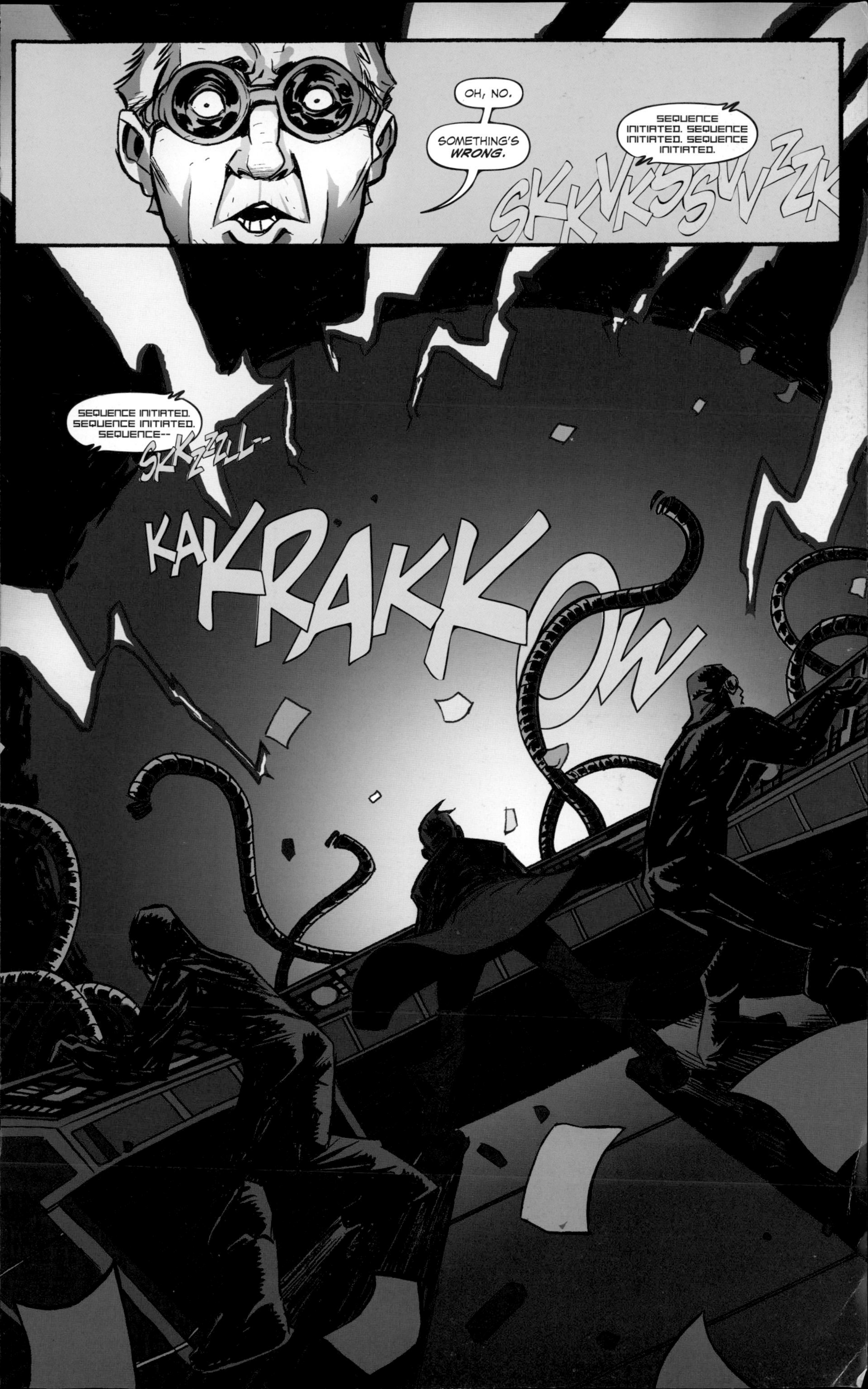
OH, NO.
SOMETHING'S *WRONG*.
SEQUENCE INITIATED. SEQUENCE INITIATED. SEQUENCE INITIATED.
SKKVKSSUVZZK
SEQUENCE INITIATED. SEQUENCE INITIATED. SEQUENCE--
SKKZZZLL--
KAKKRAKKOW

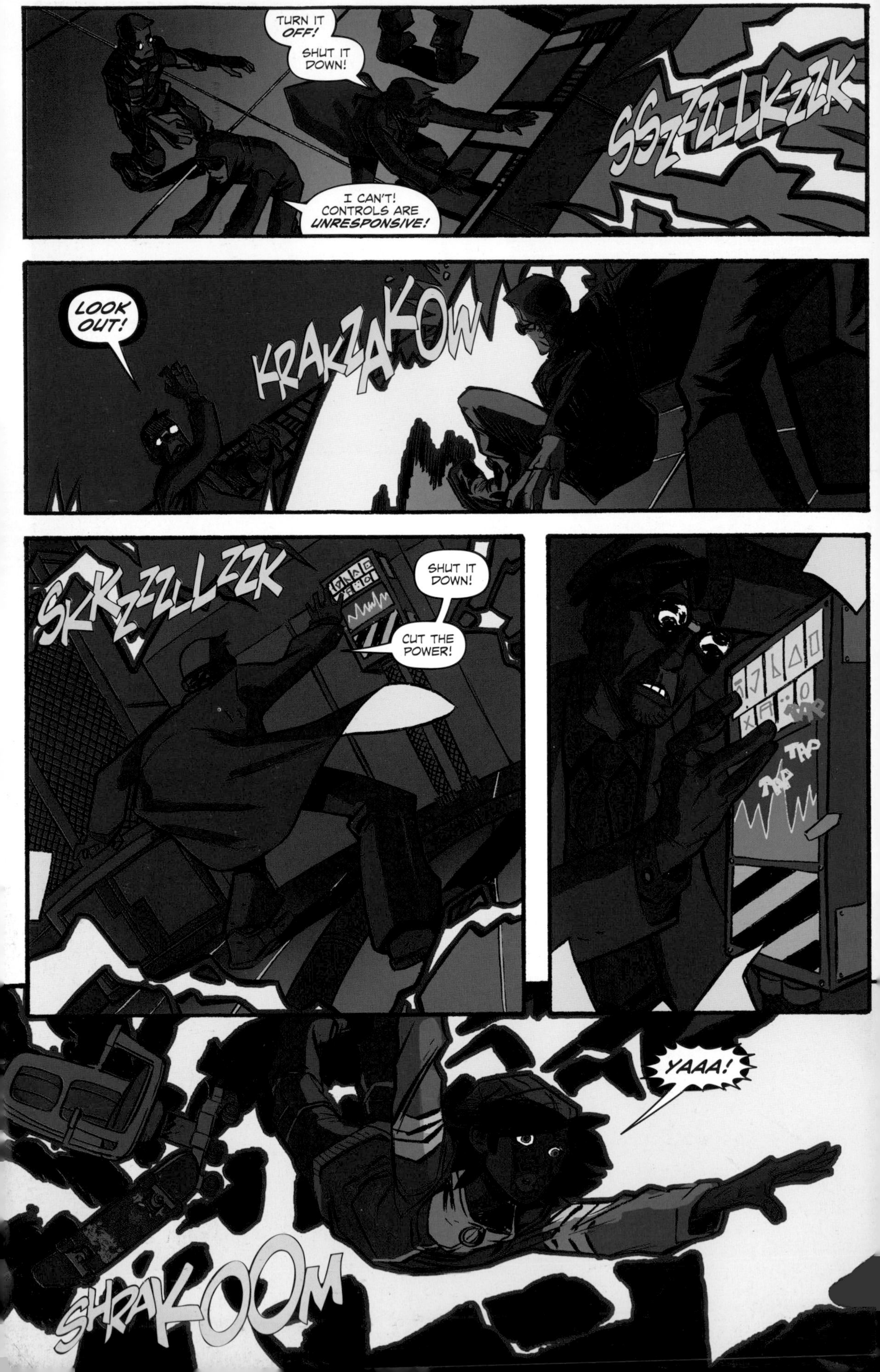
TURN IT OFF! SHUT IT DOWN!
I CAN'T! CONTROLS ARE UNRESPONSIVE!
SSZZZLLKZZK
LOOK OUT!
KRAKZAKOW
SKKZZZLLZZK
SHUT IT DOWN!
CUT THE POWER!
TAP TAP TAP
YAAA!
SHRAKOOM

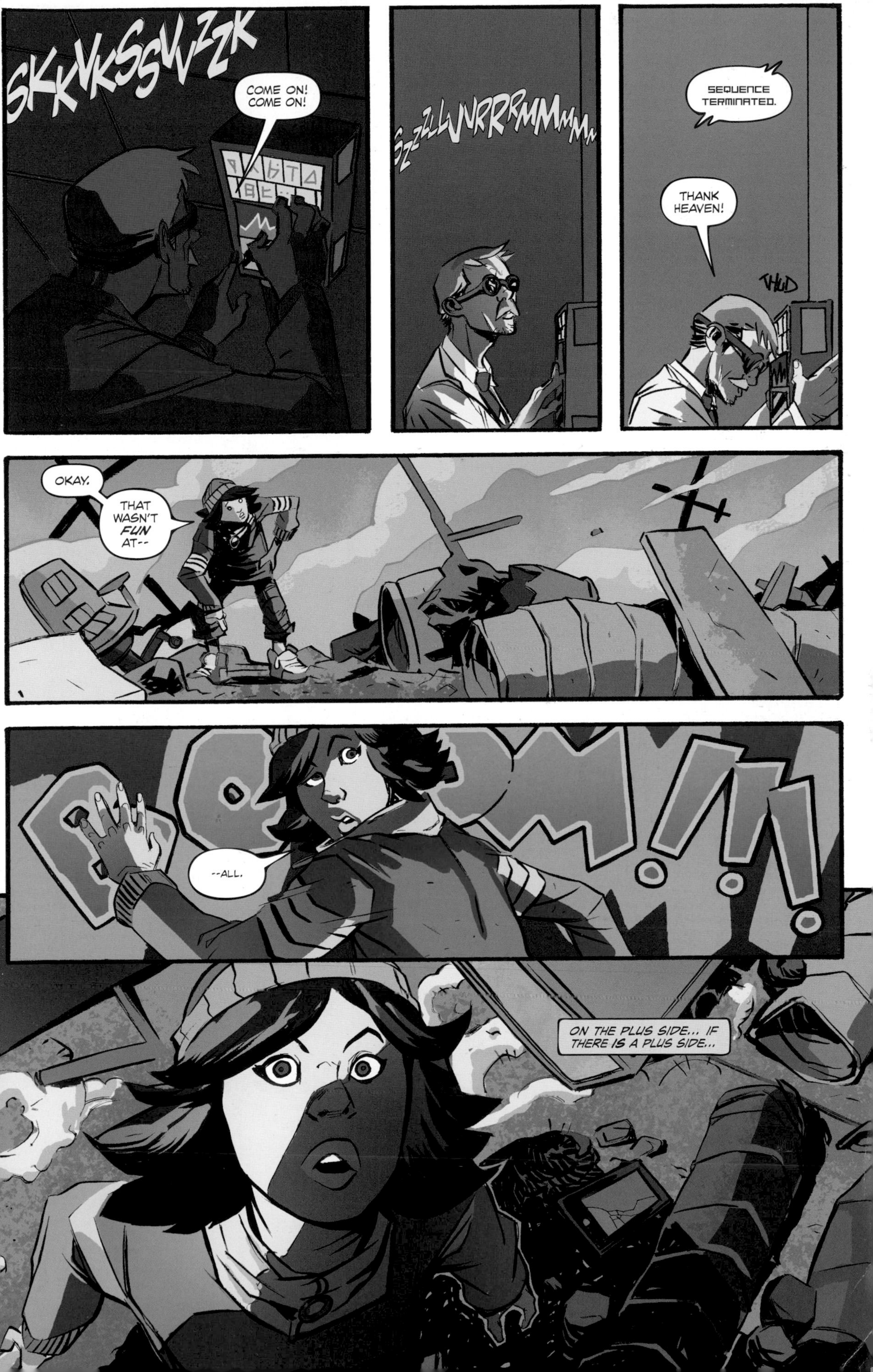
SKKVKSSVVZZK
COME ON! COME ON!
SZZZLLVVRRRMMMMM
SEQUENCE TERMINATED.
THANK HEAVEN!
THUD
OKAY.
THAT WASN'T FUN AT--
--ALL.
ON THE PLUS SIDE... IF THERE IS A PLUS SIDE...

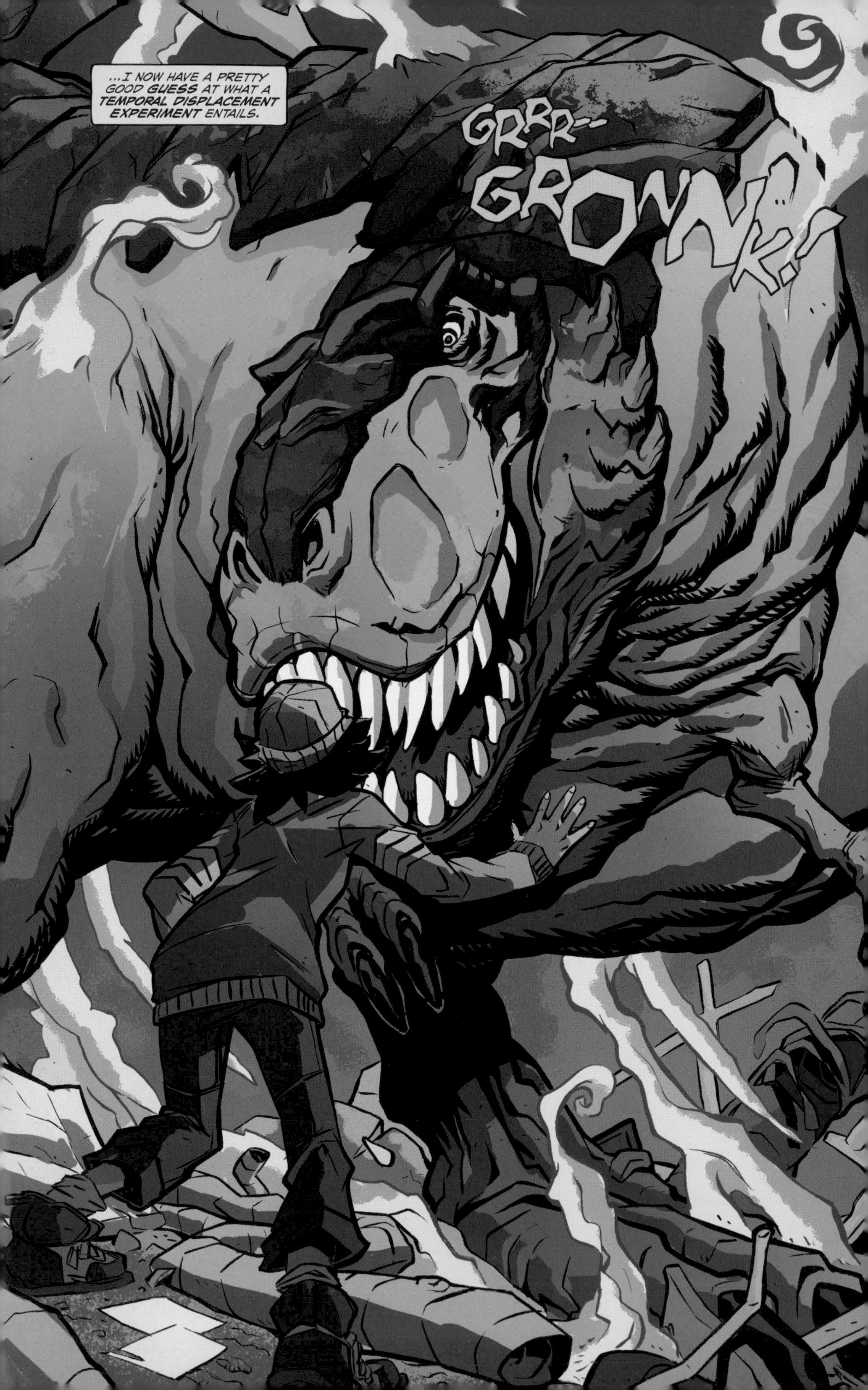
...I NOW HAVE A PRETTY GOOD GUESS AT WHAT A TEMPORAL DISPLACEMENT EXPERIMENT ENTAILS.
GRRR--
GRONNK!!

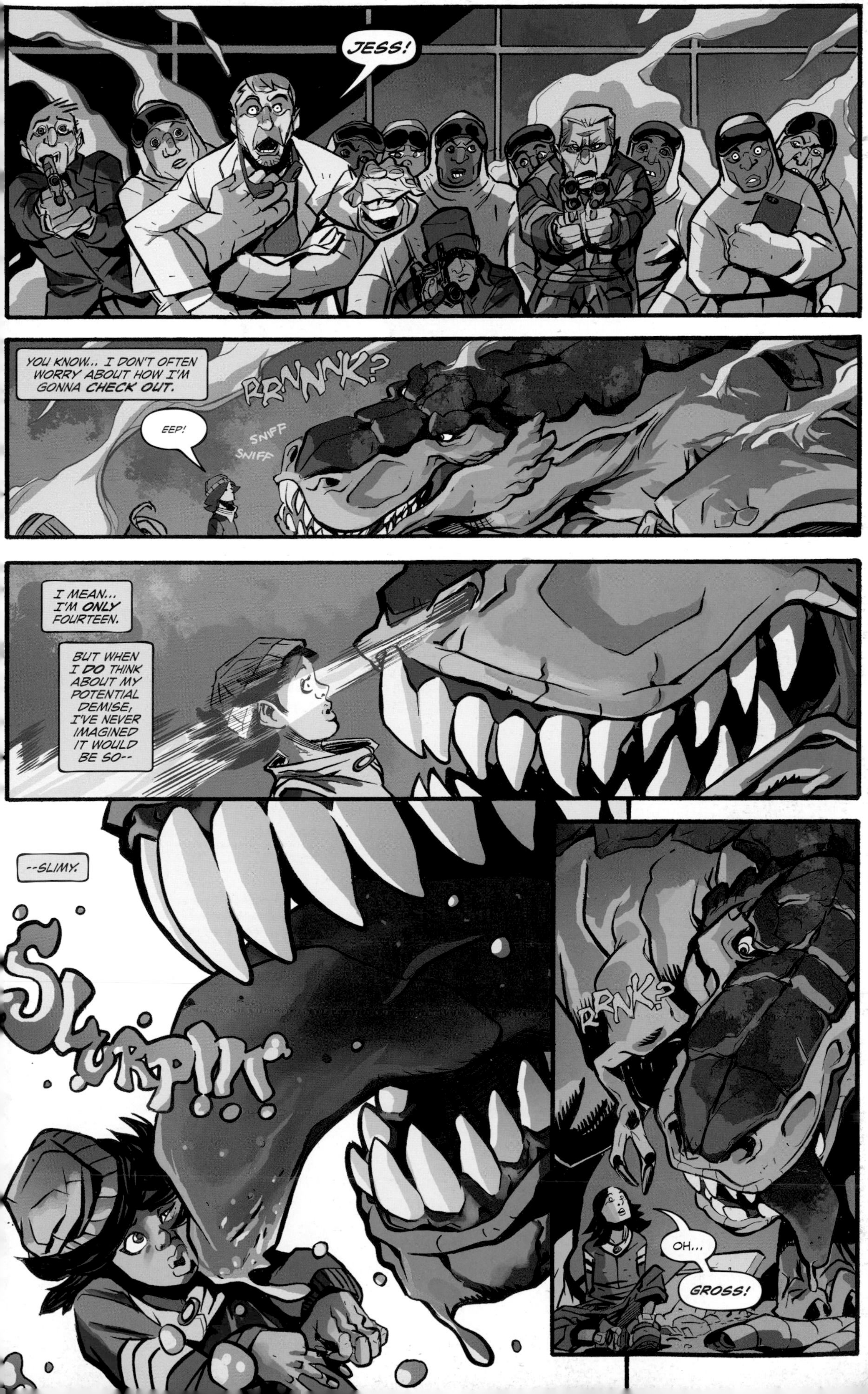

JESS!
YOU KNOW... I DON'T OFTEN WORRY ABOUT HOW I'M GONNA CHECK OUT.
RRNNNK?
EEP!
SNIFF
SNIFF
I MEAN... I'M ONLY FOURTEEN.
BUT WHEN I DO THINK ABOUT MY POTENTIAL DEMISE, I'VE NEVER IMAGINED IT WOULD BE SO--
--SLIMY.
SLURP!!
RRNK?
OH...
GROSS!

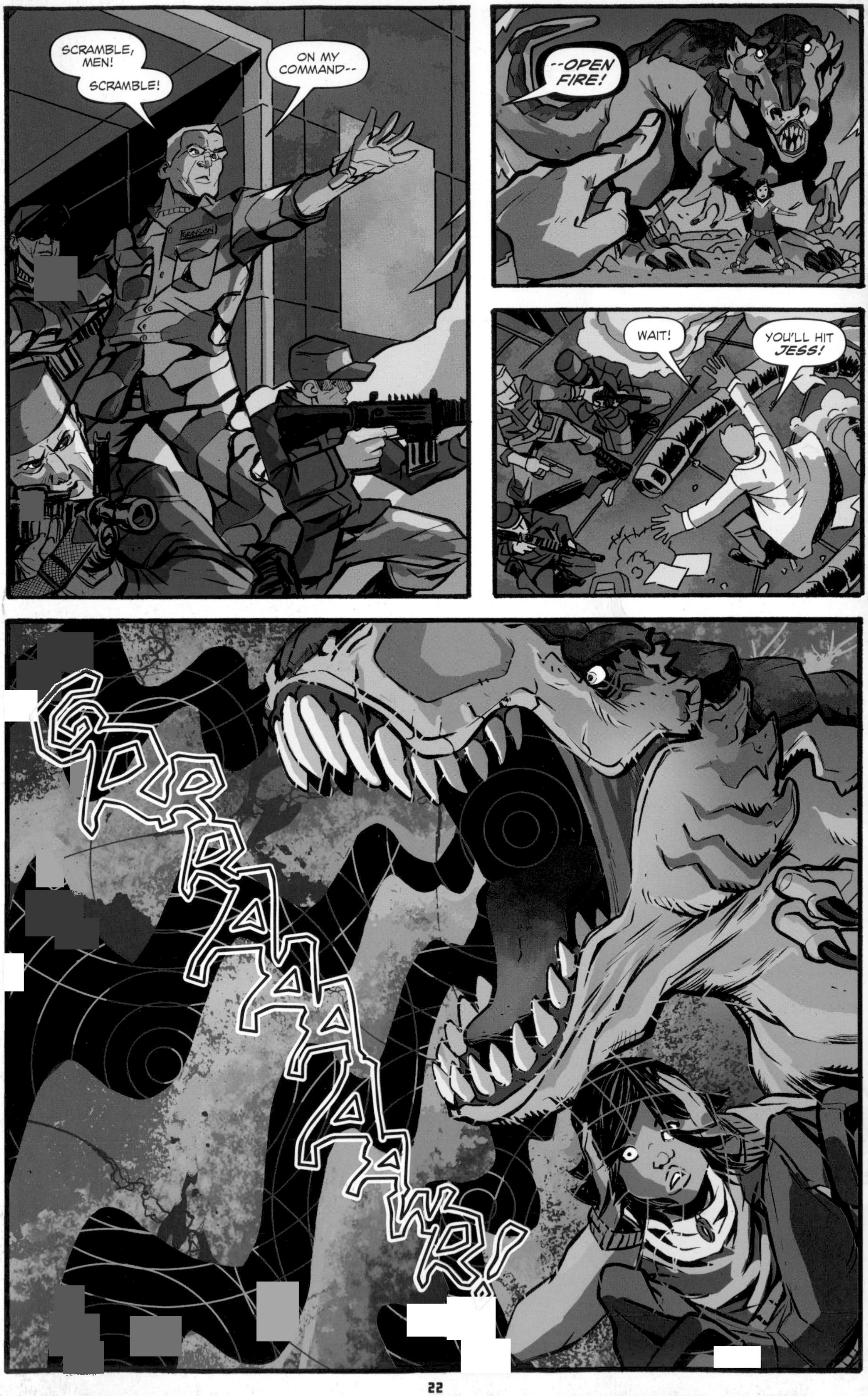
SCRAMBLE, MEN!
SCRAMBLE!
ON MY COMMAND--
--OPEN FIRE!
WAIT!
YOU'LL HIT JESS!
GRRAAAAAWR!

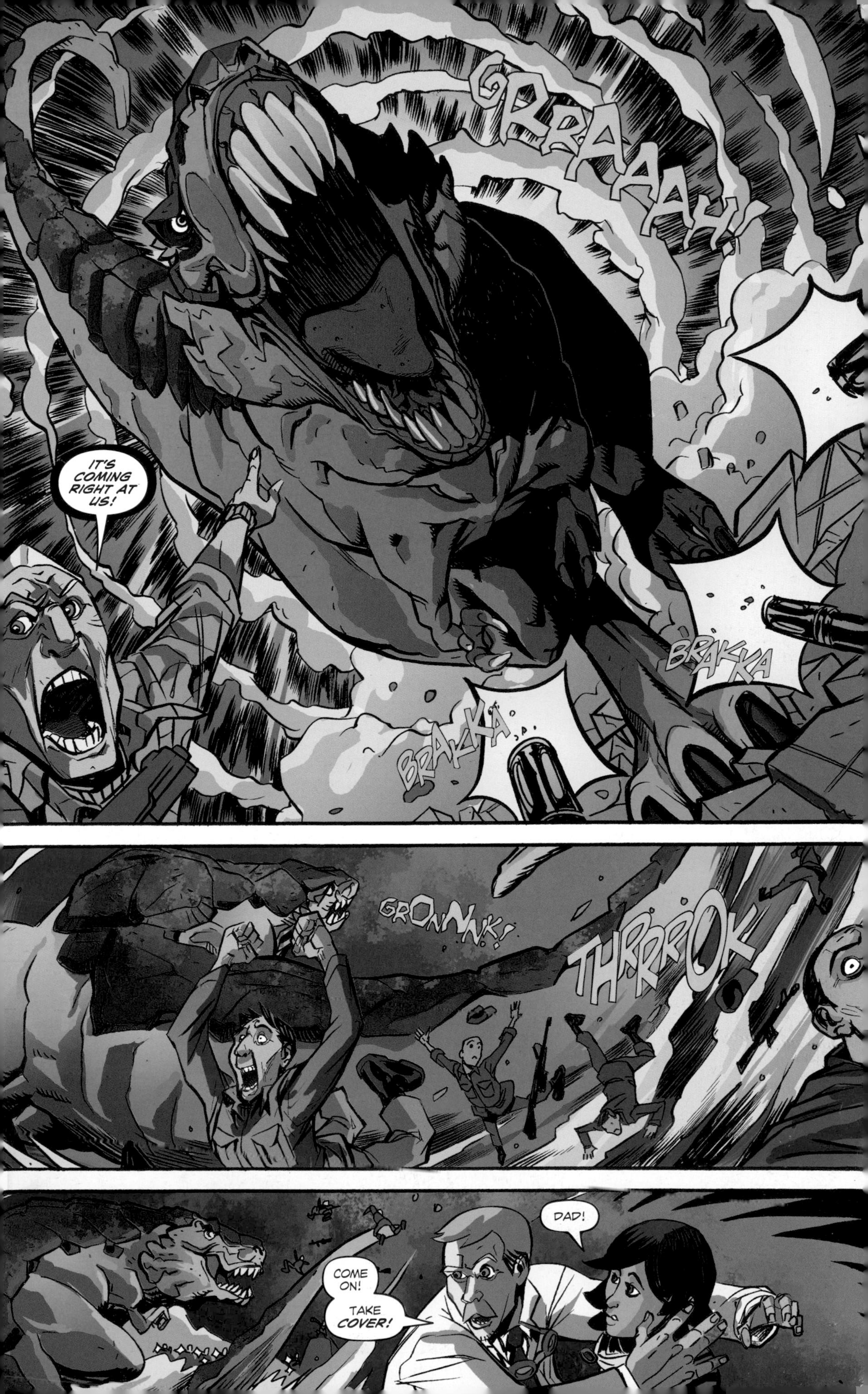
GRRAAAAH!
IT'S COMING RIGHT AT US!
BRAKKA
BRAKKA
GRONNNK!
THRRROK
DAD!
COME ON!
TAKE COVER!

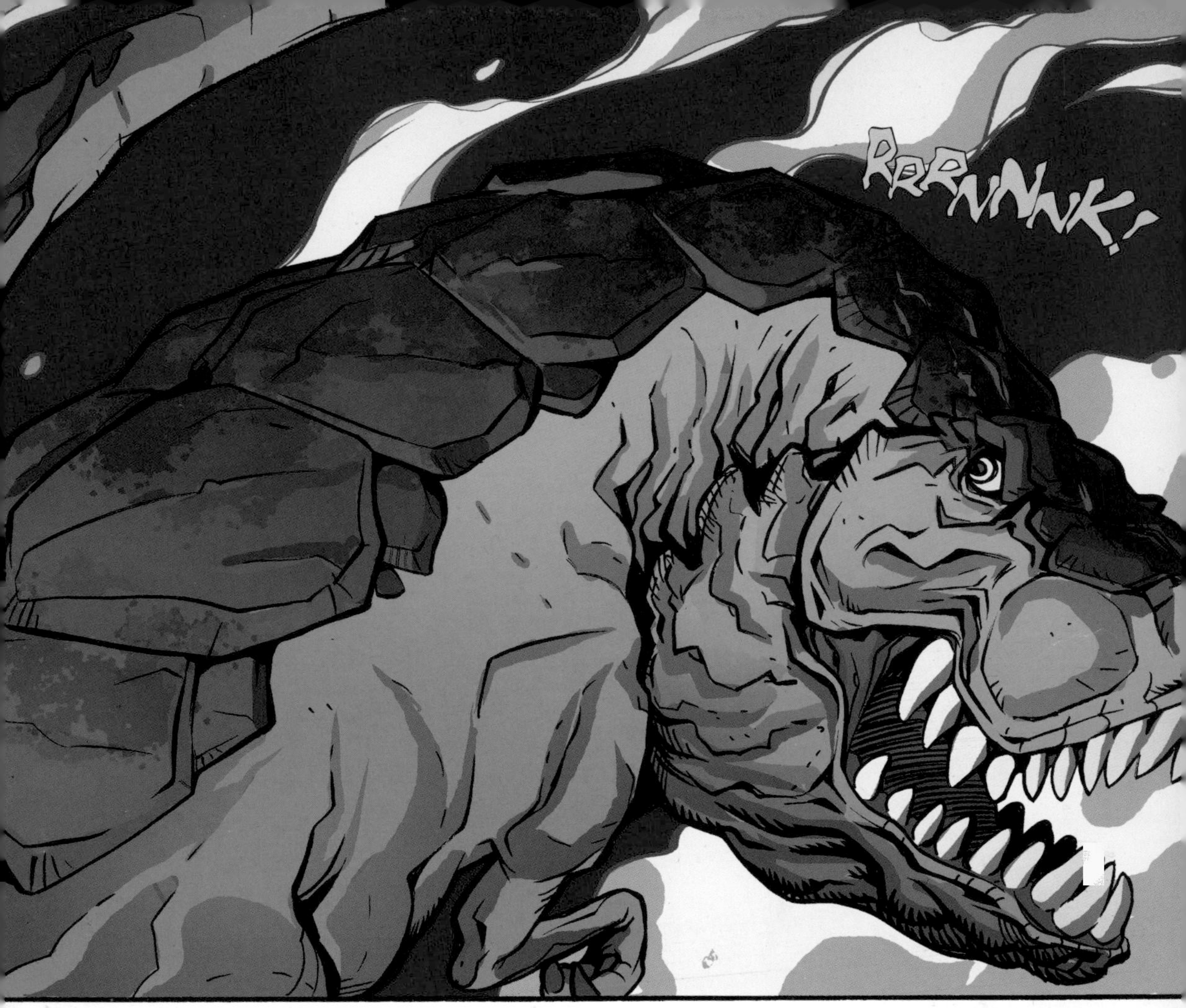
RRRNNNK!

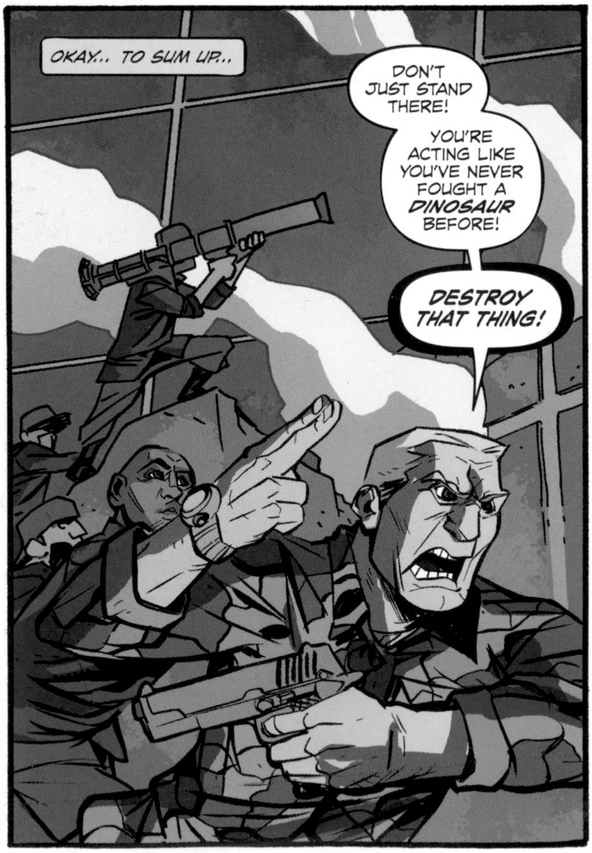
OKAY... TO SUM UP...
DON'T JUST STAND THERE!
YOU'RE ACTING LIKE YOU'VE NEVER FOUGHT A DINOSAUR BEFORE!
DESTROY THAT THING!

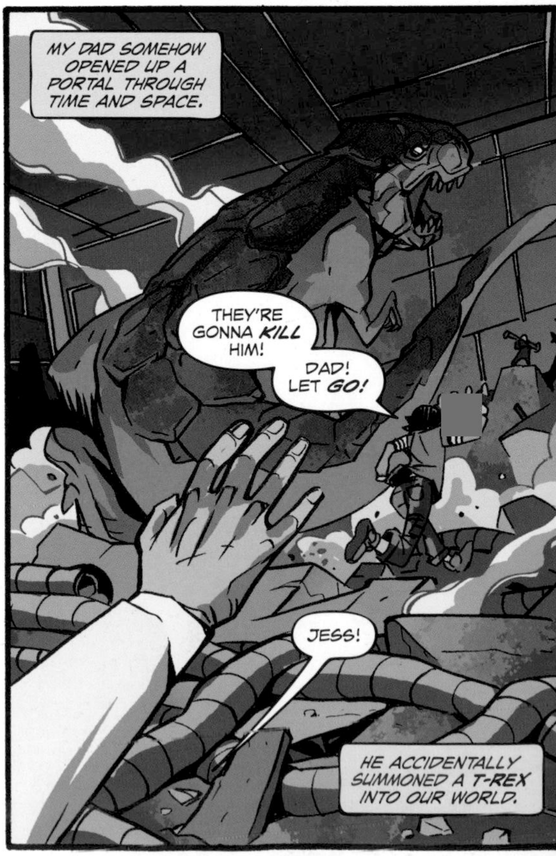
MY DAD SOMEHOW OPENED UP A PORTAL THROUGH TIME AND SPACE.
THEY'RE GONNA KILL HIM!
DAD! LET GO!
JESS!
HE ACCIDENTALLY SUMMONED A T-REX INTO OUR WORLD.

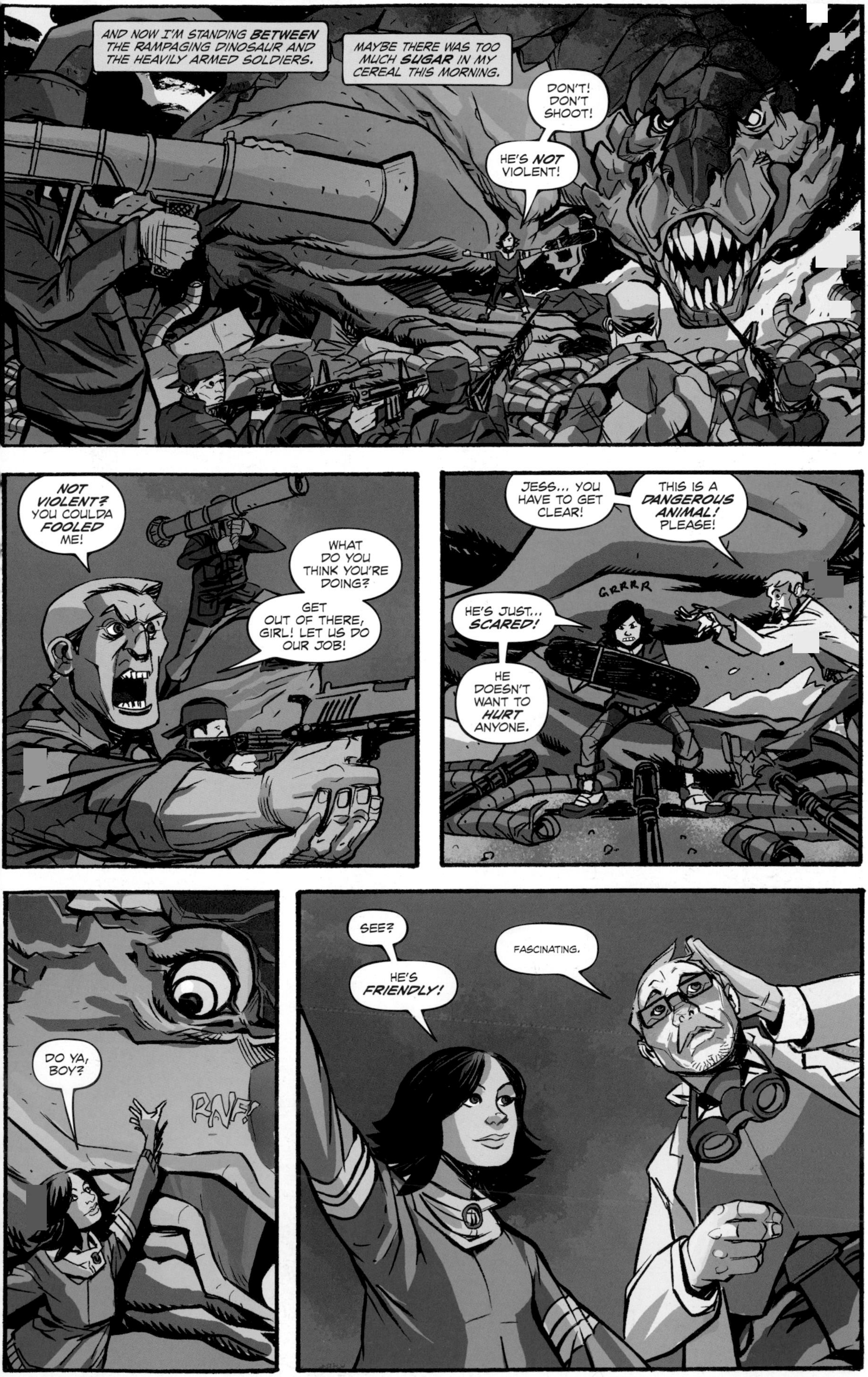
AND NOW I'M STANDING BETWEEN THE RAMPAGING DINOSAUR AND THE HEAVILY ARMED SOLDIERS.
MAYBE THERE WAS TOO MUCH SUGAR IN MY CEREAL THIS MORNING.
DON'T! DON'T SHOOT!
HE'S NOT VIOLENT!
NOT VIOLENT? YOU COULDA FOOLED ME!
WHAT DO YOU THINK YOU'RE DOING?
GET OUT OF THERE, GIRL! LET US DO OUR JOB!
JESS... YOU HAVE TO GET CLEAR!
THIS IS A DANGEROUS ANIMAL! PLEASE!
GRRRR
HE'S JUST... SCARED!
HE DOESN'T WANT TO HURT ANYONE.
DO YA, BOY?
RNF!
SEE?
HE'S FRIENDLY!
FASCINATING.

ANDERS!

GET THAT GIRL OF YOURS OUT OF THE WAY SO I CAN GET ON WITH SOME *GRATUITOUS VIOLENCE!*

NO! SHE'S *RIGHT!*

I *AM?*

GRRNK?

SEE FOR YOURSELF. THE CREATURE HAS ALREADY CALMED DOWN. IT'S NO LONGER ATTACKING.

I THINK IT MIGHT HAVE BEEN LASHING OUT IN AN EFFORT TO *PROTECT* MY DAUGHTER.

SHE WAS THE FIRST LIVING CREATURE IT SAW WHEN HE CAME THROUGH THE *CHRONO-RIFT.*

I BELIEVE IT *IMPRINTED* ON HER.

THEY'VE *BONDED.*

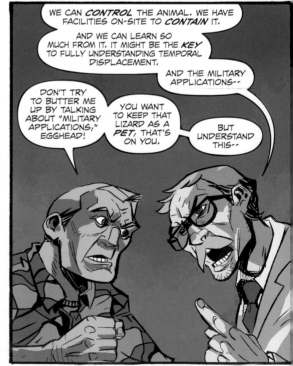

WE CAN *CONTROL* THE ANIMAL. WE HAVE FACILITIES ON-SITE TO *CONTAIN* IT.

AND WE CAN LEARN SO MUCH FROM IT. IT MIGHT BE THE *KEY* TO FULLY UNDERSTANDING TEMPORAL DISPLACEMENT.

AND THE MILITARY APPLICATIONS--

DON'T TRY TO BUTTER ME UP BY TALKING ABOUT "MILITARY APPLICATIONS," EGGHEAD!

YOU WANT TO KEEP THAT *LIZARD* AS A *PET,* THAT'S ON YOU.

BUT UNDERSTAND THIS--

26

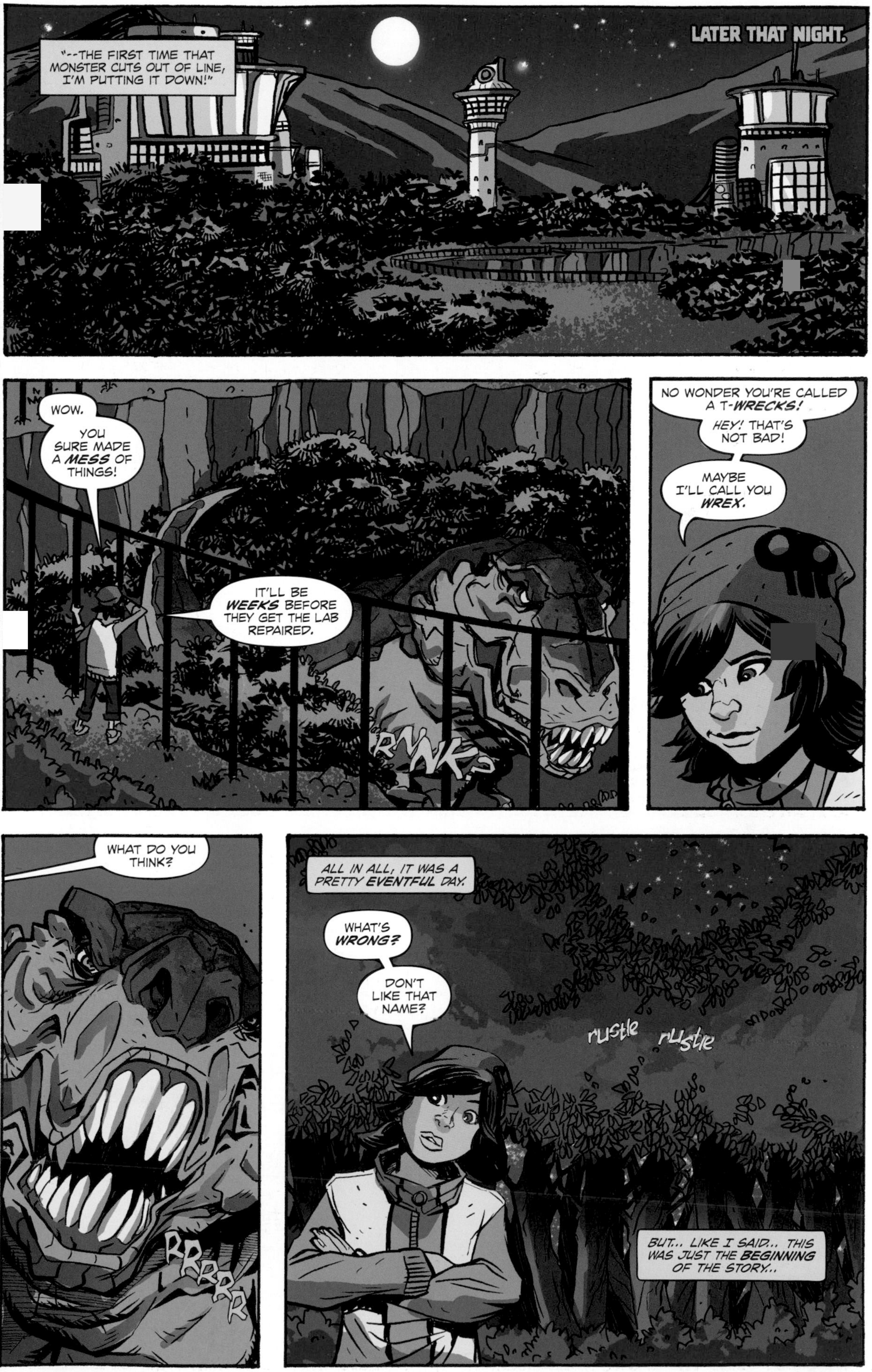
LATER THAT NIGHT.
"--THE FIRST TIME THAT MONSTER CUTS OUT OF LINE, I'M PUTTING IT DOWN!"
WOW.
YOU SURE MADE A MESS OF THINGS!
IT'LL BE WEEKS BEFORE THEY GET THE LAB REPAIRED.
RNNK?
NO WONDER YOU'RE CALLED A T-WRECKS!
HEY! THAT'S NOT BAD!
MAYBE I'LL CALL YOU WREX.
WHAT DO YOU THINK?
RRRRR
ALL IN ALL, IT WAS A PRETTY EVENTFUL DAY.
WHAT'S WRONG?
DON'T LIKE THAT NAME?
rustle rustle
BUT... LIKE I SAID... THIS WAS JUST THE BEGINNING OF THE STORY...

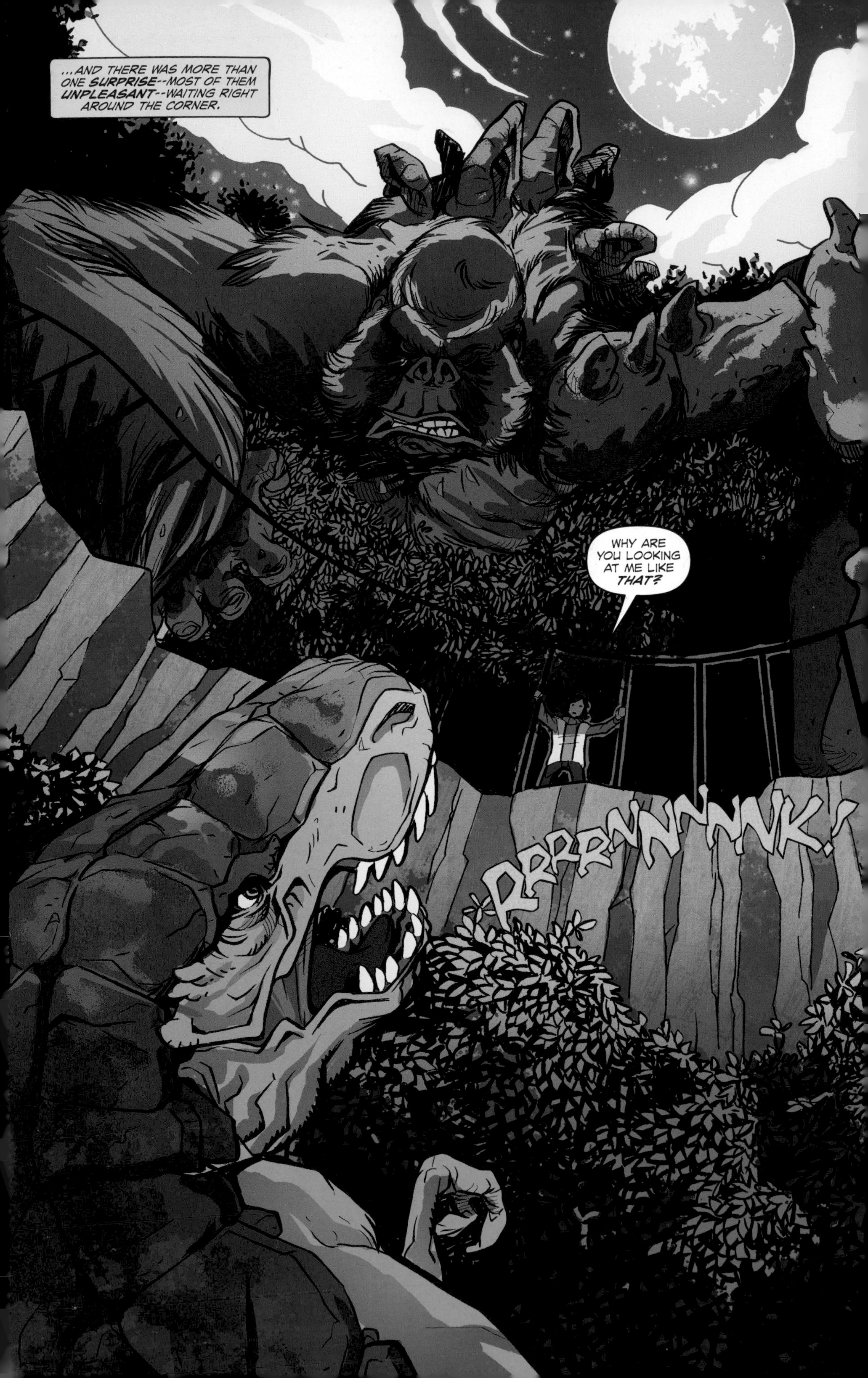
...AND THERE WAS MORE THAN ONE SURPRISE--MOST OF THEM UNPLEASANT--WAITING RIGHT AROUND THE CORNER.
WHY ARE YOU LOOKING AT ME LIKE THAT?
RRRRNNNNNK!

CHAPTER TWO

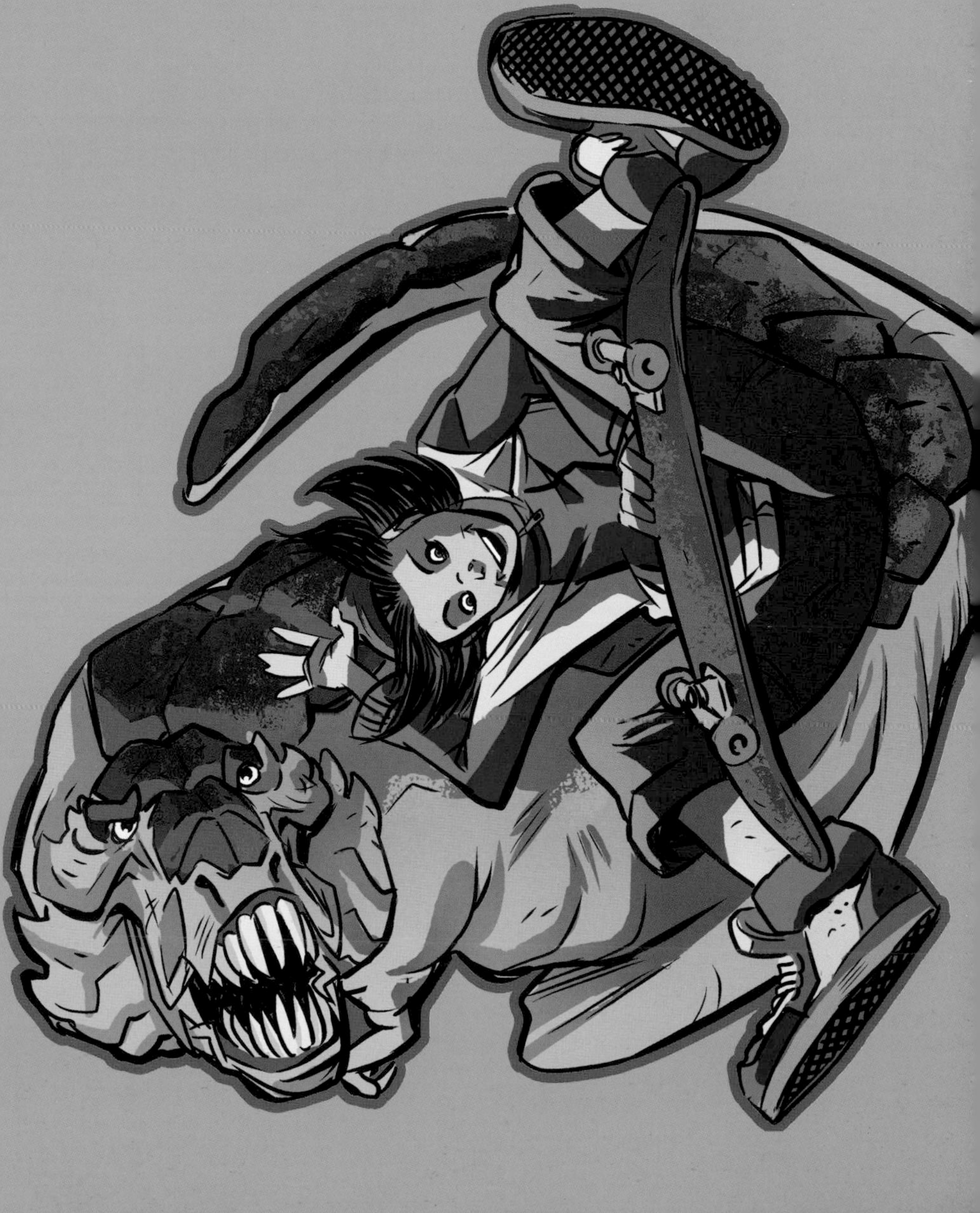

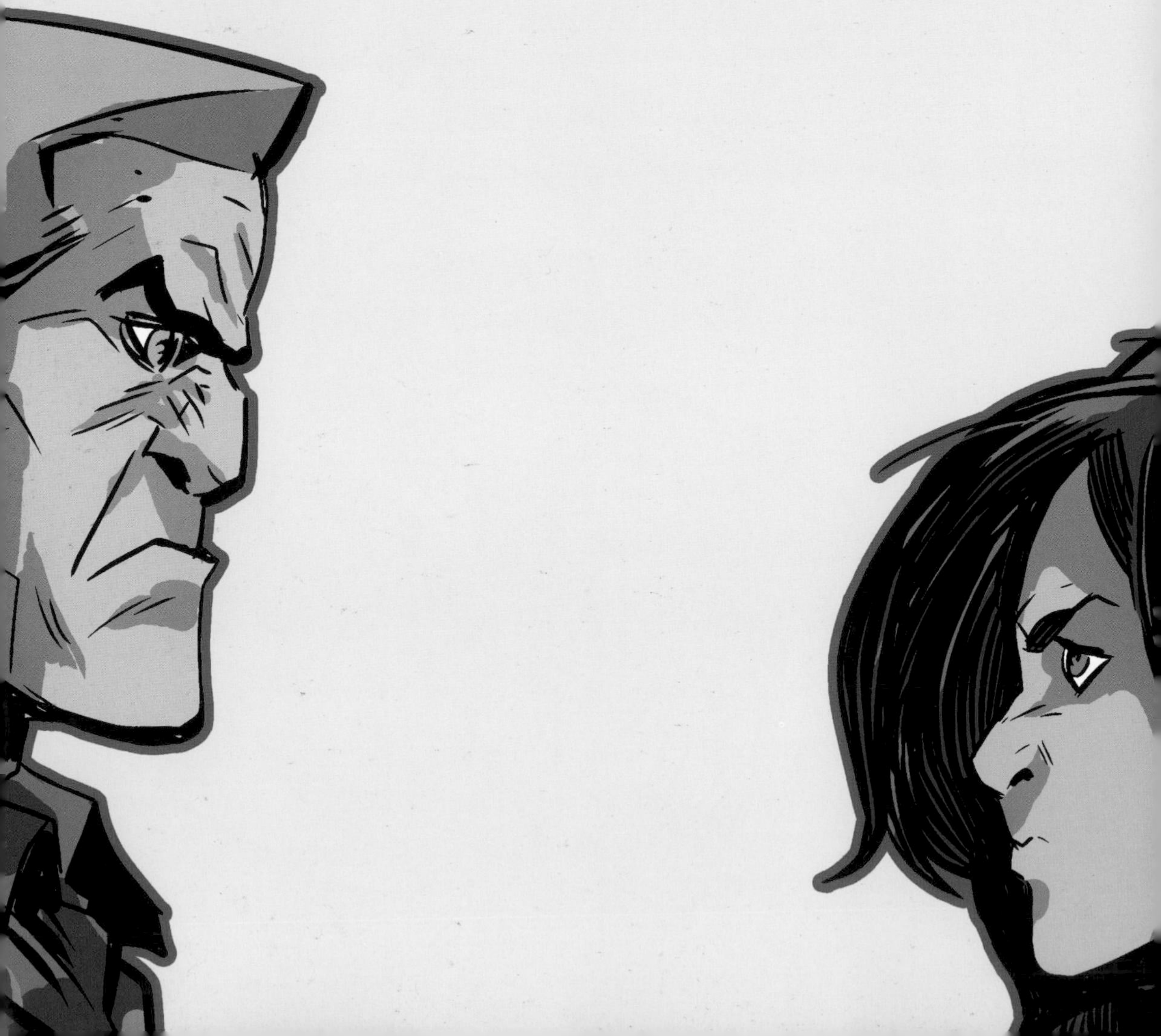

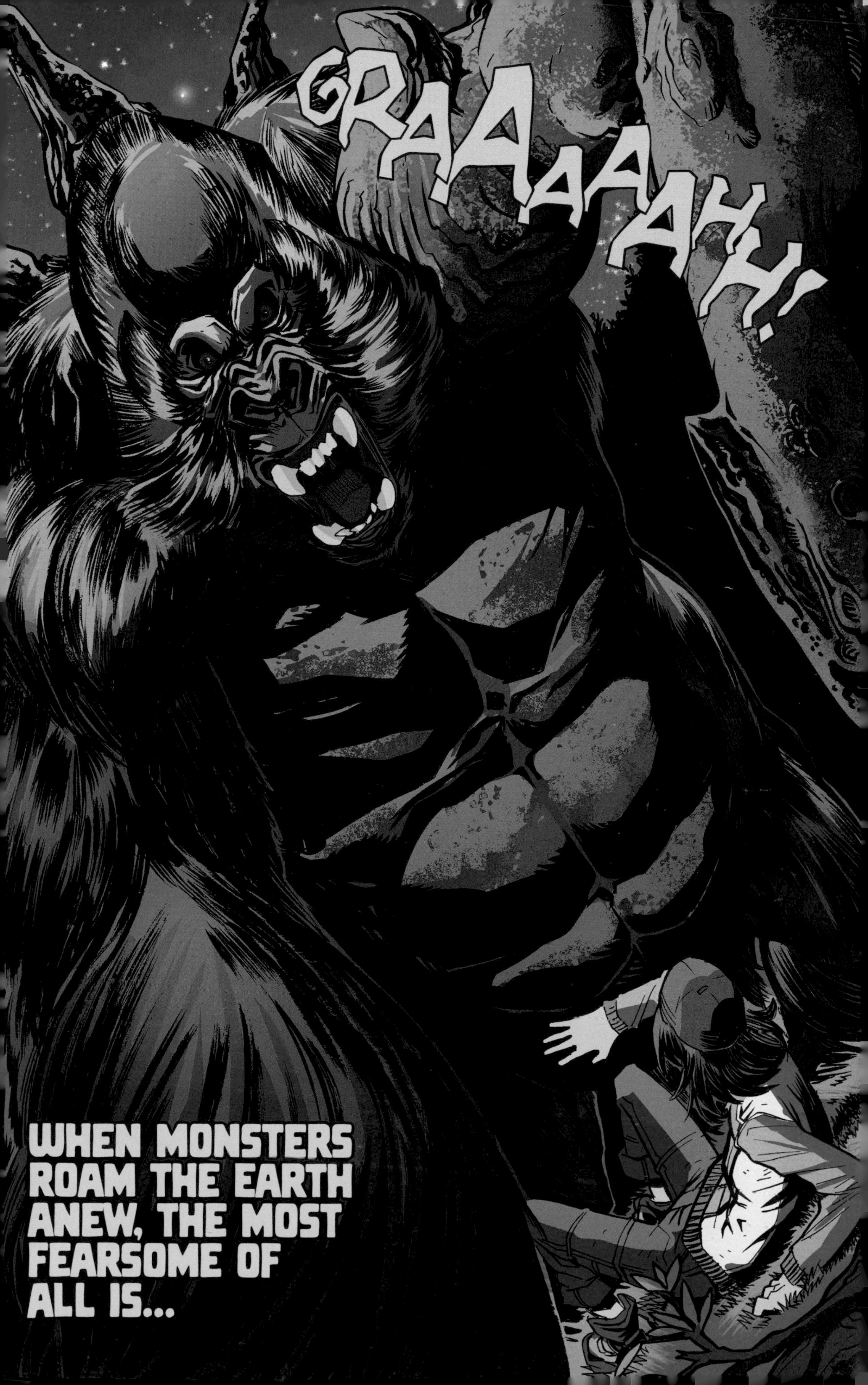
GRAAAAAHH!
WHEN MONSTERS ROAM THE EARTH ANEW, THE MOST FEARSOME OF ALL IS...

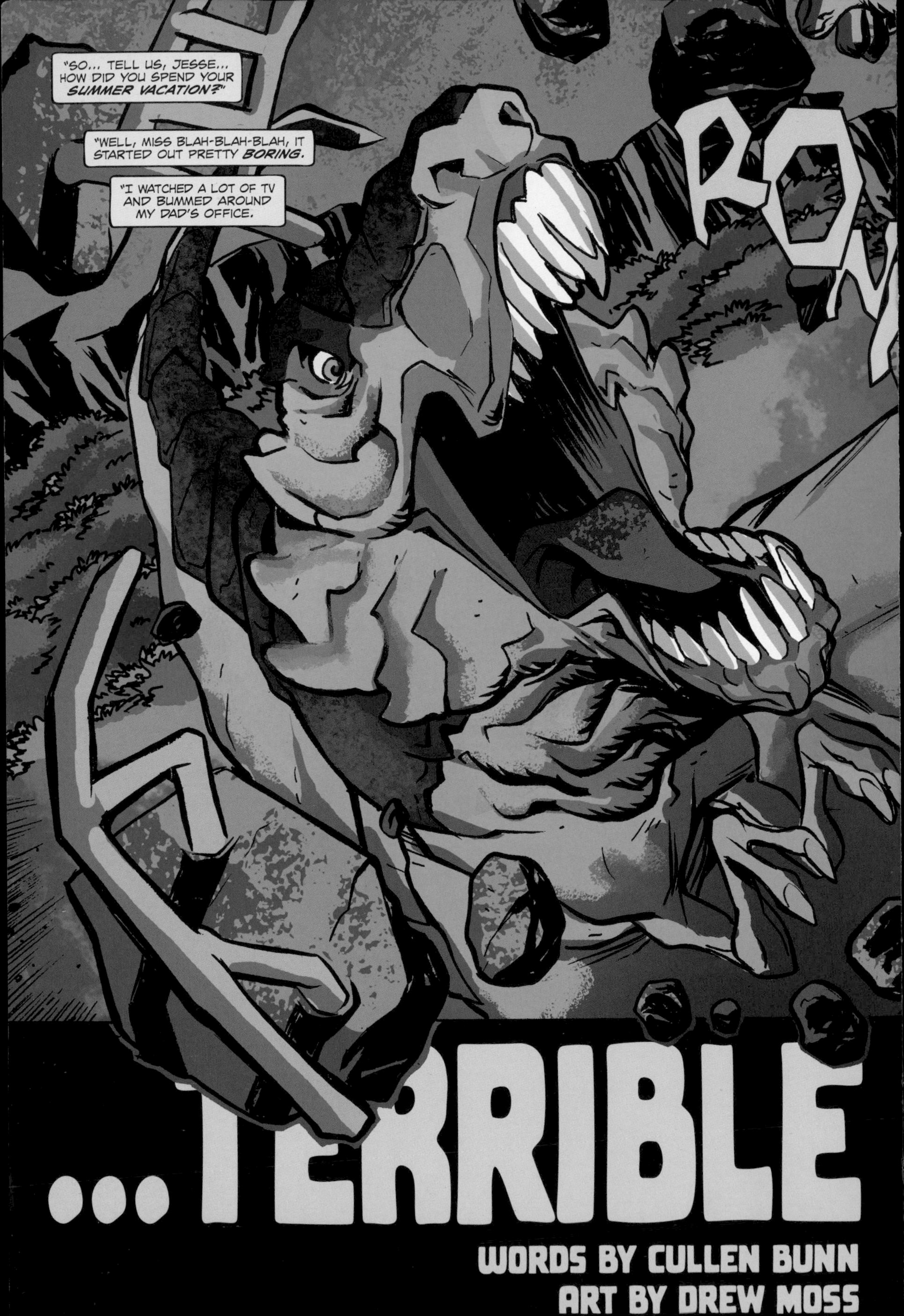
"SO... TELL US, JESSE... HOW DID YOU SPEND YOUR SUMMER VACATION?"
"WELL, MISS BLAH-BLAH-BLAH, IT STARTED OUT PRETTY BORING.
"I WATCHED A LOT OF TV AND BUMMED AROUND MY DAD'S OFFICE.
...TERRIBLE
WORDS BY CULLEN BUNN
ART BY DREW MOSS

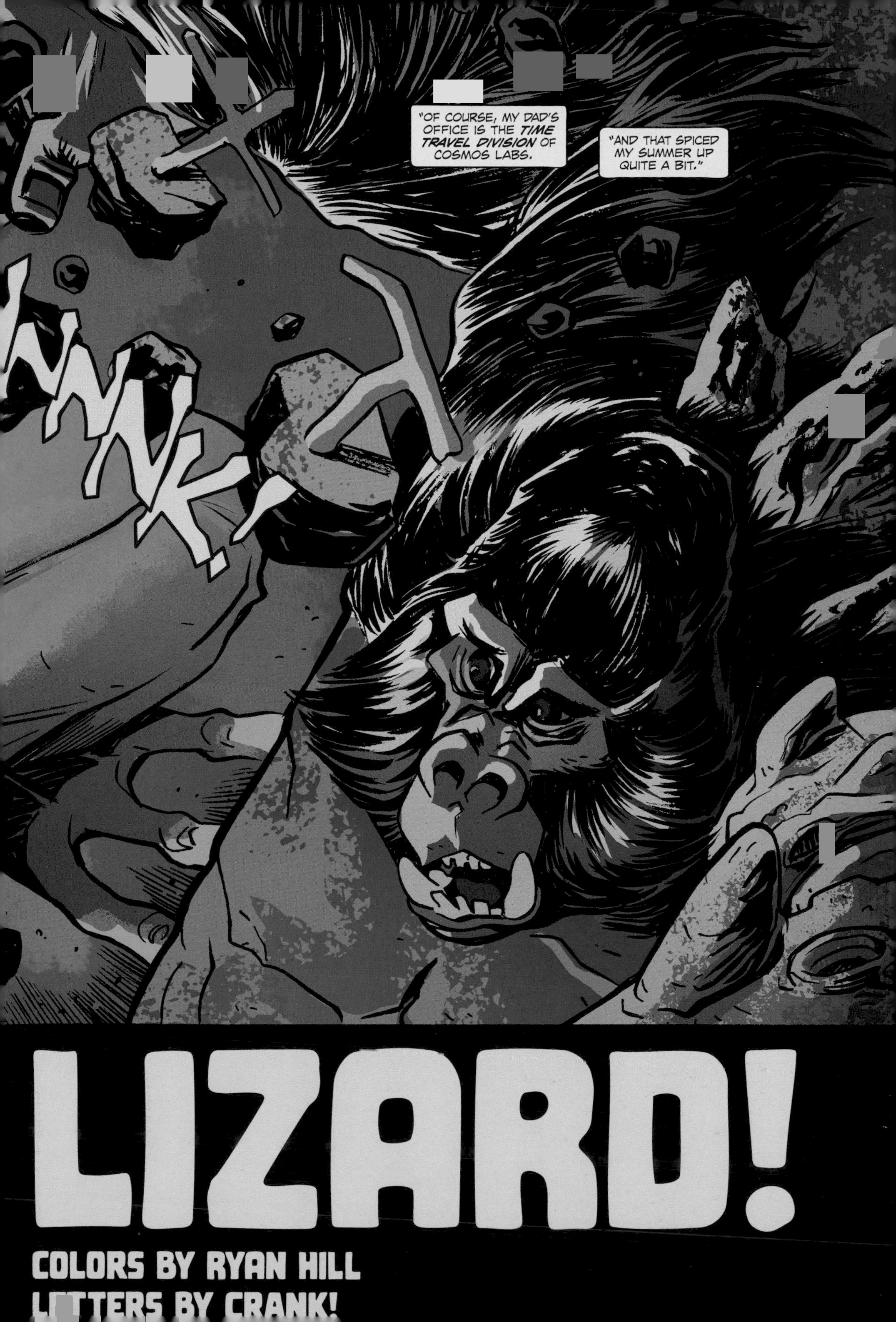
"OF COURSE, MY DAD'S OFFICE IS THE *TIME TRAVEL DIVISION* OF COSMOS LABS.
"AND THAT SPICED MY SUMMER UP QUITE A BIT."

LIZARD!

COLORS BY RYAN HILL
LETTERS BY CRANK!

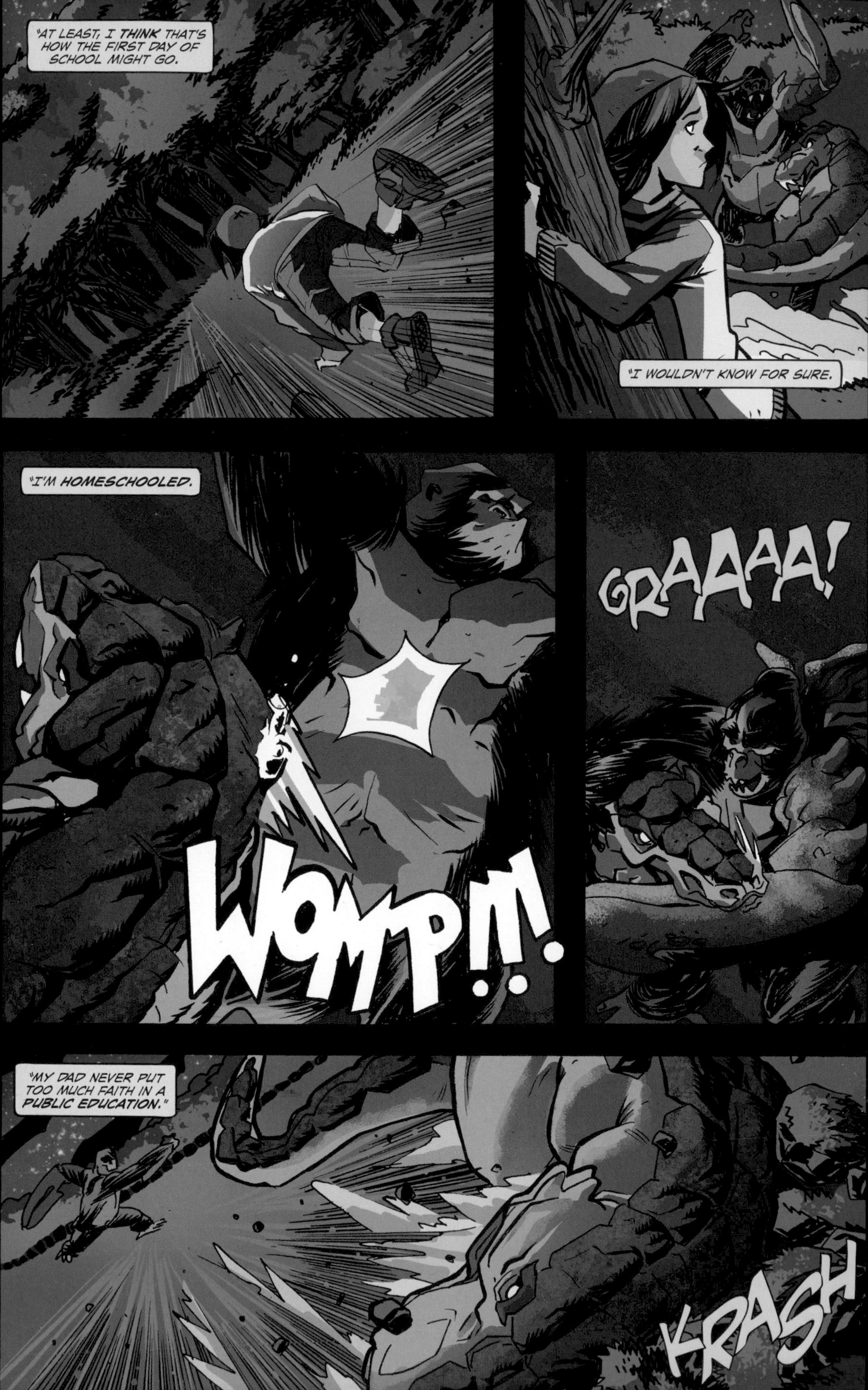

"AT LEAST, I THINK THAT'S HOW THE FIRST DAY OF SCHOOL MIGHT GO.
"I WOULDN'T KNOW FOR SURE.
"I'M HOMESCHOOLED.
WOMP!!!
GRAAAA!
"MY DAD NEVER PUT TOO MUCH FAITH IN A PUBLIC EDUCATION."
KRASH

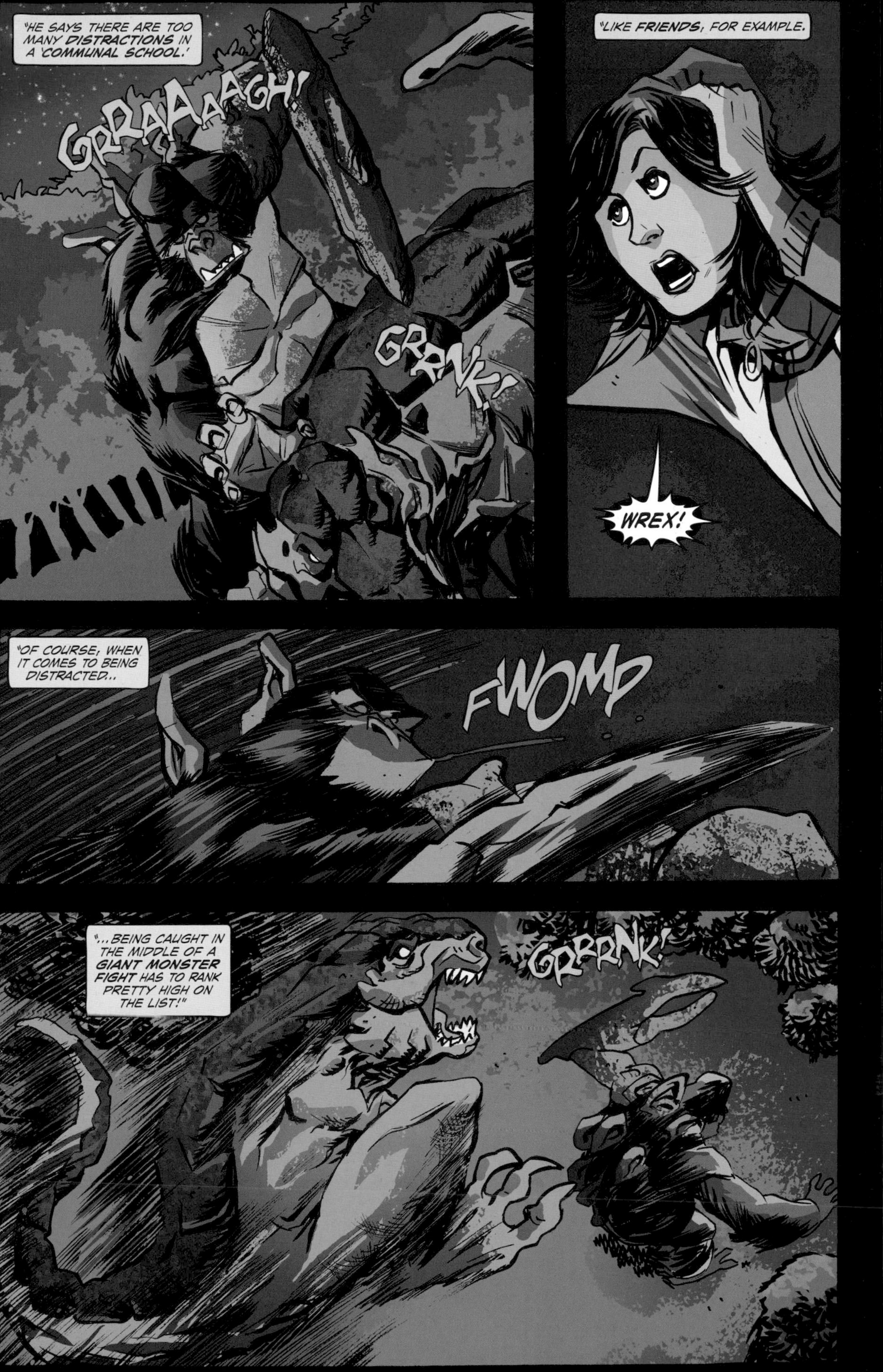
"HE SAYS THERE ARE TOO MANY DISTRACTIONS IN A 'COMMUNAL SCHOOL.'
GRRAAAAAGH!
GRRNK!
"LIKE FRIENDS, FOR EXAMPLE.
WREX!
"OF COURSE, WHEN IT COMES TO BEING DISTRACTED...
FWOMP
"...BEING CAUGHT IN THE MIDDLE OF A GIANT MONSTER FIGHT HAS TO RANK PRETTY HIGH ON THE LIST!"
GRRRNK!

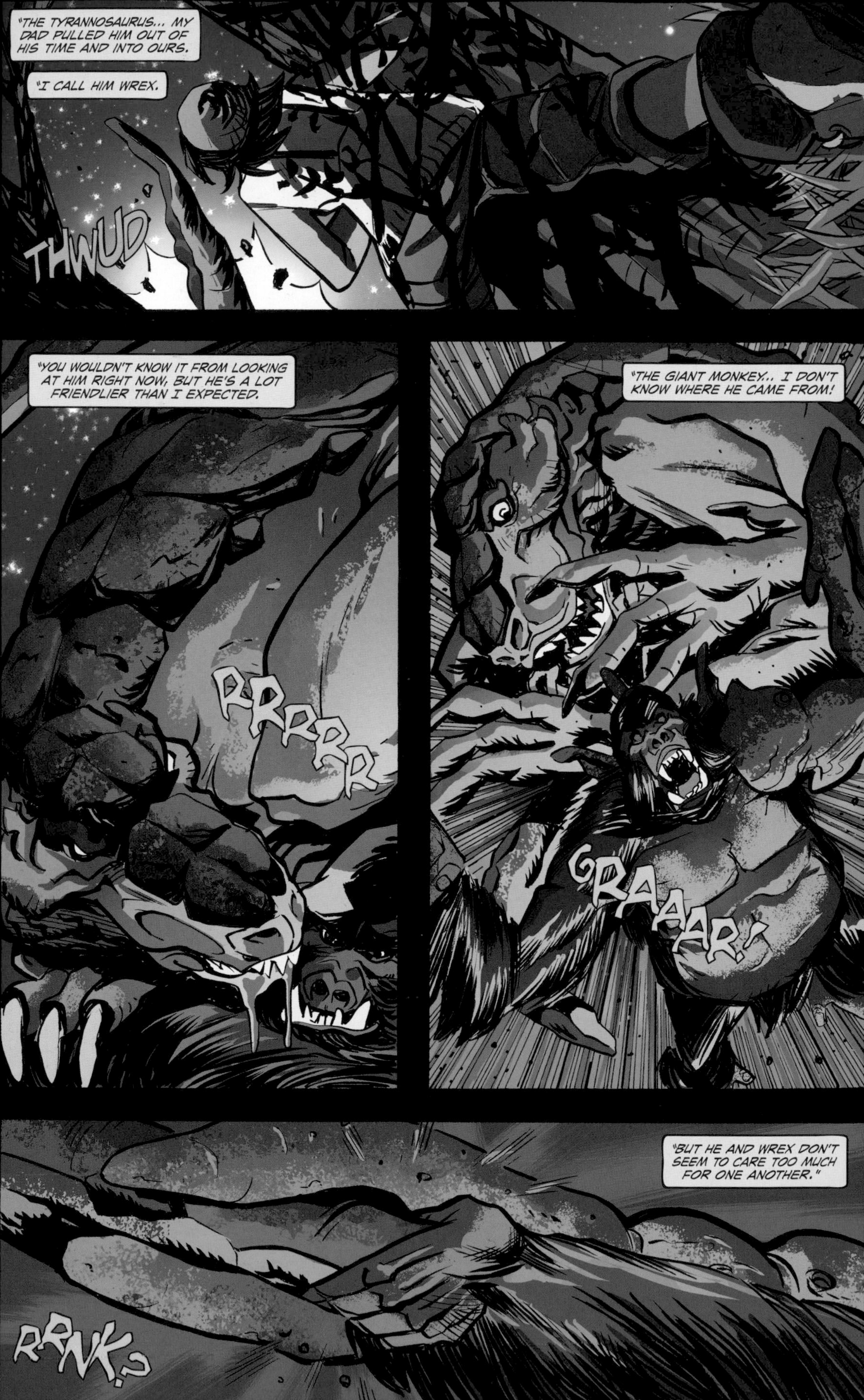
"THE TYRANNOSAURUS... MY DAD PULLED HIM OUT OF HIS TIME AND INTO OURS.
"I CALL HIM WREX.
THWUD
"YOU WOULDN'T KNOW IT FROM LOOKING AT HIM RIGHT NOW, BUT HE'S A LOT FRIENDLIER THAN I EXPECTED.
RRRRRR
"THE GIANT MONKEY.. I DON'T KNOW WHERE HE CAME FROM!
GRAAAAR!
"BUT HE AND WREX DON'T SEEM TO CARE TOO MUCH FOR ONE ANOTHER."
RRNK?

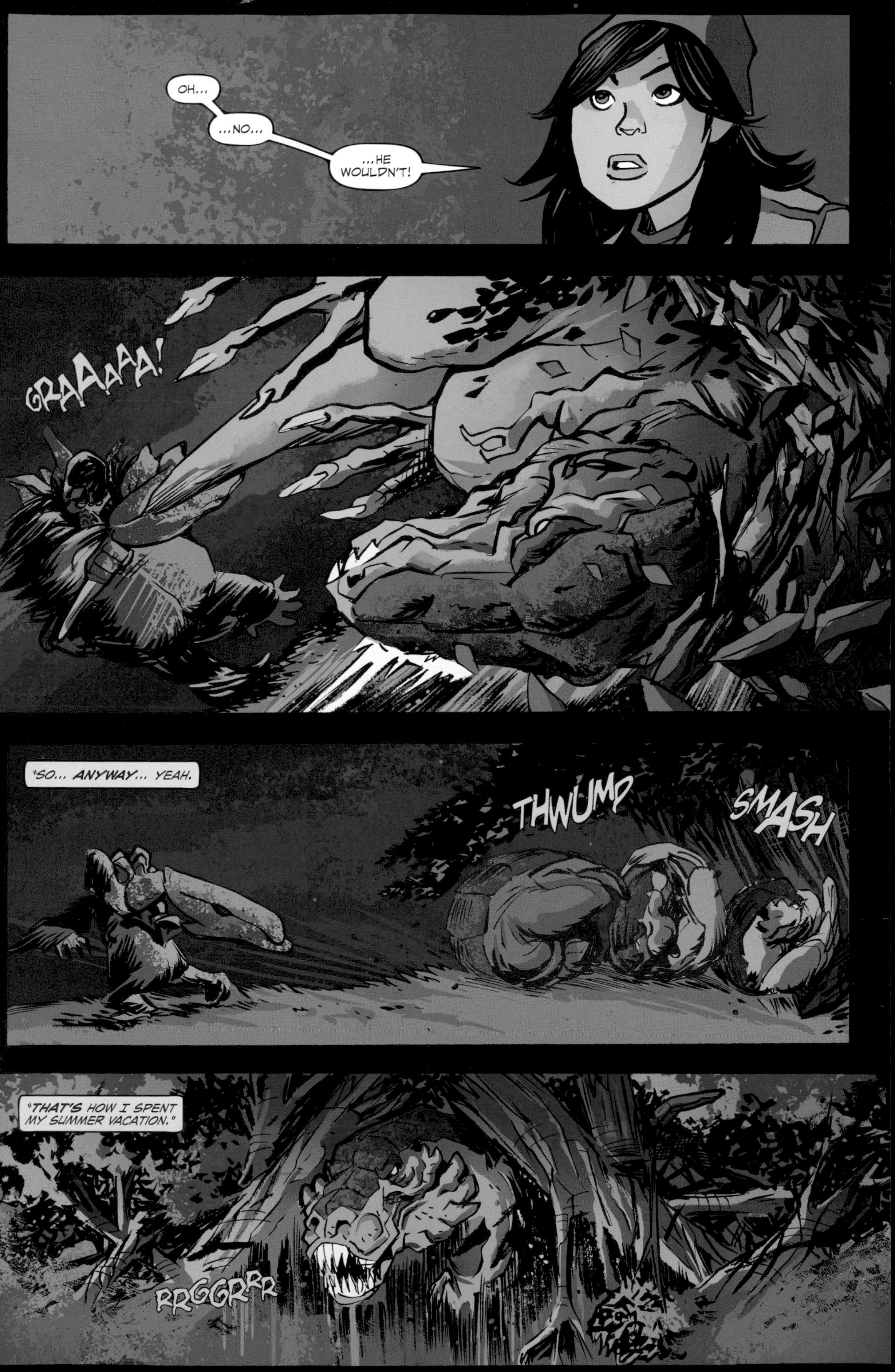
OH...
...NO...
...HE WOULDN'T!
GRAAAAA!
"SO... ANYWAY... YEAH.
THWUMP
SMASH
"THAT'S HOW I SPENT MY SUMMER VACATION."
RRGGRRR

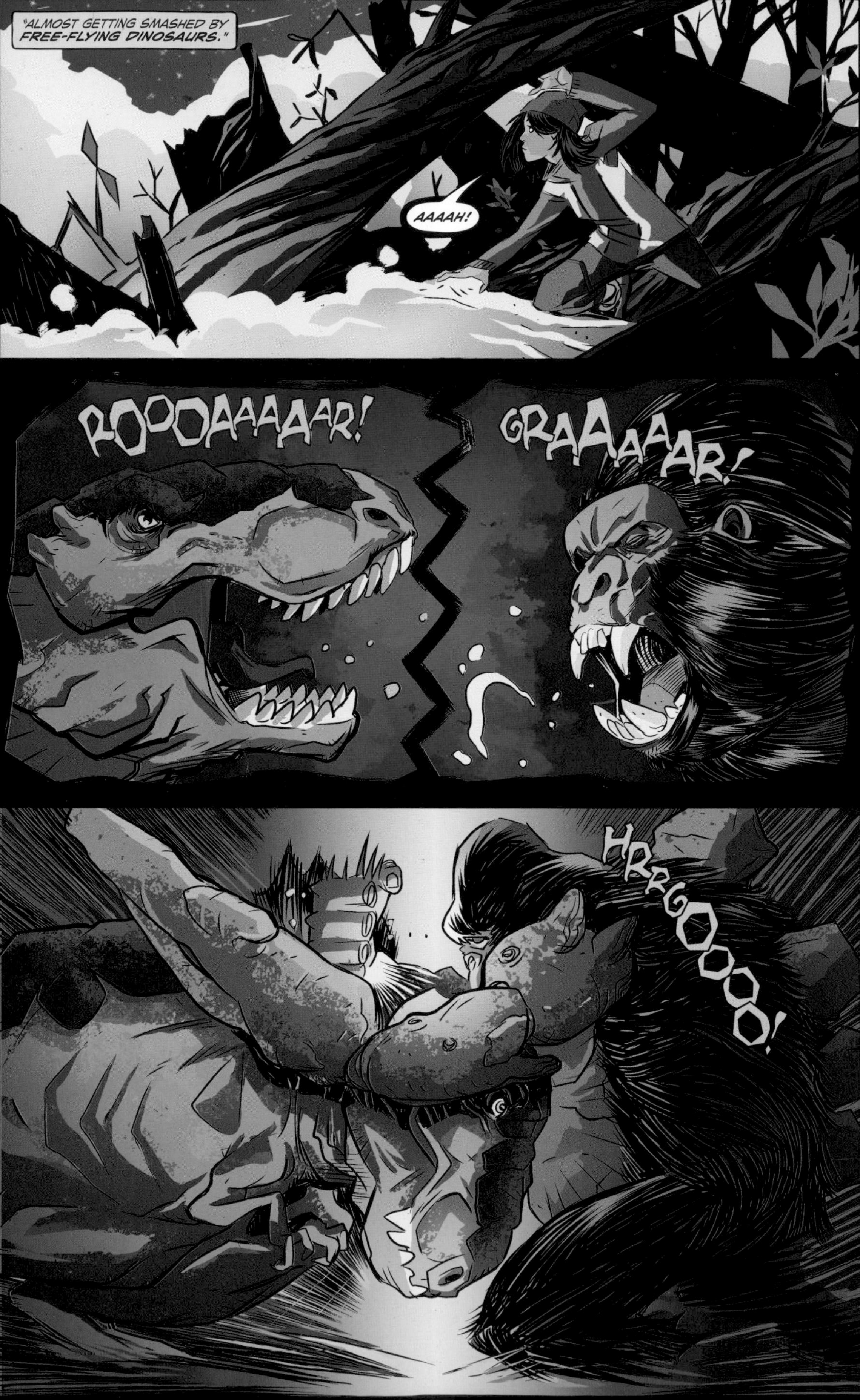
"ALMOST GETTING SMASHED BY FREE-FLYING DINOSAURS."
AAAAH!
ROOOAAAAAAR!
GRAAAAAAR!
HRRGOOOOO!

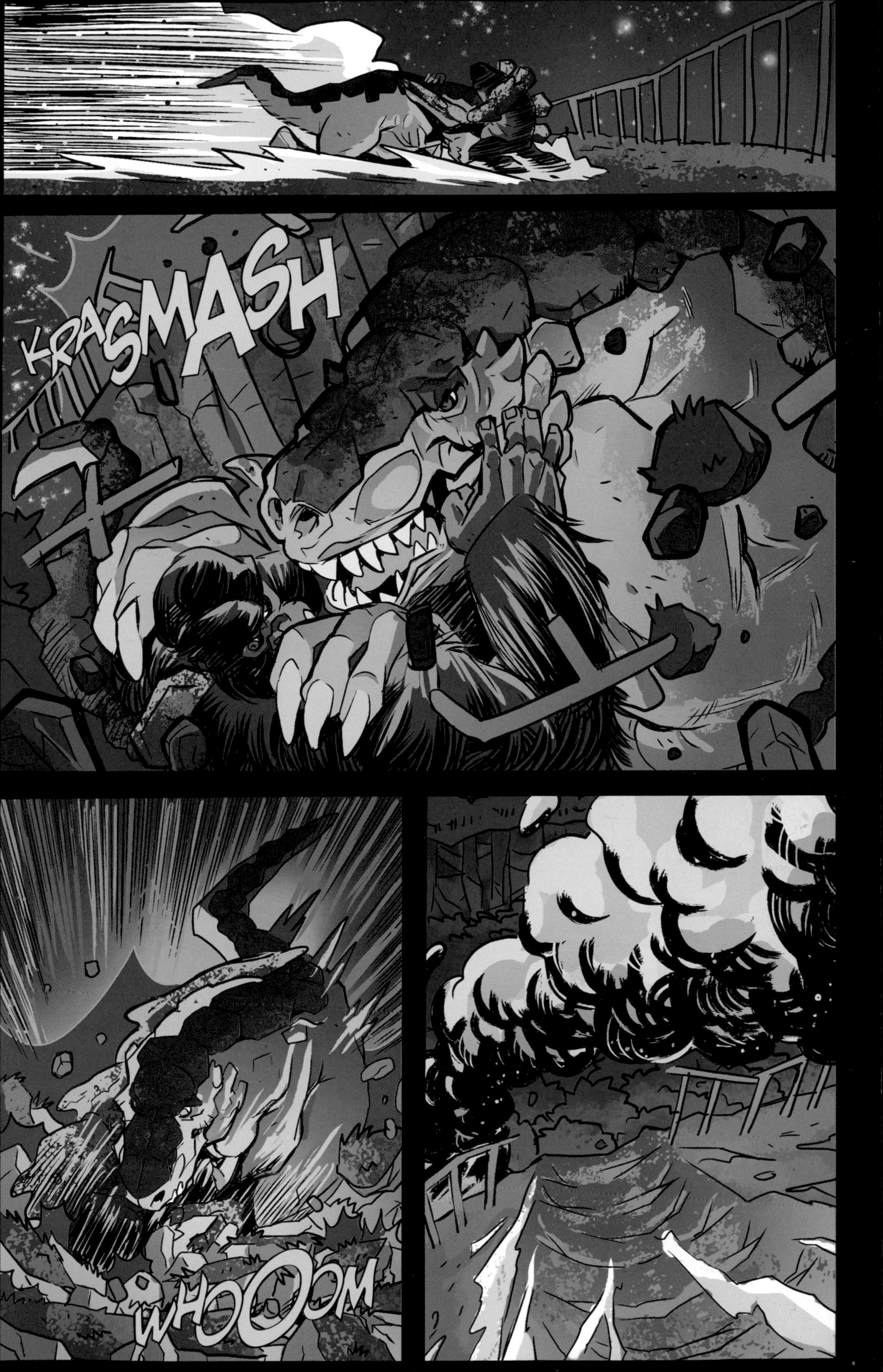
KRASMASH
WHOOOOM

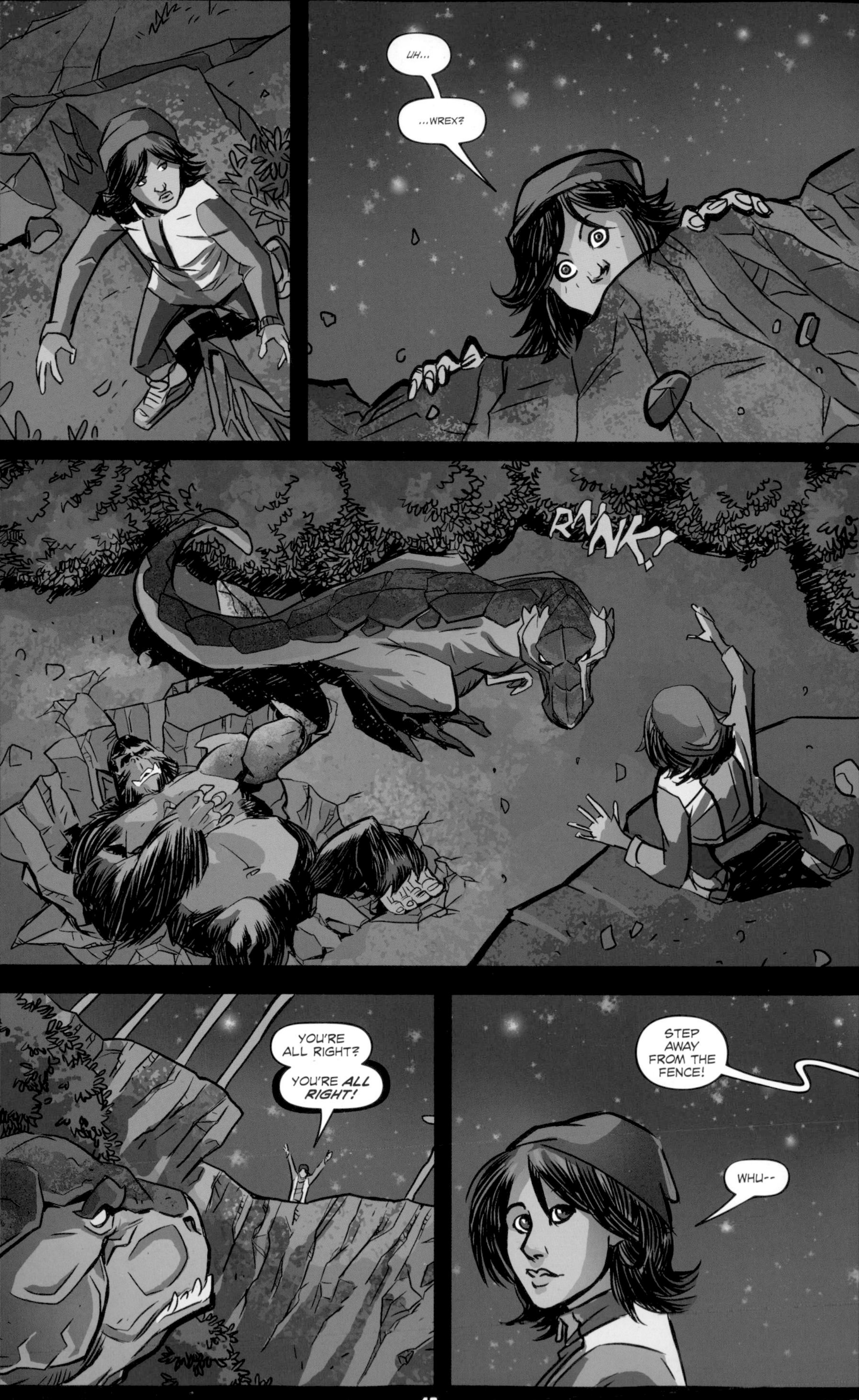
UH...
...WREX?
RNNK!
YOU'RE ALL RIGHT?
YOU'RE ALL RIGHT!
STEP AWAY FROM THE FENCE!
WHU--

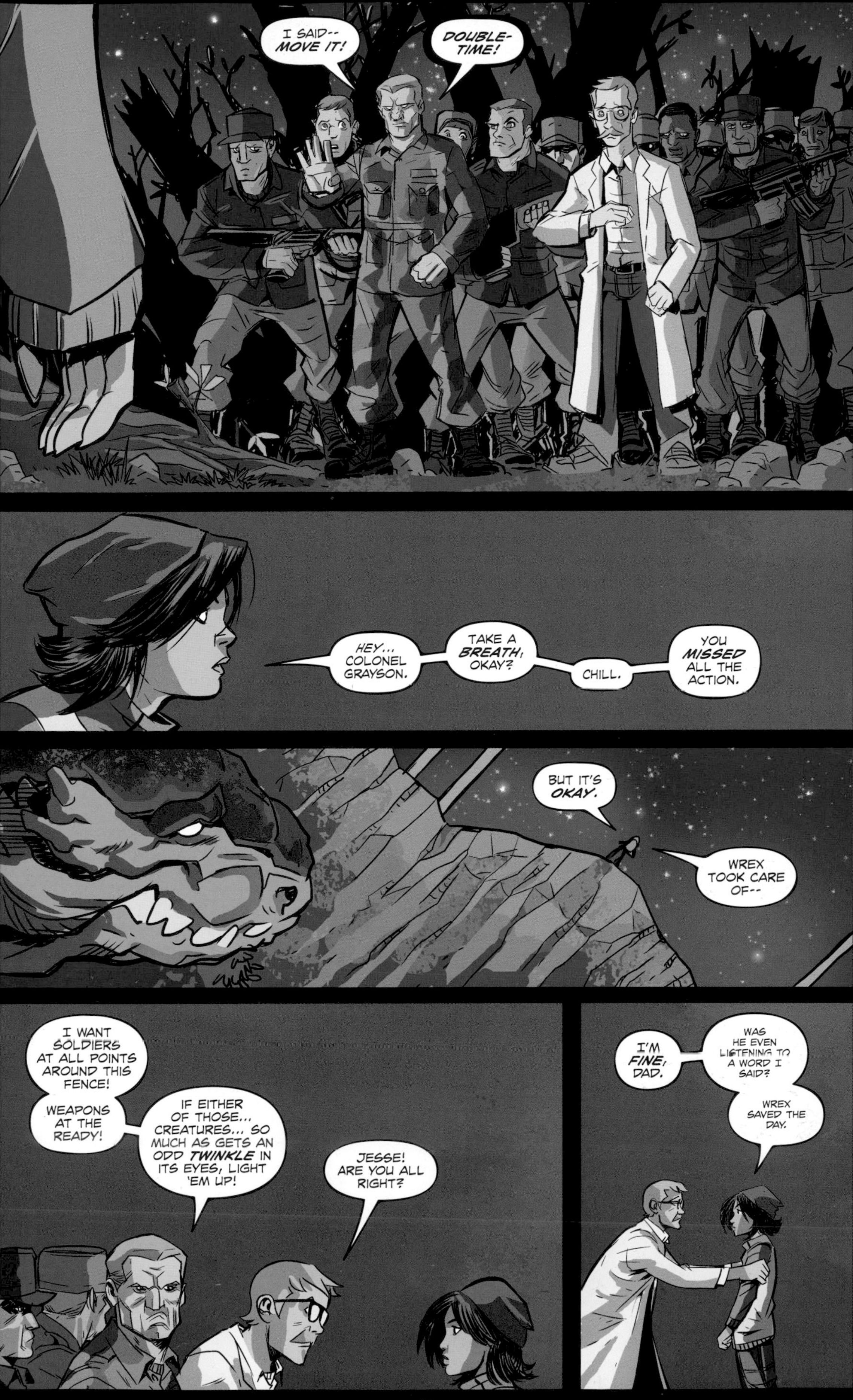
I SAID-- MOVE IT!
DOUBLE-TIME!
HEY... COLONEL GRAYSON.
TAKE A BREATH, OKAY?
CHILL.
YOU MISSED ALL THE ACTION.
BUT IT'S OKAY.
WREX TOOK CARE OF--
I WANT SOLDIERS AT ALL POINTS AROUND THIS FENCE!
WEAPONS AT THE READY!
IF EITHER OF THOSE... CREATURES... SO MUCH AS GETS AN ODD TWINKLE IN ITS EYES, LIGHT 'EM UP!
JESSE! ARE YOU ALL RIGHT?
I'M FINE, DAD.
WAS HE EVEN LISTENING TO A WORD I SAID?
WREX SAVED THE DAY.

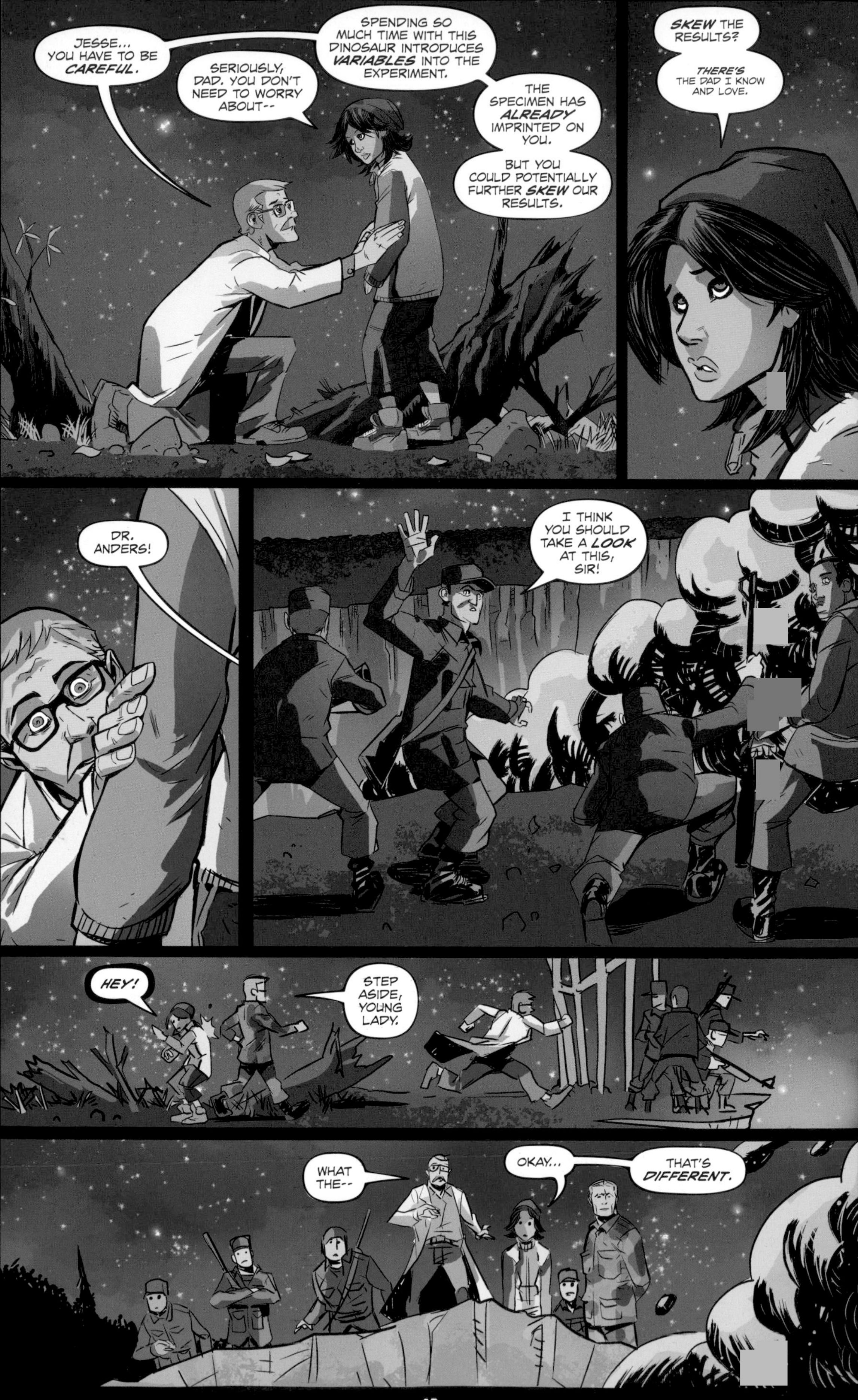
JESSE... YOU HAVE TO BE CAREFUL.
SPENDING SO MUCH TIME WITH THIS DINOSAUR INTRODUCES VARIABLES INTO THE EXPERIMENT.
SERIOUSLY, DAD. YOU DON'T NEED TO WORRY ABOUT--
THE SPECIMEN HAS ALREADY IMPRINTED ON YOU.
BUT YOU COULD POTENTIALLY FURTHER SKEW OUR RESULTS.
SKEW THE RESULTS?
THERE'S THE DAD I KNOW AND LOVE.
DR. ANDERS!
I THINK YOU SHOULD TAKE A LOOK AT THIS, SIR!
HEY!
STEP ASIDE, YOUNG LADY.
WHAT THE--
OKAY...
THAT'S DIFFERENT.

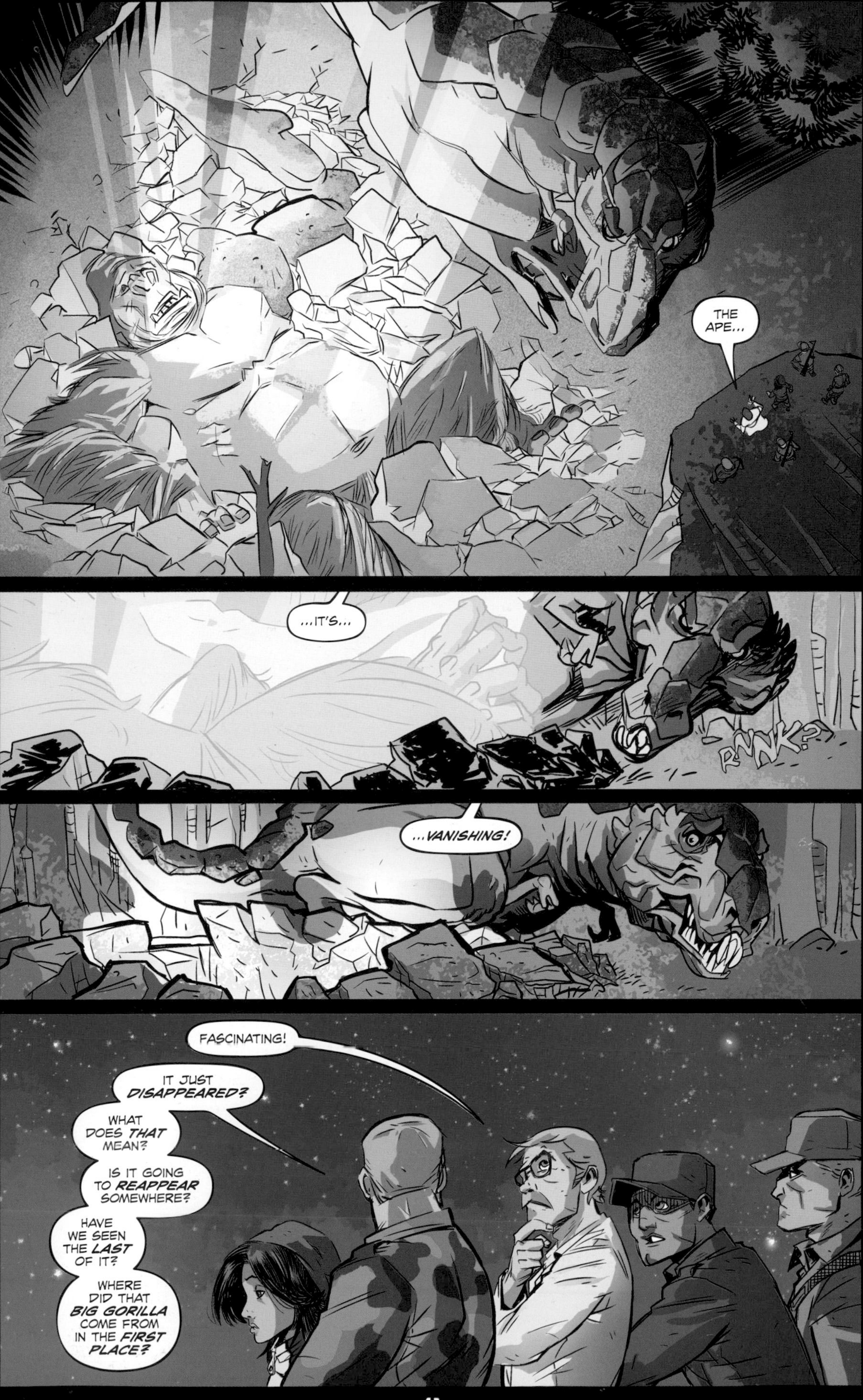
THE APE...
...IT'S...
RNNK?
...VANISHING!
FASCINATING!
IT JUST DISAPPEARED?
WHAT DOES THAT MEAN?
IS IT GOING TO REAPPEAR SOMEWHERE?
HAVE WE SEEN THE LAST OF IT?
WHERE DID THAT BIG GORILLA COME FROM IN THE FIRST PLACE?

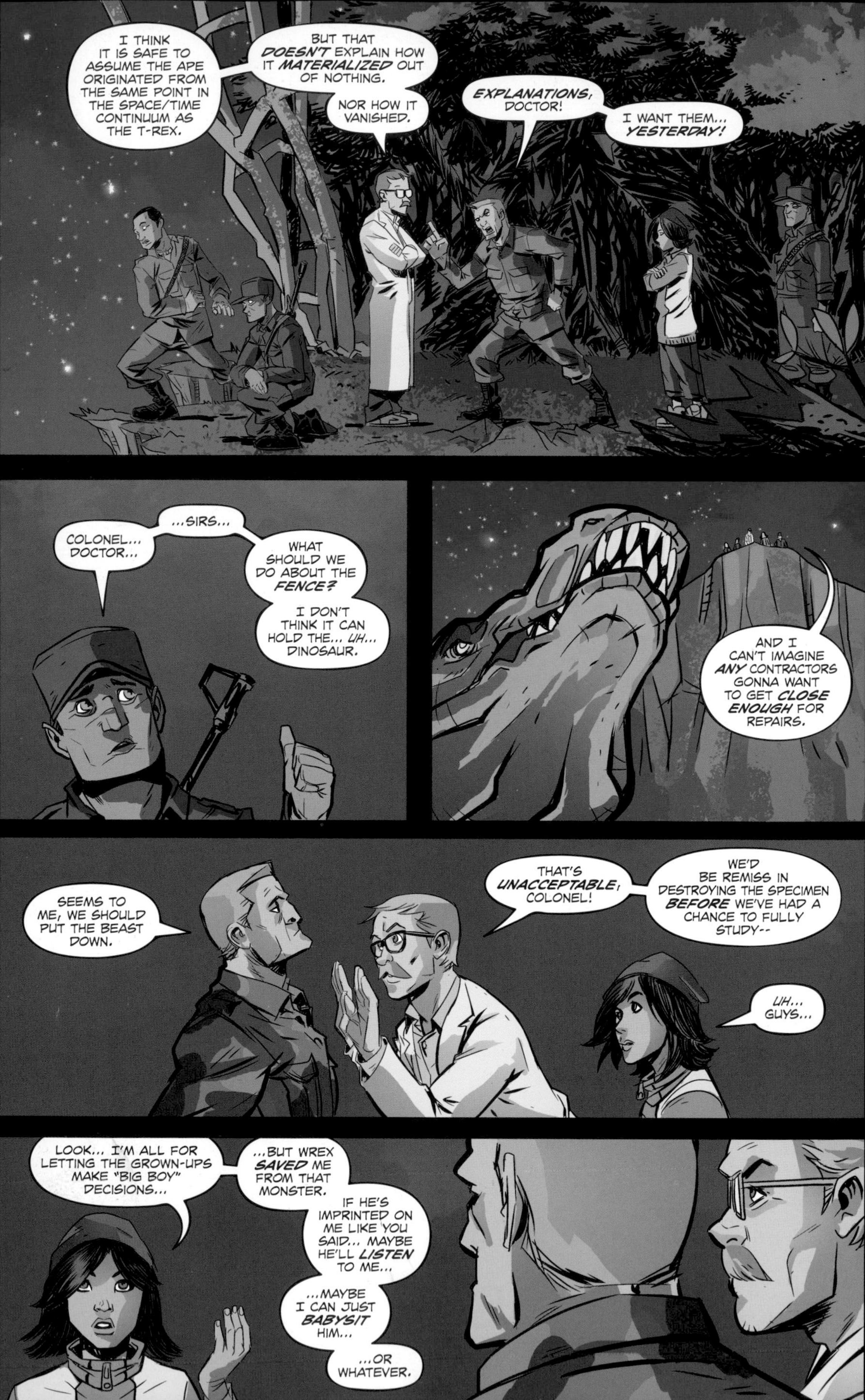
I THINK IT IS SAFE TO ASSUME THE APE ORIGINATED FROM THE SAME POINT IN THE SPACE/TIME CONTINUUM AS THE T-REX.
BUT THAT *DOESN'T* EXPLAIN HOW IT *MATERIALIZED* OUT OF NOTHING.
NOR HOW IT VANISHED.
EXPLANATIONS, DOCTOR!
I WANT THEM... *YESTERDAY!*
COLONEL... DOCTOR...
...SIRS...
WHAT SHOULD WE DO ABOUT THE *FENCE?*
I DON'T THINK IT CAN HOLD THE... *UH*... DINOSAUR.
AND I CAN'T IMAGINE *ANY* CONTRACTORS GONNA WANT TO GET *CLOSE ENOUGH* FOR REPAIRS.
SEEMS TO ME, WE SHOULD PUT THE BEAST DOWN.
THAT'S *UNACCEPTABLE*, COLONEL!
WE'D BE REMISS IN DESTROYING THE SPECIMEN *BEFORE* WE'VE HAD A CHANCE TO FULLY STUDY--
UH... GUYS...
LOOK... I'M ALL FOR LETTING THE GROWN-UPS MAKE "BIG BOY" DECISIONS...
...BUT WREX *SAVED* ME FROM THAT MONSTER.
IF HE'S IMPRINTED ON ME LIKE YOU SAID... MAYBE HE'LL *LISTEN* TO ME...
...MAYBE I CAN JUST *BABYSIT* HIM...
...OR WHATEVER.

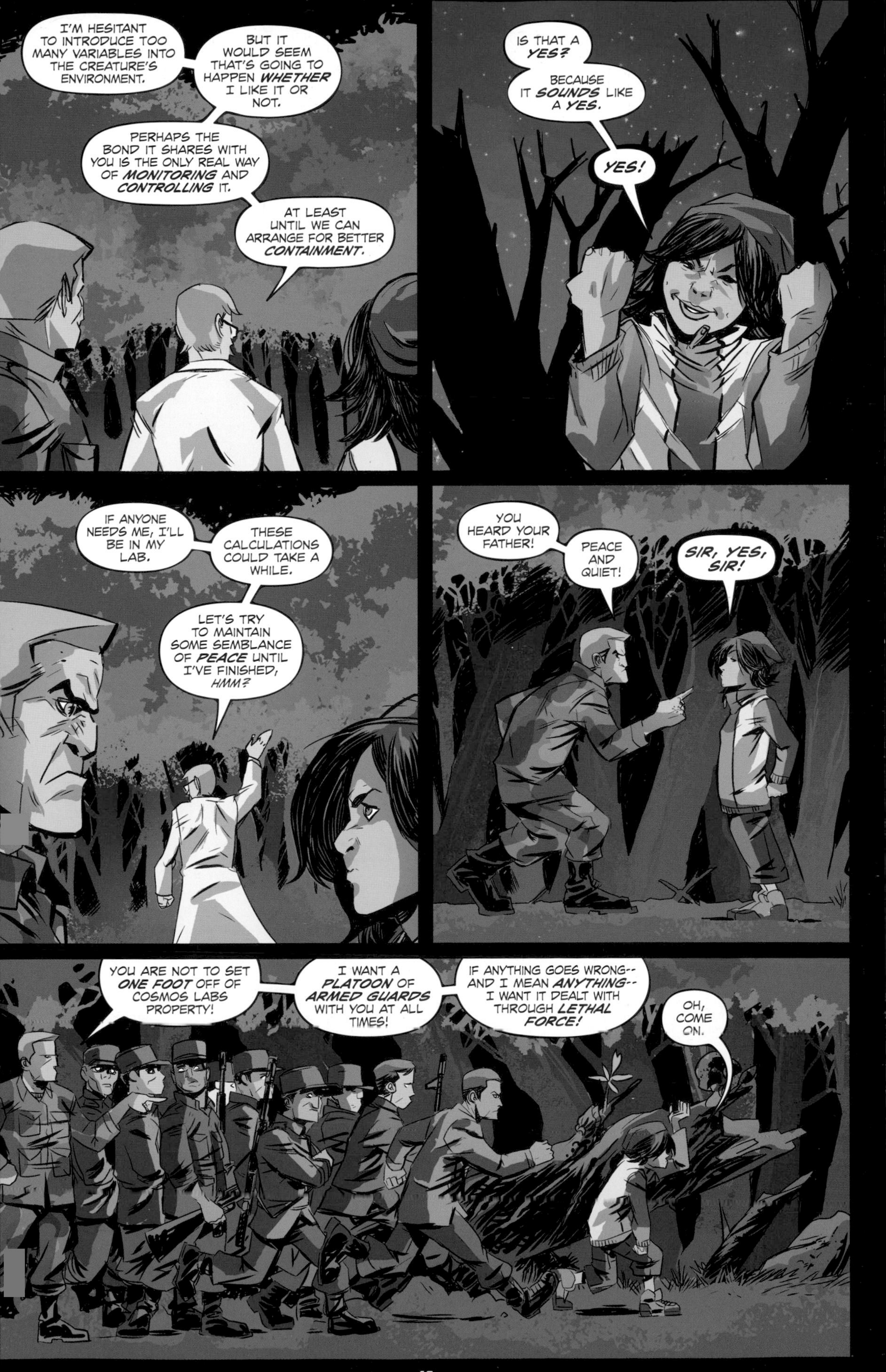

I'M HESITANT TO INTRODUCE TOO MANY VARIABLES INTO THE CREATURE'S ENVIRONMENT.
BUT IT WOULD SEEM THAT'S GOING TO HAPPEN *WHETHER* I LIKE IT OR NOT.
PERHAPS THE BOND IT SHARES WITH YOU IS THE ONLY REAL WAY OF *MONITORING* AND *CONTROLLING* IT.
AT LEAST UNTIL WE CAN ARRANGE FOR BETTER *CONTAINMENT*.
IS THAT A *YES?*
BECAUSE IT *SOUNDS* LIKE A *YES*.
YES!
IF ANYONE NEEDS ME, I'LL BE IN MY LAB.
THESE CALCULATIONS COULD TAKE A WHILE.
LET'S TRY TO MAINTAIN SOME SEMBLANCE OF *PEACE* UNTIL I'VE FINISHED, *HMM?*
YOU HEARD YOUR FATHER!
PEACE AND QUIET!
SIR, YES, SIR!
YOU ARE NOT TO SET *ONE FOOT* OFF OF COSMOS LABS PROPERTY!
I WANT A *PLATOON* OF *ARMED GUARDS* WITH YOU AT ALL TIMES!
IF ANYTHING GOES WRONG-- AND I MEAN *ANYTHING*-- I WANT IT DEALT WITH THROUGH *LETHAL FORCE!*
OH, COME ON.

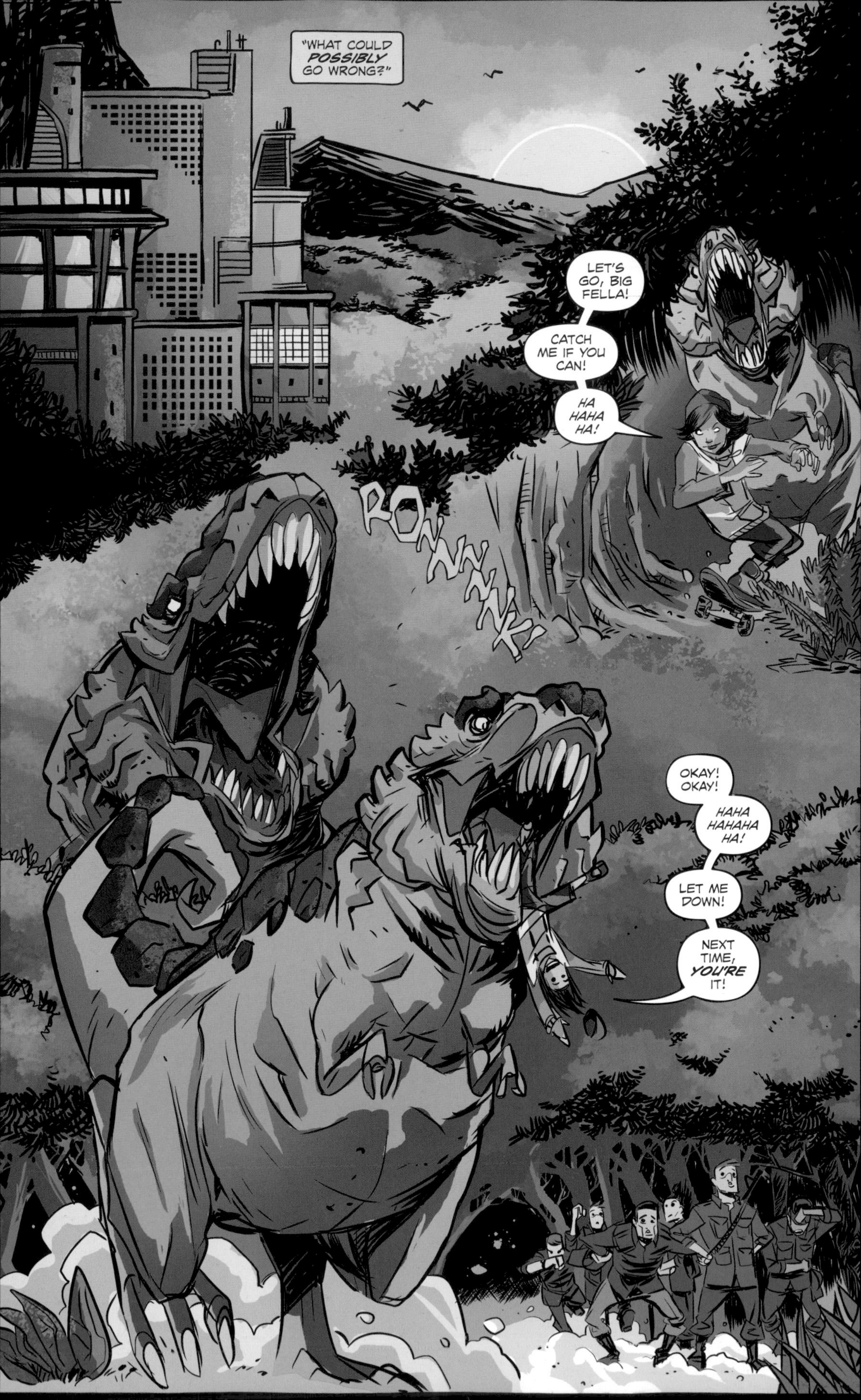
"WHAT COULD POSSIBLY GO WRONG?"
LET'S GO, BIG FELLA!
CATCH ME IF YOU CAN!
HA HAHAHA HA!
RONNNNNK!
OKAY! OKAY!
HAHA HAHAHA HA!
LET ME DOWN!
NEXT TIME, YOU'RE IT!

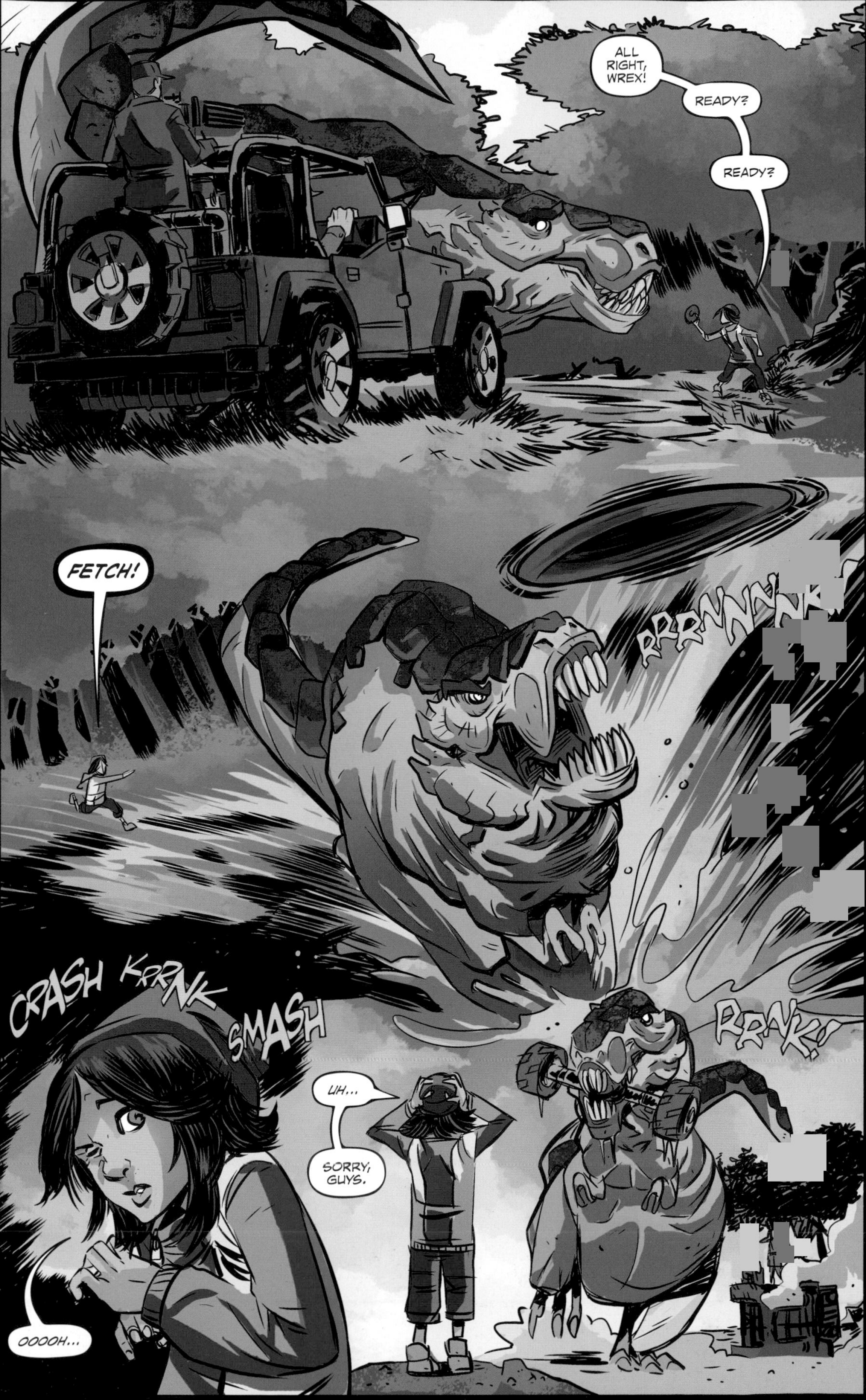
ALL RIGHT, WREX!
READY?
READY?
FETCH!
CRASH KRRNK
SMASH
RRNK!
UH...
SORRY, GUYS.
OOOOH...

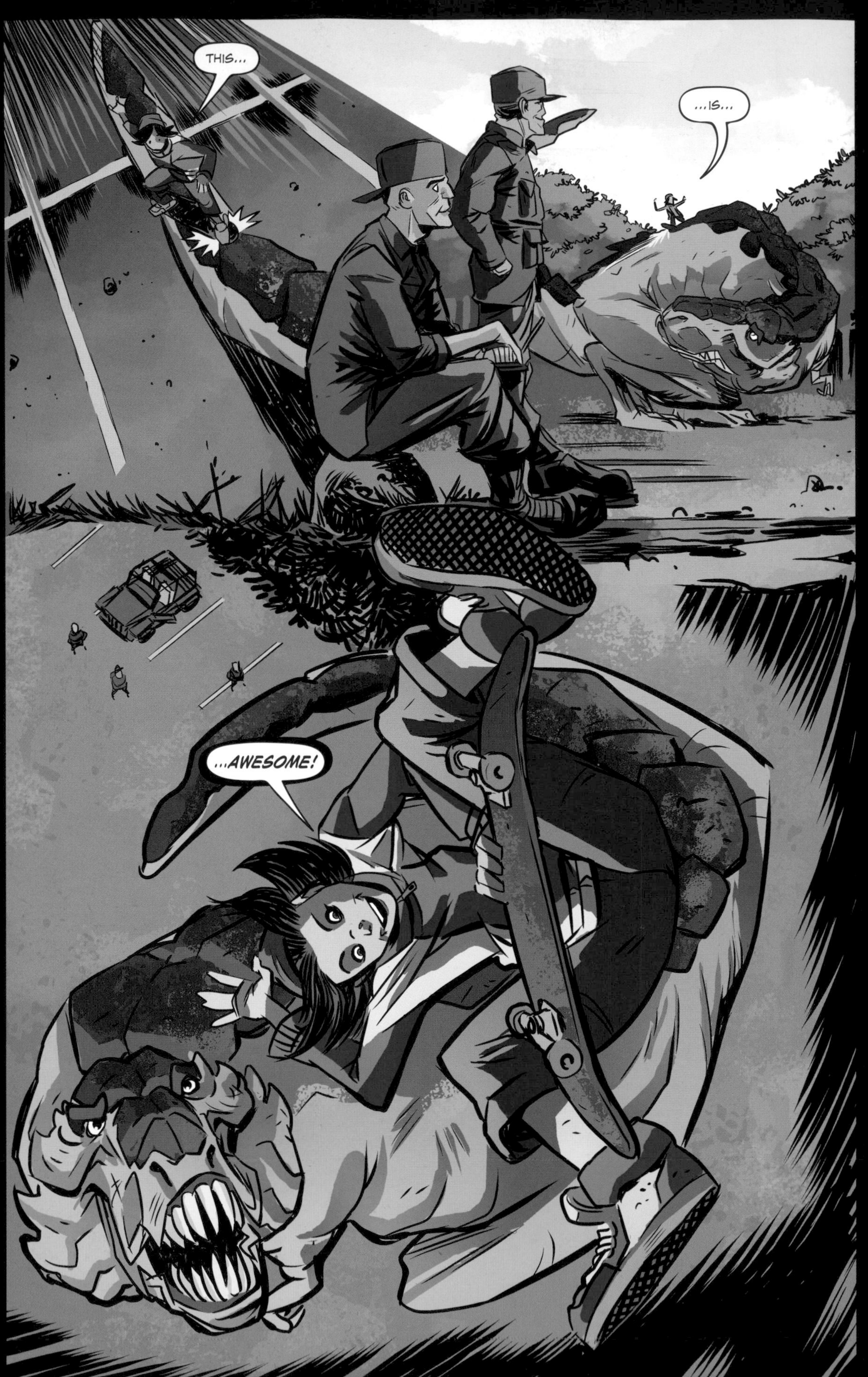
THIS...
...IS...
...AWESOME!

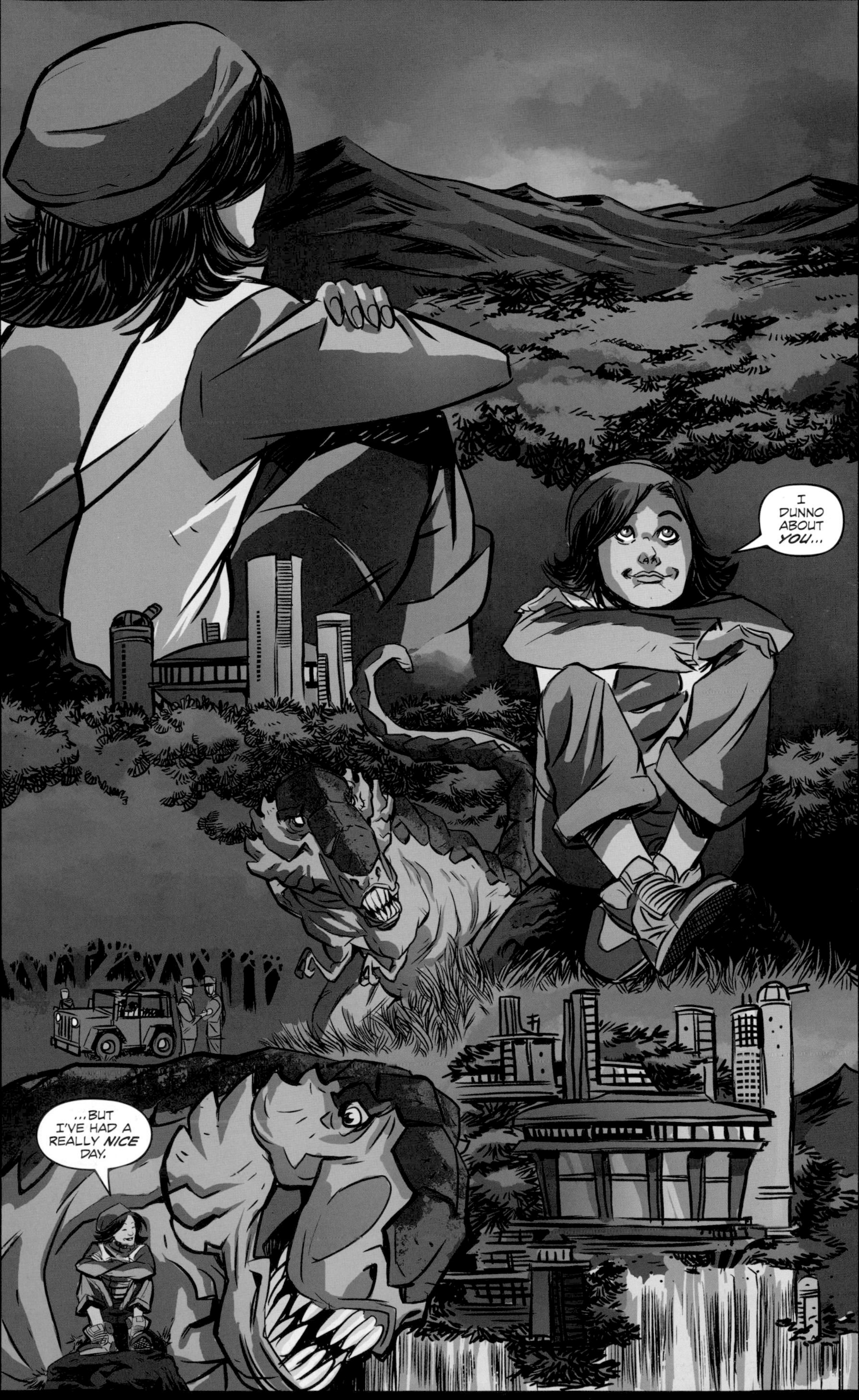
I DUNNO ABOUT YOU...
...BUT I'VE HAD A REALLY NICE DAY.

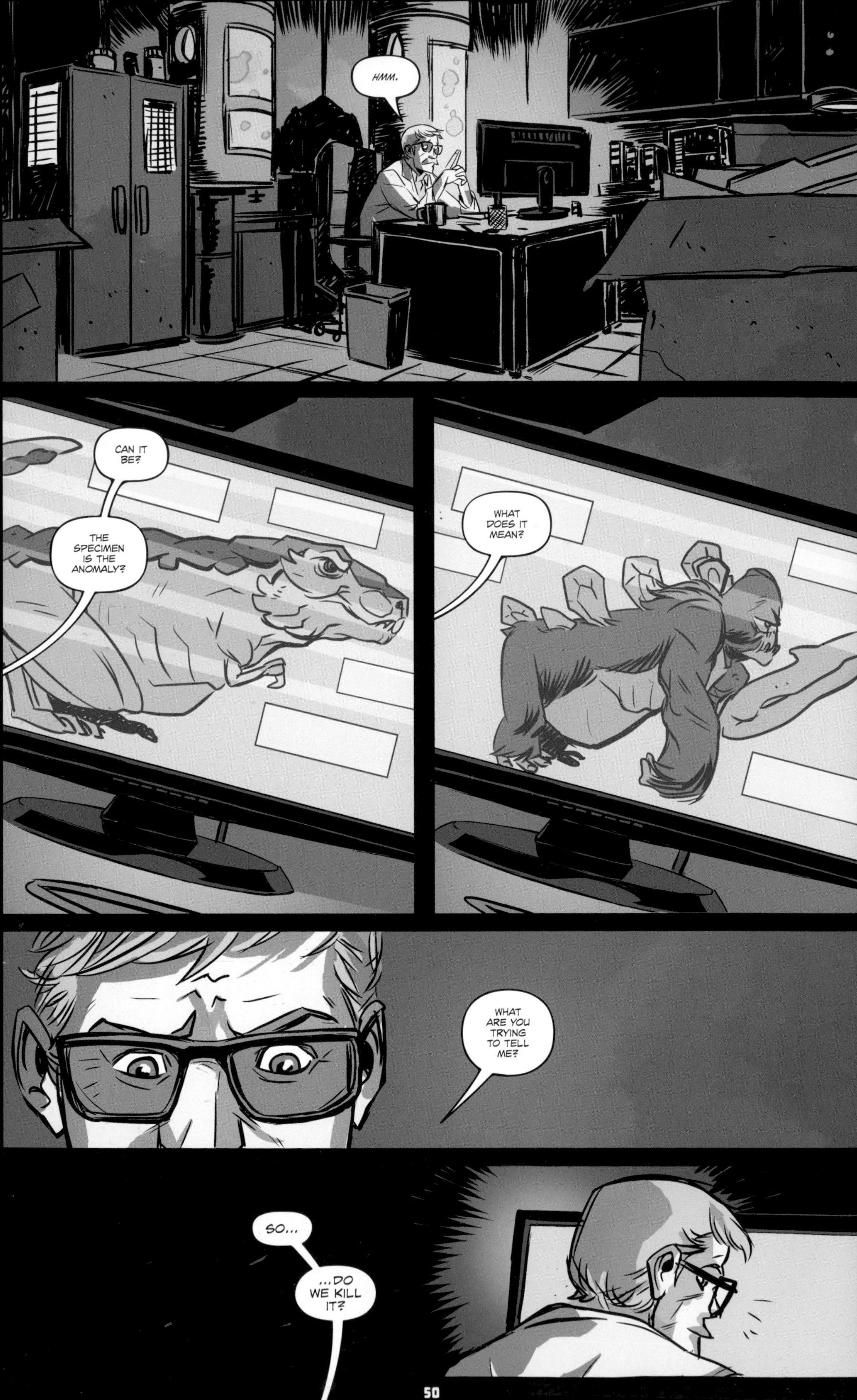
HMM.
CAN IT BE?
THE SPECIMEN IS THE ANOMALY?
WHAT DOES IT MEAN?
WHAT ARE YOU TRYING TO TELL ME?
SO...
...DO WE KILL IT?

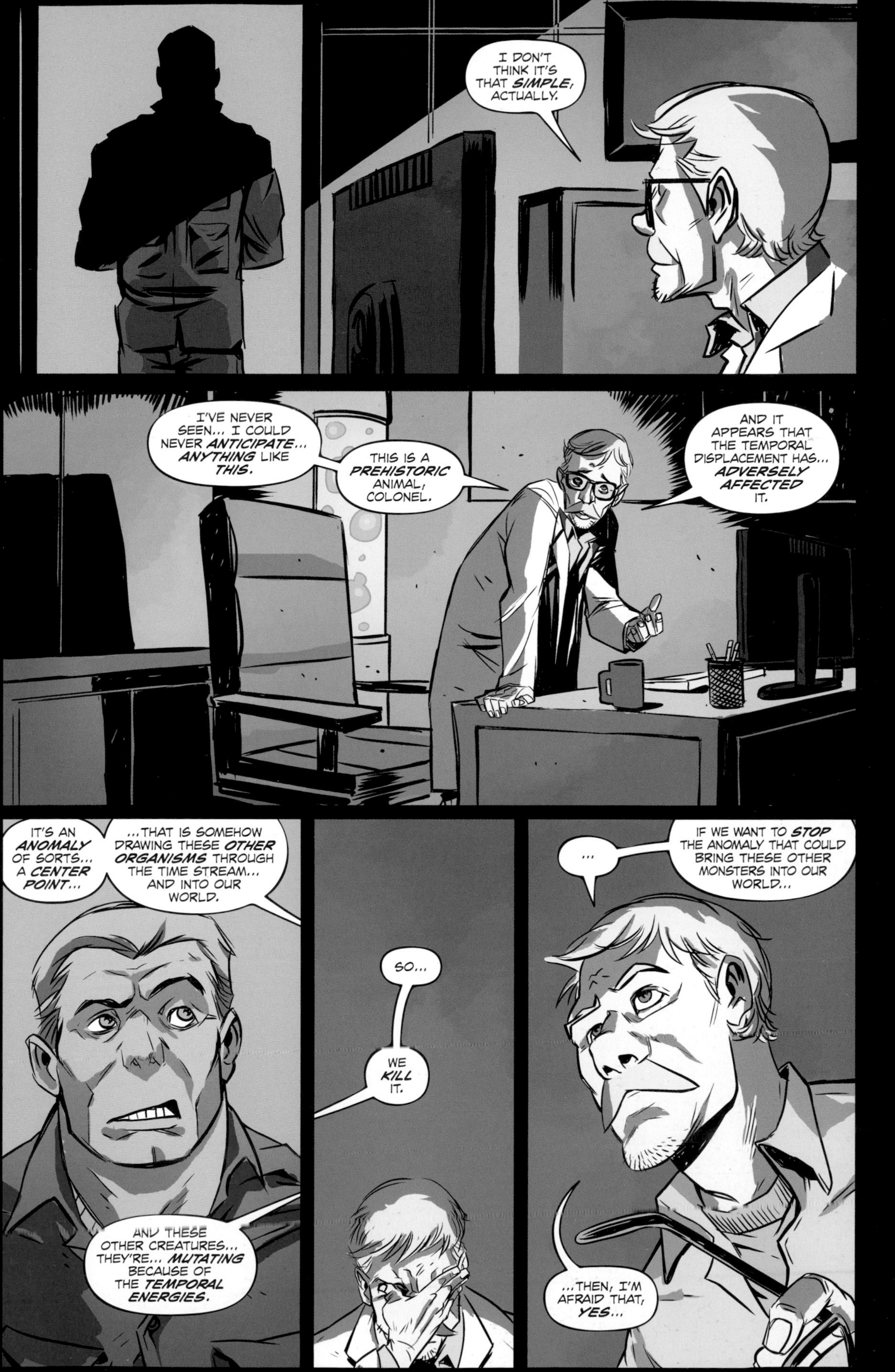
I DON'T THINK IT'S THAT SIMPLE, ACTUALLY.
I'VE NEVER SEEN... I COULD NEVER ANTICIPATE... ANYTHING LIKE THIS.
THIS IS A PREHISTORIC ANIMAL, COLONEL.
AND IT APPEARS THAT THE TEMPORAL DISPLACEMENT HAS... ADVERSELY AFFECTED IT.
IT'S AN ANOMALY OF SORTS... A CENTER POINT...
...THAT IS SOMEHOW DRAWING THESE OTHER ORGANISMS THROUGH THE TIME STREAM... AND INTO OUR WORLD.
AND THESE OTHER CREATURES... THEY'RE... MUTATING BECAUSE OF THE TEMPORAL ENERGIES.
SO...
WE KILL IT.
...
IF WE WANT TO STOP THE ANOMALY THAT COULD BRING THESE OTHER MONSTERS INTO OUR WORLD...
...THEN, I'M AFRAID THAT, YES...

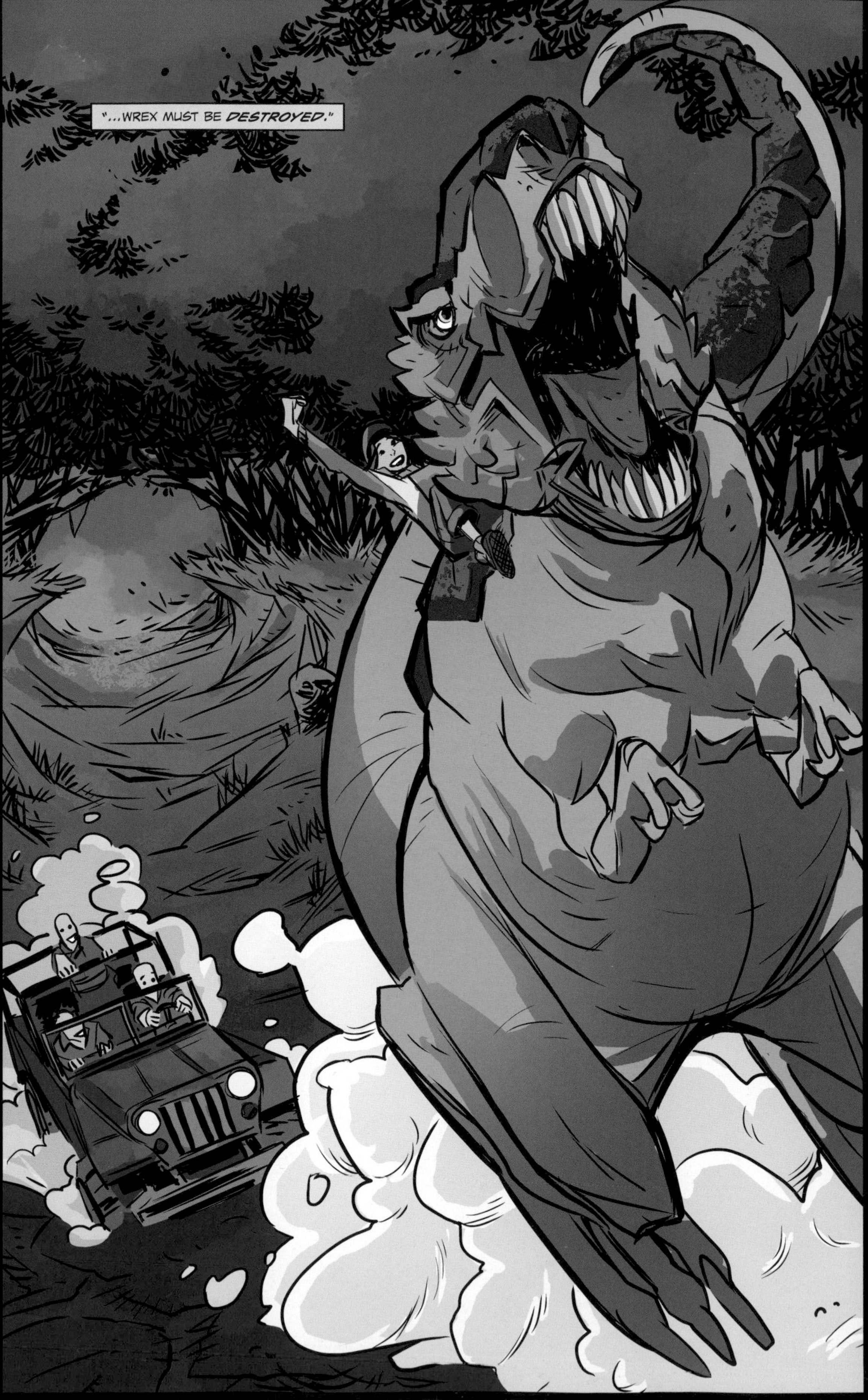
"...WREX MUST BE *DESTROYED.*"

CHAPTER THREE

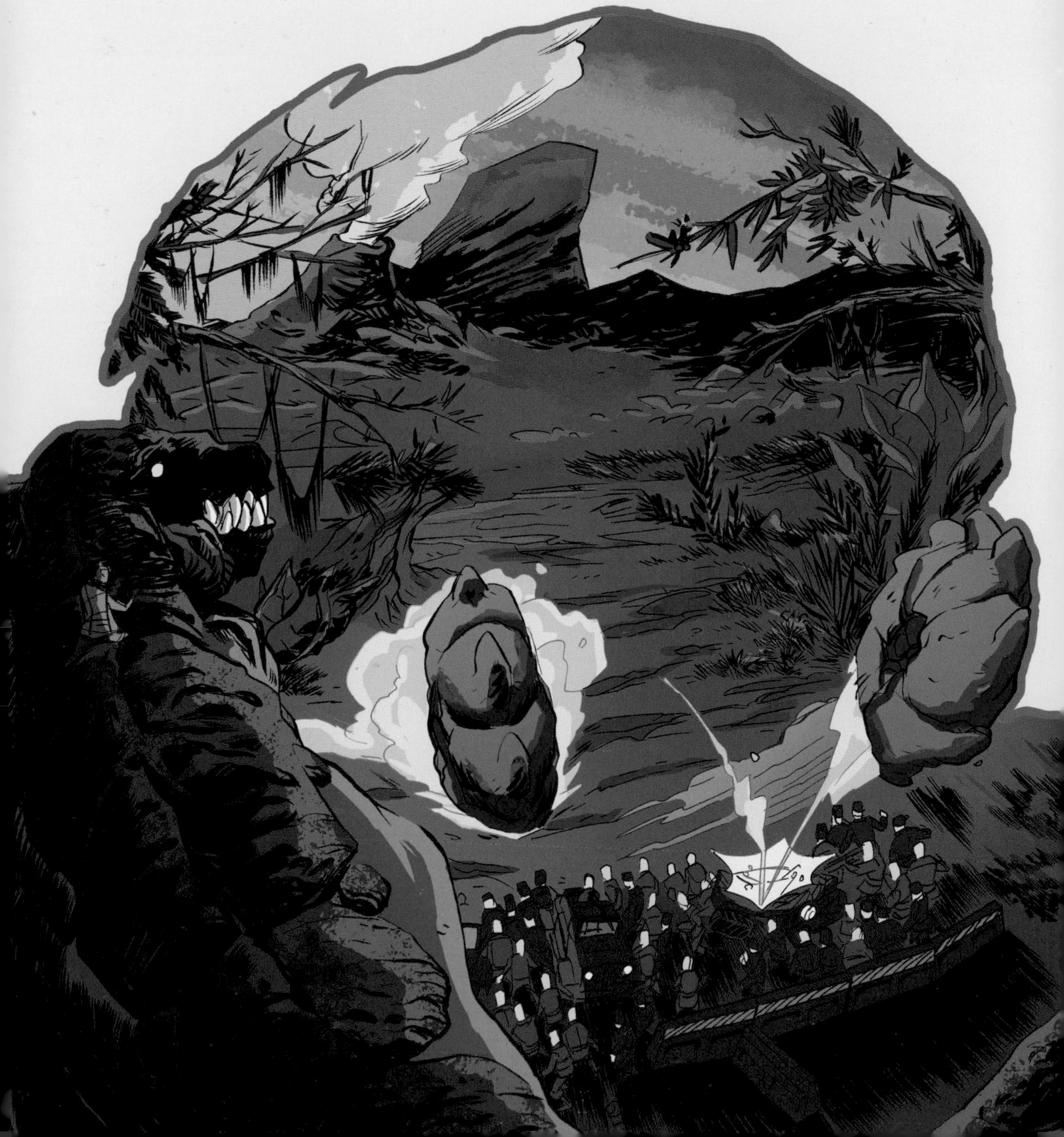

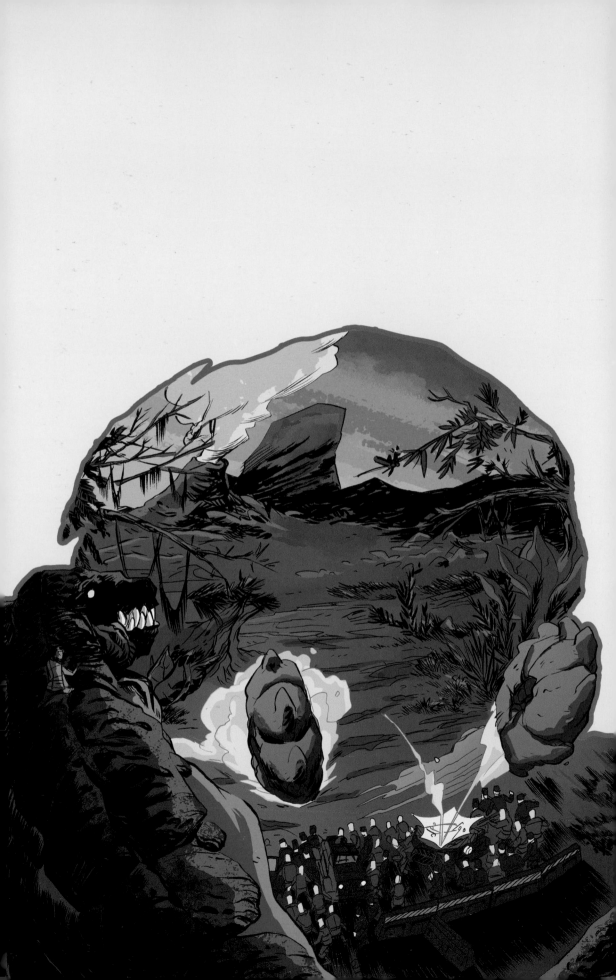

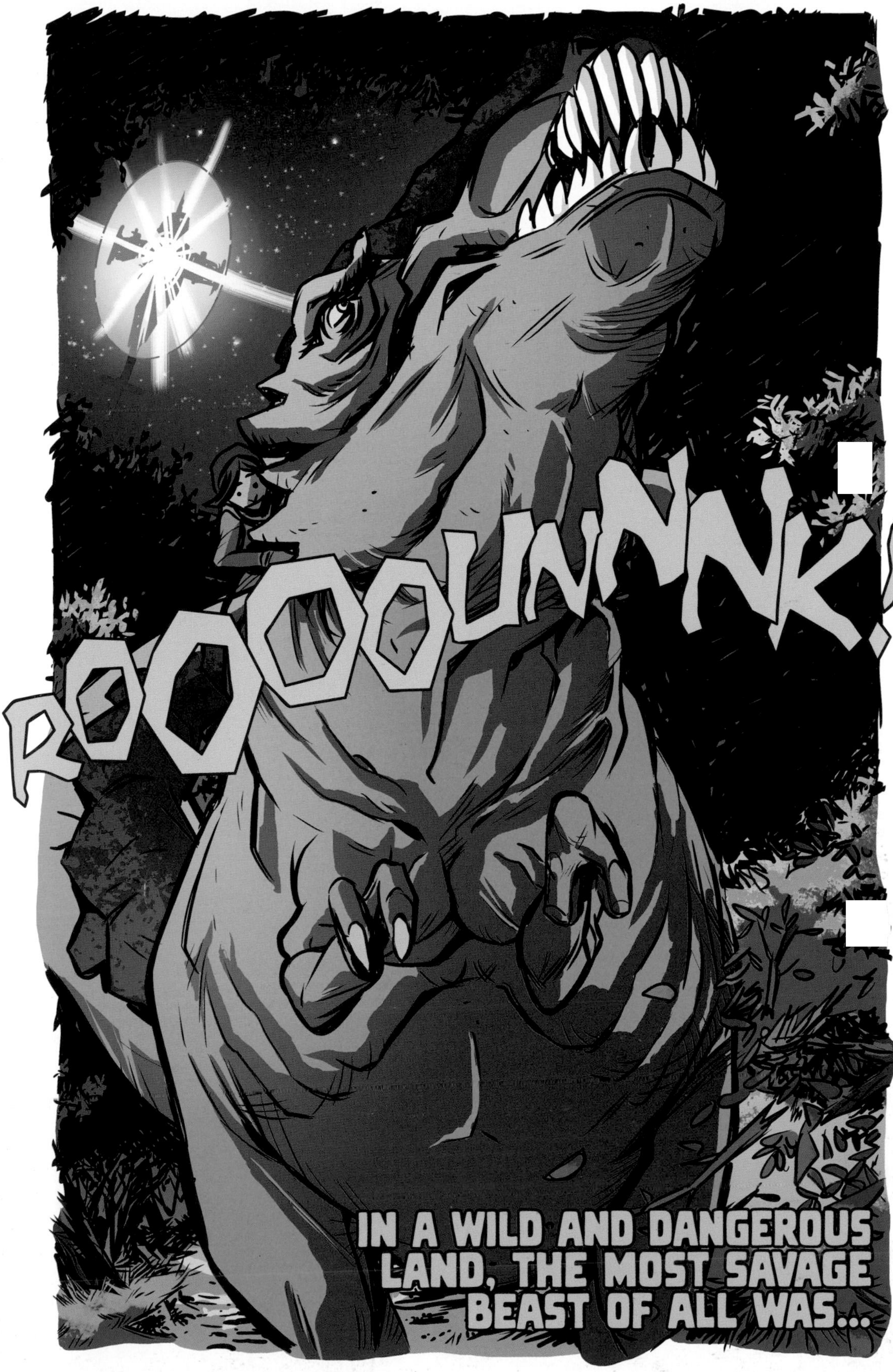
ROOOOOUNNNK!
IN A WILD AND DANGEROUS LAND, THE MOST SAVAGE BEAST OF ALL WAS...

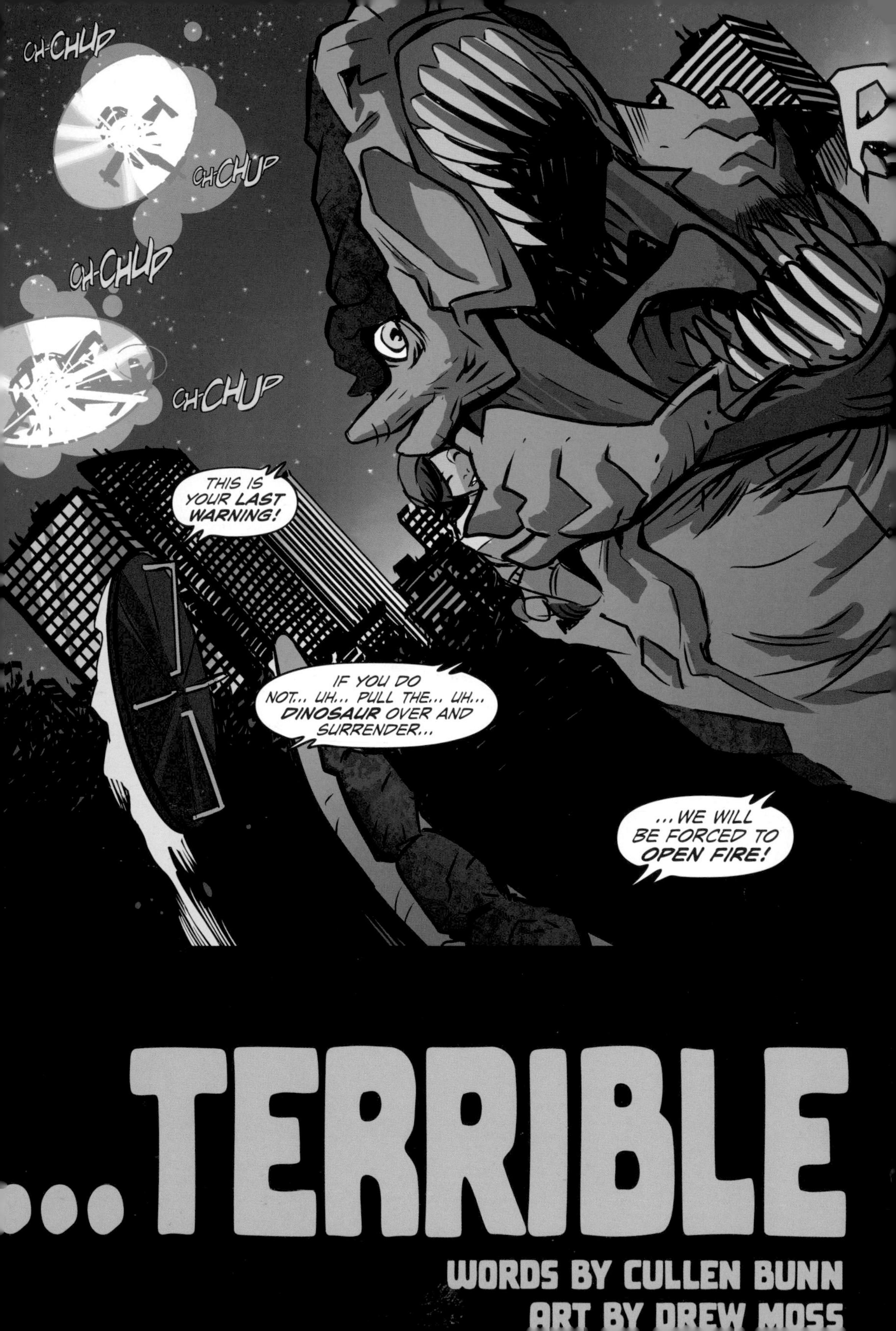
CH-CHUP
CH-CHUP
CH-CHUP
CH-CHUP
THIS IS YOUR LAST WARNING!
IF YOU DO NOT... UH... PULL THE... UH... DINOSAUR OVER AND SURRENDER...
...WE WILL BE FORCED TO OPEN FIRE!

...TERRIBLE

WORDS BY CULLEN BUNN
ART BY DREW MOSS

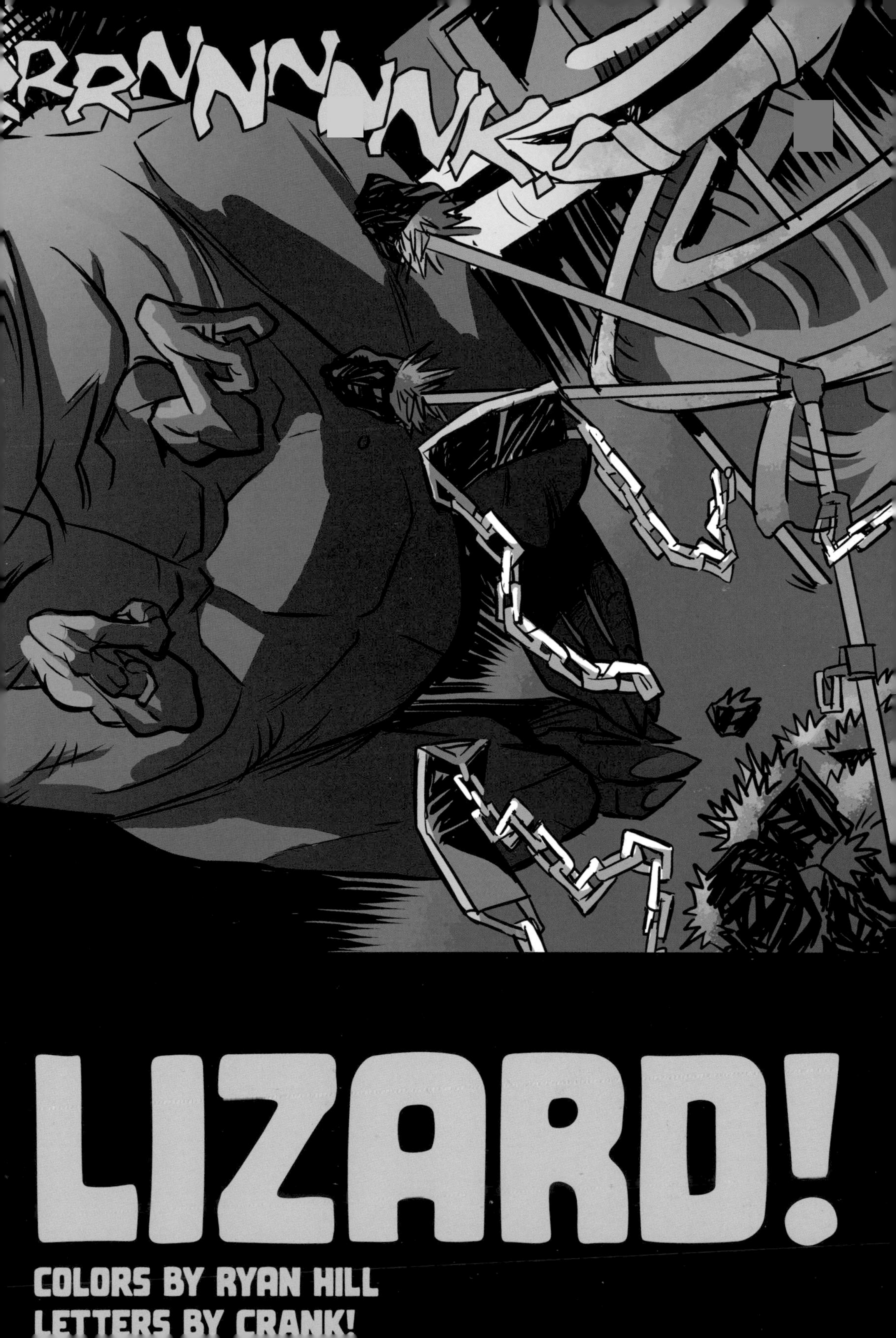
RRNNNNNK

LIZARD!

COLORS BY RYAN HILL
LETTERS BY CRANK!

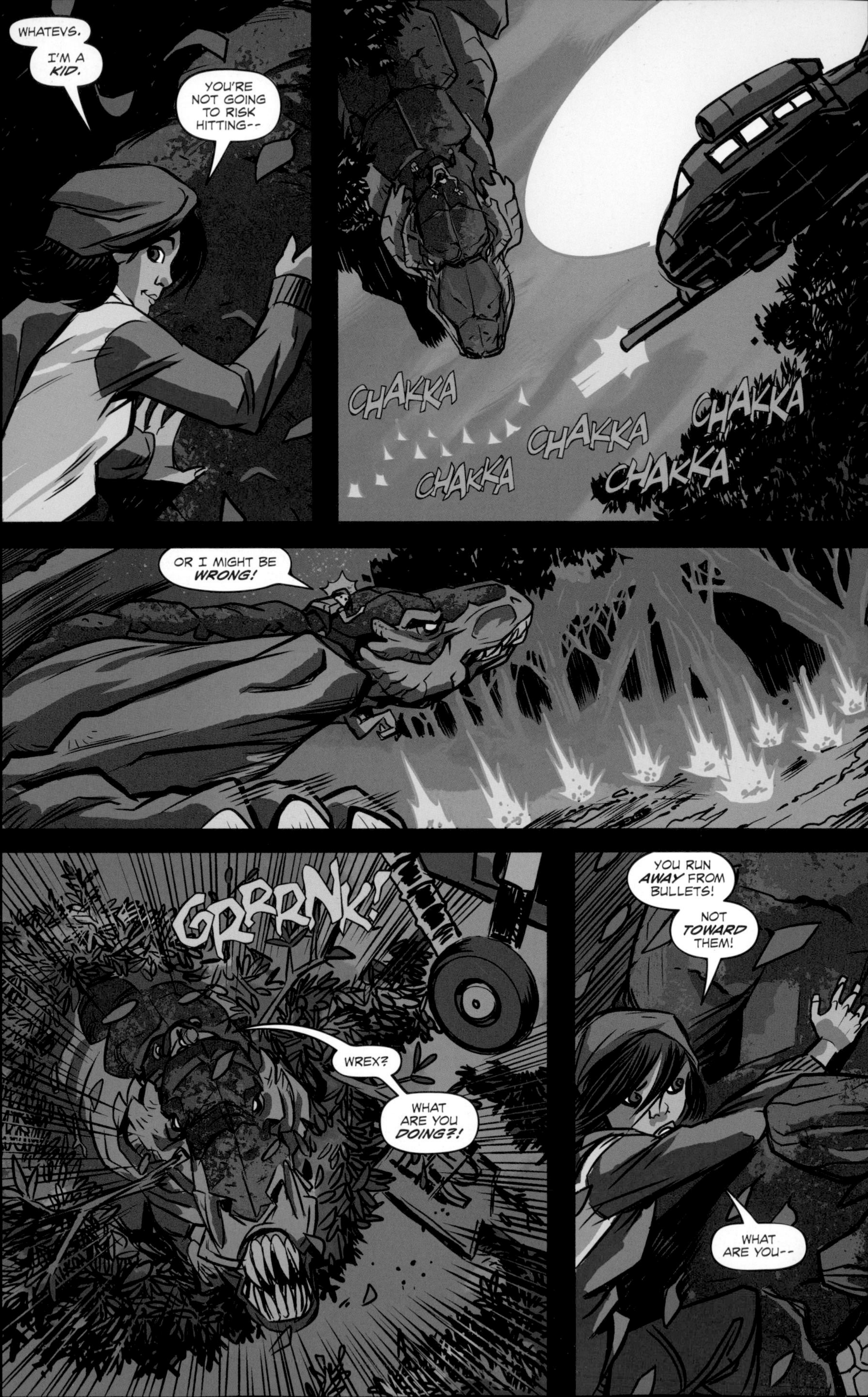
WHATEVS.
I'M A KID.
YOU'RE NOT GOING TO RISK HITTING--
CHAKKA
CHAKKA
CHAKKA
CHAKKA
CHAKKA
OR I MIGHT BE WRONG!
GRRRNK!
WREX?
WHAT ARE YOU DOING?!
YOU RUN AWAY FROM BULLETS!
NOT TOWARD THEM!
WHAT ARE YOU--

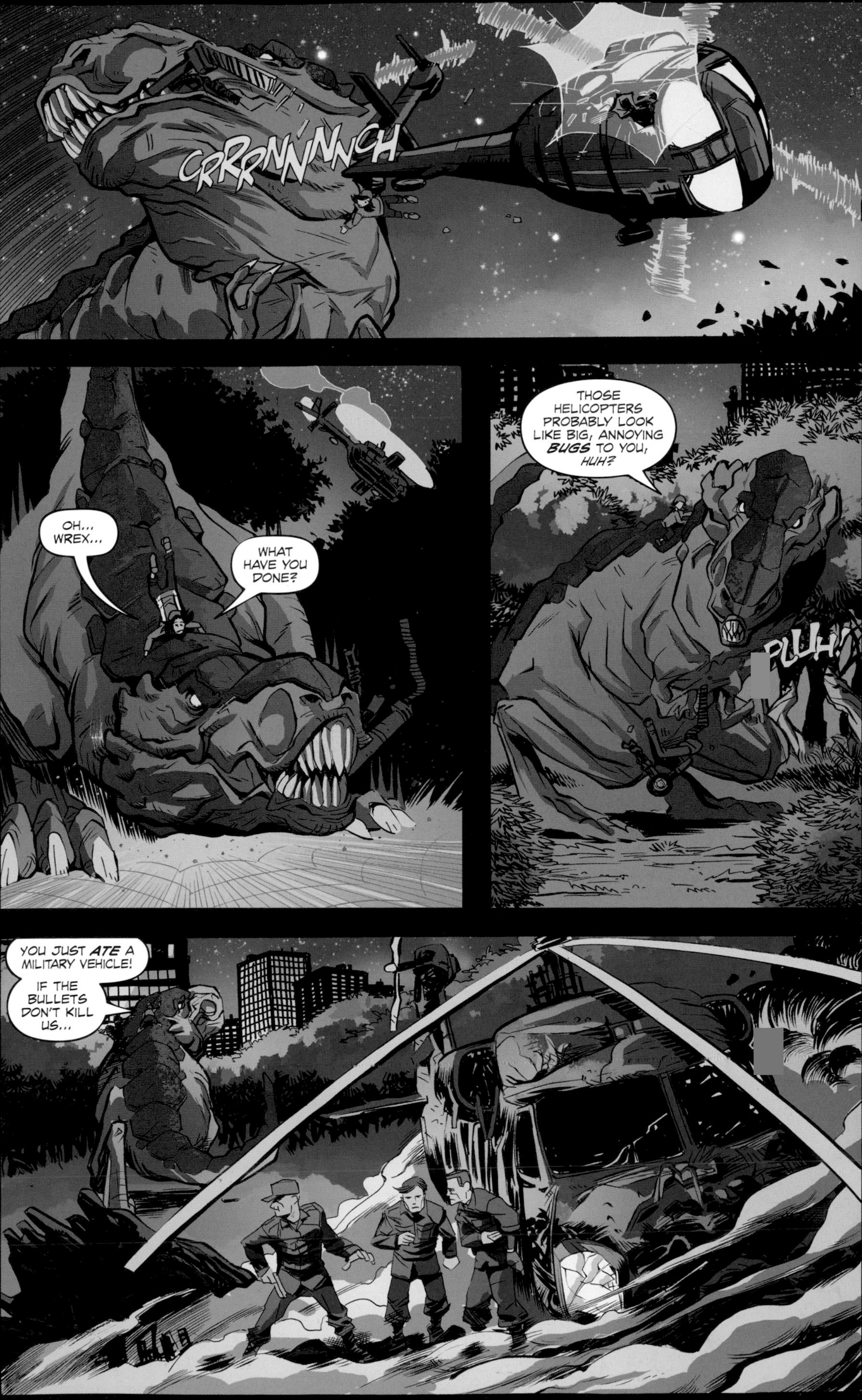
CRRRNNNNCH
OH... WREX...
WHAT HAVE YOU DONE?
THOSE HELICOPTERS PROBABLY LOOK LIKE BIG, ANNOYING BUGS TO YOU, HUH?
PLUH!
YOU JUST ATE A MILITARY VEHICLE!
IF THE BULLETS DON'T KILL US...

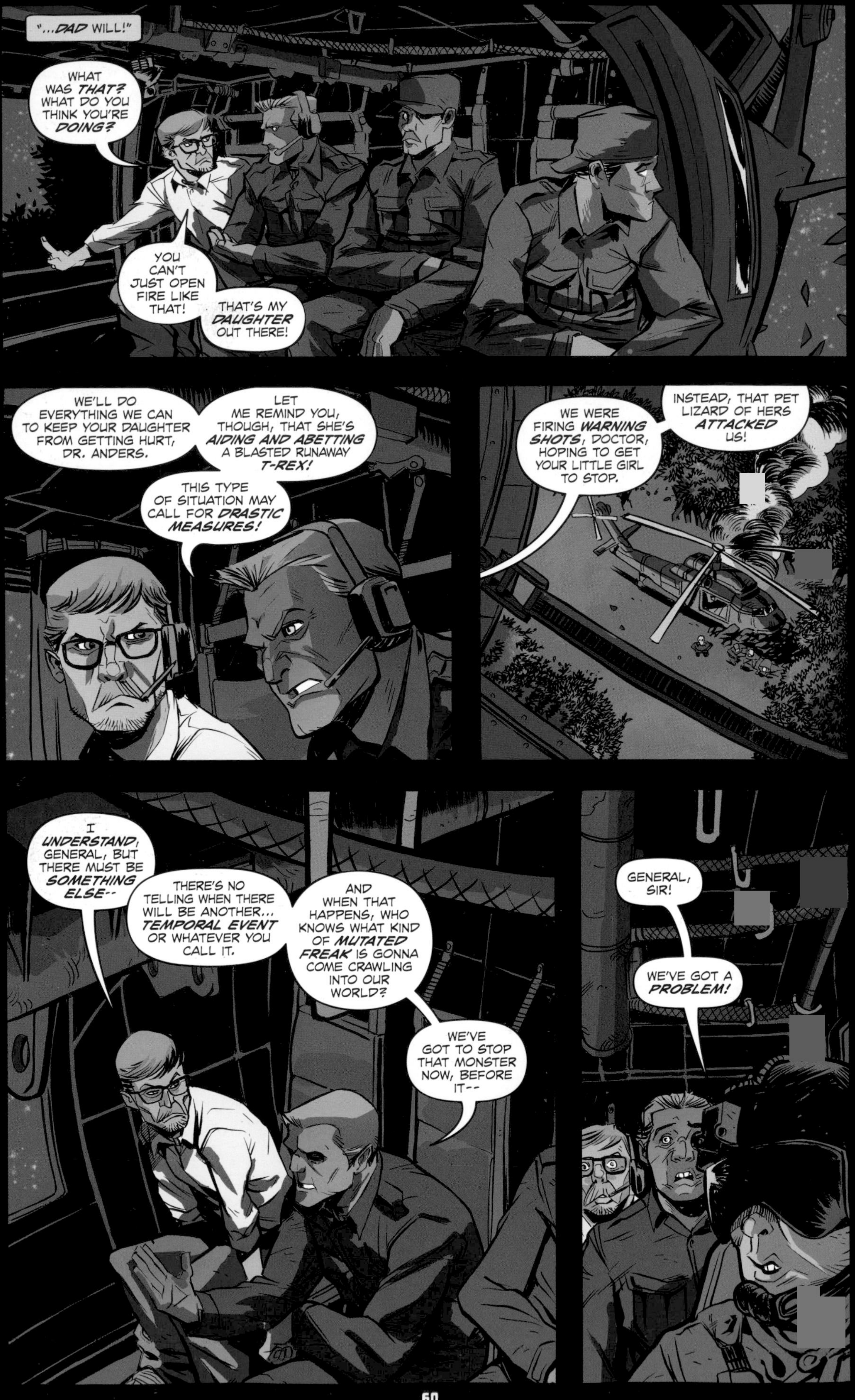
"...DAD WILL!"
WHAT WAS THAT? WHAT DO YOU THINK YOU'RE DOING?
YOU CAN'T JUST OPEN FIRE LIKE THAT!
THAT'S MY DAUGHTER OUT THERE!
WE'LL DO EVERYTHING WE CAN TO KEEP YOUR DAUGHTER FROM GETTING HURT, DR. ANDERS.
LET ME REMIND YOU, THOUGH, THAT SHE'S AIDING AND ABETTING A BLASTED RUNAWAY T-REX!
THIS TYPE OF SITUATION MAY CALL FOR DRASTIC MEASURES!
WE WERE FIRING WARNING SHOTS, DOCTOR, HOPING TO GET YOUR LITTLE GIRL TO STOP.
INSTEAD, THAT PET LIZARD OF HERS ATTACKED US!
I UNDERSTAND, GENERAL, BUT THERE MUST BE SOMETHING ELSE--
THERE'S NO TELLING WHEN THERE WILL BE ANOTHER... TEMPORAL EVENT OR WHATEVER YOU CALL IT.
AND WHEN THAT HAPPENS, WHO KNOWS WHAT KIND OF MUTATED FREAK IS GONNA COME CRAWLING INTO OUR WORLD?
WE'VE GOT TO STOP THAT MONSTER NOW, BEFORE IT--
GENERAL, SIR!
WE'VE GOT A PROBLEM!

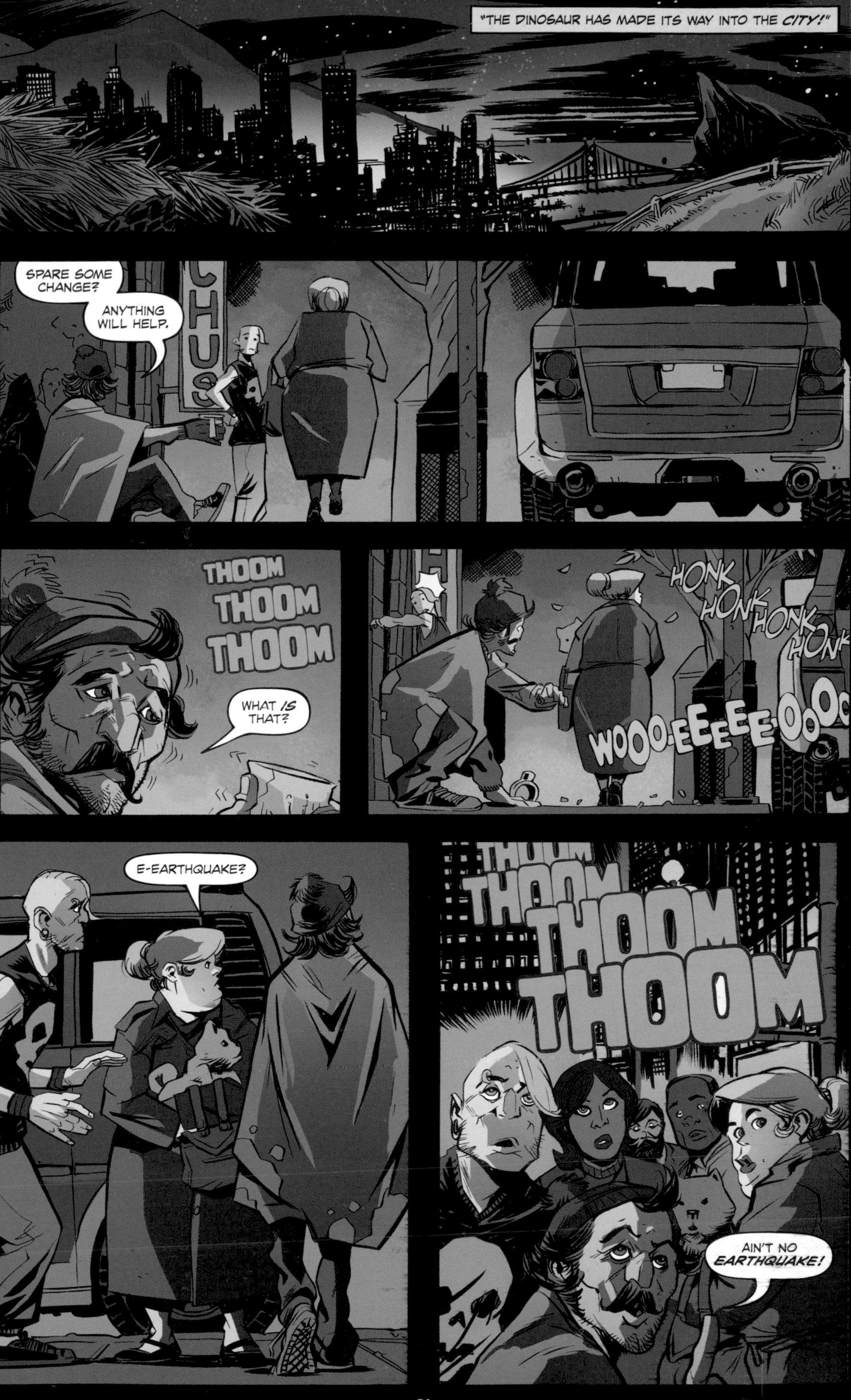
"THE DINOSAUR HAS MADE ITS WAY INTO THE CITY!"
SPARE SOME CHANGE?
ANYTHING WILL HELP.
THOOM THOOM THOOM
WHAT IS THAT?
HONK HONK HONK HONK
WOOO-EEEEE-OOOO
E-EARTHQUAKE?
THOOM THOOM THOOM THOOM
AIN'T NO EARTHQUAKE!

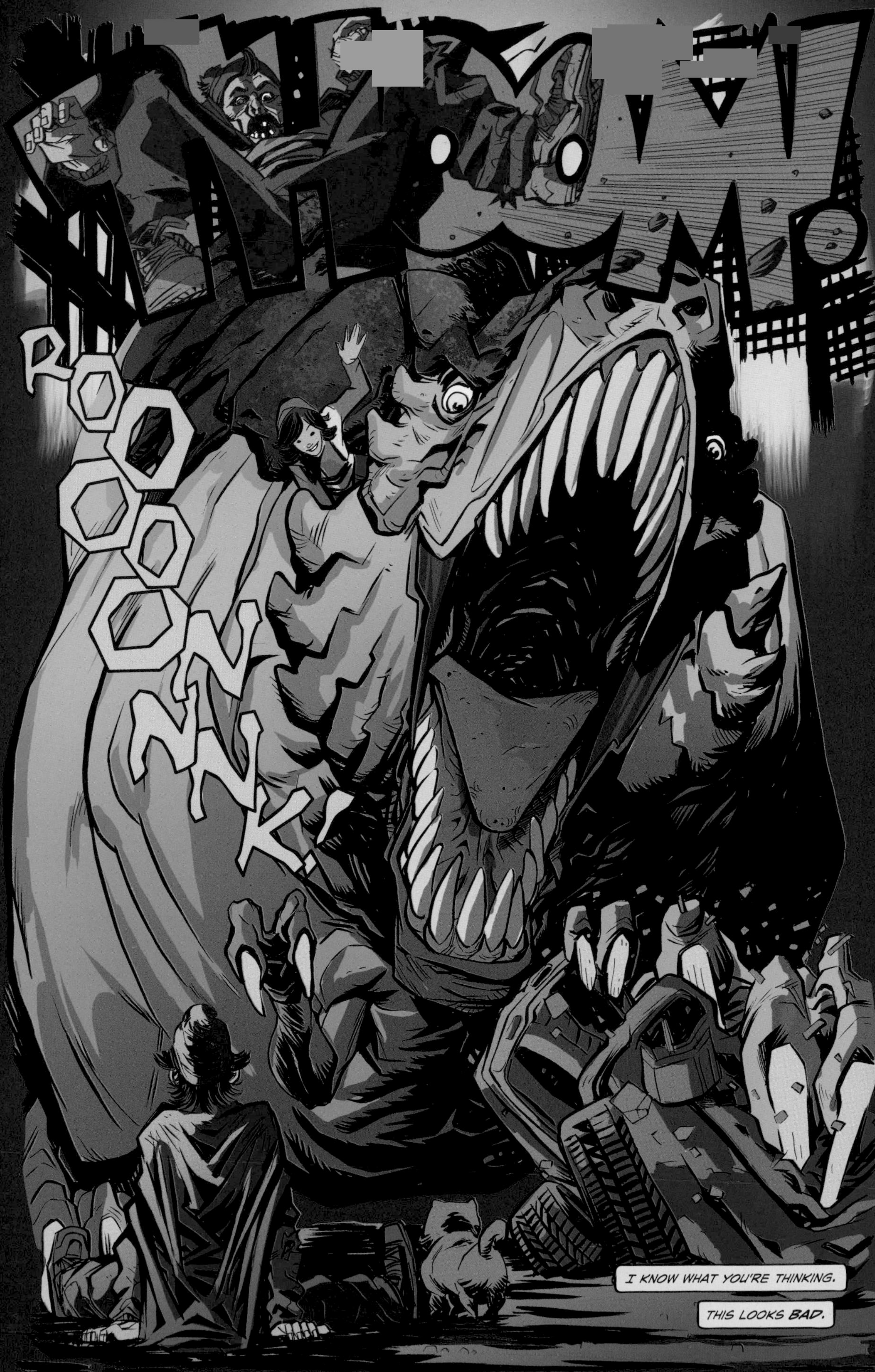
ROOOOONNK!
I KNOW WHAT YOU'RE THINKING.
THIS LOOKS BAD.

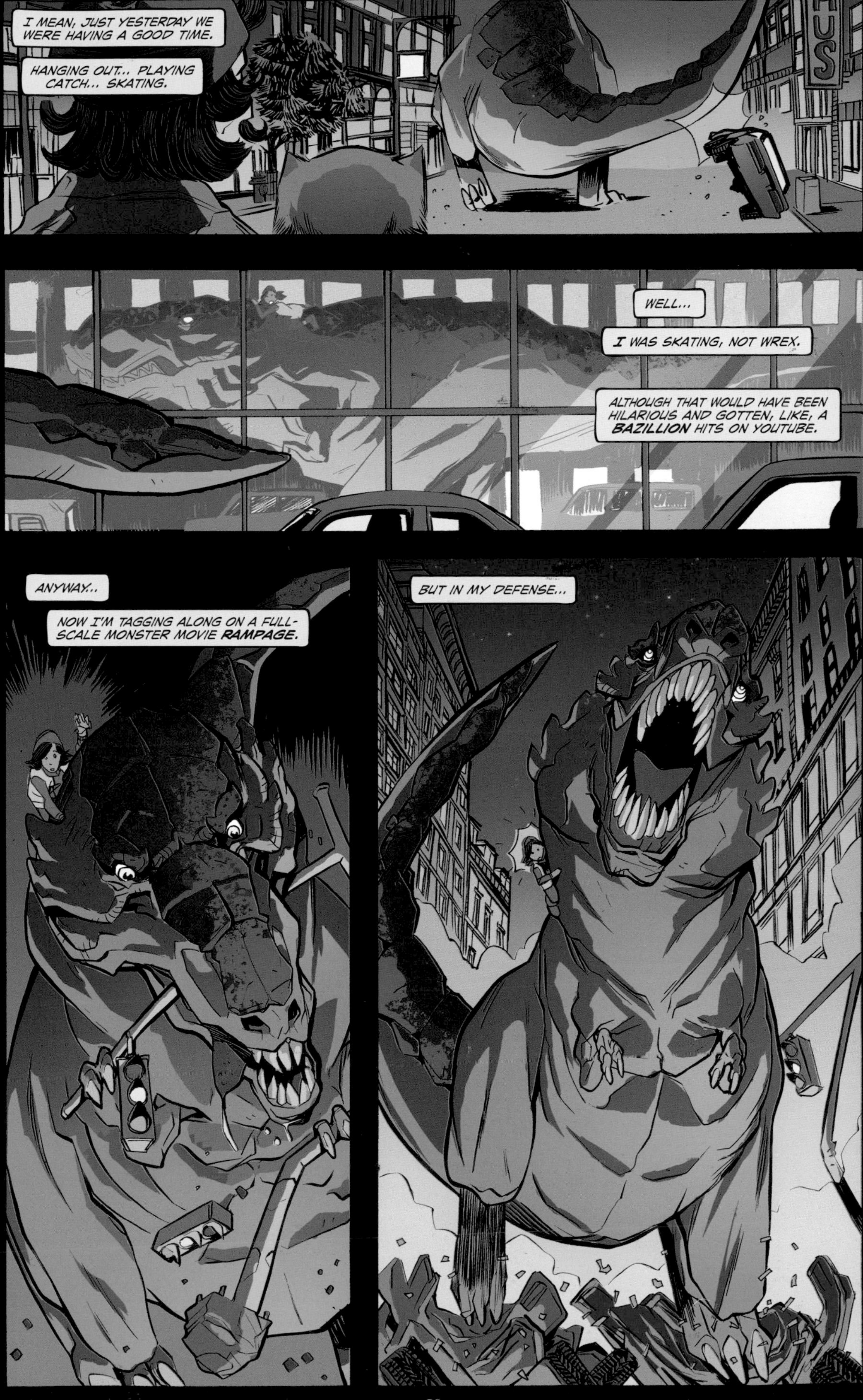
I MEAN, JUST YESTERDAY WE WERE HAVING A GOOD TIME.
HANGING OUT... PLAYING CATCH... SKATING.
WELL...
I WAS SKATING, NOT WREX.
ALTHOUGH THAT WOULD HAVE BEEN HILARIOUS AND GOTTEN, LIKE, A **BAZILLION** HITS ON YOUTUBE.
ANYWAY...
NOW I'M TAGGING ALONG ON A FULL-SCALE MONSTER MOVIE **RAMPAGE**.
BUT IN MY DEFENSE...

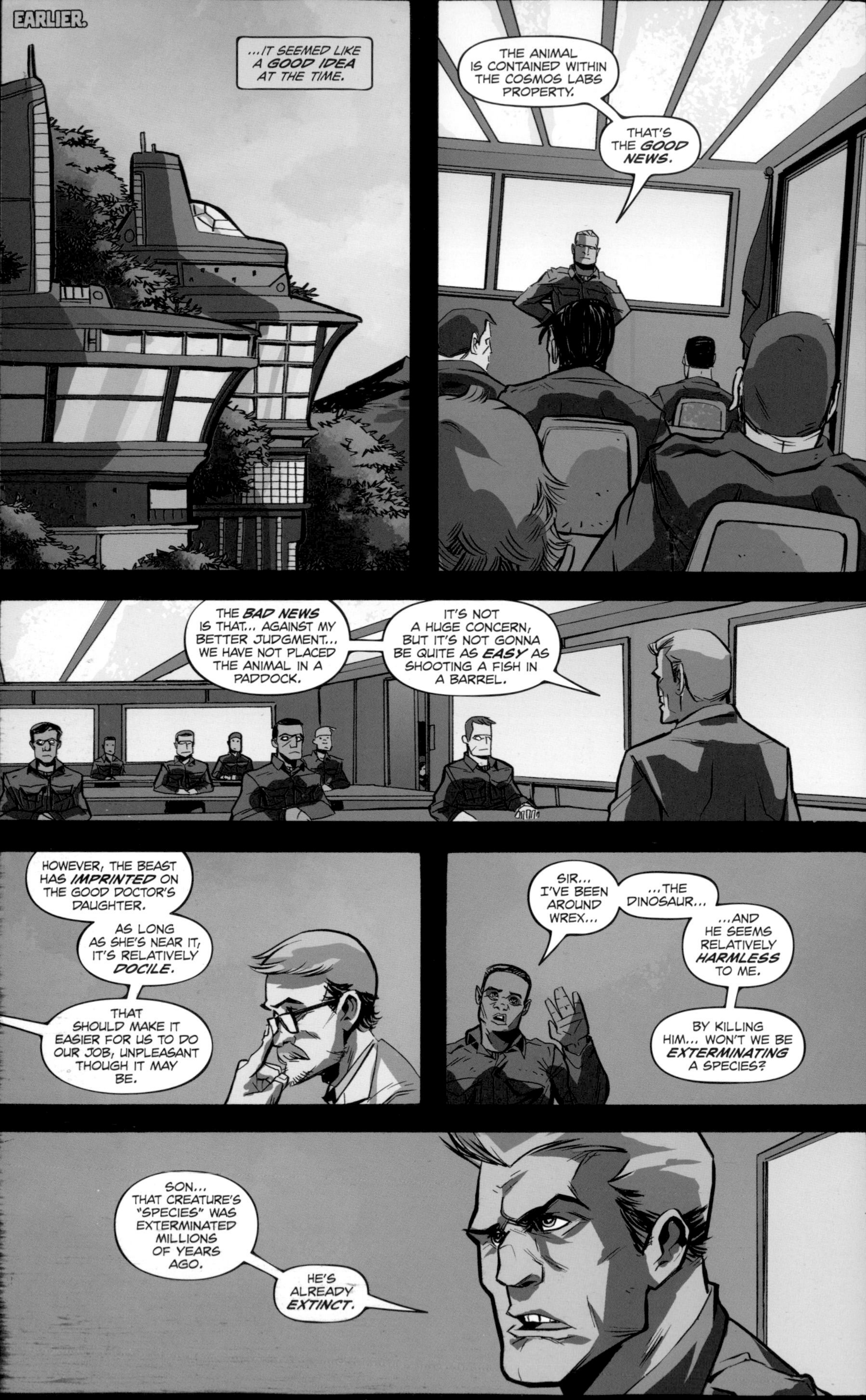
EARLIER.
...IT SEEMED LIKE A GOOD IDEA AT THE TIME.
THE ANIMAL IS CONTAINED WITHIN THE COSMOS LABS PROPERTY.
THAT'S THE GOOD NEWS.
THE BAD NEWS IS THAT... AGAINST MY BETTER JUDGMENT... WE HAVE NOT PLACED THE ANIMAL IN A PADDOCK.
IT'S NOT A HUGE CONCERN, BUT IT'S NOT GONNA BE QUITE AS EASY AS SHOOTING A FISH IN A BARREL.
HOWEVER, THE BEAST HAS IMPRINTED ON THE GOOD DOCTOR'S DAUGHTER.
AS LONG AS SHE'S NEAR IT, IT'S RELATIVELY DOCILE.
THAT SHOULD MAKE IT EASIER FOR US TO DO OUR JOB, UNPLEASANT THOUGH IT MAY BE.
SIR... I'VE BEEN AROUND WREX...
...THE DINOSAUR...
...AND HE SEEMS RELATIVELY HARMLESS TO ME.
BY KILLING HIM... WON'T WE BE EXTERMINATING A SPECIES?
SON... THAT CREATURE'S "SPECIES" WAS EXTERMINATED MILLIONS OF YEARS AGO.
HE'S ALREADY EXTINCT.

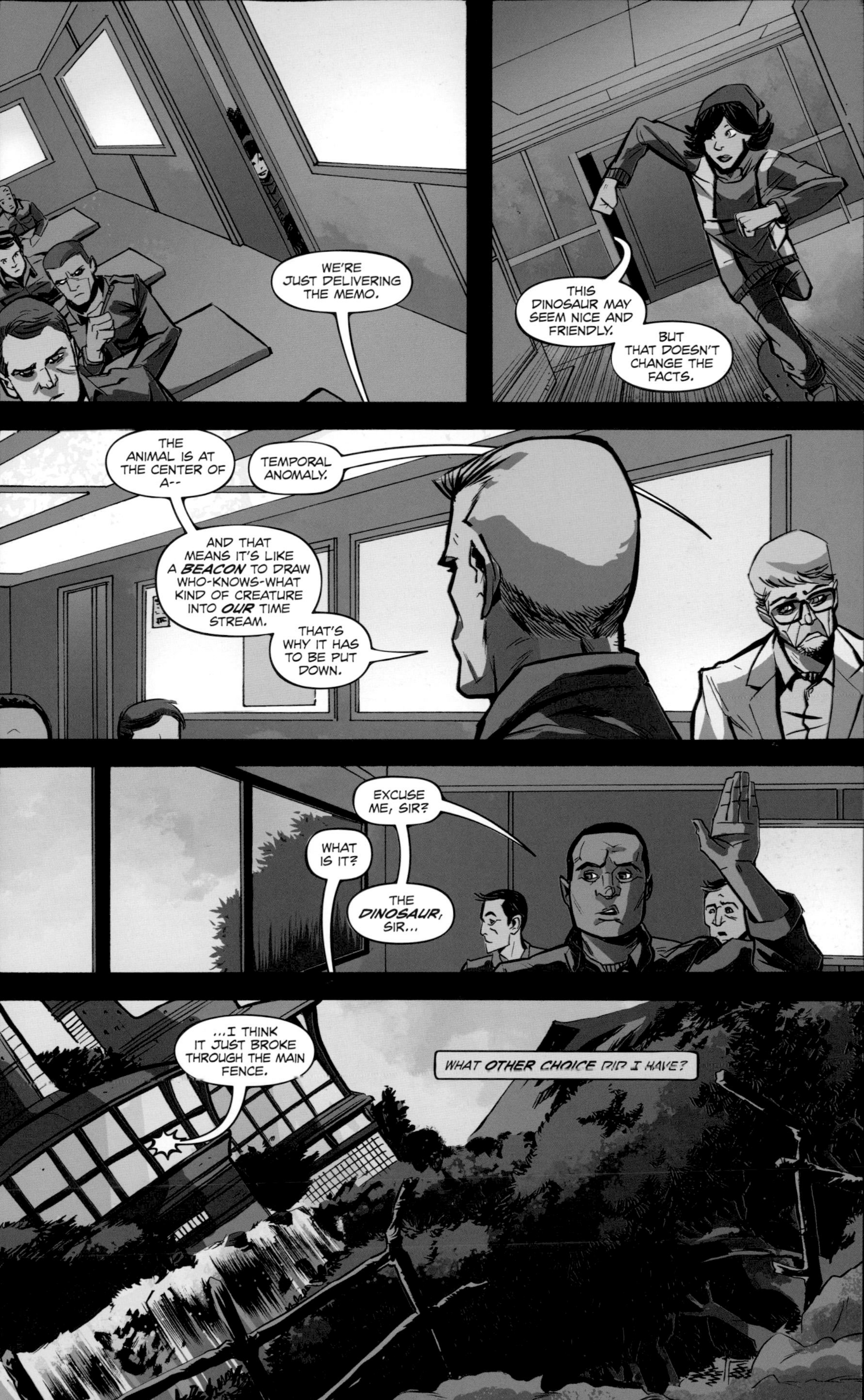
WE'RE JUST DELIVERING THE MEMO.
THIS DINOSAUR MAY SEEM NICE AND FRIENDLY.
BUT THAT DOESN'T CHANGE THE FACTS.
THE ANIMAL IS AT THE CENTER OF A--
TEMPORAL ANOMALY.
AND THAT MEANS IT'S LIKE A BEACON TO DRAW WHO-KNOWS-WHAT KIND OF CREATURE INTO OUR TIME STREAM.
THAT'S WHY IT HAS TO BE PUT DOWN.
EXCUSE ME, SIR?
WHAT IS IT?
THE DINOSAUR, SIR...
...I THINK IT JUST BROKE THROUGH THE MAIN FENCE.
WHAT OTHER CHOICE DID I HAVE?

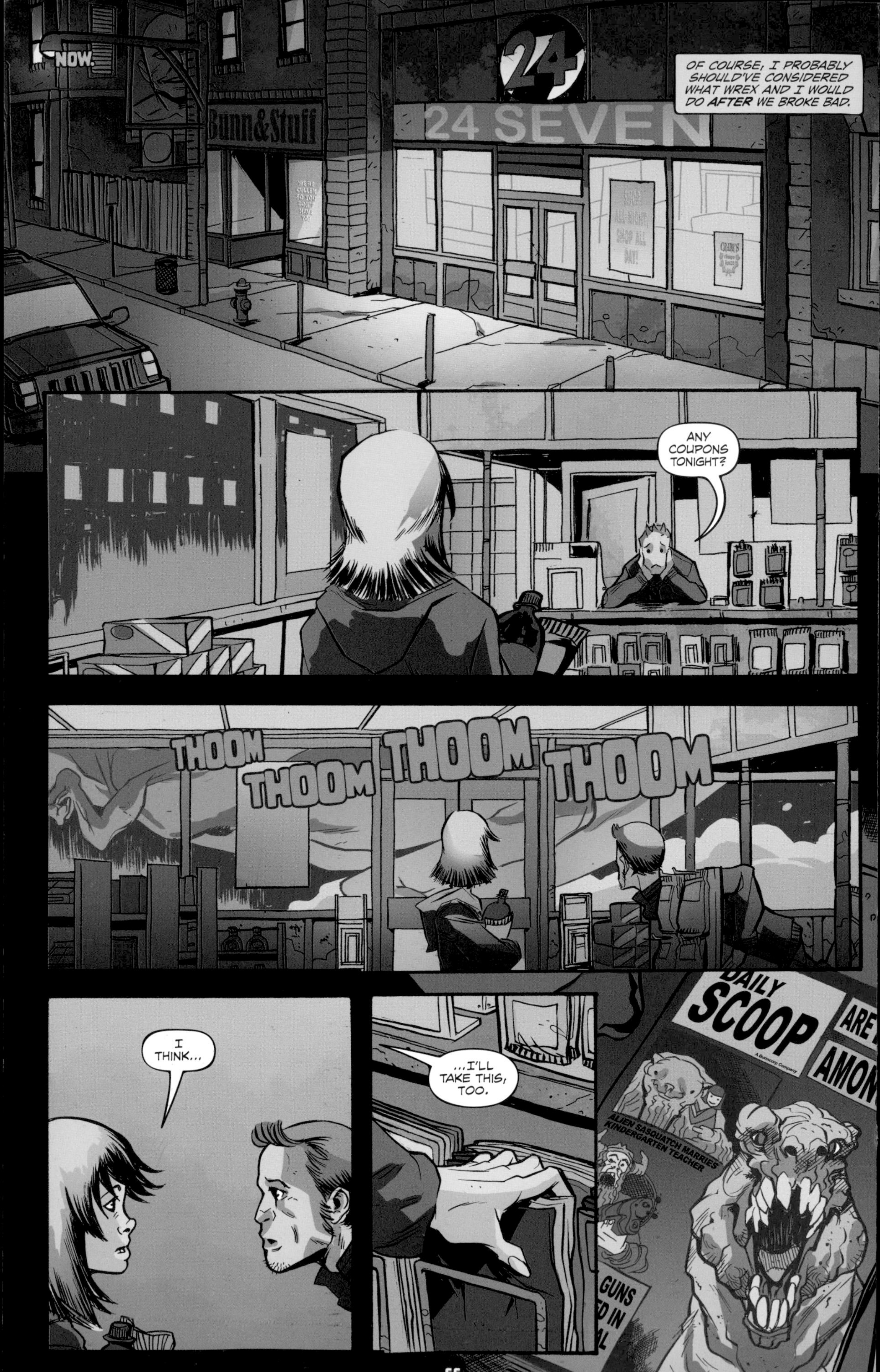
NOW.
OF COURSE, I PROBABLY SHOULD'VE CONSIDERED WHAT WREX AND I WOULD DO **AFTER** WE BROKE BAD.
24
24 SEVEN
Bunn&Stuff
SHOP ALL NIGHT, SHOP ALL DAY!
ANY COUPONS TONIGHT?
THOOM
THOOM
THOOM
THOOM
I THINK...
...I'LL TAKE THIS, TOO.
DAILY SCOOP
A Bunncorp Company
ALIEN SASQUATCH MARRIES KINDERGARTEN TEACHER

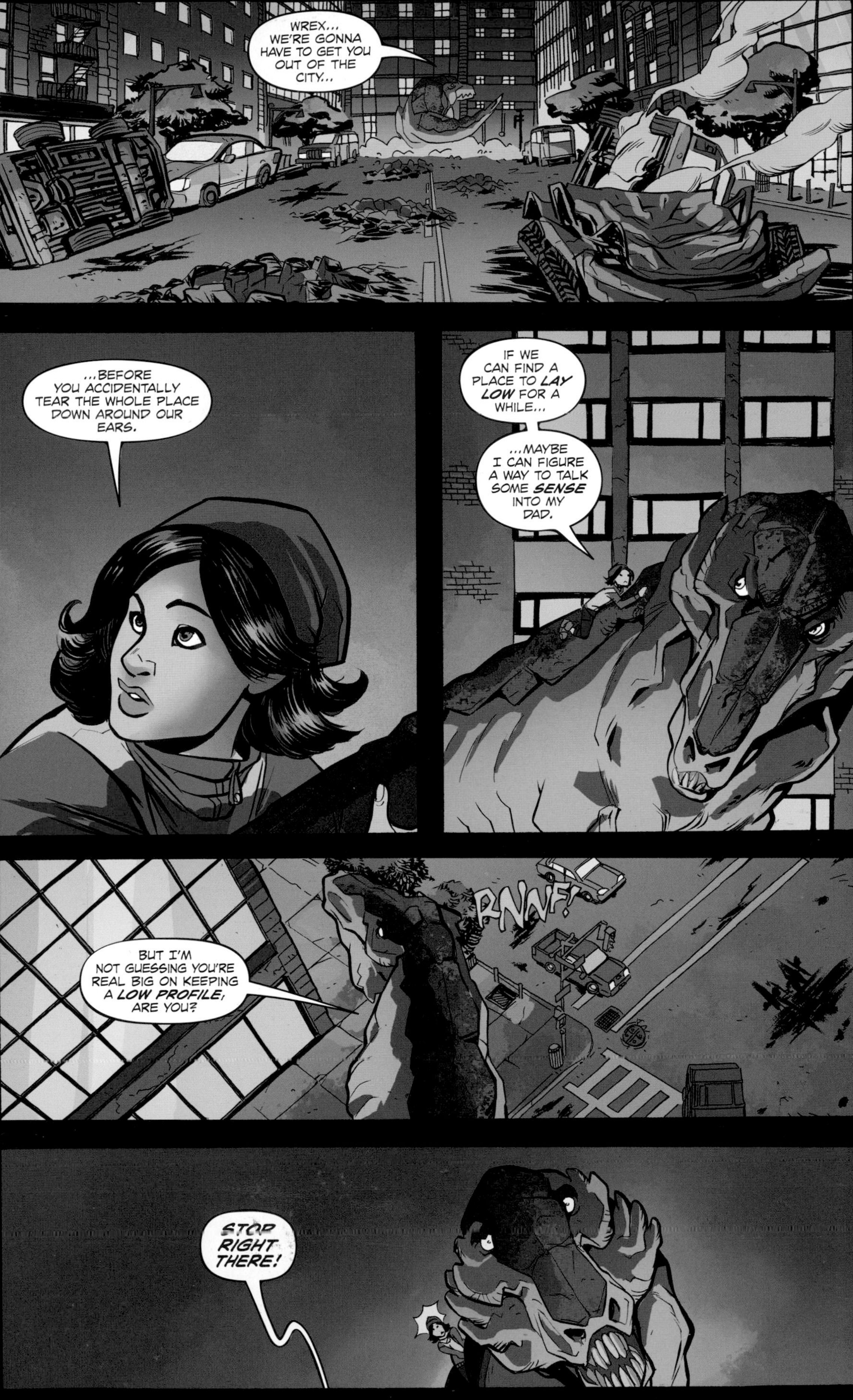
WREX... WE'RE GONNA HAVE TO GET YOU OUT OF THE CITY...
...BEFORE YOU ACCIDENTALLY TEAR THE WHOLE PLACE DOWN AROUND OUR EARS.
IF WE CAN FIND A PLACE TO LAY LOW FOR A WHILE...
...MAYBE I CAN FIGURE A WAY TO TALK SOME SENSE INTO MY DAD.
RNNF!
BUT I'M NOT GUESSING YOU'RE REAL BIG ON KEEPING A LOW PROFILE, ARE YOU?
STOP RIGHT THERE!

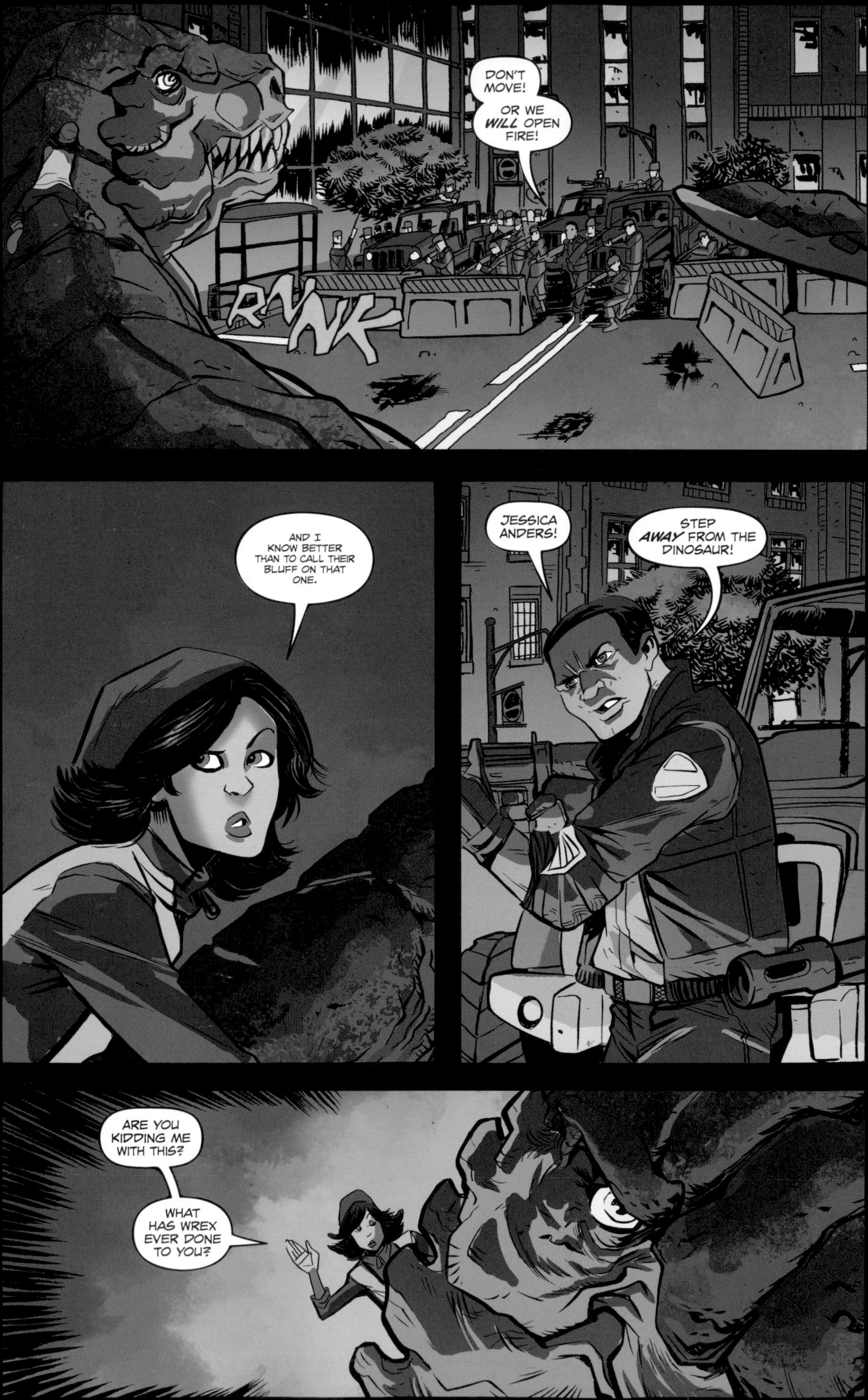
DON'T MOVE!
OR WE WILL OPEN FIRE!
RNNK
AND I KNOW BETTER THAN TO CALL THEIR BLUFF ON THAT ONE.
JESSICA ANDERS!
STEP AWAY FROM THE DINOSAUR!
ARE YOU KIDDING ME WITH THIS?
WHAT HAS WREX EVER DONE TO YOU?

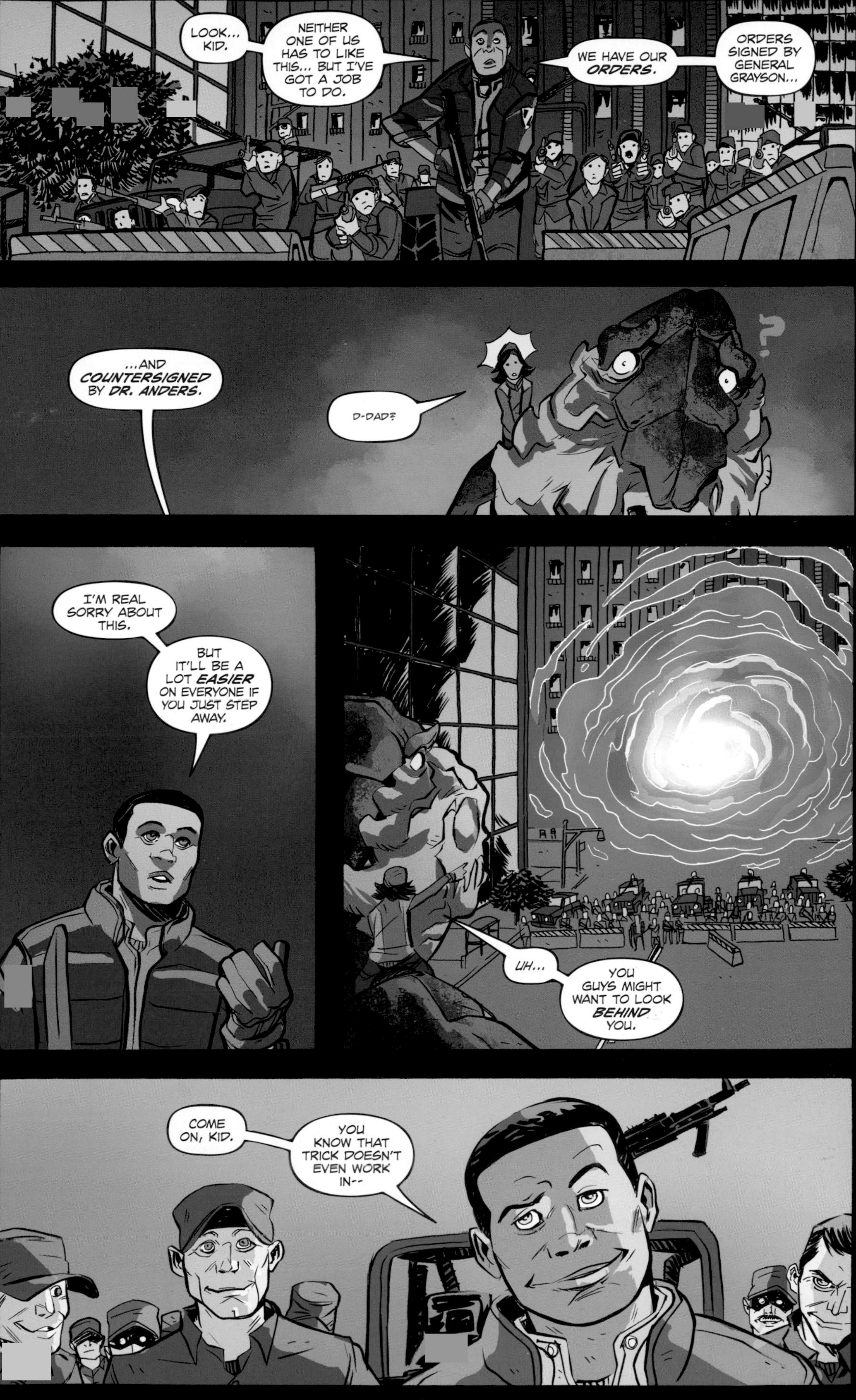
LOOK... KID.
NEITHER ONE OF US HAS TO LIKE THIS... BUT I'VE GOT A JOB TO DO.
WE HAVE OUR ORDERS.
ORDERS SIGNED BY GENERAL GRAYSON...
...AND COUNTERSIGNED BY DR. ANDERS.
D-DAD?
?
I'M REAL SORRY ABOUT THIS.
BUT IT'LL BE A LOT EASIER ON EVERYONE IF YOU JUST STEP AWAY.
UH...
YOU GUYS MIGHT WANT TO LOOK BEHIND YOU.
COME ON, KID.
YOU KNOW THAT TRICK DOESN'T EVEN WORK IN--

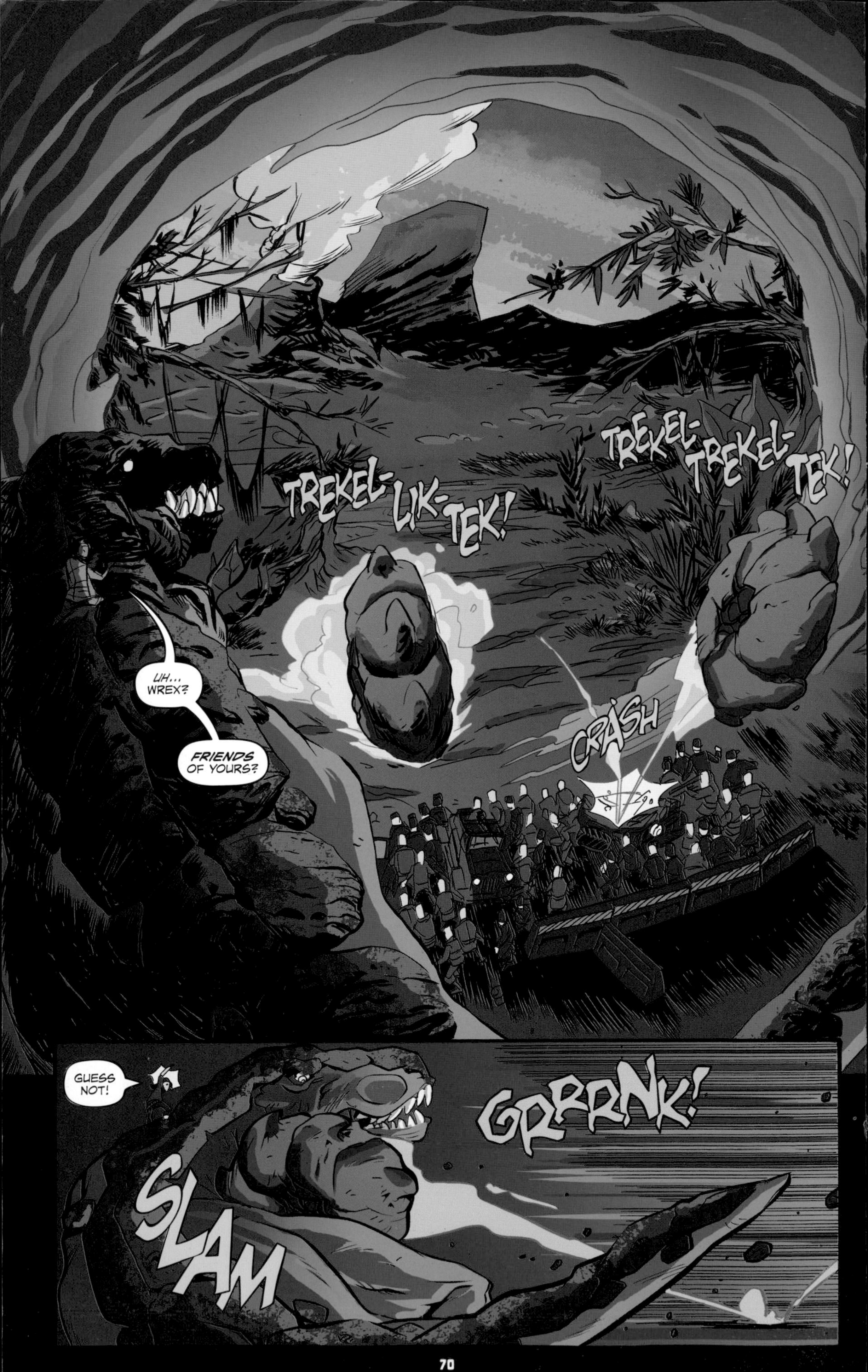
TREKEL-LIK-TEK!
TREKEL-TREKEL-TREKEL-TEK!
UH... WREX?
FRIENDS OF YOURS?
CRASH
GUESS NOT!
GRRRNK!
SLAM

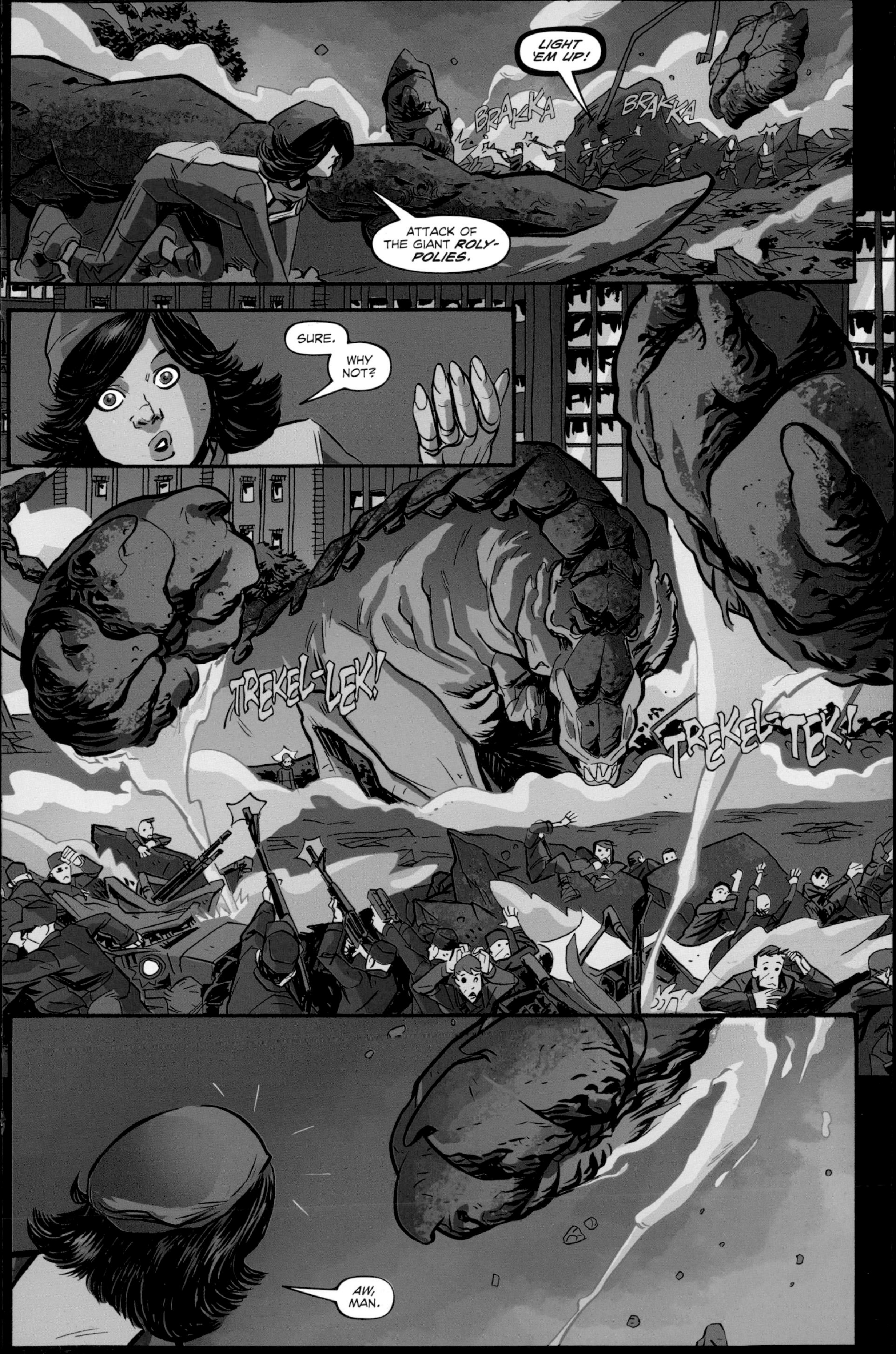
BRAKKA
BRAKKA
LIGHT 'EM UP!
ATTACK OF THE GIANT ROLY-POLIES.
SURE.
WHY NOT?
TREKEL-LEK!
TREKEL-TEK!
AW, MAN.

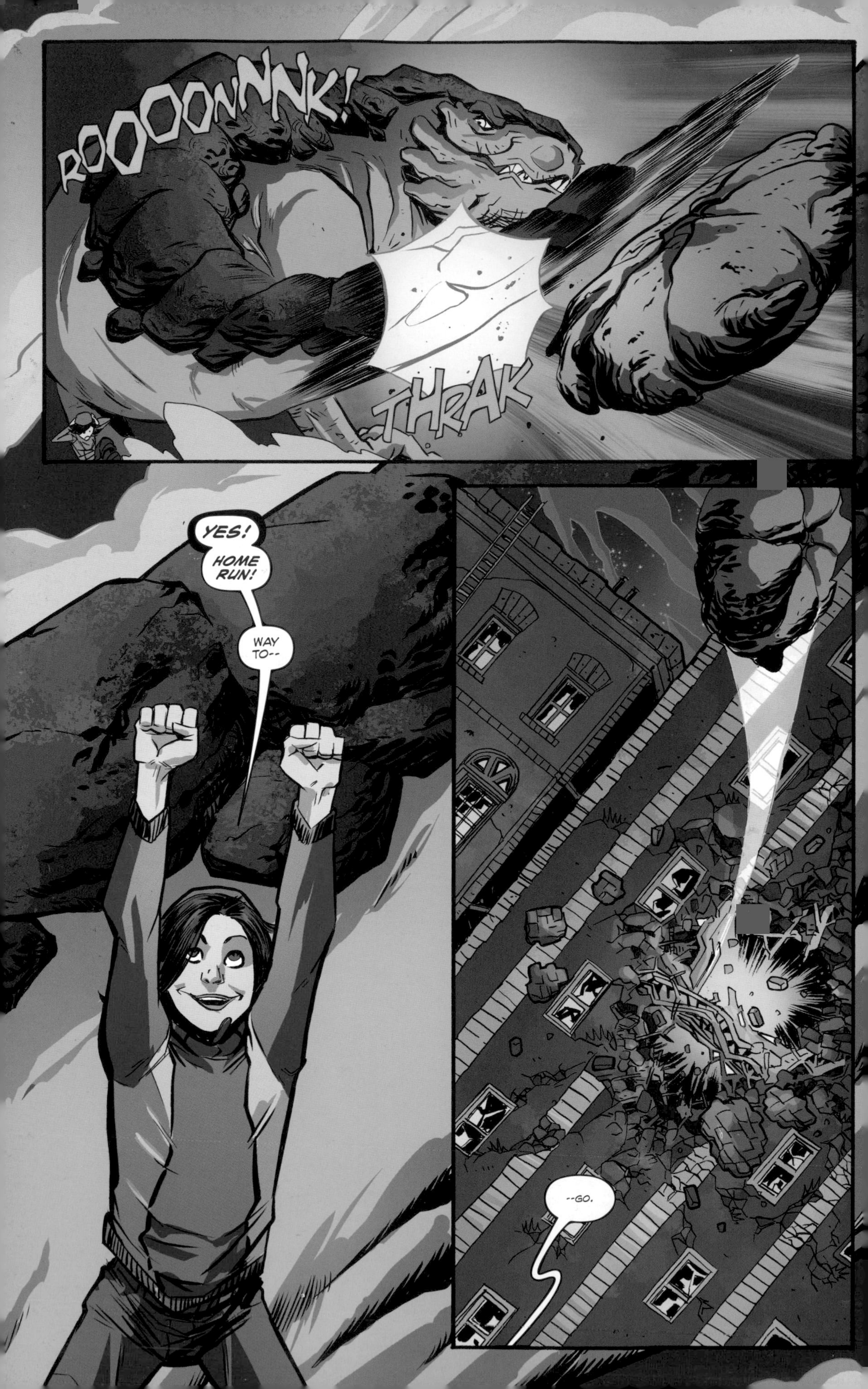
ROOOONNNK!
THRAK
YES!
HOME RUN!
WAY TO--
--GO.

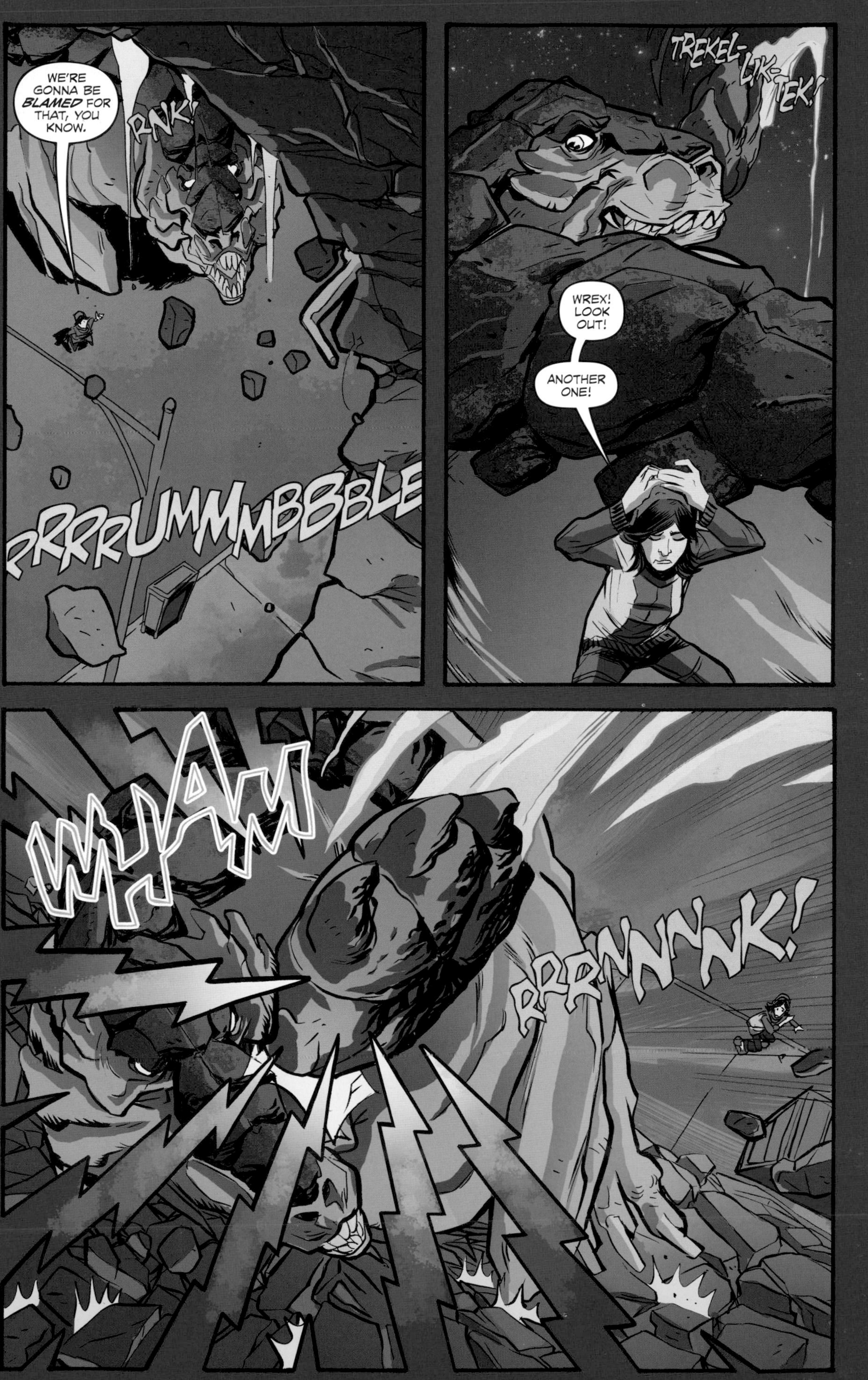
WE'RE GONNA BE *BLAMED* FOR THAT, YOU KNOW.
RNK!
PRRRUMMMBBBLE
TREKEL-LIK-TEK!
WREX! LOOK OUT!
ANOTHER ONE!
WHAM
RRRNNNNK!

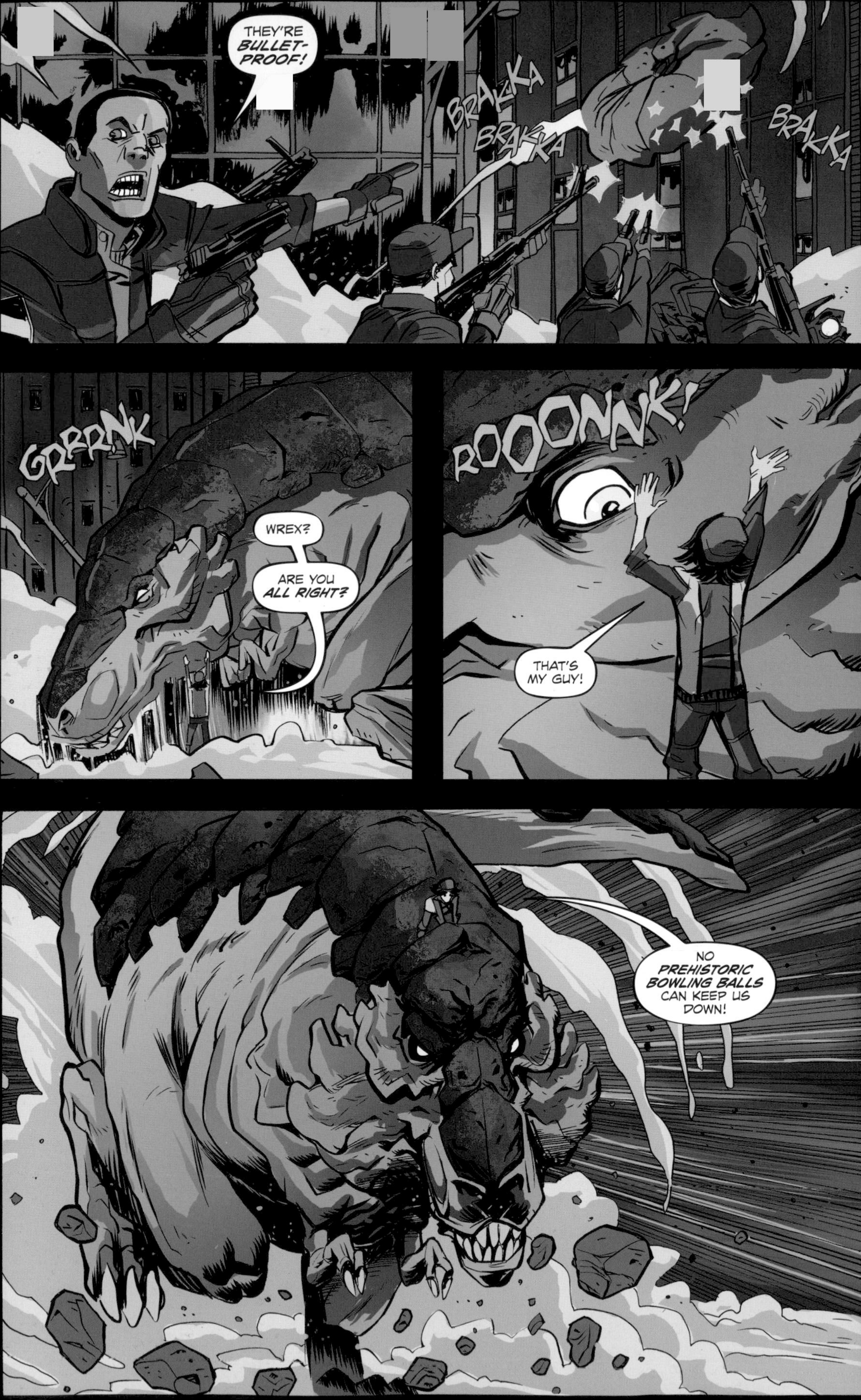
THEY'RE BULLET-PROOF!
BRAKKA
BRAKKA
BRAKKA
GRRRNK
WREX?
ARE YOU ALL RIGHT?
ROOONNK!
THAT'S MY GUY!
NO PREHISTORIC BOWLING BALLS CAN KEEP US DOWN!

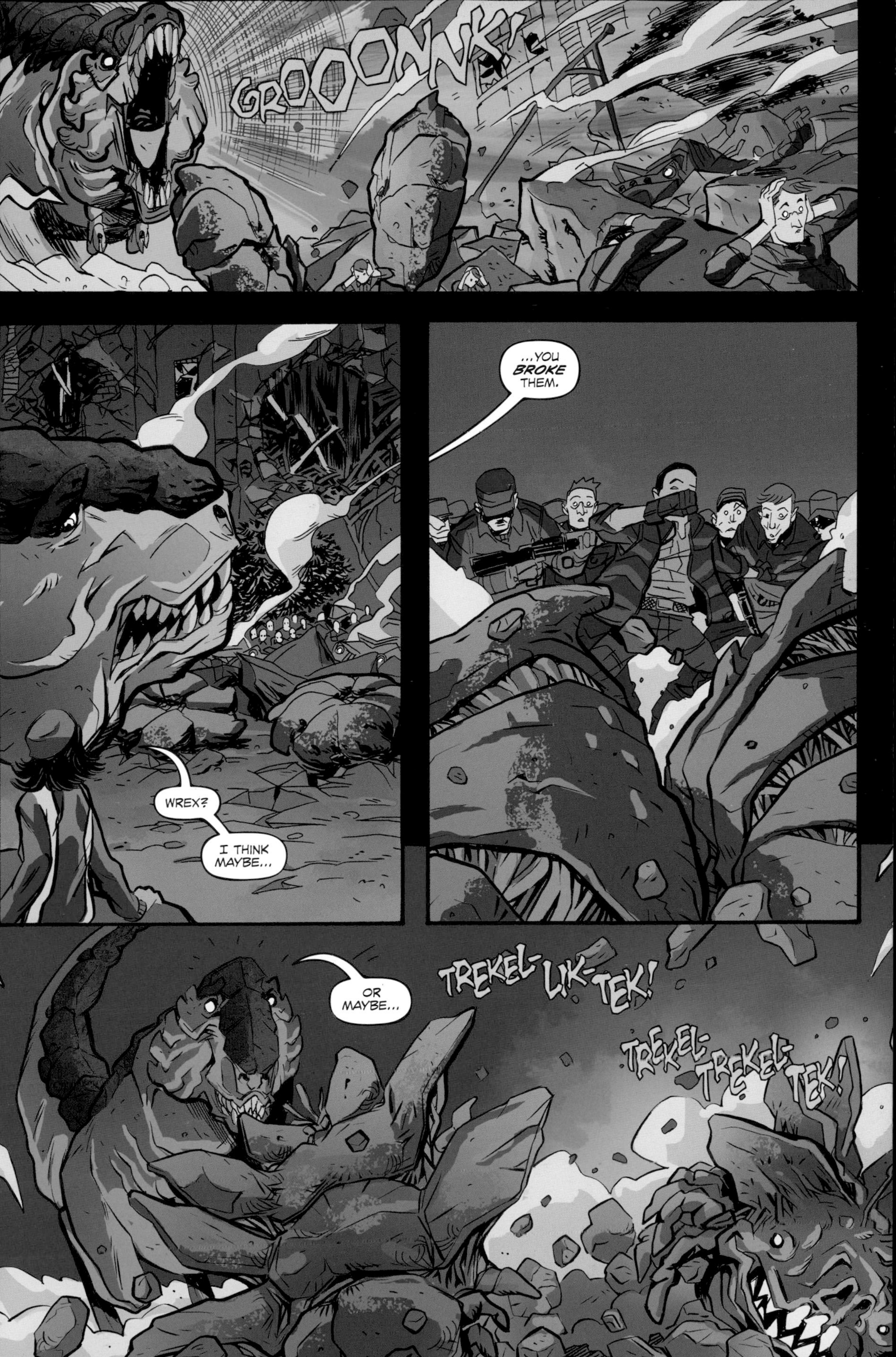
GROOONNK!
WREX?
I THINK MAYBE...
...YOU *BROKE* THEM.
OR MAYBE...
TREKEL-LIK-TEK!
TREKEL-TREKEL-TEK!

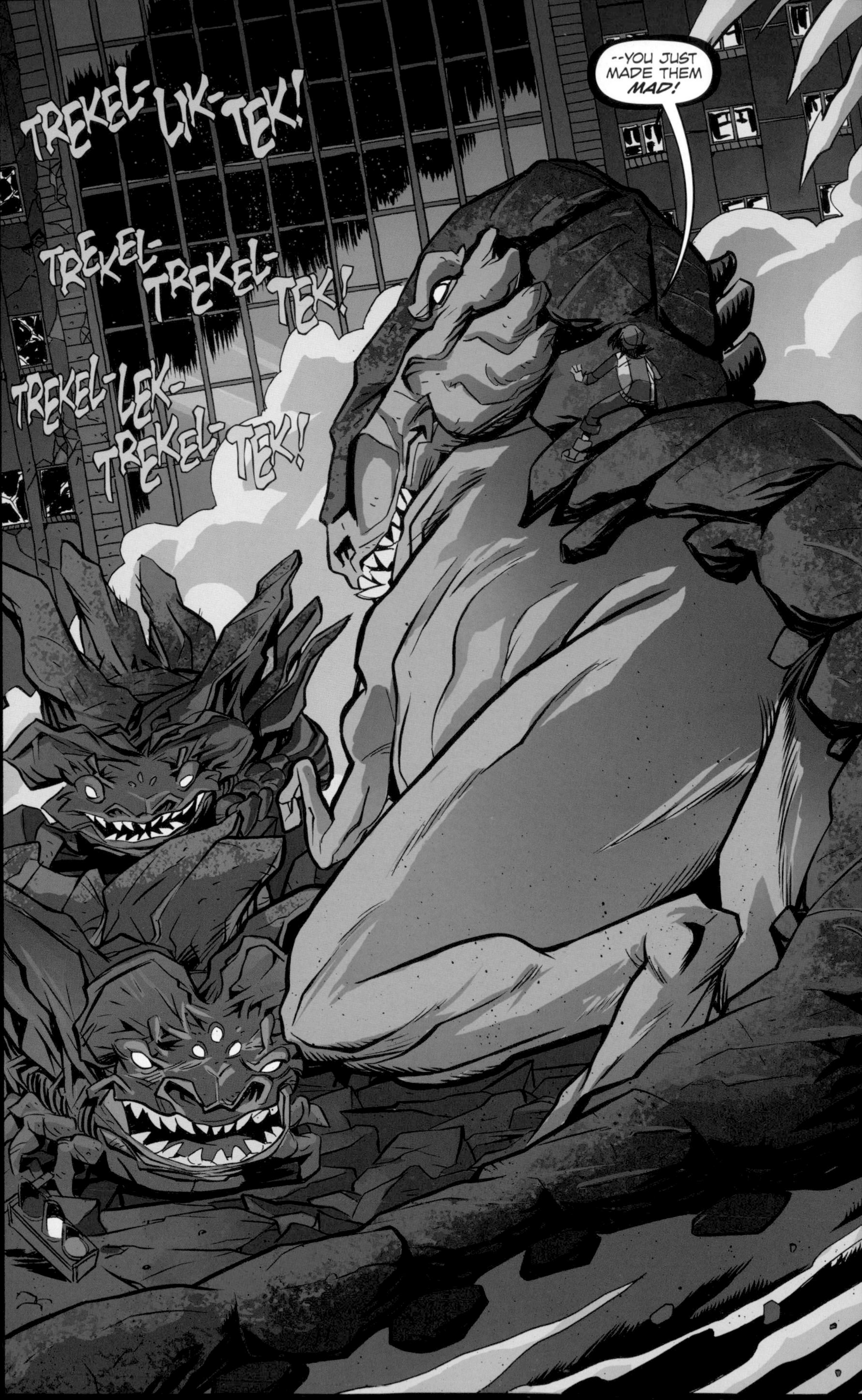
--YOU JUST MADE THEM MAD!
TREKEL-LIK-TEK!
TREKEL-TREKEL-TREKEL-TEK!
TREKEL-LEK-TREKEL-TEK!

CHAPTER FOUR

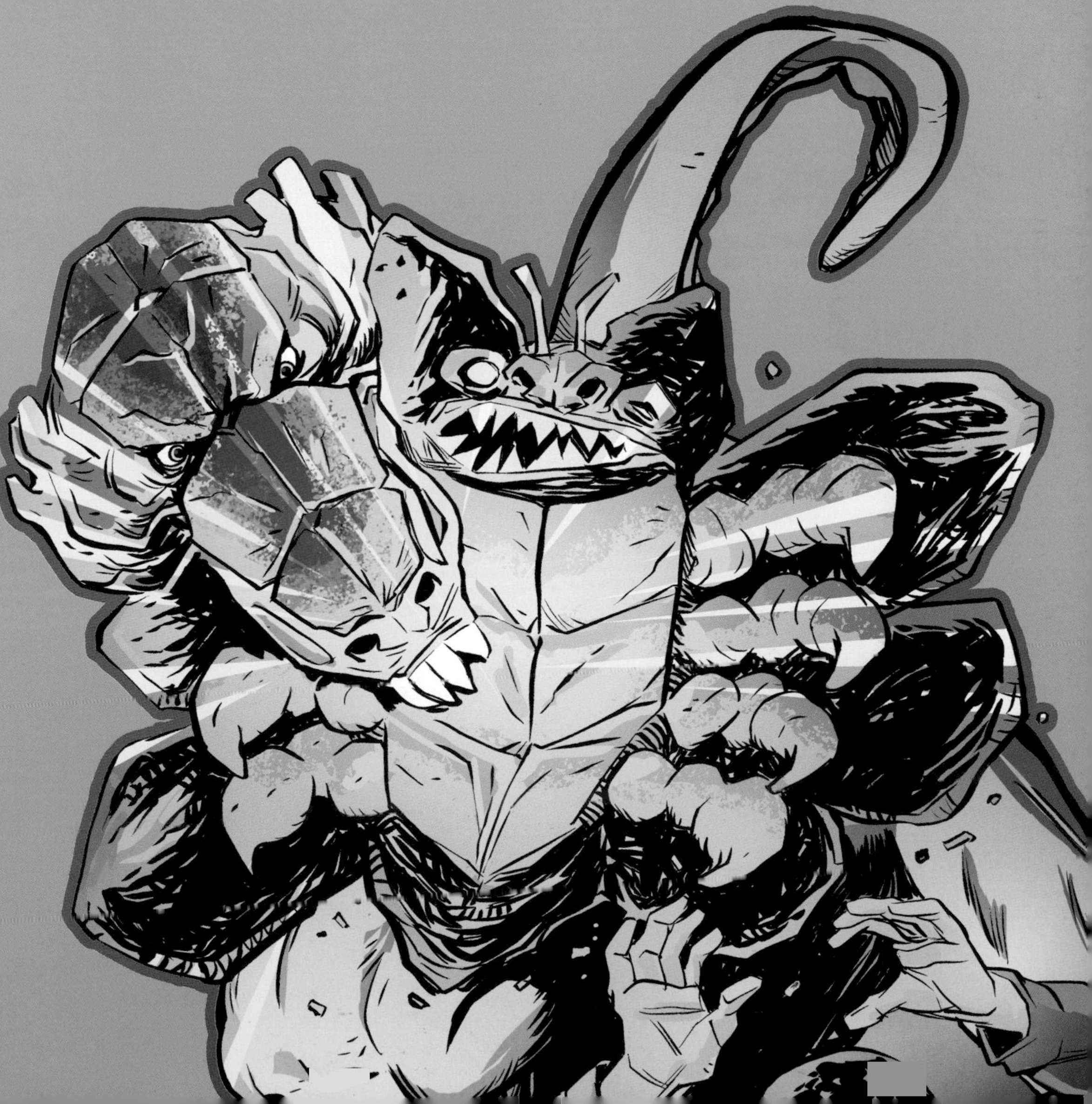

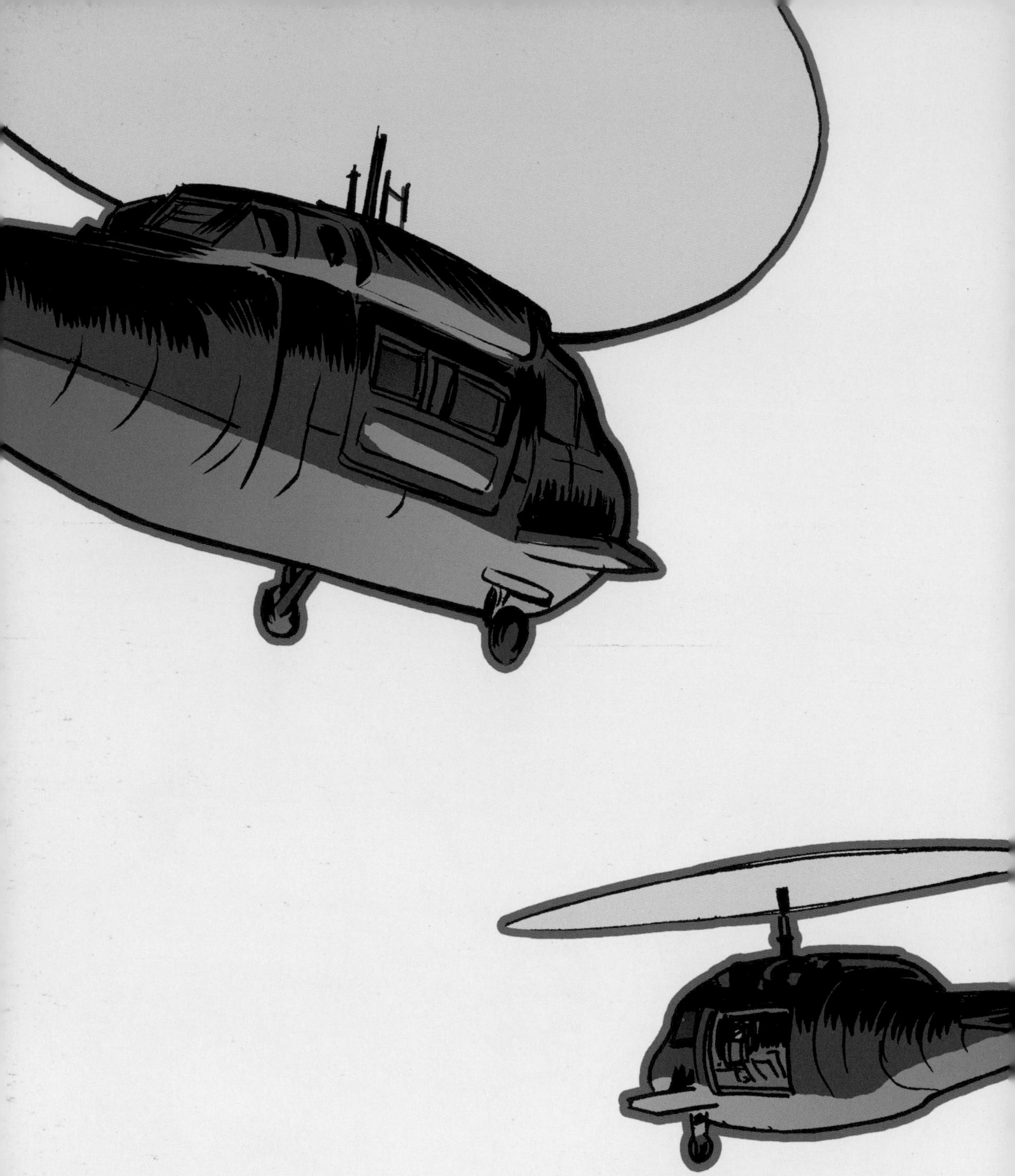

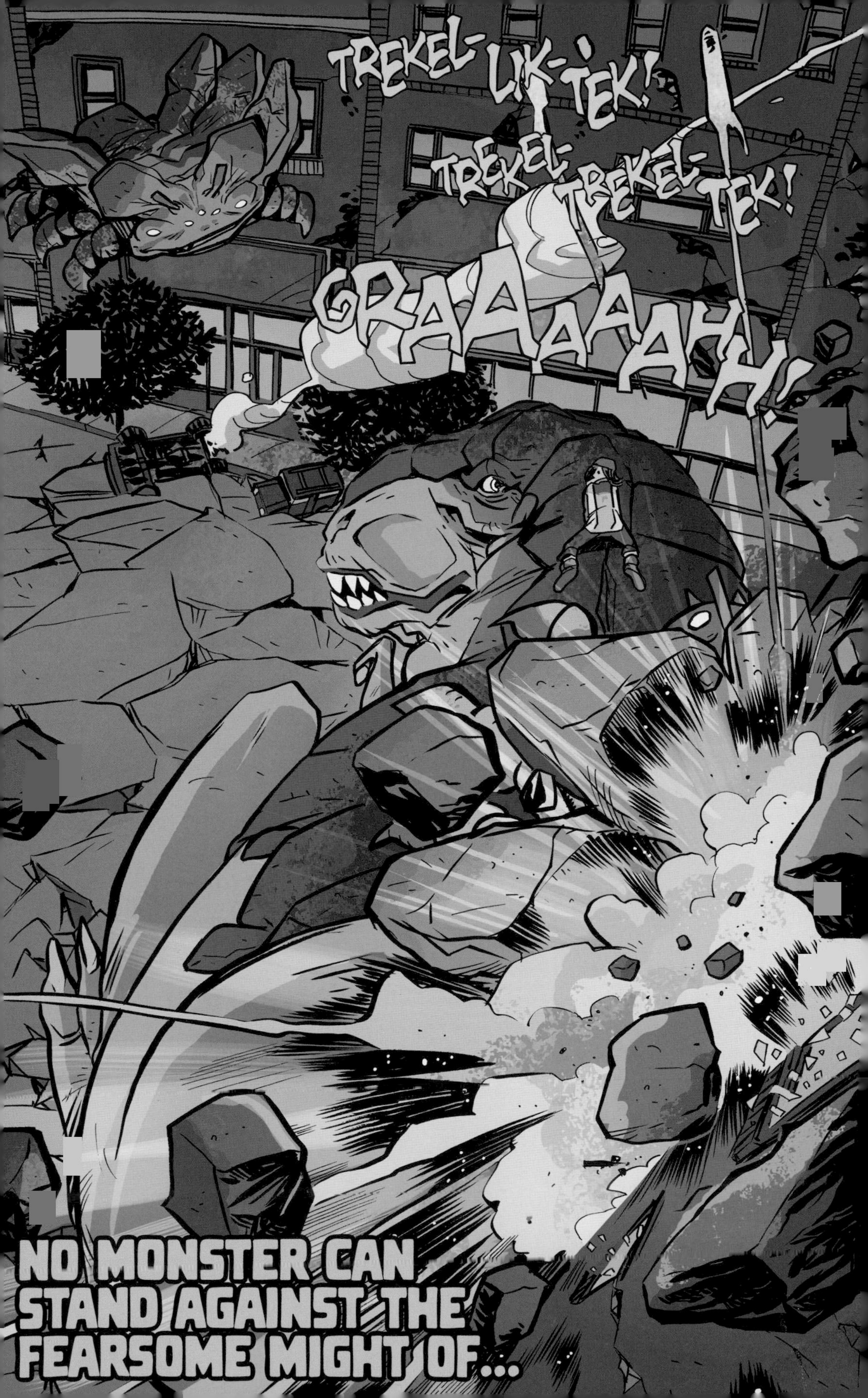

TREKEL-LIK-TEK!
TREKEL-TREKEL-TEK!
GRAAAAAHH!
NO MONSTER CAN STAND AGAINST THE FEARSOME MIGHT OF...

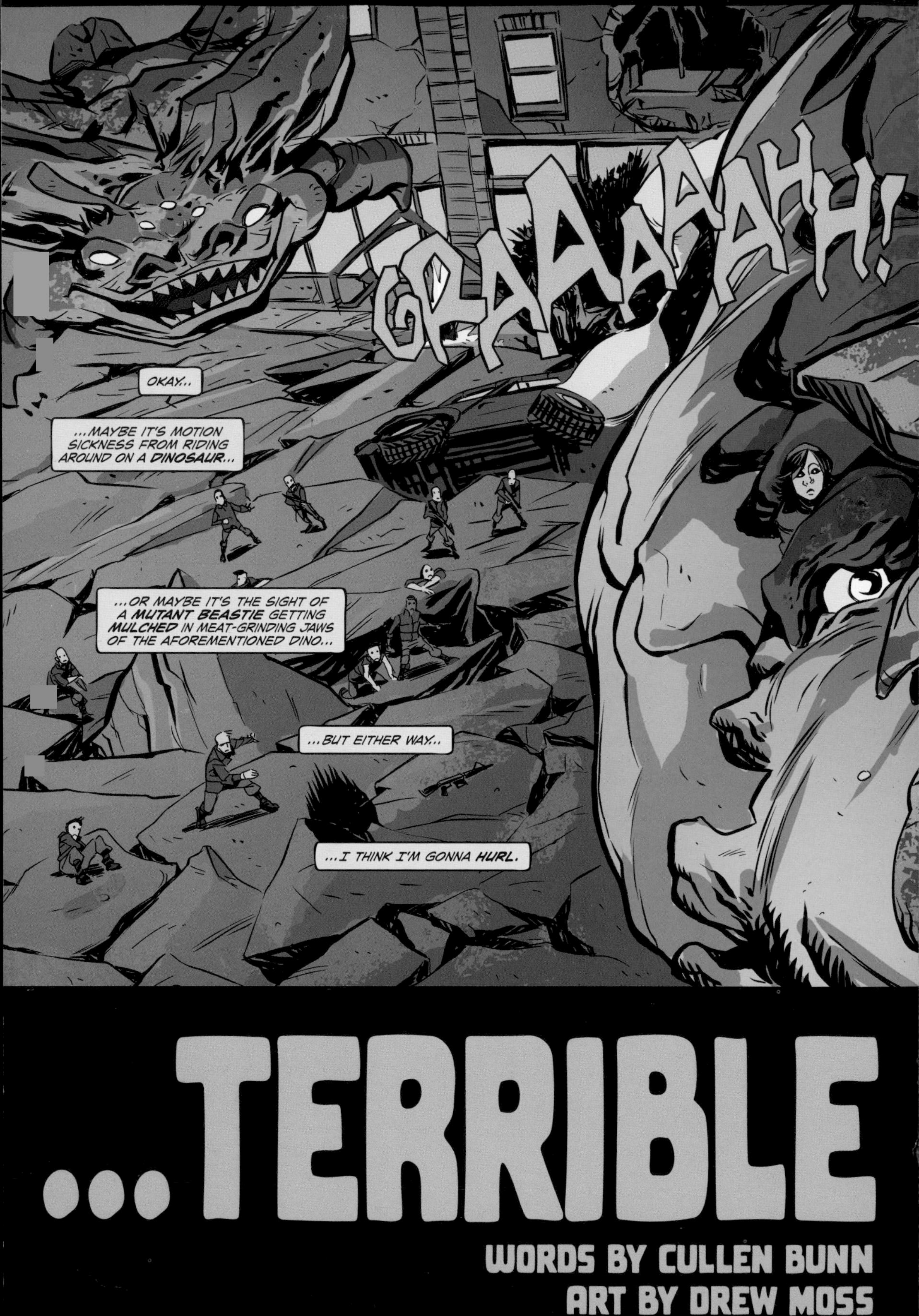
GRAAAAAAHH!
OKAY...
...MAYBE IT'S MOTION SICKNESS FROM RIDING AROUND ON A DINOSAUR...
...OR MAYBE IT'S THE SIGHT OF A MUTANT BEASTIE GETTING MULCHED IN MEAT-GRINDING JAWS OF THE AFOREMENTIONED DINO...
...BUT EITHER WAY...
...I THINK I'M GONNA HURL.

...TERRIBLE

WORDS BY CULLEN BUNN
ART BY DREW MOSS

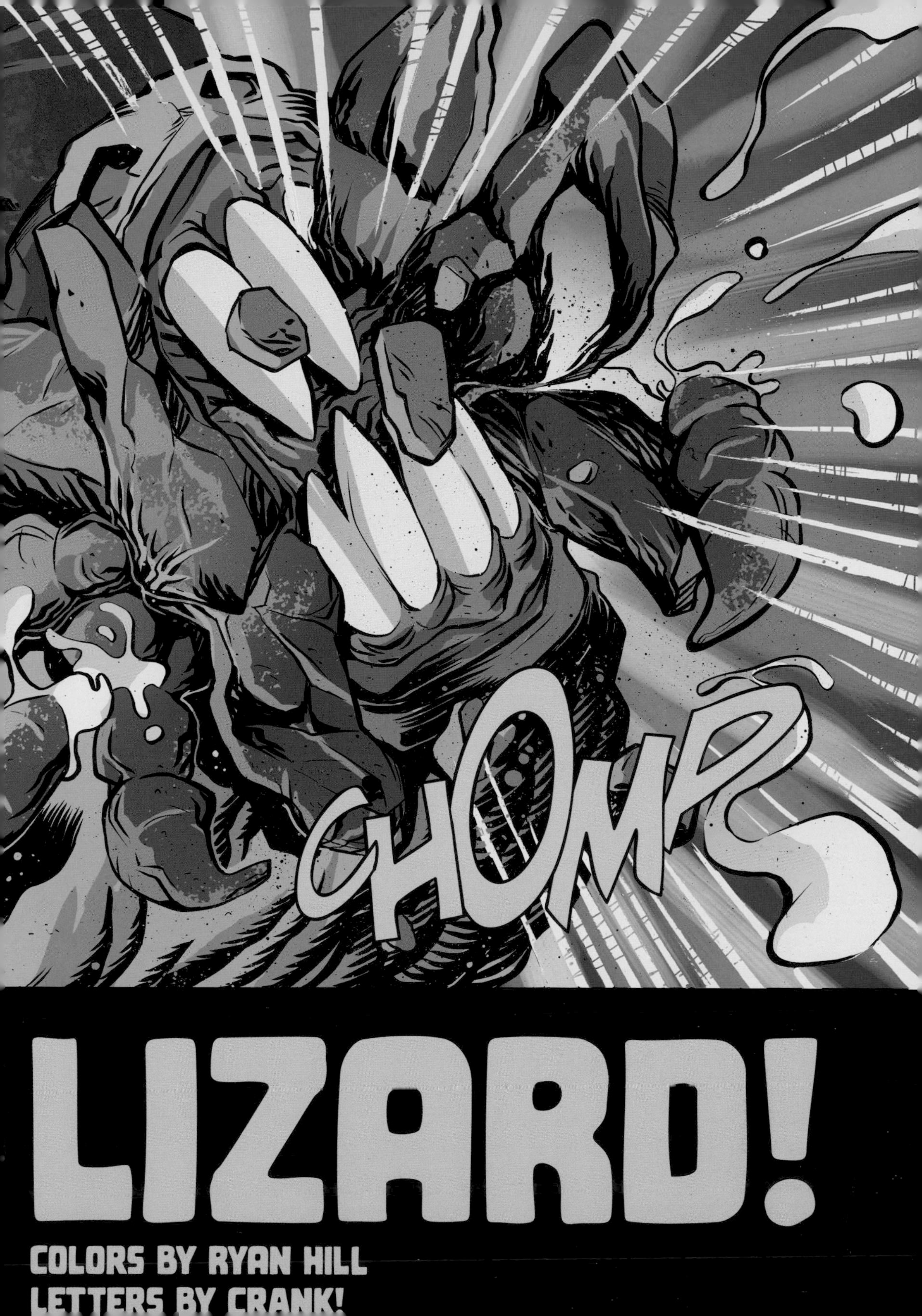
CHOMP

LIZARD!

COLORS BY RYAN HILL
LETTERS BY CRANK!

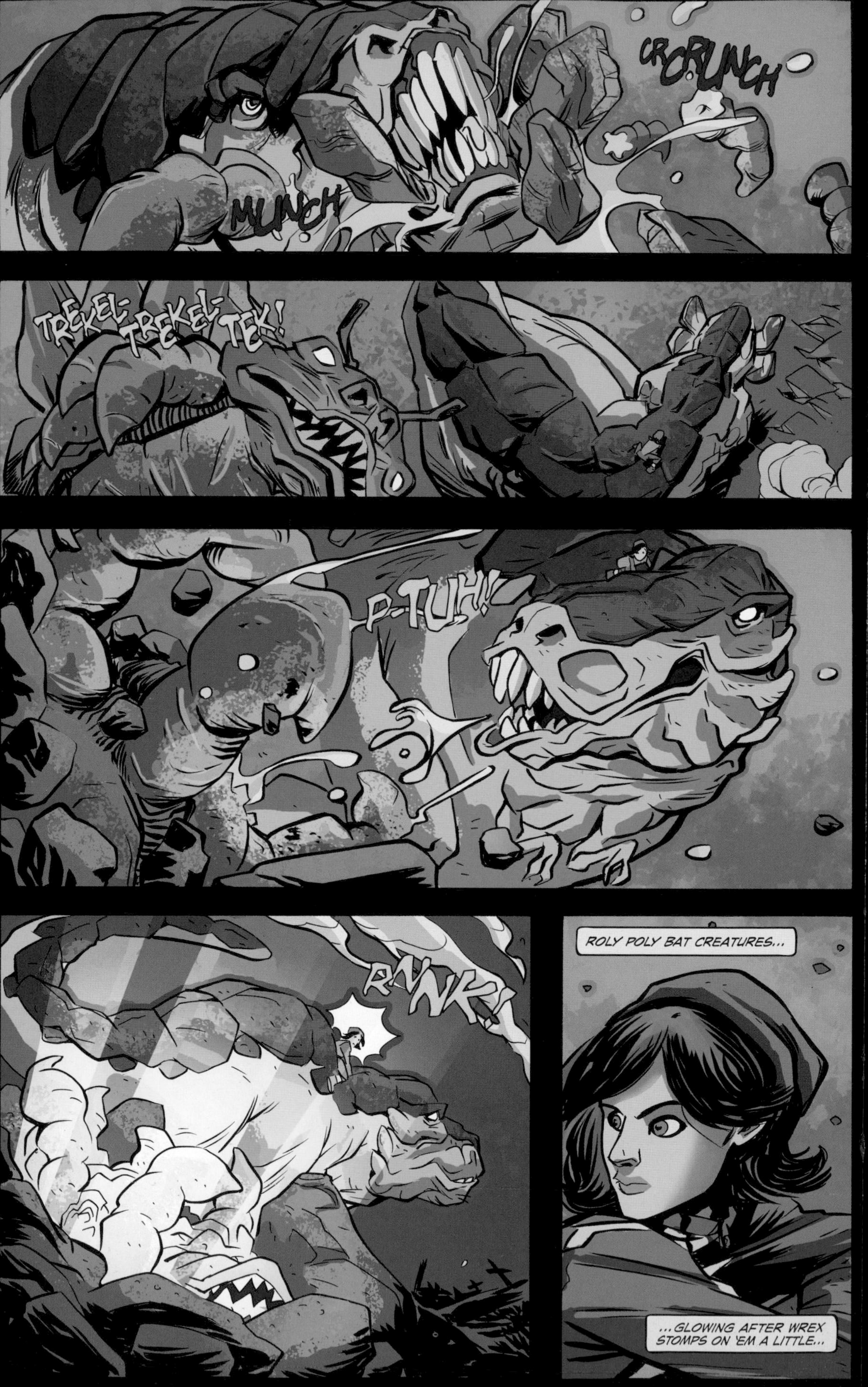
CRCRUNCH
MUNCH
TREKEL-TREKEL-TEK!
P-TUH!
RNNK!
ROLY POLY BAT CREATURES...
...GLOWING AFTER WREX STOMPS ON 'EM A LITTLE...

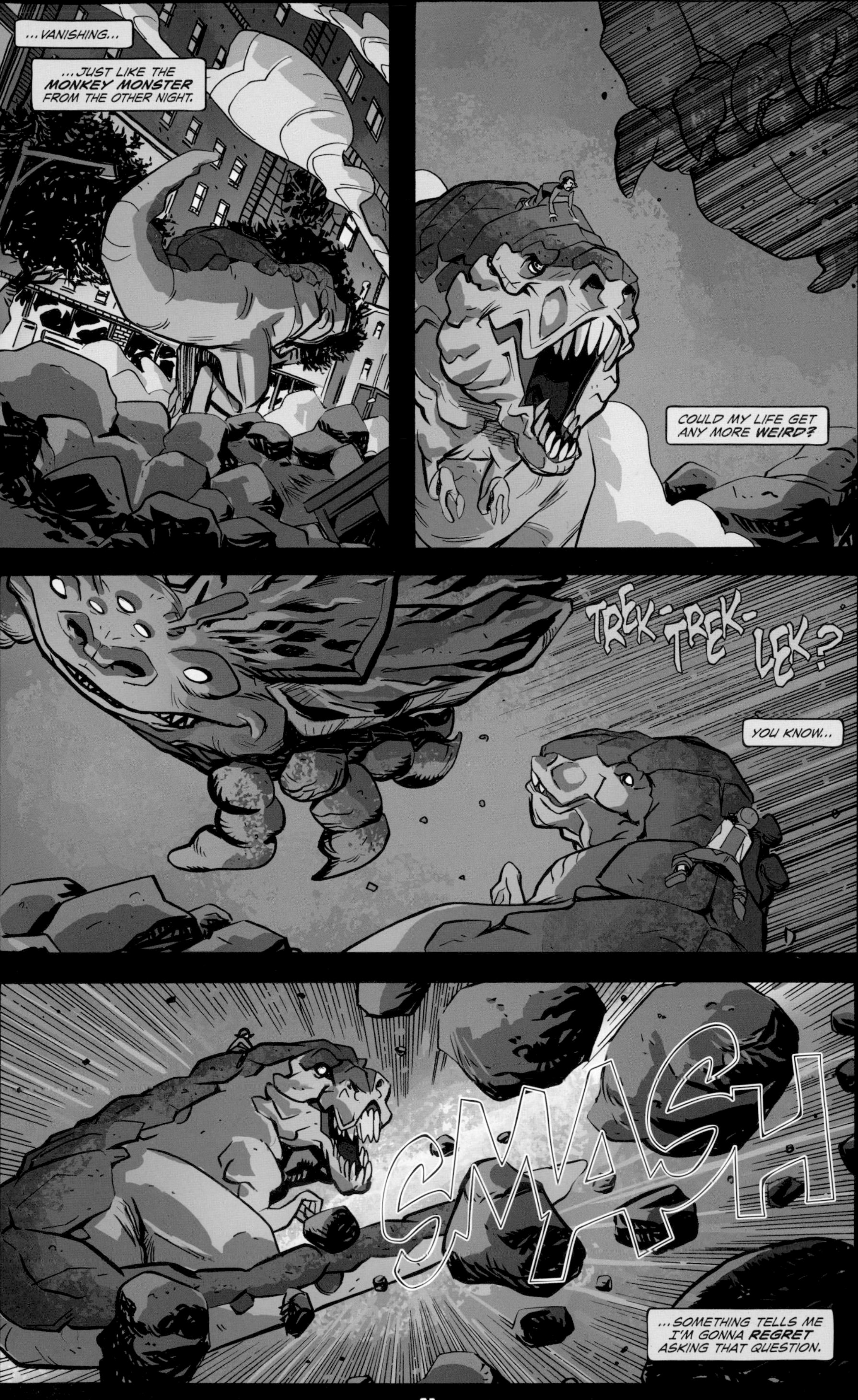
...VANISHING...
...JUST LIKE THE MONKEY MONSTER FROM THE OTHER NIGHT.
COULD MY LIFE GET ANY MORE WEIRD?
TREK-TREK-LEK?
YOU KNOW...
SMASH
...SOMETHING TELLS ME I'M GONNA REGRET ASKING THAT QUESTION.

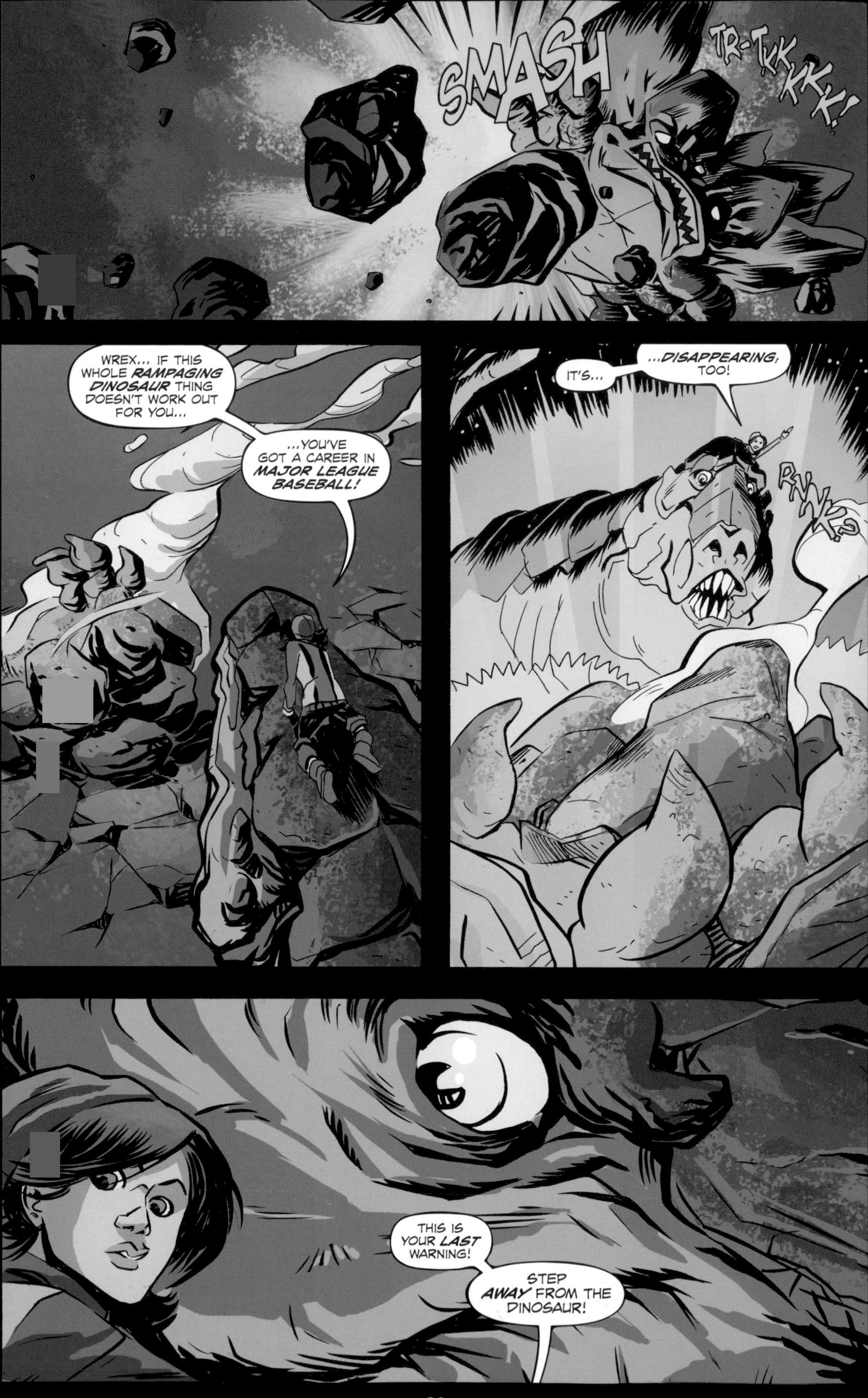
SMASH
TR-TKKKKK!
WREX... IF THIS WHOLE *RAMPAGING DINOSAUR* THING DOESN'T WORK OUT FOR YOU...
...YOU'VE GOT A CAREER IN *MAJOR LEAGUE BASEBALL!*
IT'S...
...*DISAPPEARING,* TOO!
RNNK?
THIS IS YOUR *LAST* WARNING!
STEP *AWAY* FROM THE DINOSAUR!

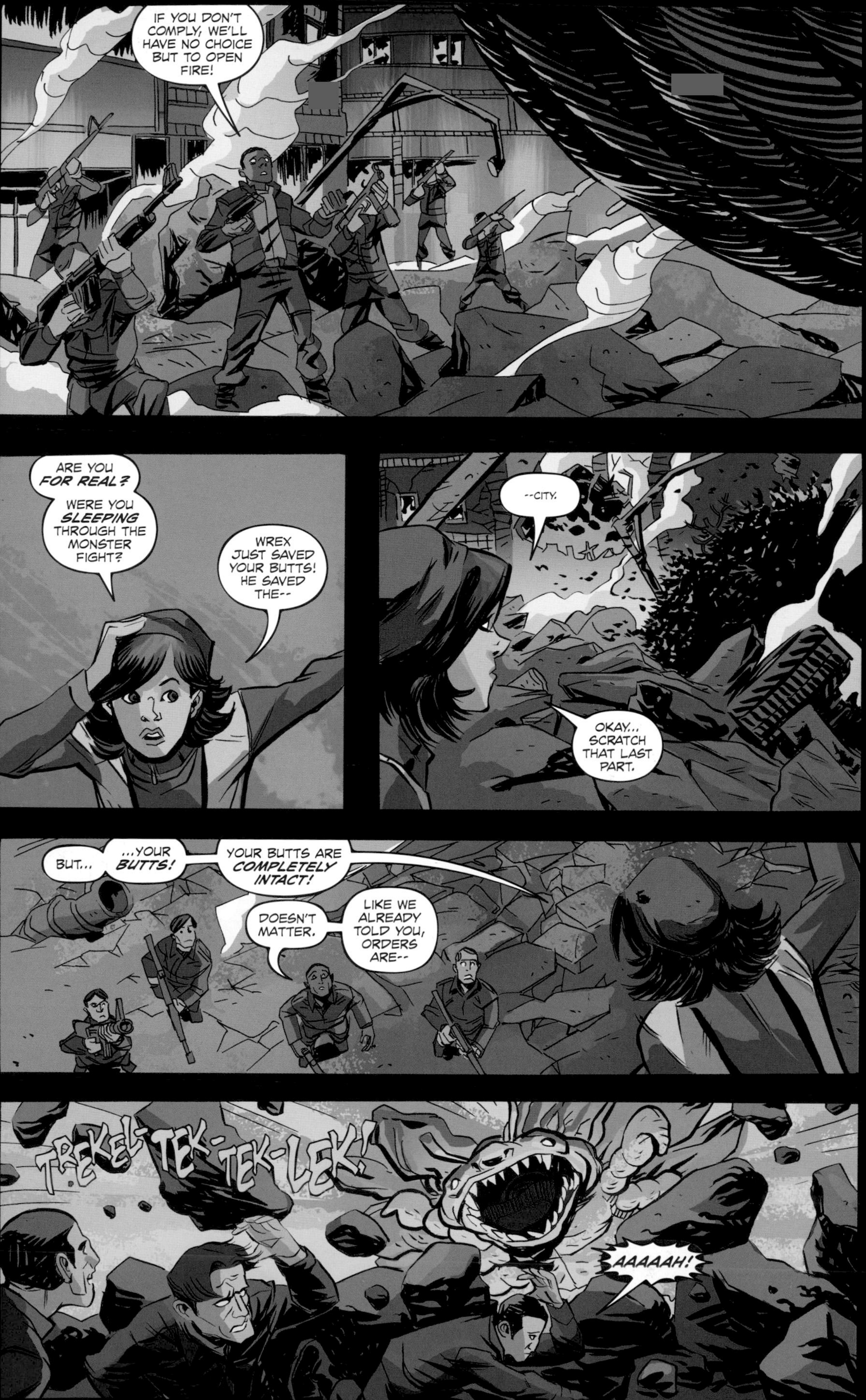
IF YOU DON'T COMPLY, WE'LL HAVE NO CHOICE BUT TO OPEN FIRE!
ARE YOU FOR REAL?
WERE YOU SLEEPING THROUGH THE MONSTER FIGHT?
WREX JUST SAVED YOUR BUTTS! HE SAVED THE--
--CITY.
OKAY.. SCRATCH THAT LAST PART.
BUT...
...YOUR BUTTS!
YOUR BUTTS ARE COMPLETELY INTACT!
DOESN'T MATTER.
LIKE WE ALREADY TOLD YOU, ORDERS ARE--
TREKEL-TEK-TEK-LEK!
AAAAAH!

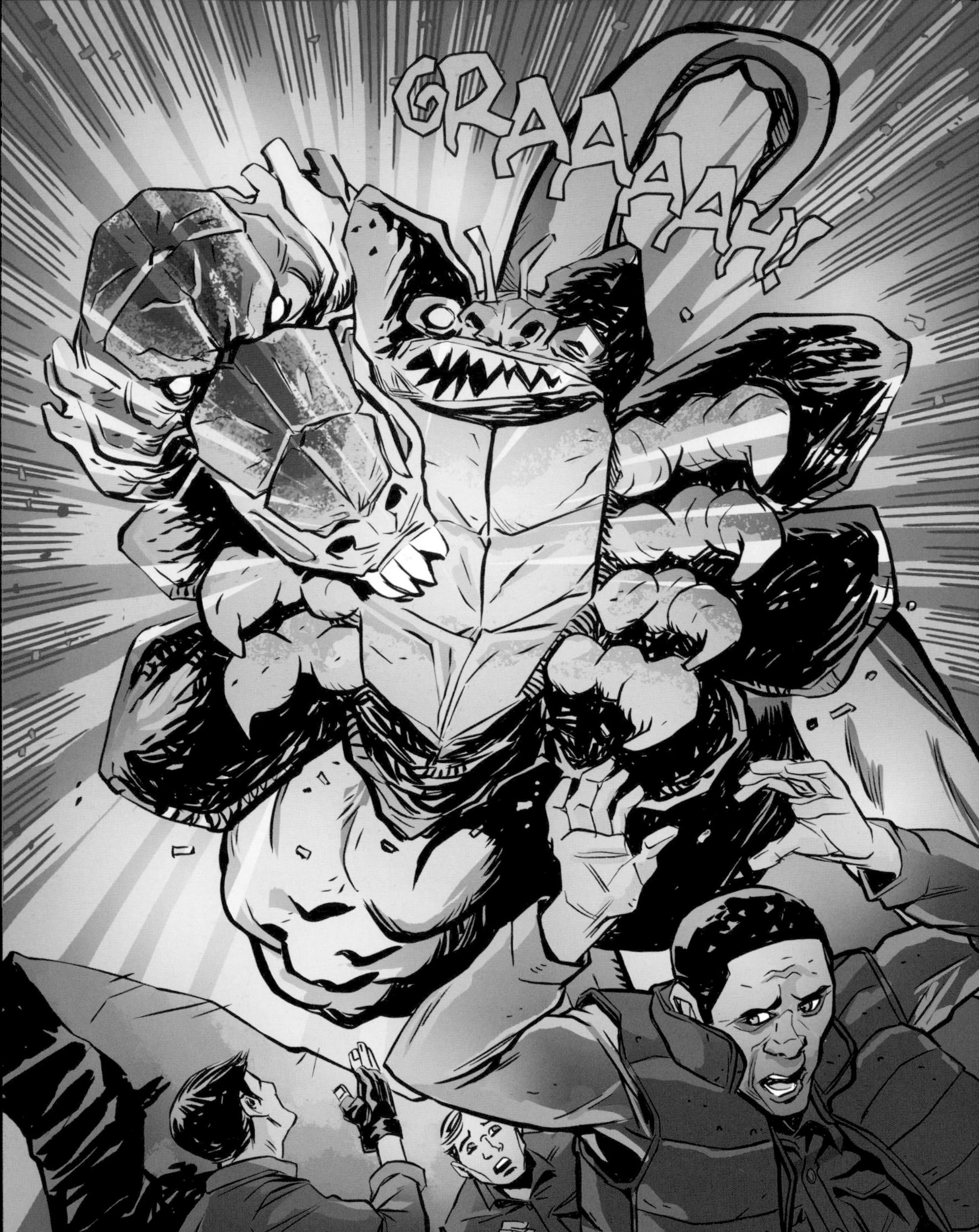
GRAAAAAH!!

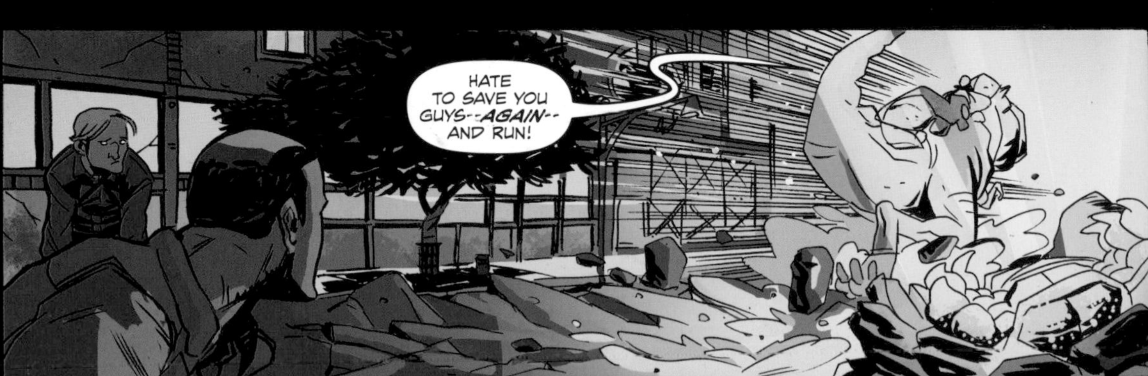
HATE TO SAVE YOU GUYS--*AGAIN*--AND RUN!

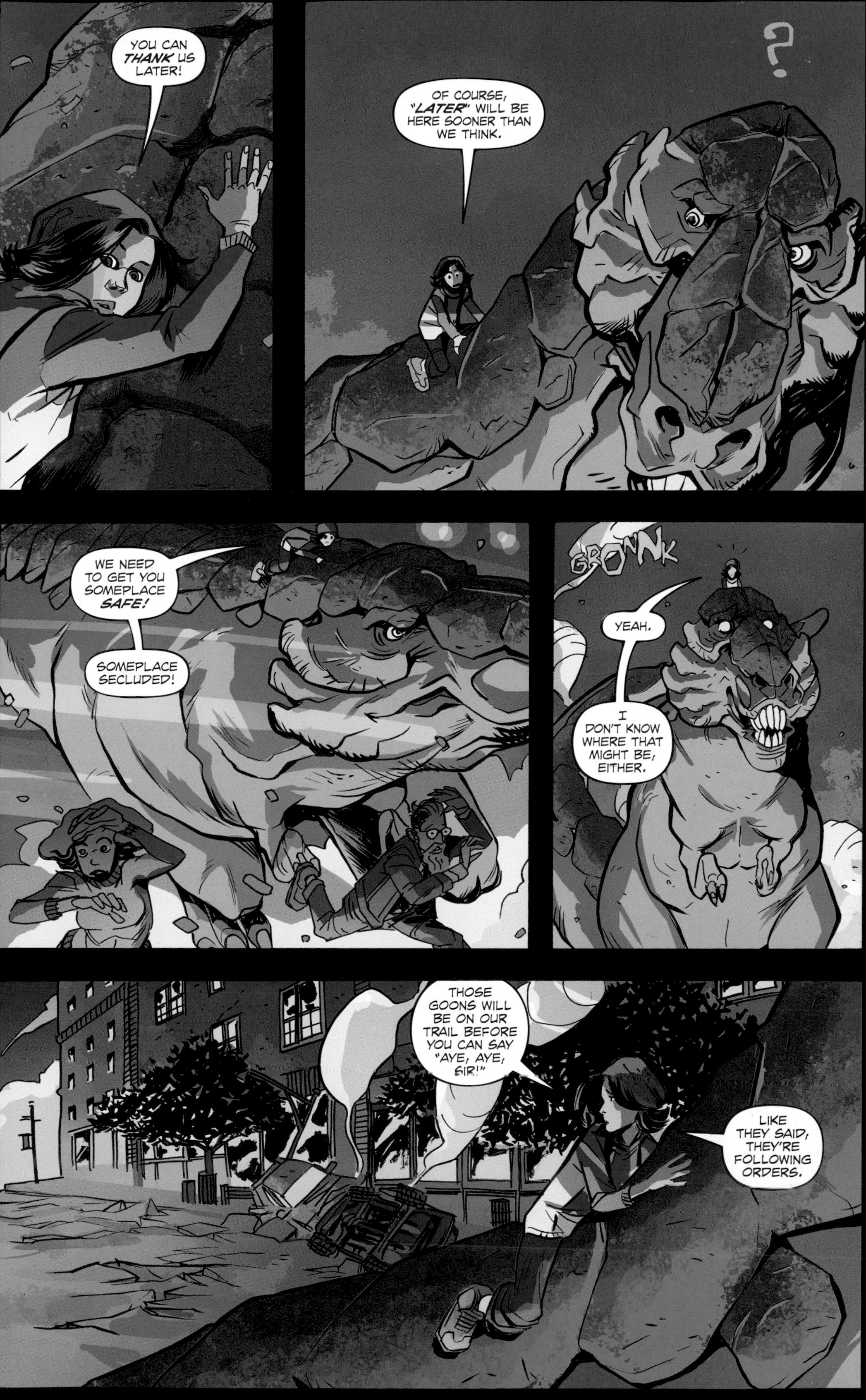
YOU CAN *THANK* US LATER!
?
OF COURSE, "*LATER*" WILL BE HERE SOONER THAN WE THINK.
WE NEED TO GET YOU SOMEPLACE *SAFE!*
SOMEPLACE SECLUDED!
GRONNK
YEAH.
I DON'T KNOW WHERE THAT MIGHT BE, EITHER.
THOSE GOONS WILL BE ON OUR TRAIL BEFORE YOU CAN SAY "AYE, AYE, SIR!"
LIKE THEY SAID, THEY'RE FOLLOWING ORDERS.

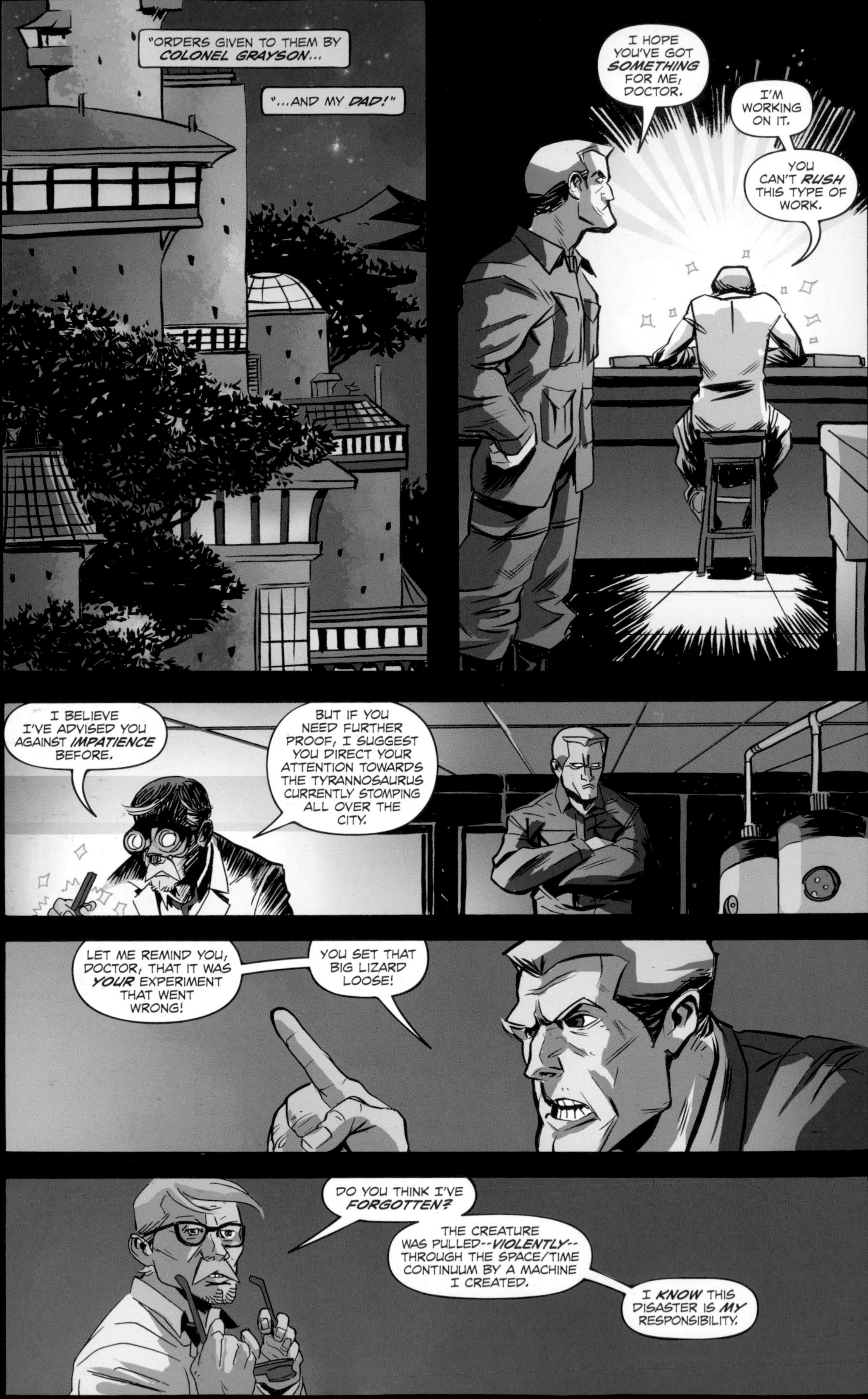
"ORDERS GIVEN TO THEM BY COLONEL GRAYSON...
"...AND MY DAD!"
I HOPE YOU'VE GOT SOMETHING FOR ME, DOCTOR.
I'M WORKING ON IT.
YOU CAN'T RUSH THIS TYPE OF WORK.
I BELIEVE I'VE ADVISED YOU AGAINST IMPATIENCE BEFORE.
BUT IF YOU NEED FURTHER PROOF, I SUGGEST YOU DIRECT YOUR ATTENTION TOWARDS THE TYRANNOSAURUS CURRENTLY STOMPING ALL OVER THE CITY.
LET ME REMIND YOU, DOCTOR, THAT IT WAS YOUR EXPERIMENT THAT WENT WRONG!
YOU SET THAT BIG LIZARD LOOSE!
DO YOU THINK I'VE FORGOTTEN?
THE CREATURE WAS PULLED--VIOLENTLY--THROUGH THE SPACE/TIME CONTINUUM BY A MACHINE I CREATED.
I KNOW THIS DISASTER IS MY RESPONSIBILITY.

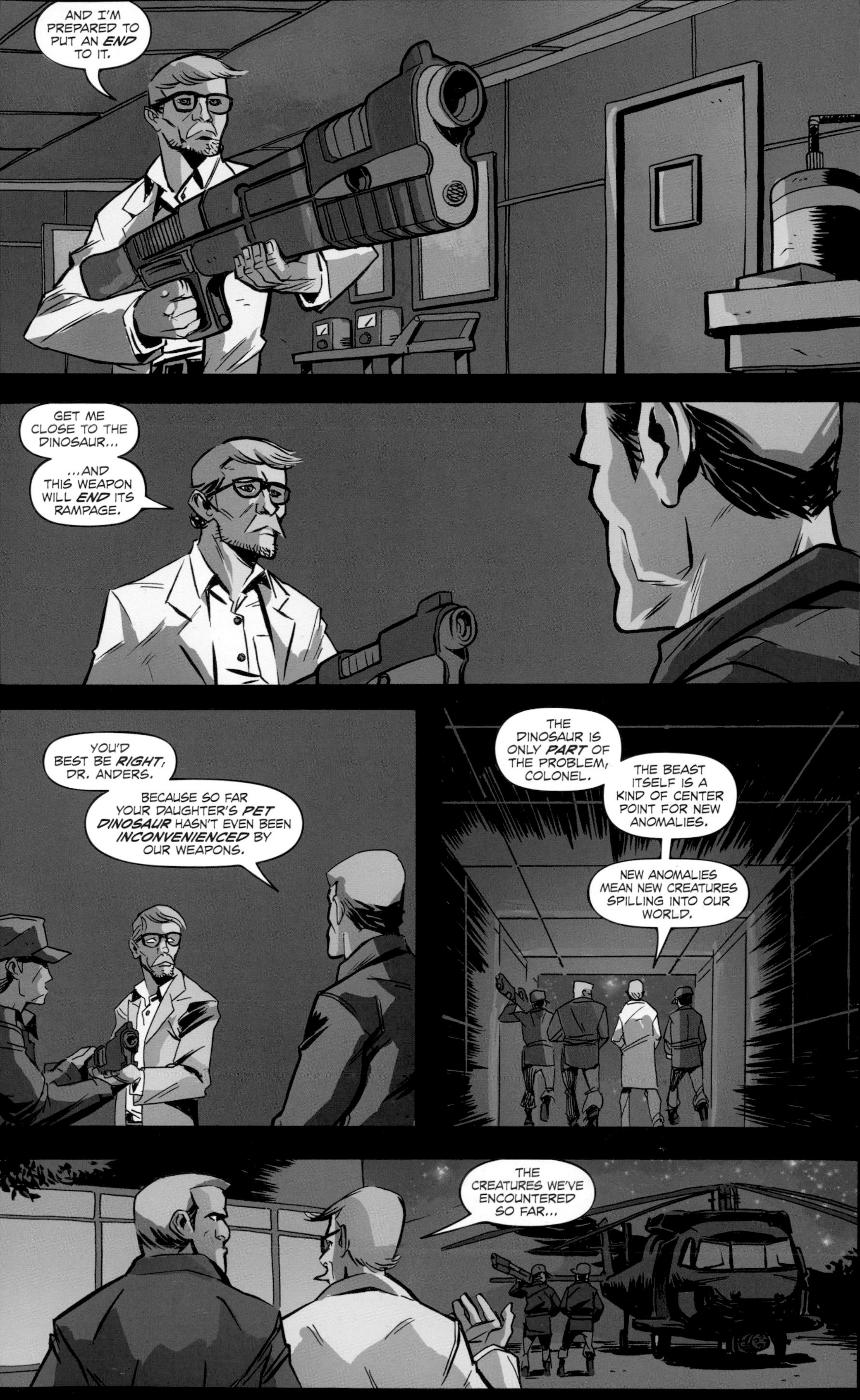
AND I'M PREPARED TO PUT AN *END* TO IT.
GET ME CLOSE TO THE DINOSAUR...
...AND THIS WEAPON WILL *END* ITS RAMPAGE.
YOU'D BEST BE *RIGHT*, DR. ANDERS.
BECAUSE SO FAR YOUR DAUGHTER'S *PET DINOSAUR* HASN'T EVEN BEEN *INCONVENIENCED* BY OUR WEAPONS.
THE DINOSAUR IS ONLY *PART* OF THE PROBLEM, COLONEL.
THE BEAST ITSELF IS A KIND OF CENTER POINT FOR NEW ANOMALIES.
NEW ANOMALIES MEAN NEW CREATURES SPILLING INTO OUR WORLD.
THE CREATURES WE'VE ENCOUNTERED SO FAR...

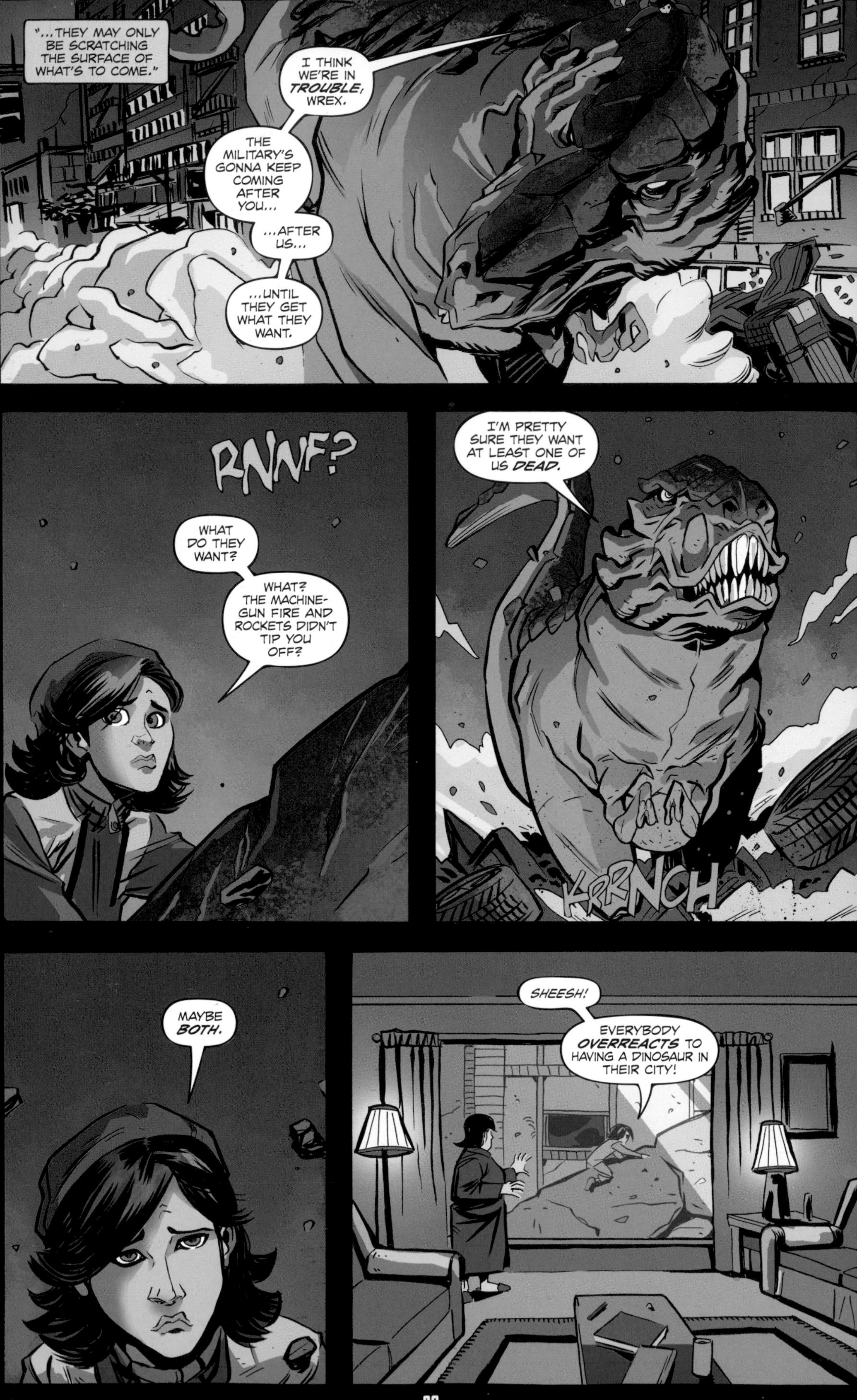
"...THEY MAY ONLY BE SCRATCHING THE SURFACE OF WHAT'S TO COME."
I THINK WE'RE IN TROUBLE, WREX.
THE MILITARY'S GONNA KEEP COMING AFTER YOU...
...AFTER US...
...UNTIL THEY GET WHAT THEY WANT.
RNNF?
WHAT DO THEY WANT?
WHAT? THE MACHINE-GUN FIRE AND ROCKETS DIDN'T TIP YOU OFF?
I'M PRETTY SURE THEY WANT AT LEAST ONE OF US DEAD.
KRRNCH
MAYBE BOTH.
SHEESH!
EVERYBODY OVERREACTS TO HAVING A DINOSAUR IN THEIR CITY!

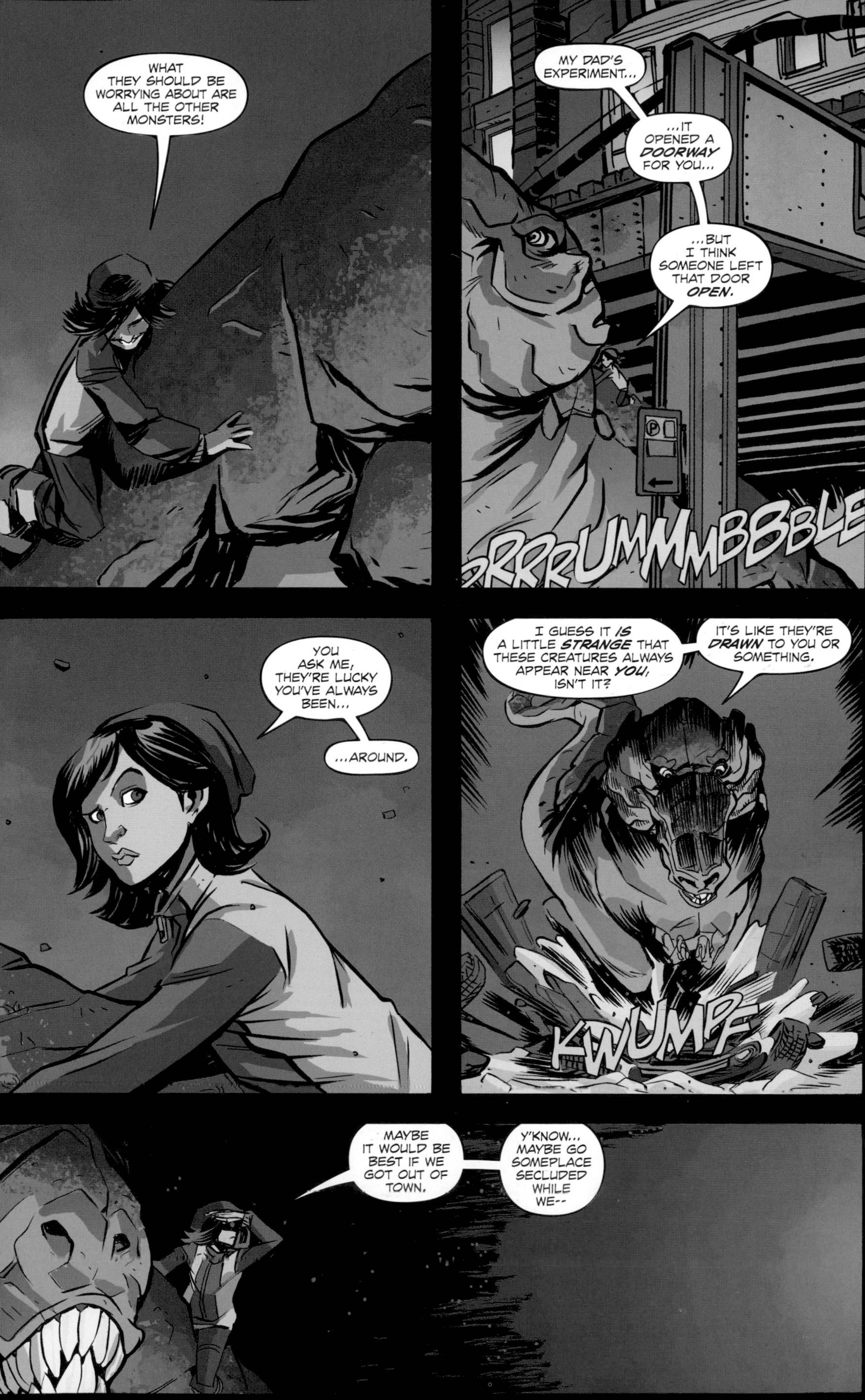
WHAT THEY SHOULD BE WORRYING ABOUT ARE ALL THE OTHER MONSTERS!
MY DAD'S EXPERIMENT...
...IT OPENED A DOORWAY FOR YOU...
...BUT I THINK SOMEONE LEFT THAT DOOR OPEN.
RRRRUMMMBBBLE
YOU ASK ME, THEY'RE LUCKY YOU'VE ALWAYS BEEN...
...AROUND.
I GUESS IT IS A LITTLE STRANGE THAT THESE CREATURES ALWAYS APPEAR NEAR YOU, ISN'T IT?
IT'S LIKE THEY'RE DRAWN TO YOU OR SOMETHING.
KWUMPF
MAYBE IT WOULD BE BEST IF WE GOT OUT OF TOWN.
Y'KNOW... MAYBE GO SOMEPLACE SECLUDED WHILE WE--

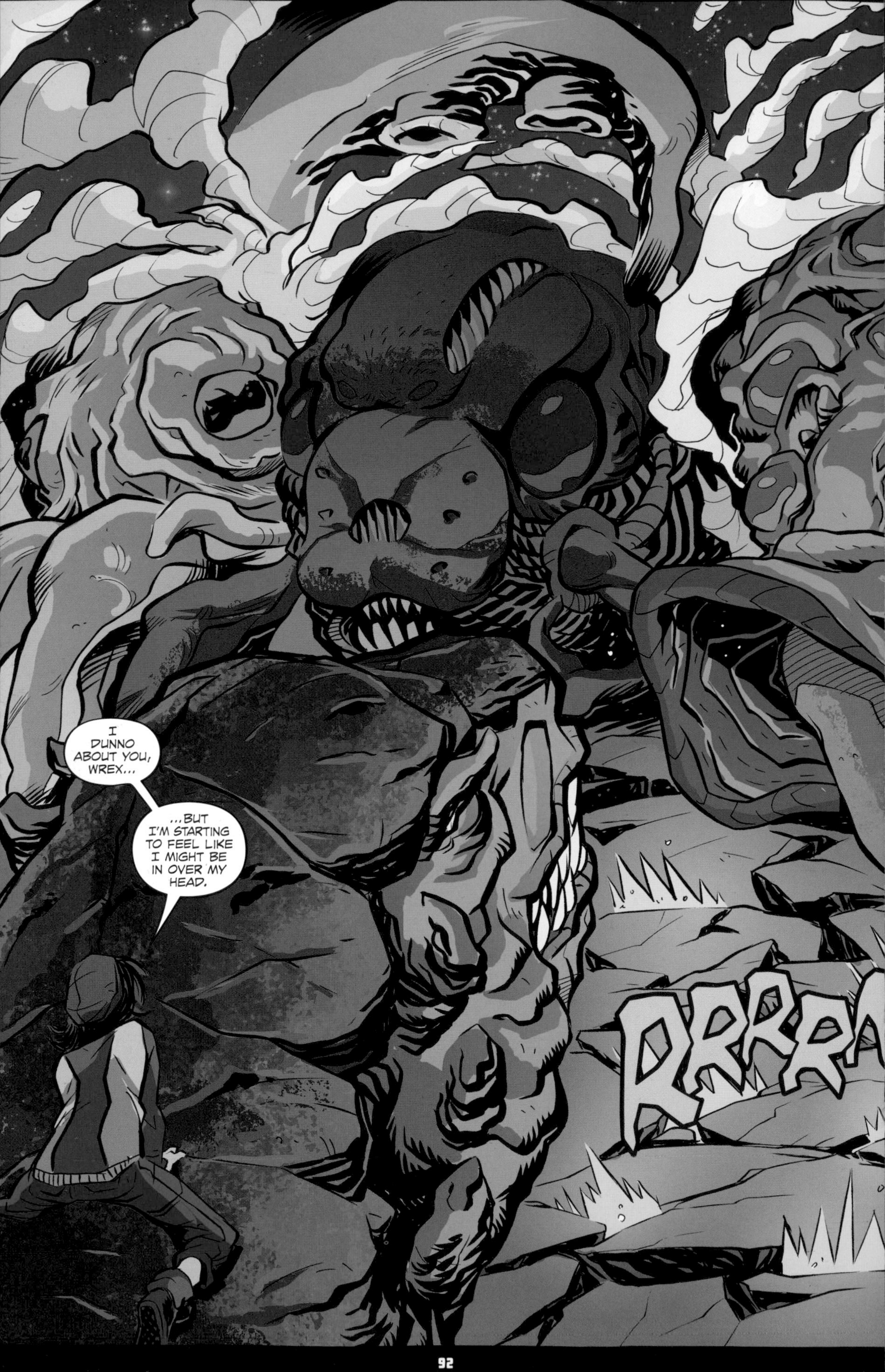
I DUNNO ABOUT YOU, WREX...
...BUT I'M STARTING TO FEEL LIKE I MIGHT BE IN OVER MY HEAD.
RRRRA

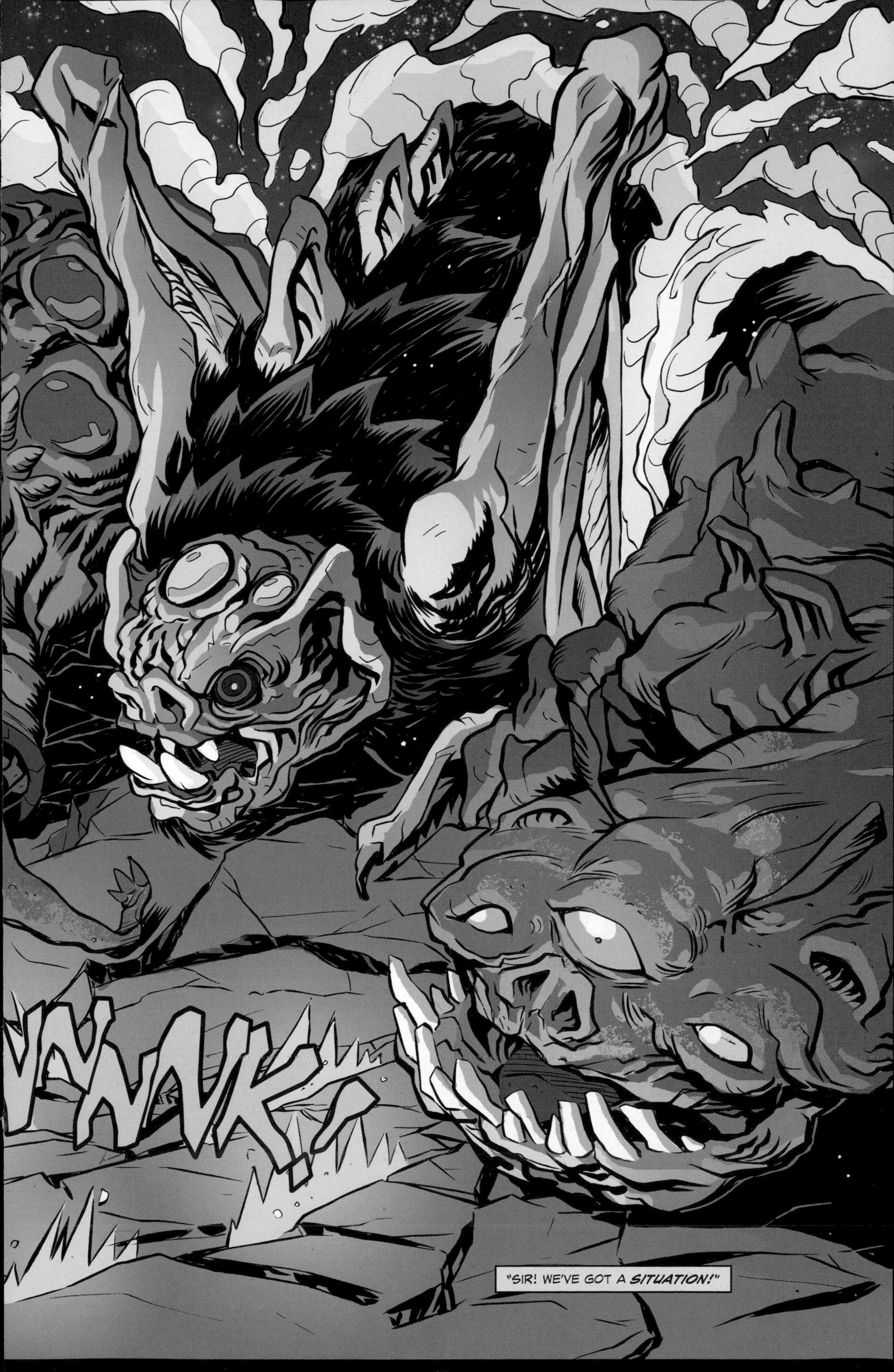
WNAK!
"SIR! WE'VE GOT A *SITUATION!*"

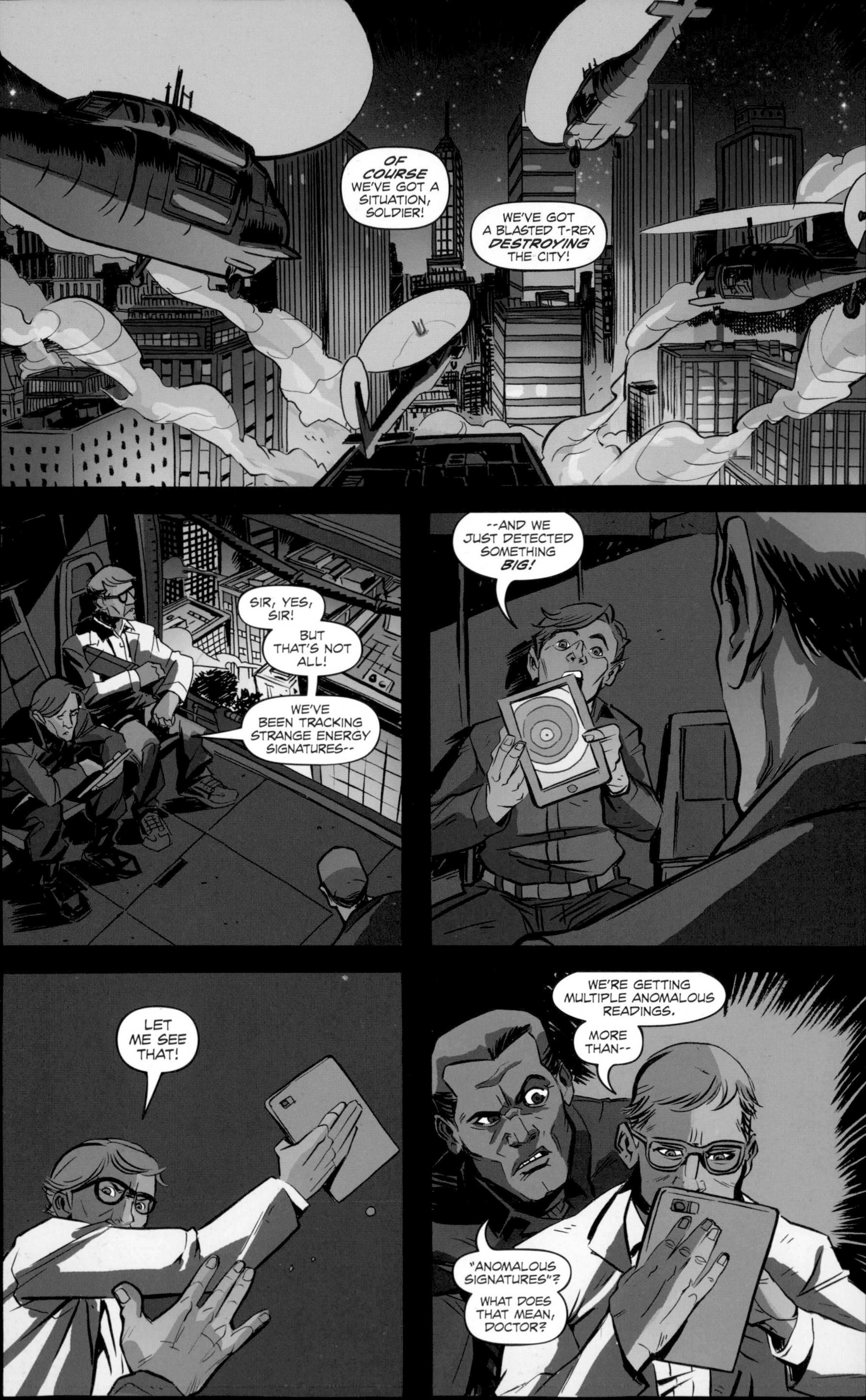
OF COURSE WE'VE GOT A SITUATION, SOLDIER!
WE'VE GOT A BLASTED T-REX DESTROYING THE CITY!
SIR, YES, SIR!
BUT THAT'S NOT ALL!
WE'VE BEEN TRACKING STRANGE ENERGY SIGNATURES--
--AND WE JUST DETECTED SOMETHING BIG!
LET ME SEE THAT!
WE'RE GETTING MULTIPLE ANOMALOUS READINGS.
MORE THAN--
"ANOMALOUS SIGNATURES"?
WHAT DOES THAT MEAN, DOCTOR?

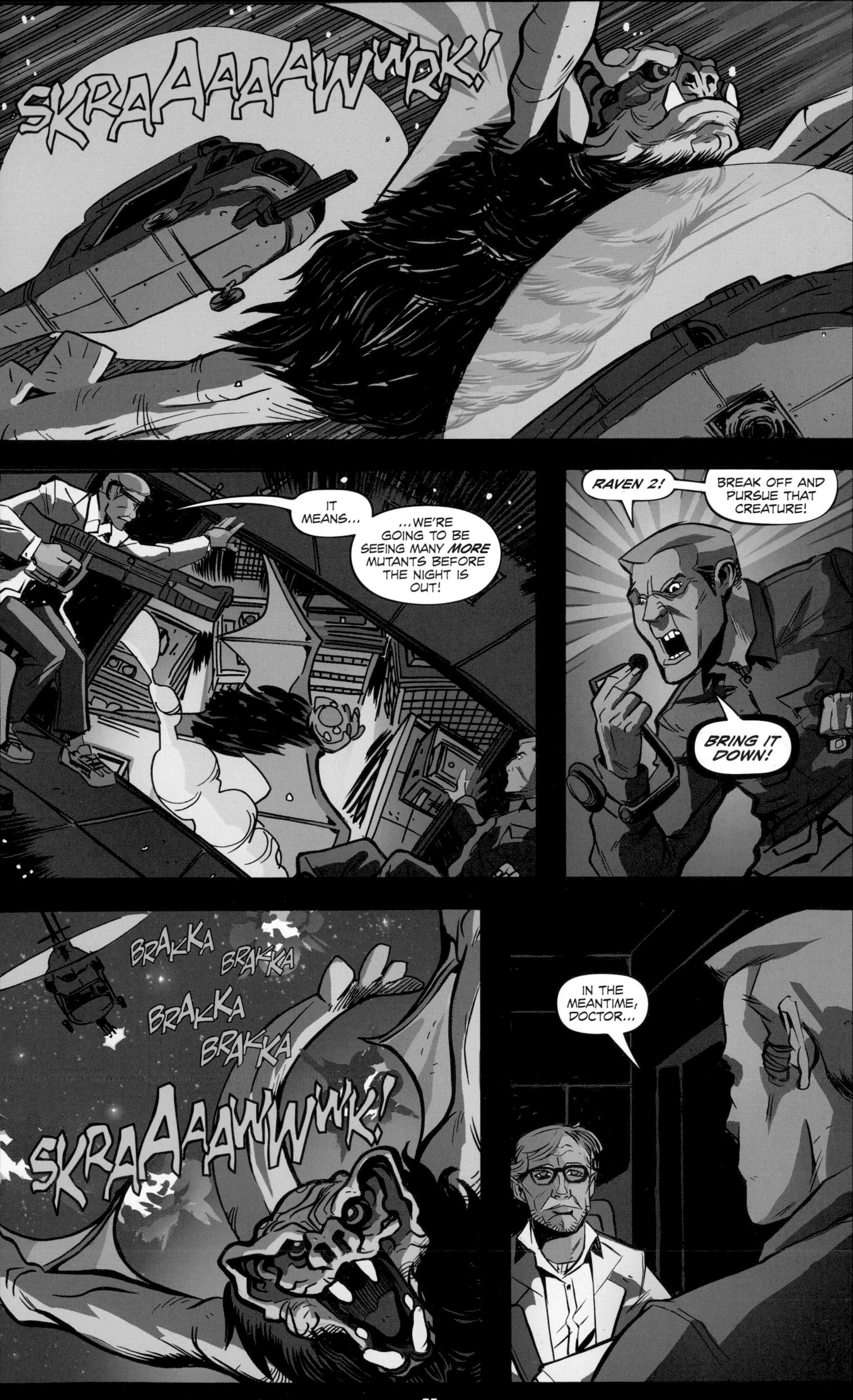
SKRAAAAAAWWRK!
IT MEANS...
...WE'RE GOING TO BE SEEING MANY MORE MUTANTS BEFORE THE NIGHT IS OUT!
RAVEN 2!
BREAK OFF AND PURSUE THAT CREATURE!
BRING IT DOWN!
BRAKKA BRAKKA
BRAKKA
BRAKKA
SKRAAAAWWWK!
IN THE MEANTIME, DOCTOR...

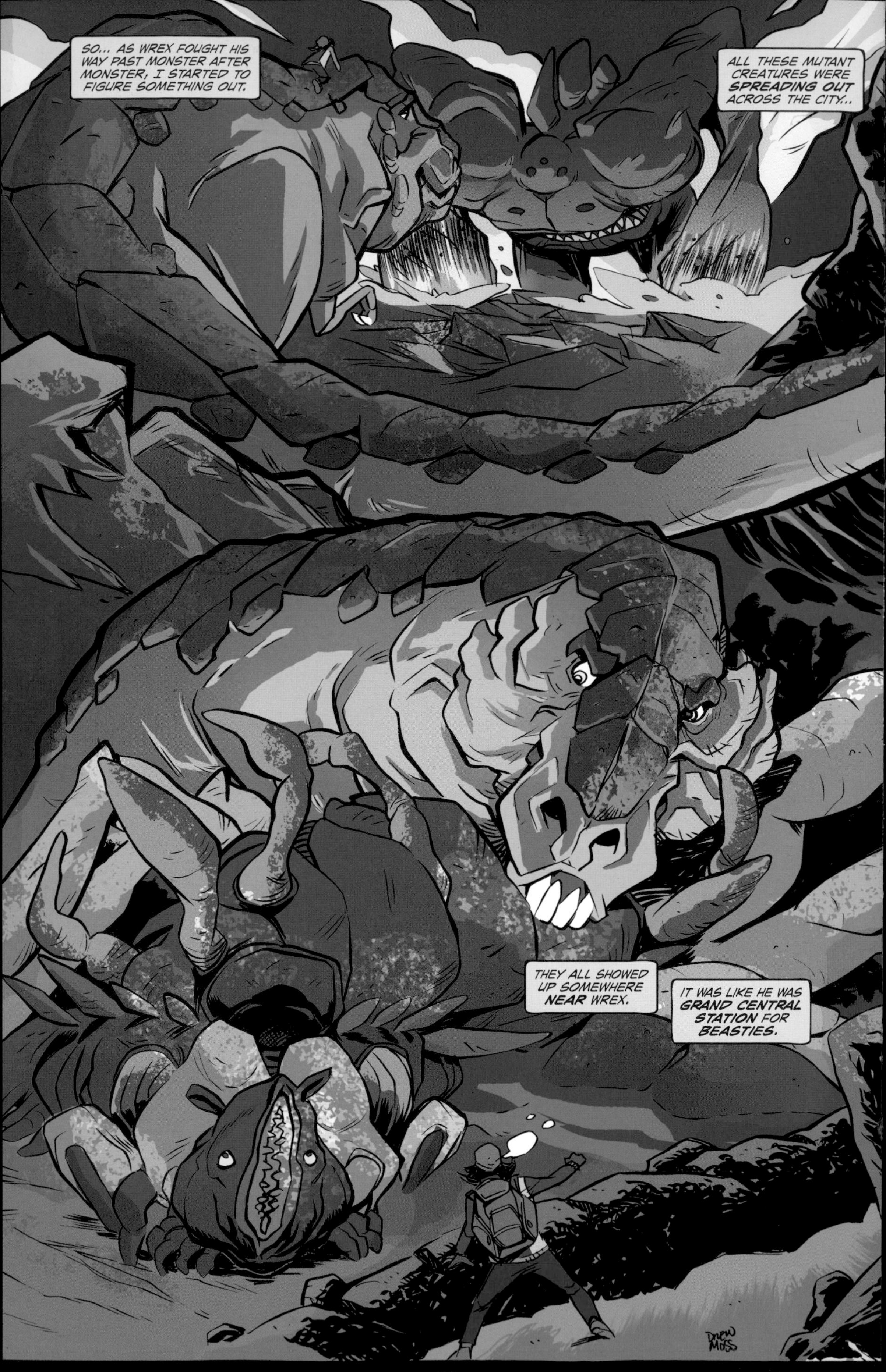
SO... AS WREX FOUGHT HIS WAY PAST MONSTER AFTER MONSTER, I STARTED TO FIGURE SOMETHING OUT.
ALL THESE MUTANT CREATURES WERE SPREADING OUT ACROSS THE CITY...
THEY ALL SHOWED UP SOMEWHERE NEAR WREX.
IT WAS LIKE HE WAS GRAND CENTRAL STATION FOR BEASTIES.
DREW MOSS

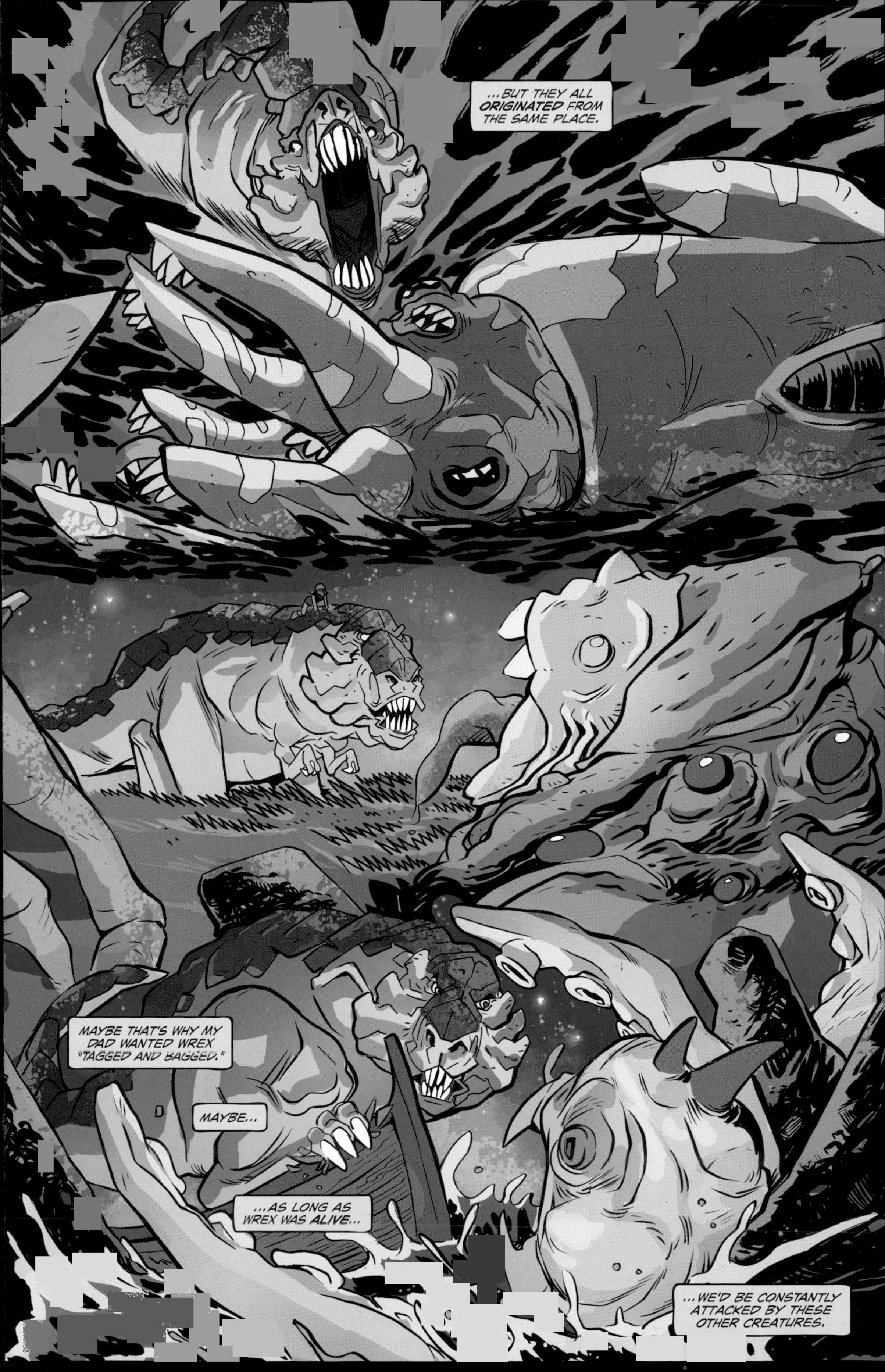
...BUT THEY ALL ORIGINATED FROM THE SAME PLACE.
MAYBE THAT'S WHY MY DAD WANTED WREX "TAGGED AND BAGGED."
MAYBE...
...AS LONG AS WREX WAS ALIVE...
...WE'D BE CONSTANTLY ATTACKED BY THESE OTHER CREATURES.

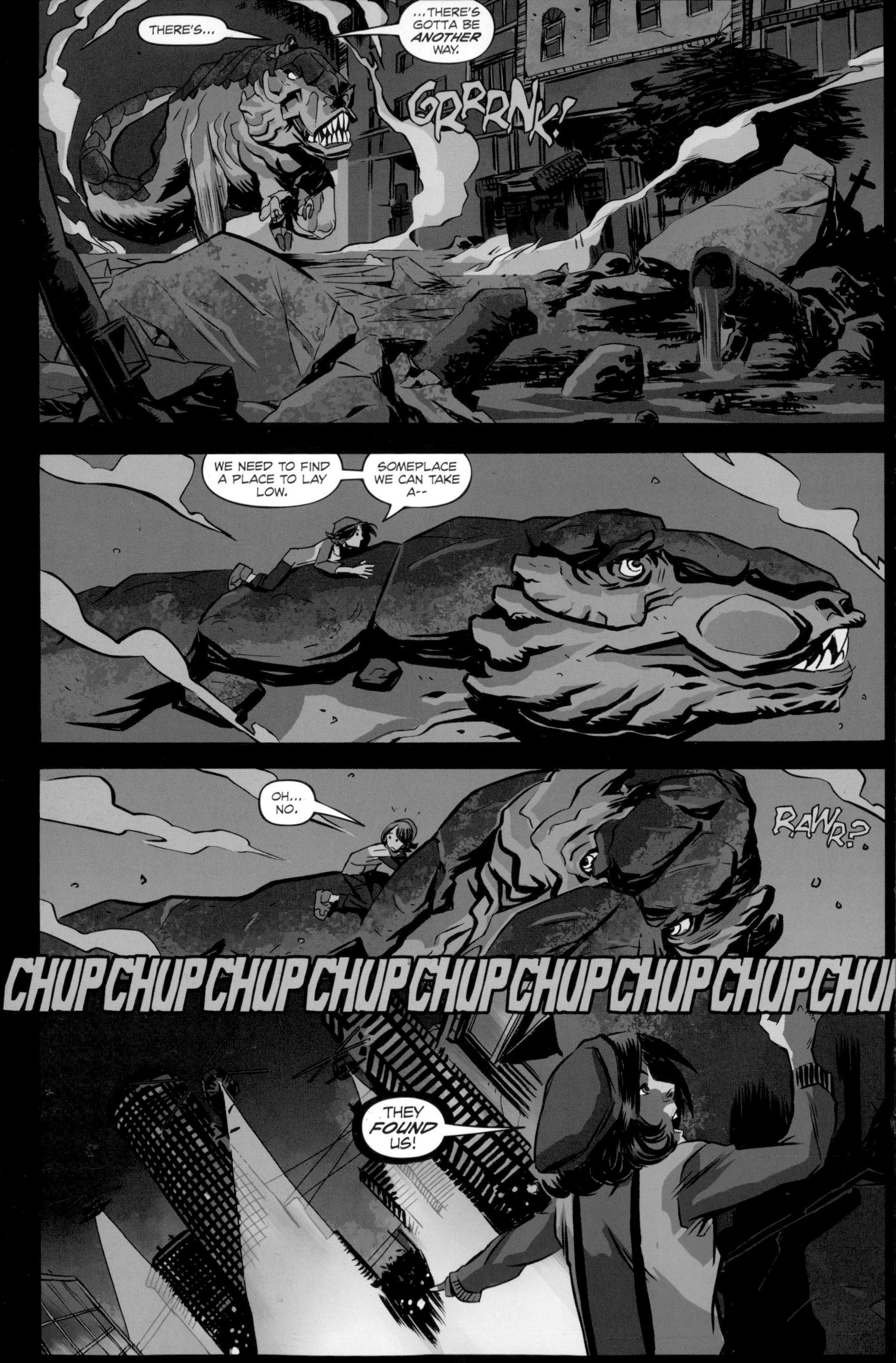
THERE'S...
...THERE'S GOTTA BE ANOTHER WAY.
GRRRNK!
WE NEED TO FIND A PLACE TO LAY LOW.
SOMEPLACE WE CAN TAKE A--
OH... NO.
RAWR?
CHUP CHUP CHUP CHUP CHUP CHUP CHUP CHUP
THEY FOUND US!

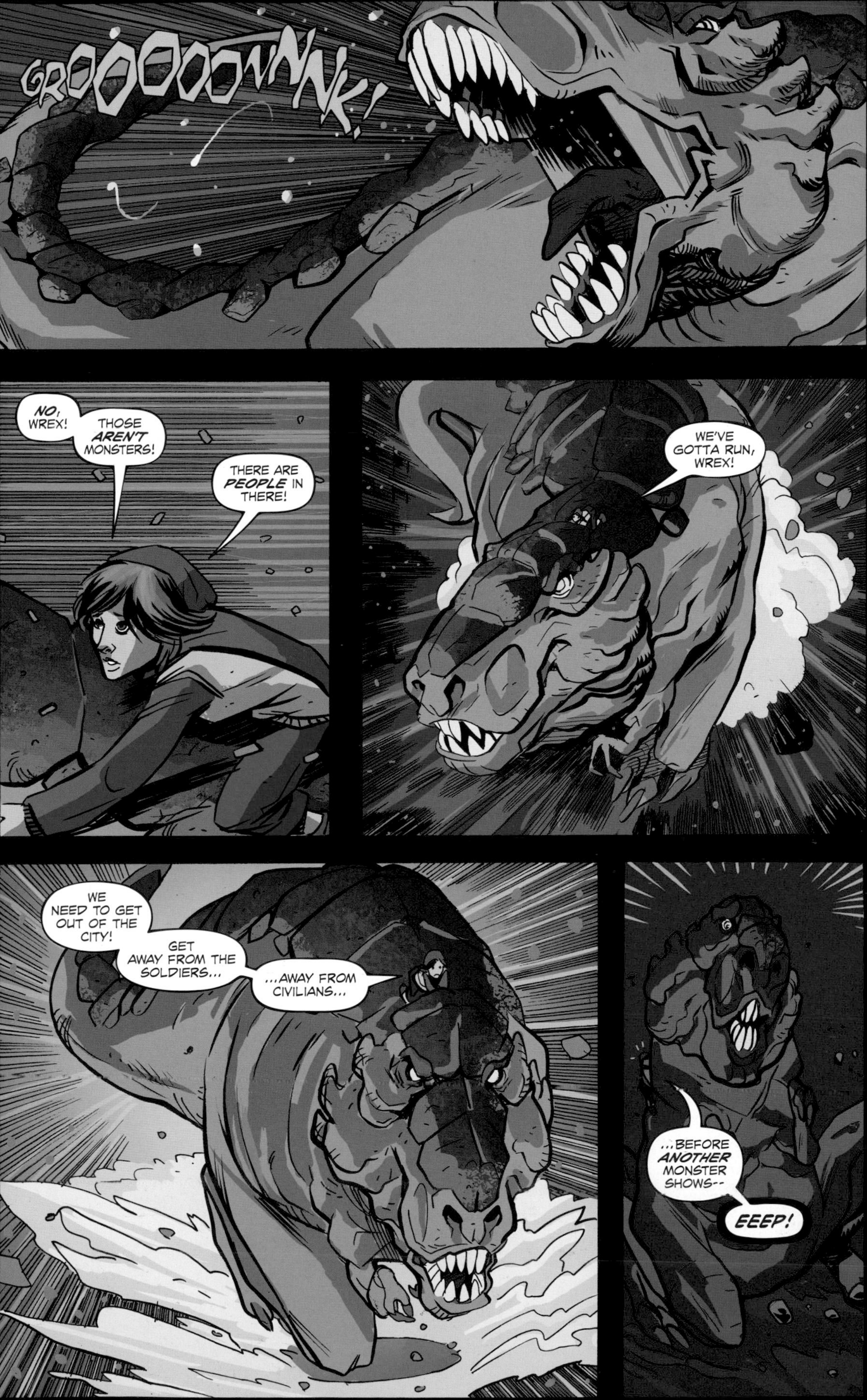
GROOOOONNNK!
NO, WREX!
THOSE AREN'T MONSTERS!
THERE ARE PEOPLE IN THERE!
WE'VE GOTTA RUN, WREX!
WE NEED TO GET OUT OF THE CITY!
GET AWAY FROM THE SOLDIERS...
...AWAY FROM CIVILIANS...
...BEFORE ANOTHER MONSTER SHOWS--
EEEP!

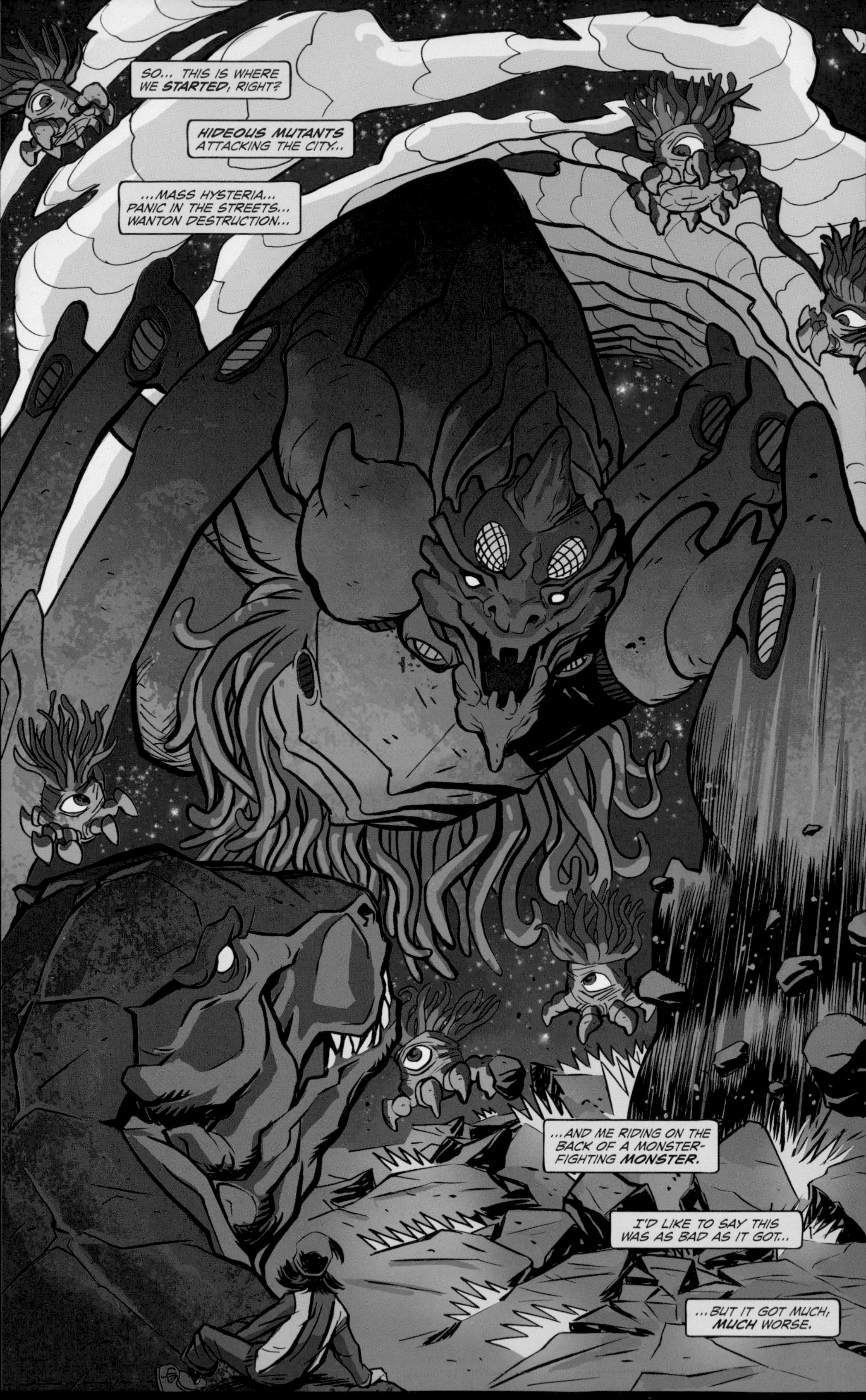
SO... THIS IS WHERE WE STARTED, RIGHT?
HIDEOUS MUTANTS ATTACKING THE CITY...
...MASS HYSTERIA... PANIC IN THE STREETS... WANTON DESTRUCTION...
...AND ME RIDING ON THE BACK OF A MONSTER-FIGHTING MONSTER.
I'D LIKE TO SAY THIS WAS AS BAD AS IT GOT...
...BUT IT GOT MUCH, MUCH WORSE.

CHAPTER FIVE

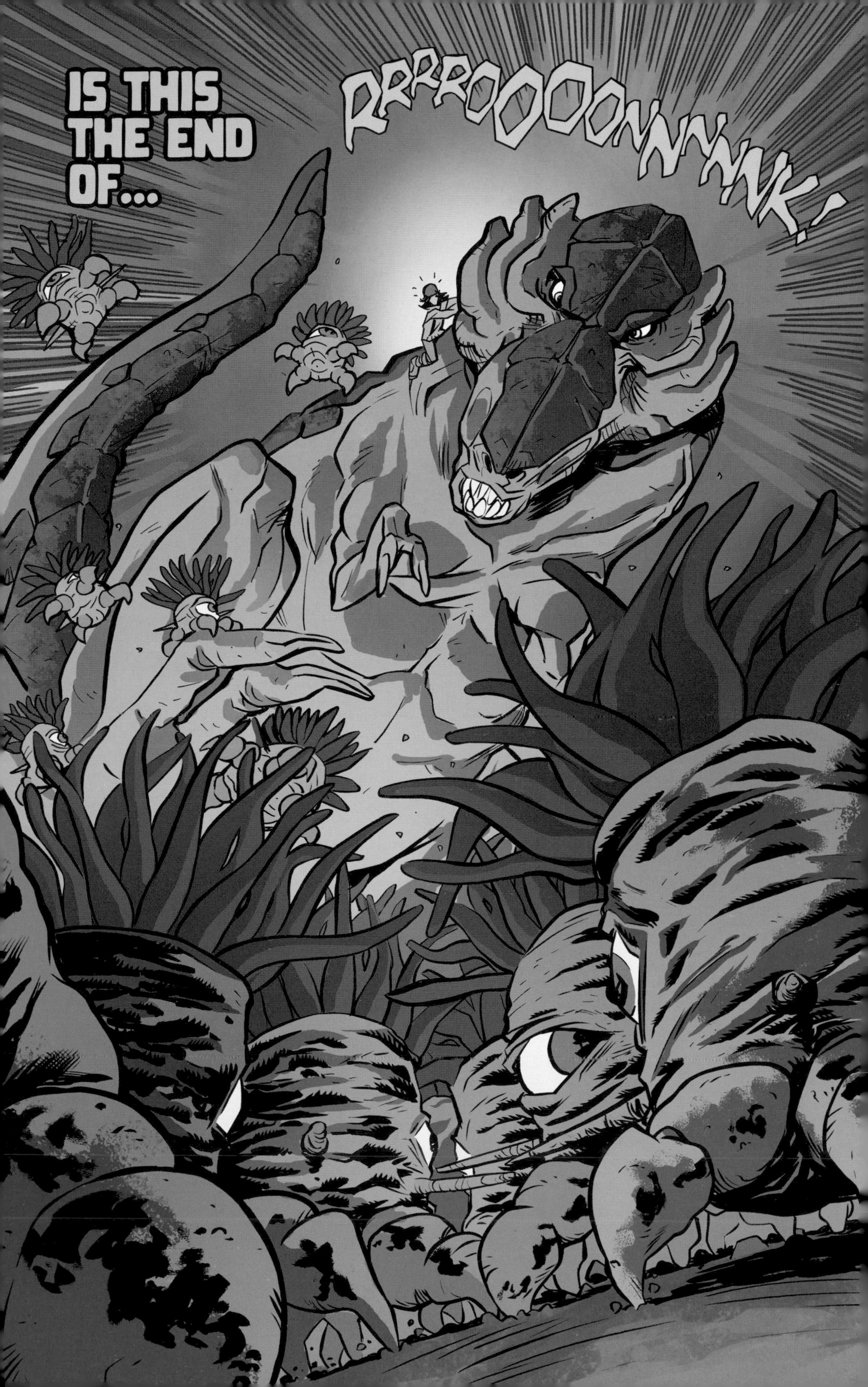
IS THIS THE END OF...
RRRROOOOONNNNNK!

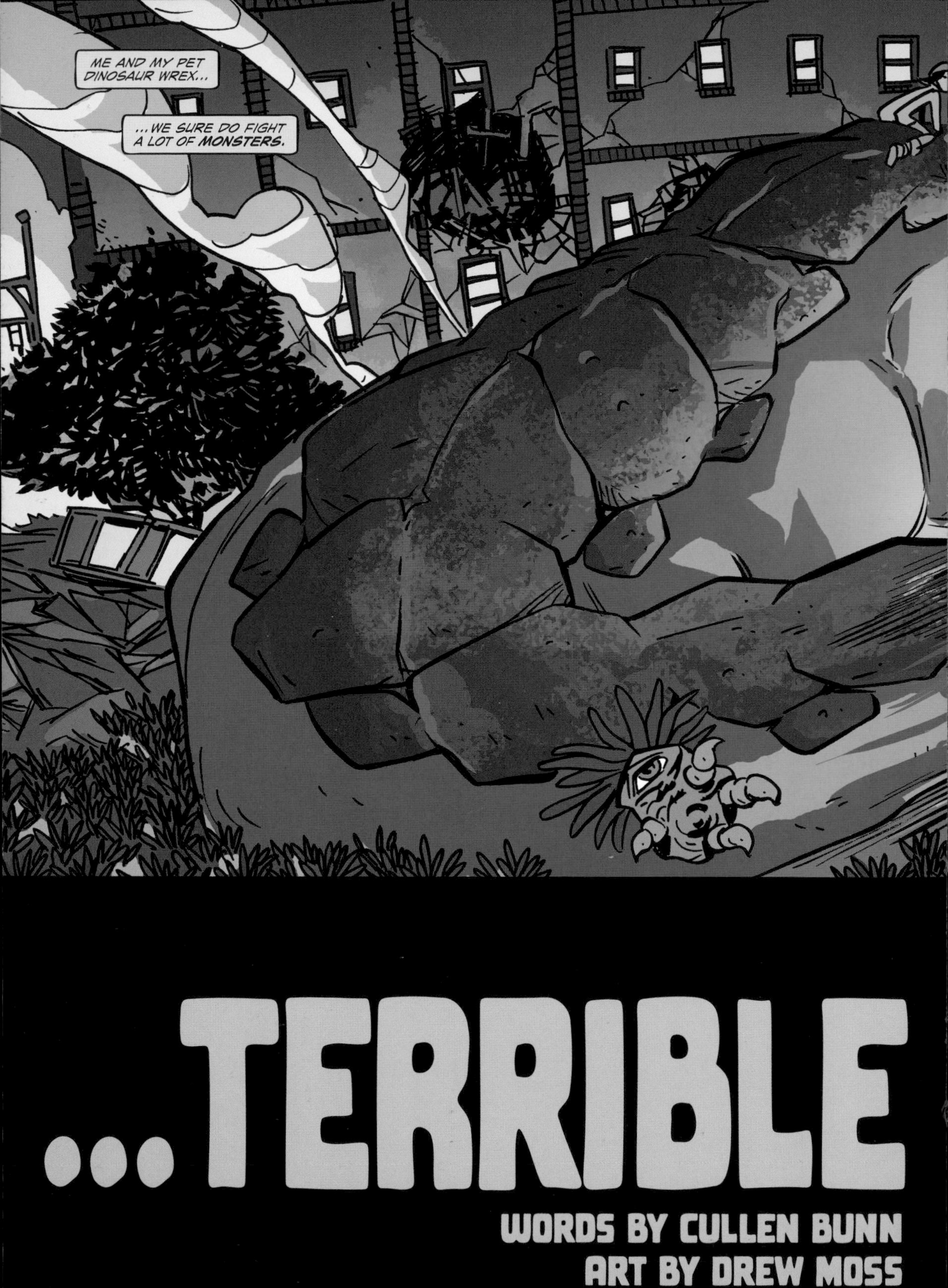
ME AND MY PET DINOSAUR WREX...
...WE SURE DO FIGHT A LOT OF MONSTERS.

...TERRIBLE

WORDS BY CULLEN BUNN
ART BY DREW MOSS

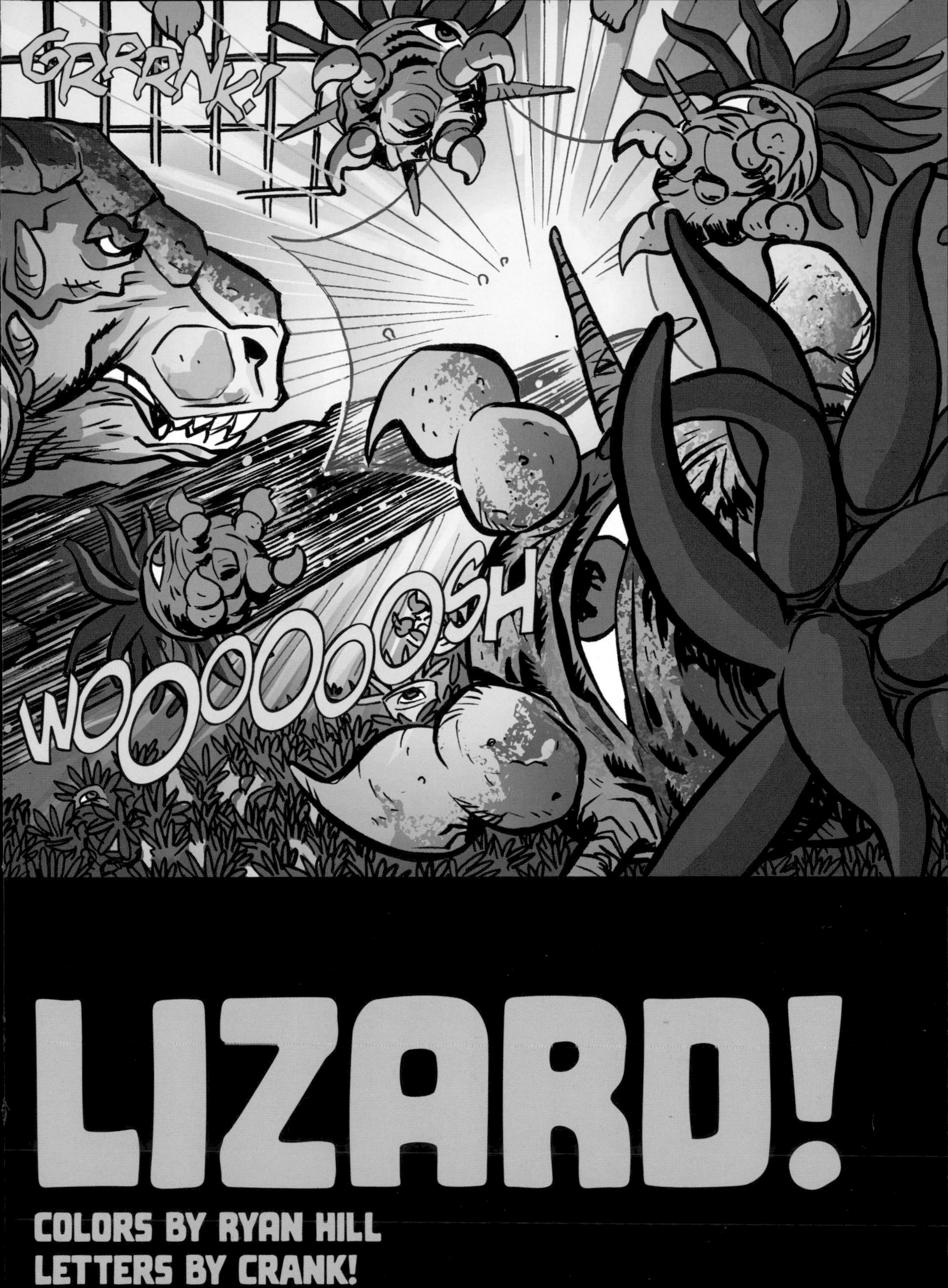
GRRRNK!
WOOOOOOSH

LIZARD!

COLORS BY RYAN HILL
LETTERS BY CRANK!

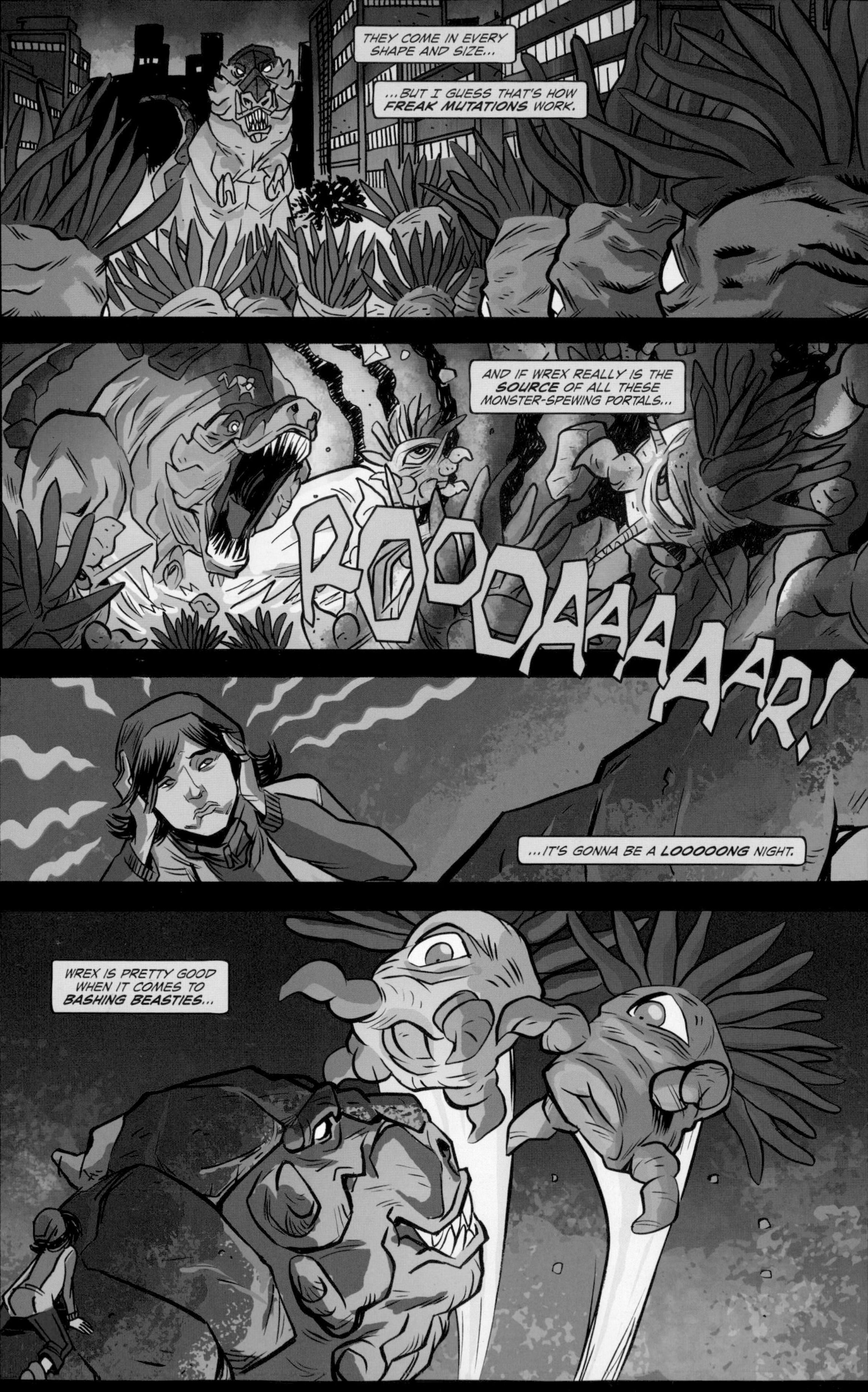
THEY COME IN EVERY SHAPE AND SIZE...
...BUT I GUESS THAT'S HOW **FREAK MUTATIONS** WORK.
AND IF WREX REALLY IS THE **SOURCE** OF ALL THESE MONSTER-SPEWING PORTALS...
ROOOAAAAAR!
...IT'S GONNA BE A **LOOOOONG** NIGHT.
WREX IS PRETTY GOOD WHEN IT COMES TO **BASHING BEASTIES**...

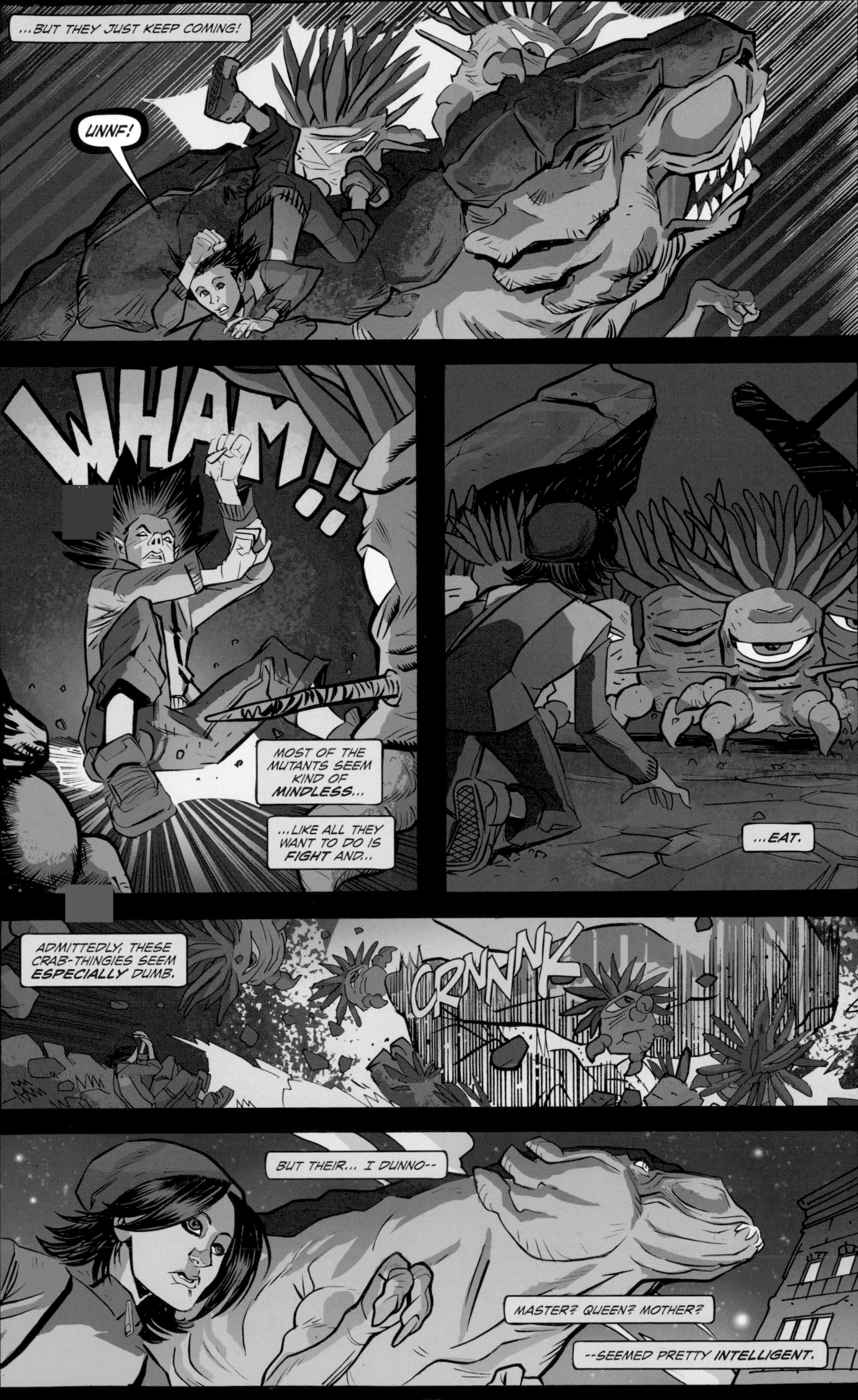
...BUT THEY JUST KEEP COMING!
UNNF!
WHAM!!!
MOST OF THE MUTANTS SEEM KIND OF MINDLESS...
...LIKE ALL THEY WANT TO DO IS FIGHT AND...
...EAT.
ADMITTEDLY, THESE CRAB-THINGIES SEEM ESPECIALLY DUMB.
CRNNNK
BUT THEIR... I DUNNO--
MASTER? QUEEN? MOTHER?
--SEEMED PRETTY INTELLIGENT.

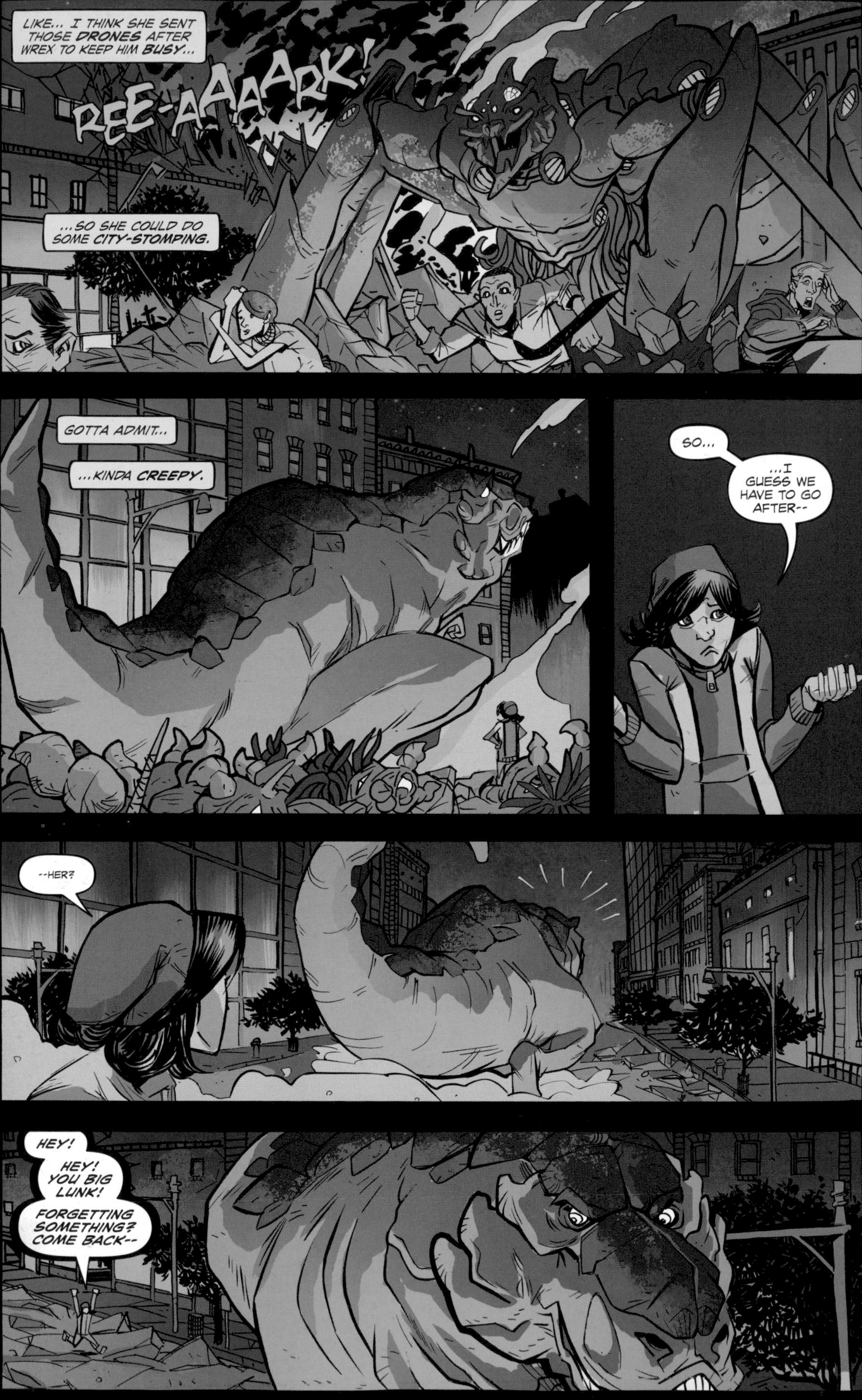
LIKE... I THINK SHE SENT THOSE DRONES AFTER WREX TO KEEP HIM BUSY...
REE-AAAARK!
...SO SHE COULD DO SOME CITY-STOMPING.
GOTTA ADMIT...
...KINDA CREEPY.
SO...
...I GUESS WE HAVE TO GO AFTER--
--HER?
HEY!
HEY! YOU BIG LUNK!
FORGETTING SOMETHING? COME BACK--

ROOOAAAAAR!

WHU-- WHAT WAS *THAT* ALL ABOUT?

GRRK?

I KNOW HOW YOU FEEL.

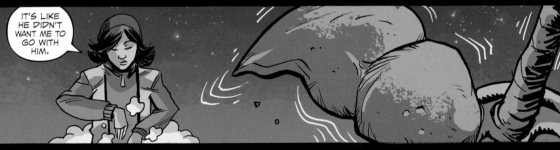

IT'S LIKE HE DIDN'T WANT ME TO GO WITH HIM.

GRONK!

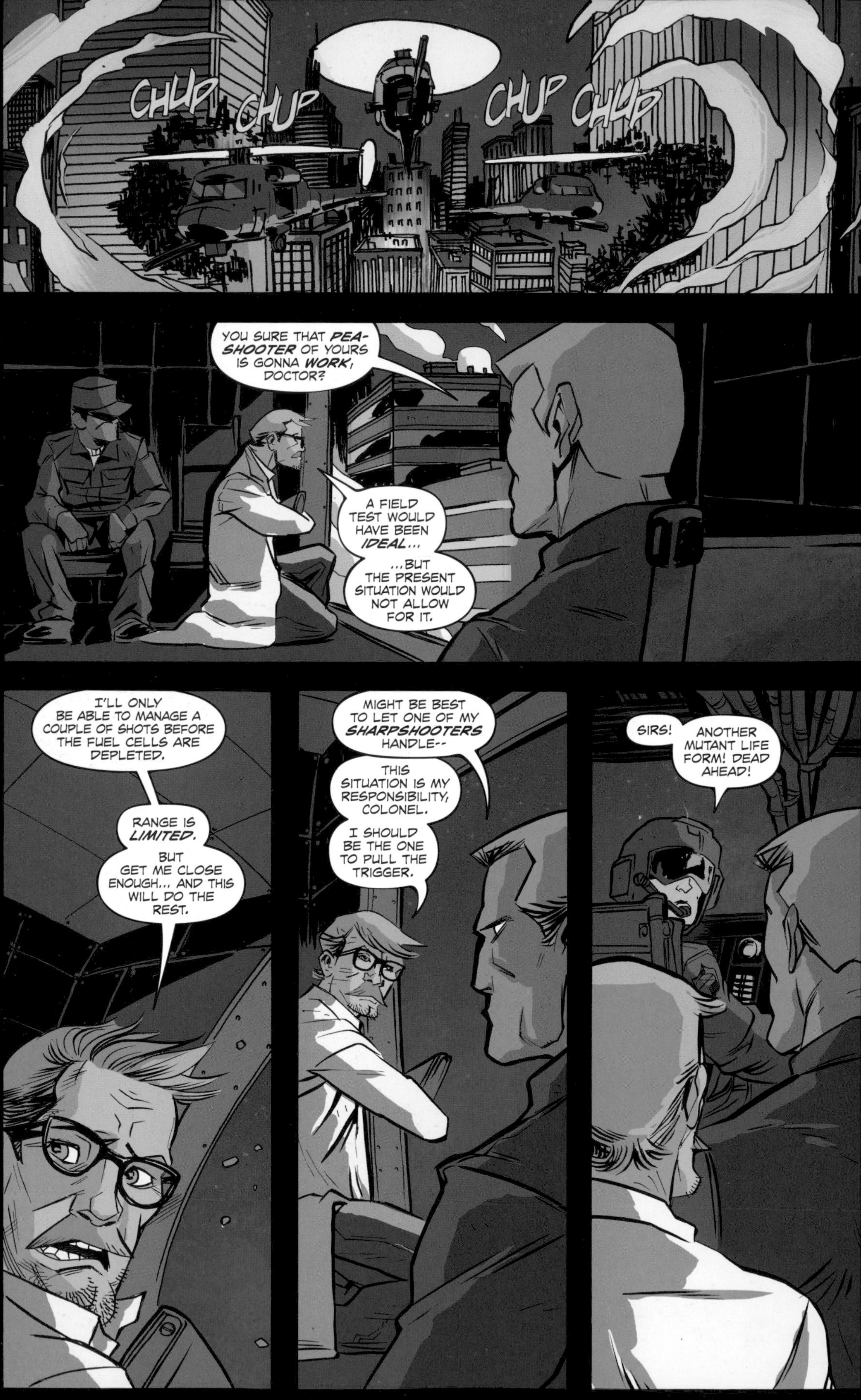
CHUP CHUP
CHUP CHUP
YOU SURE THAT PEA-SHOOTER OF YOURS IS GONNA WORK, DOCTOR?
A FIELD TEST WOULD HAVE BEEN IDEAL...
...BUT THE PRESENT SITUATION WOULD NOT ALLOW FOR IT.
I'LL ONLY BE ABLE TO MANAGE A COUPLE OF SHOTS BEFORE THE FUEL CELLS ARE DEPLETED.
RANGE IS LIMITED.
BUT GET ME CLOSE ENOUGH... AND THIS WILL DO THE REST.
MIGHT BE BEST TO LET ONE OF MY SHARPSHOOTERS HANDLE--
THIS SITUATION IS MY RESPONSIBILITY, COLONEL.
I SHOULD BE THE ONE TO PULL THE TRIGGER.
SIRS!
ANOTHER MUTANT LIFE FORM! DEAD AHEAD!

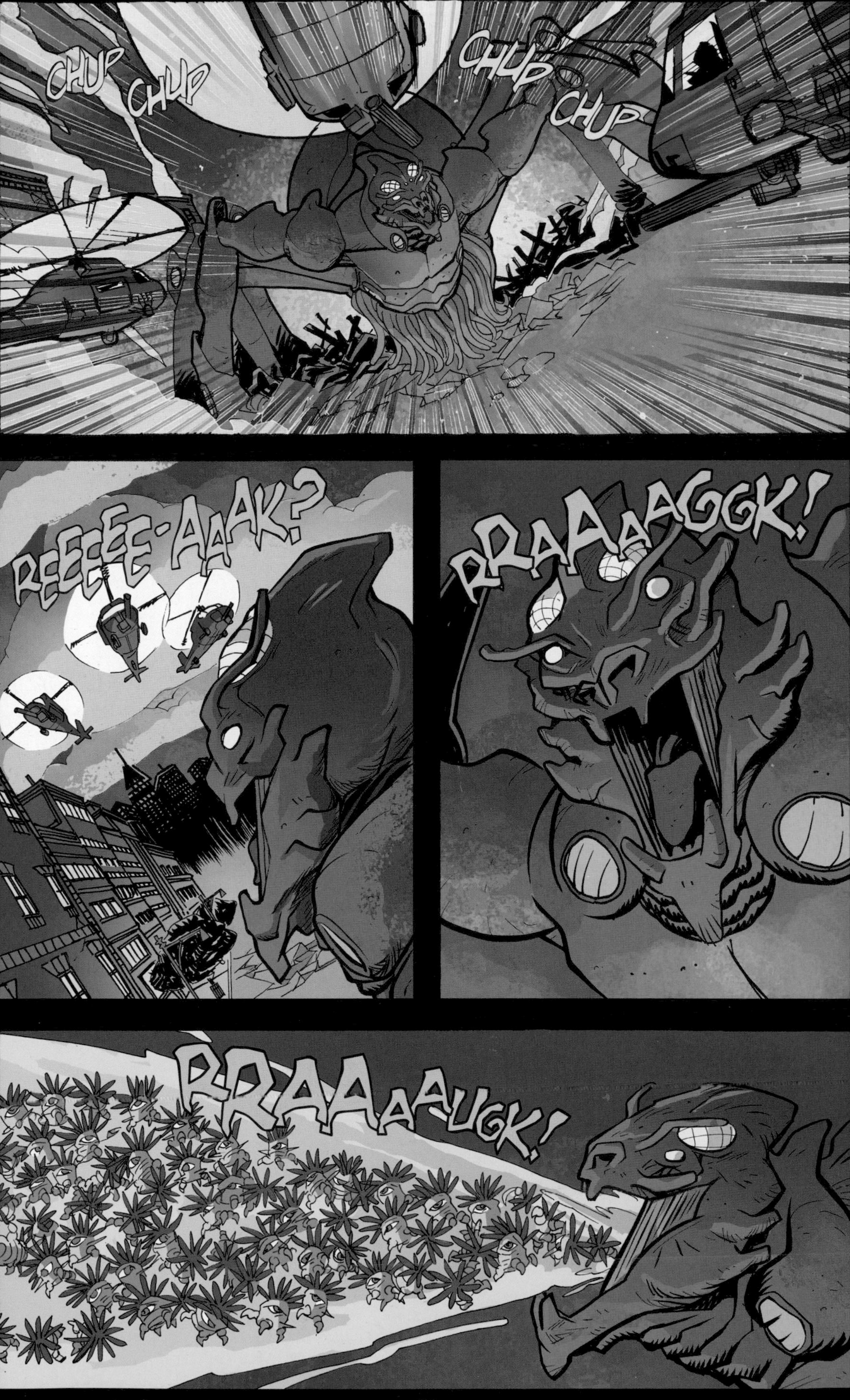
CHUP CHUP
CHUP CHUP
REEEEEE-AAAK?
RRAAAAGGK!
RRAAAAAUGK!

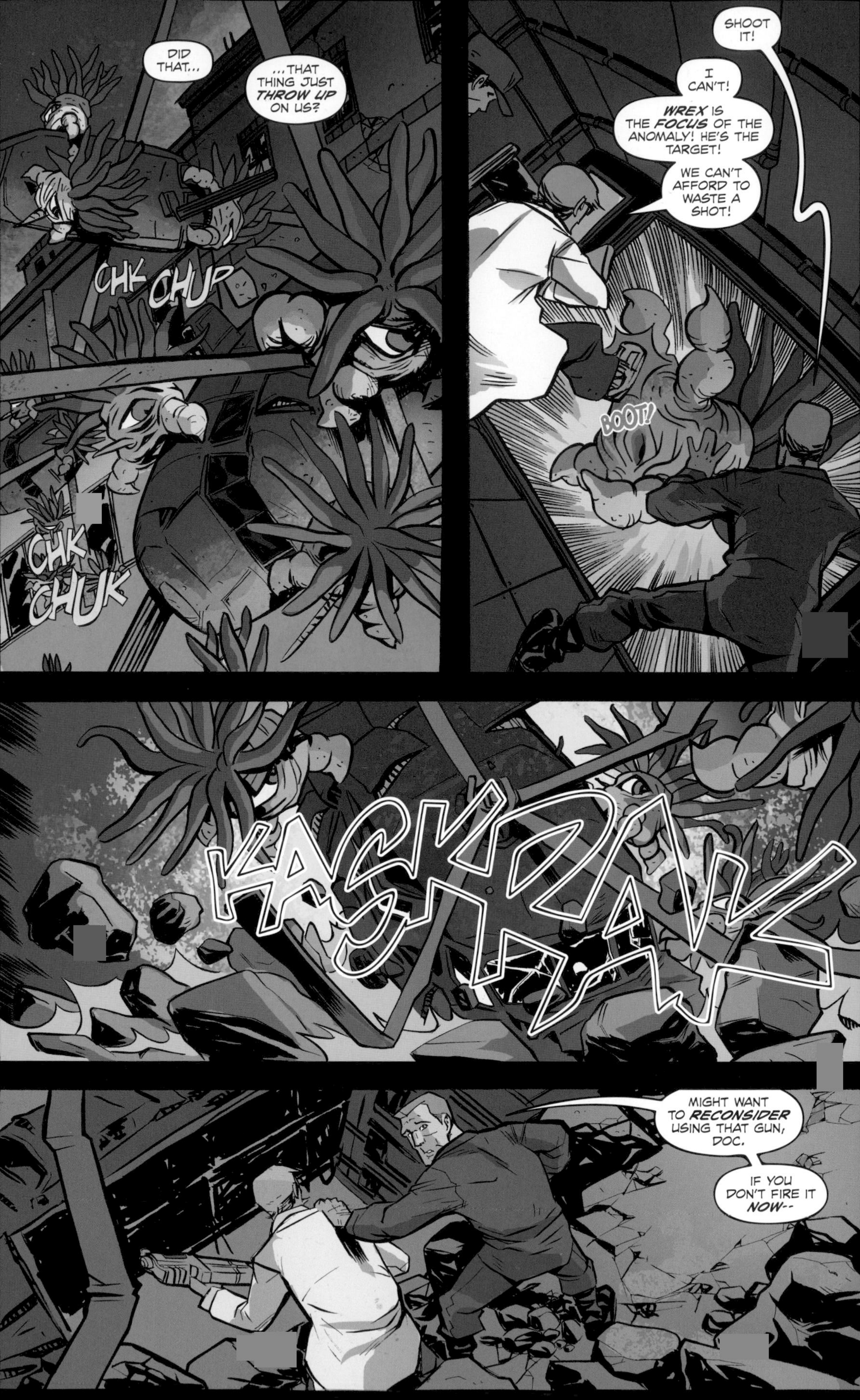
DID THAT...
...THAT THING JUST *THROW UP* ON US?
CHK CHUP
CHK CHUK
SHOOT IT!
I CAN'T!
WREX IS THE *FOCUS* OF THE ANOMALY! HE'S THE TARGET!
WE CAN'T AFFORD TO WASTE A SHOT!
BOOT!
KASKRAK
MIGHT WANT TO *RECONSIDER* USING THAT GUN, DOC.
IF YOU DON'T FIRE IT *NOW*--

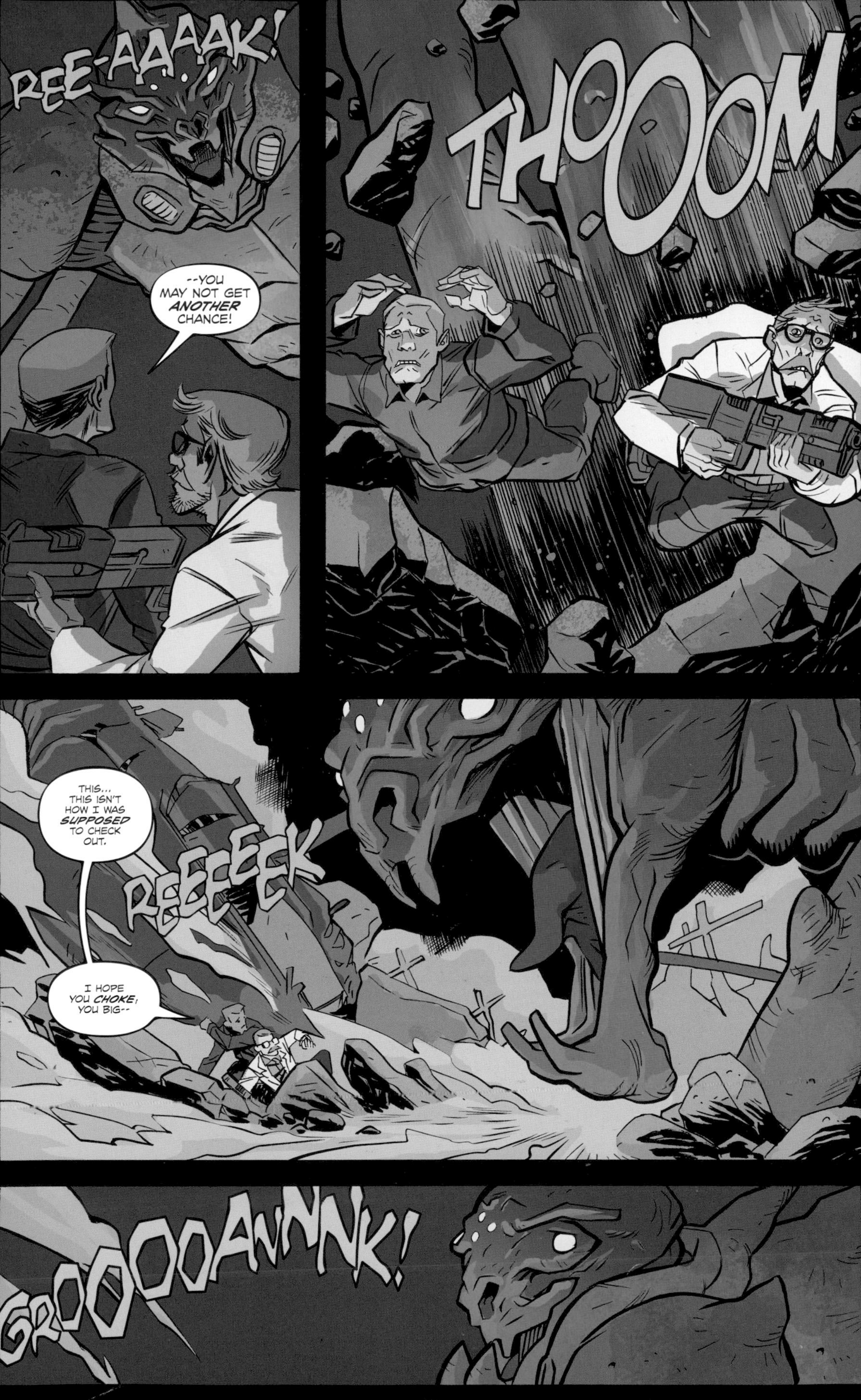
REE-AAAAK!
--YOU MAY NOT GET ANOTHER CHANCE!
THOOOOM
THIS... THIS ISN'T HOW I WAS SUPPOSED TO CHECK OUT.
REEEEEK
I HOPE YOU CHOKE, YOU BIG--
GROOOOANNNK!

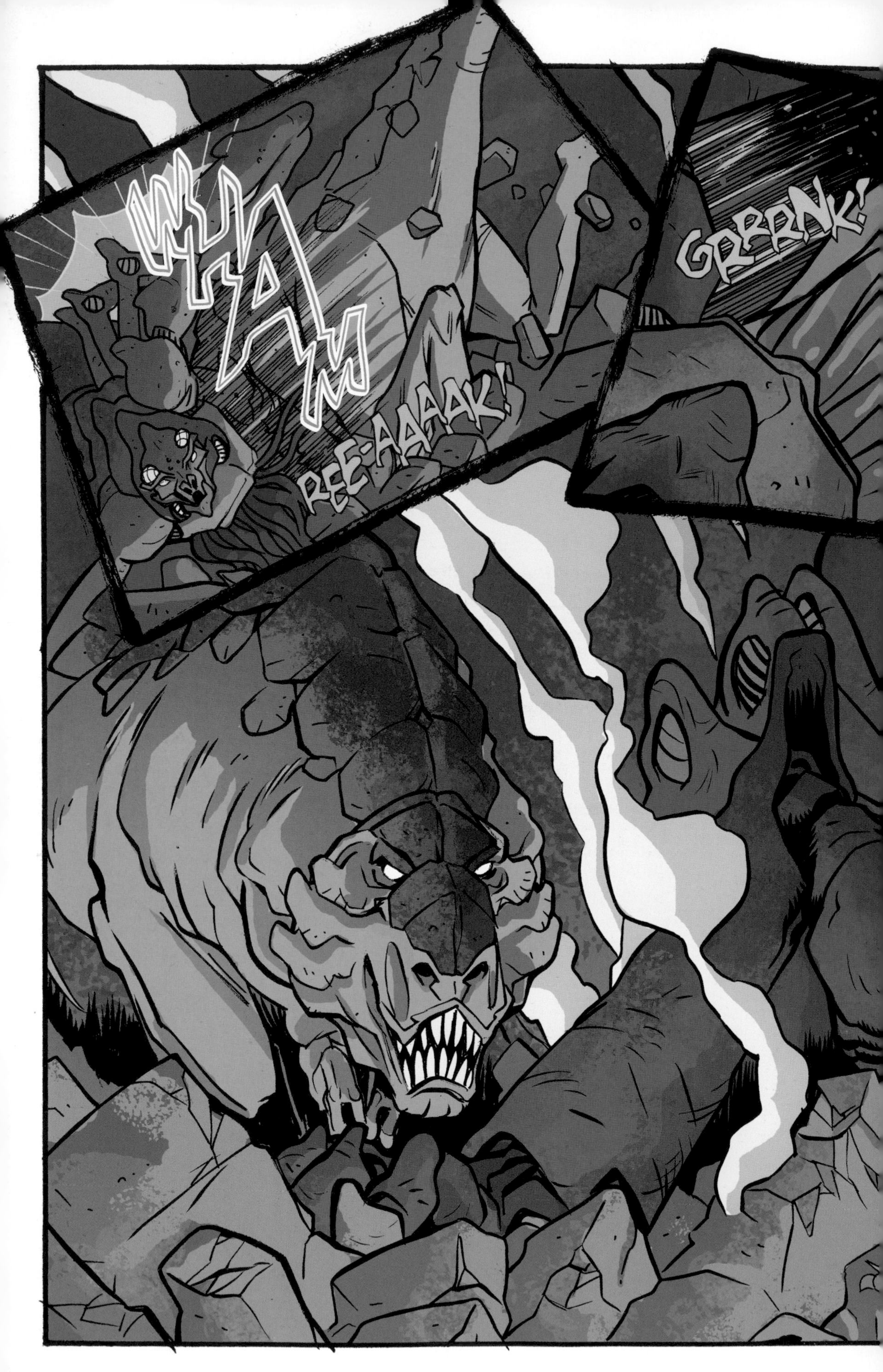
WHAM
REE-AAAAK!
GRRRNK!

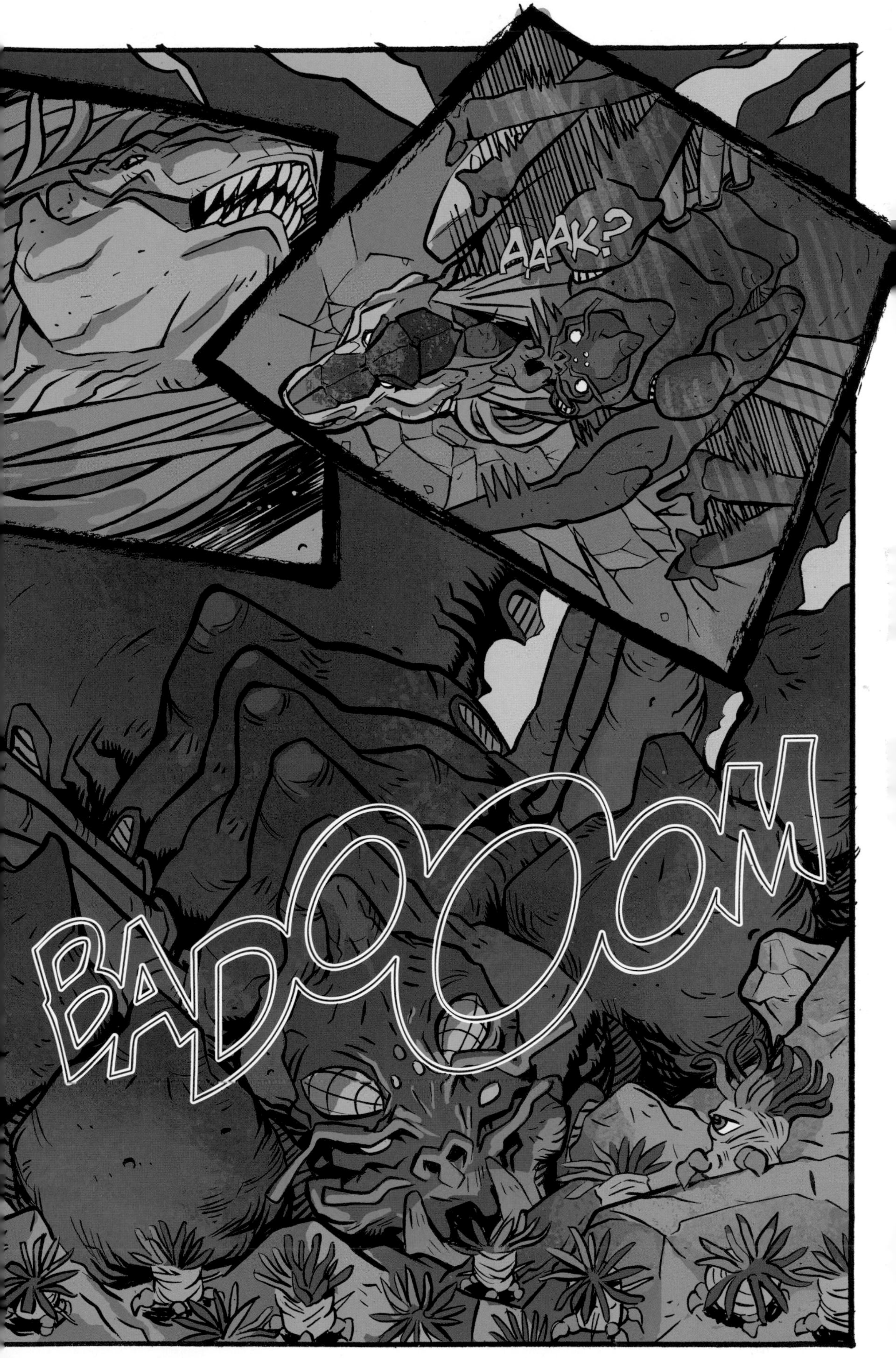
AAAK?
BADOOOOM

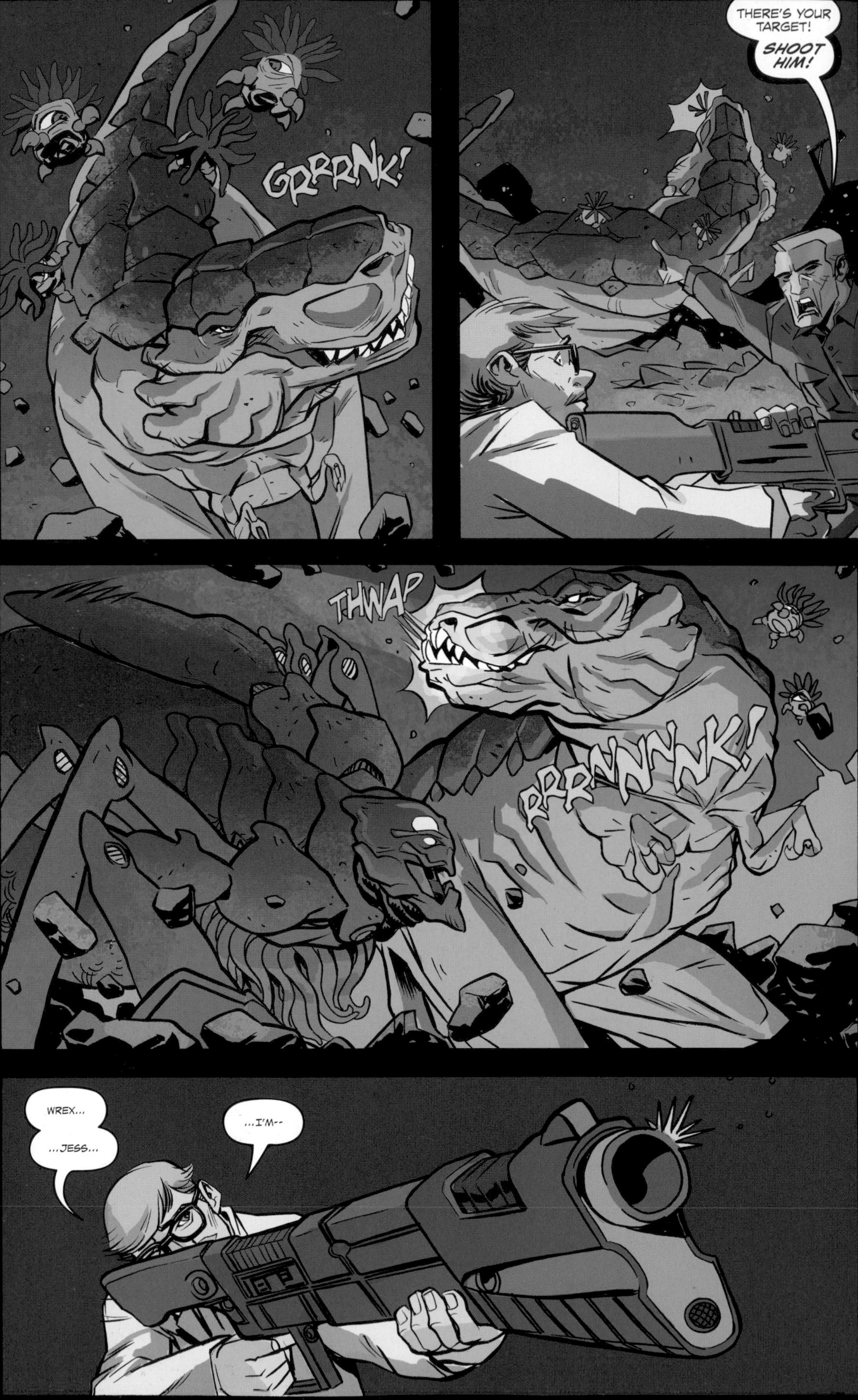
GRRRNK!
THERE'S YOUR TARGET! SHOOT HIM!
THWAP
RRRNNNNK!
WREX...
...JESS...
...I'M--

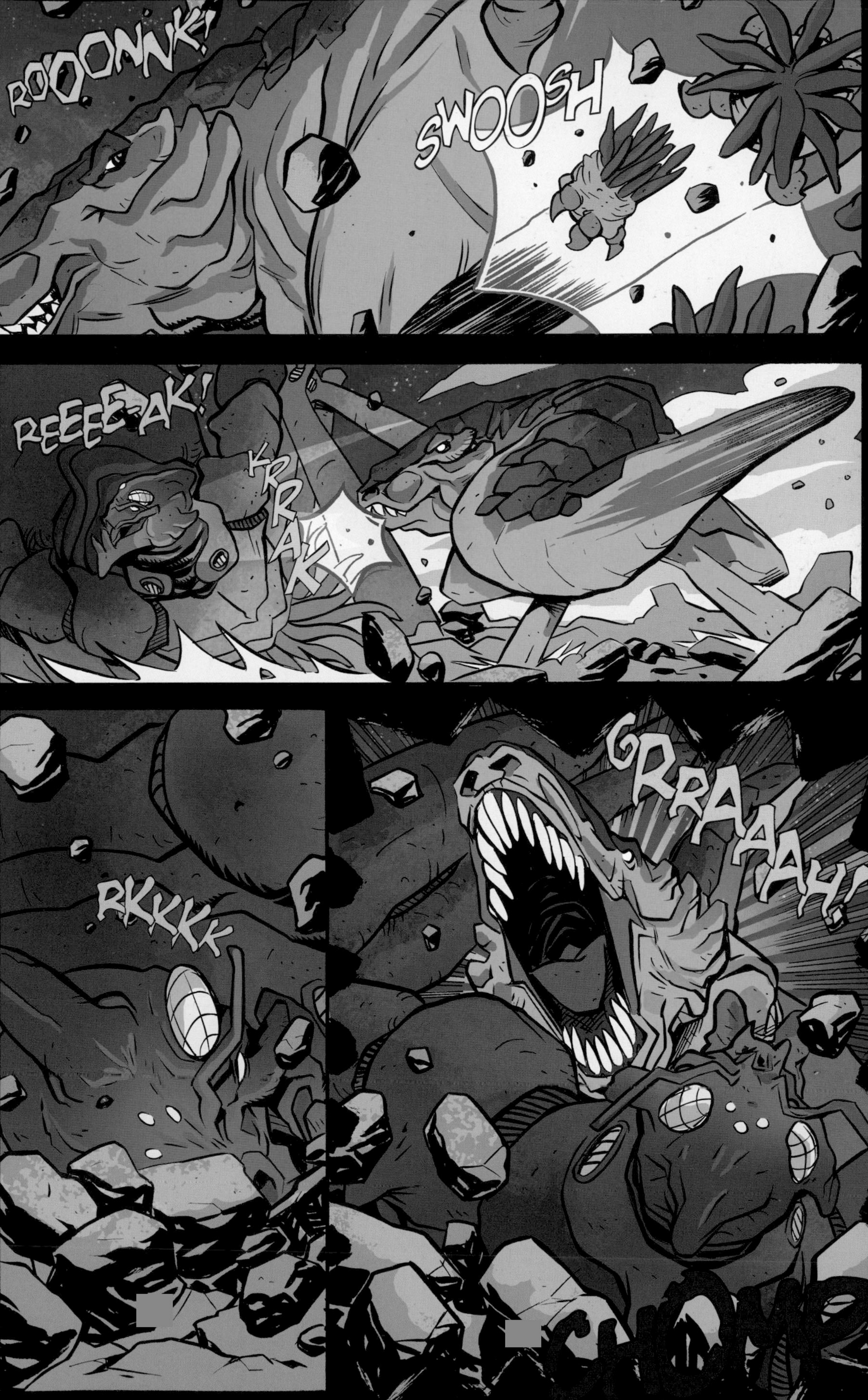
ROOONNK!
SWOOSH
REEEEEAK!
KRRAK!
RKKKK
GRRAAAAH!
CHOMP

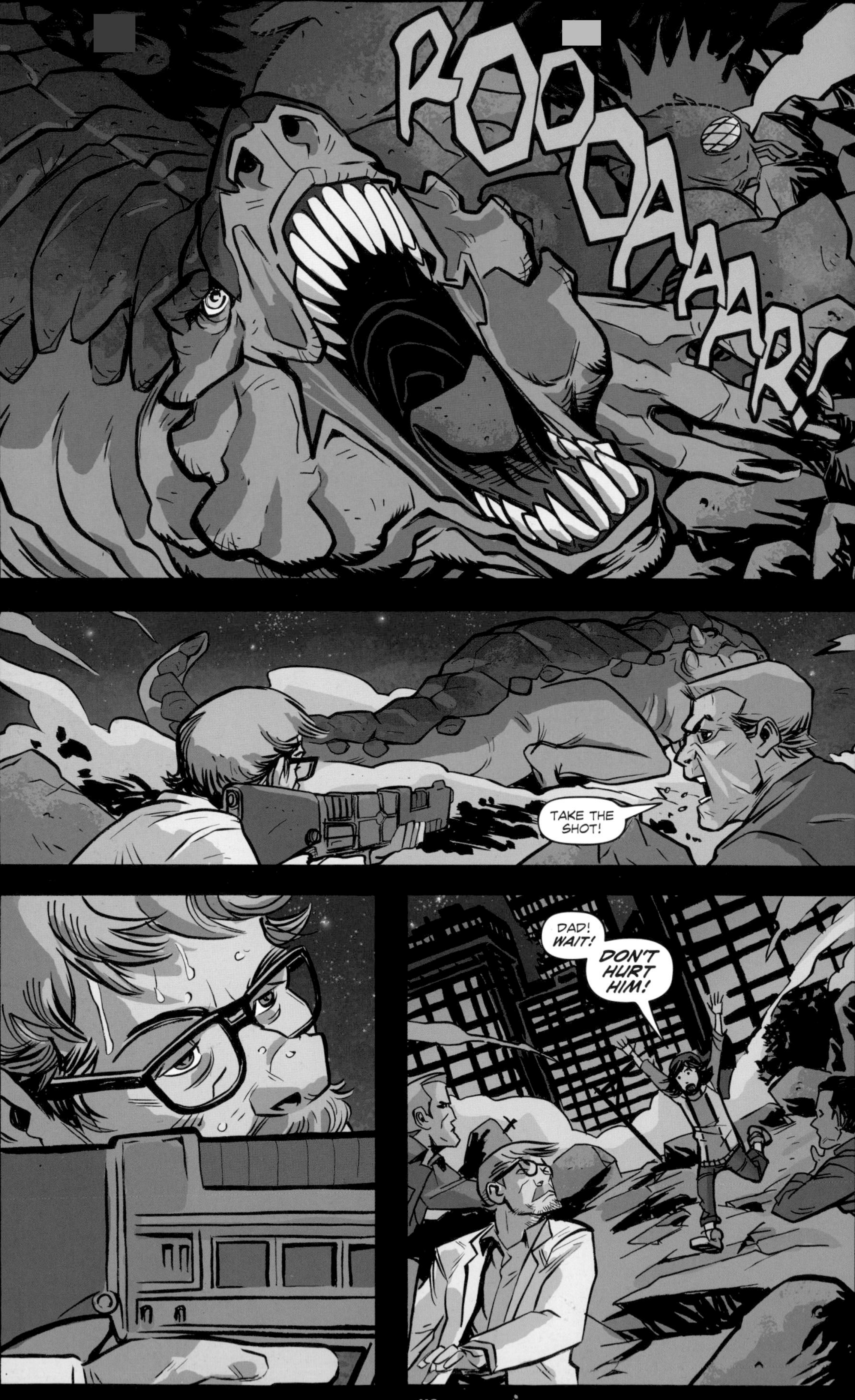
ROOOAAAR!
TAKE THE SHOT!
DAD! WAIT!
DON'T HURT HIM!

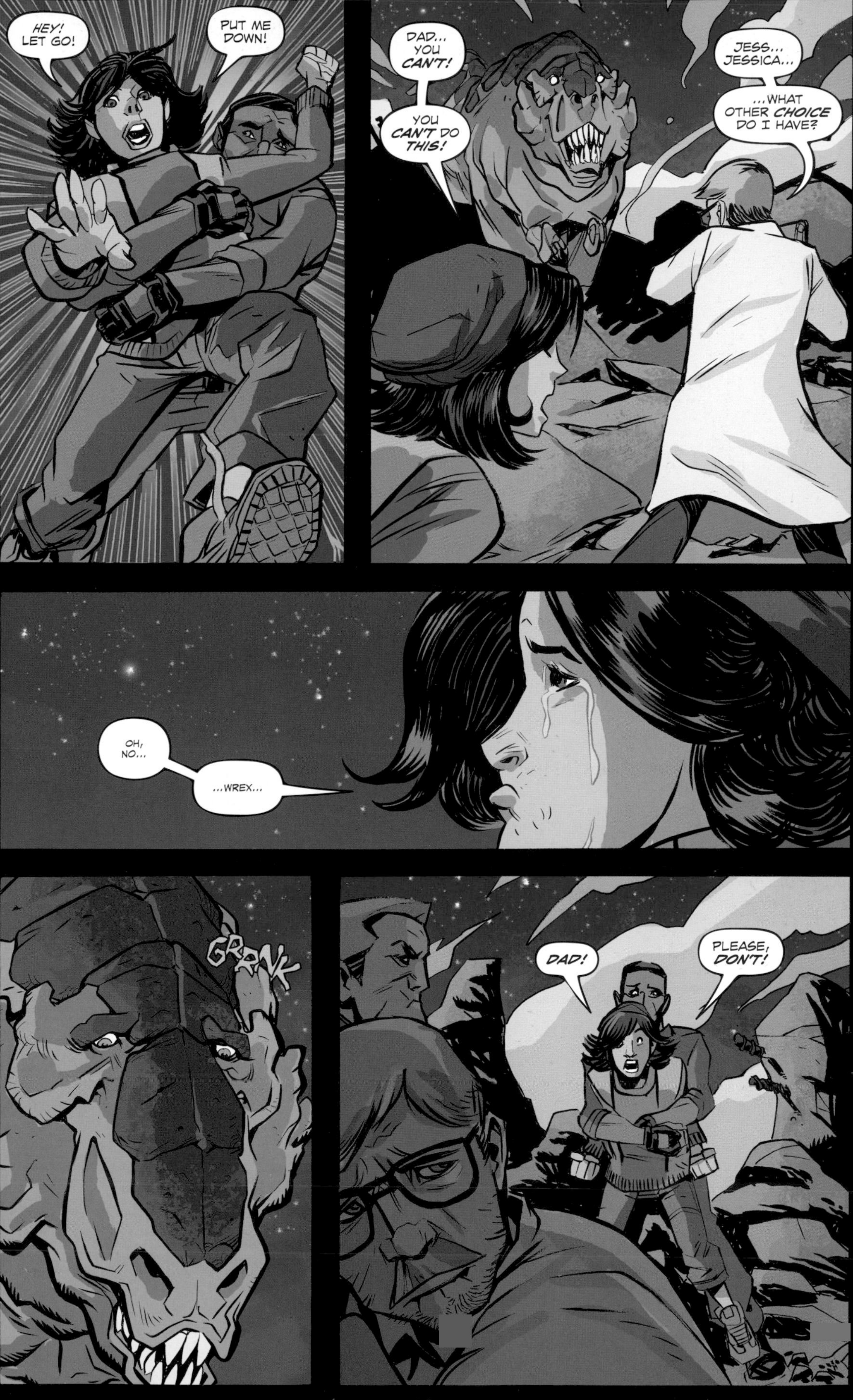
HEY! LET GO!
PUT ME DOWN!
DAD... YOU CAN'T!
YOU CAN'T DO THIS!
JESS... JESSICA...
...WHAT OTHER CHOICE DO I HAVE?
OH, NO...
...WREX...
GRRNK
DAD!
PLEASE, DON'T!

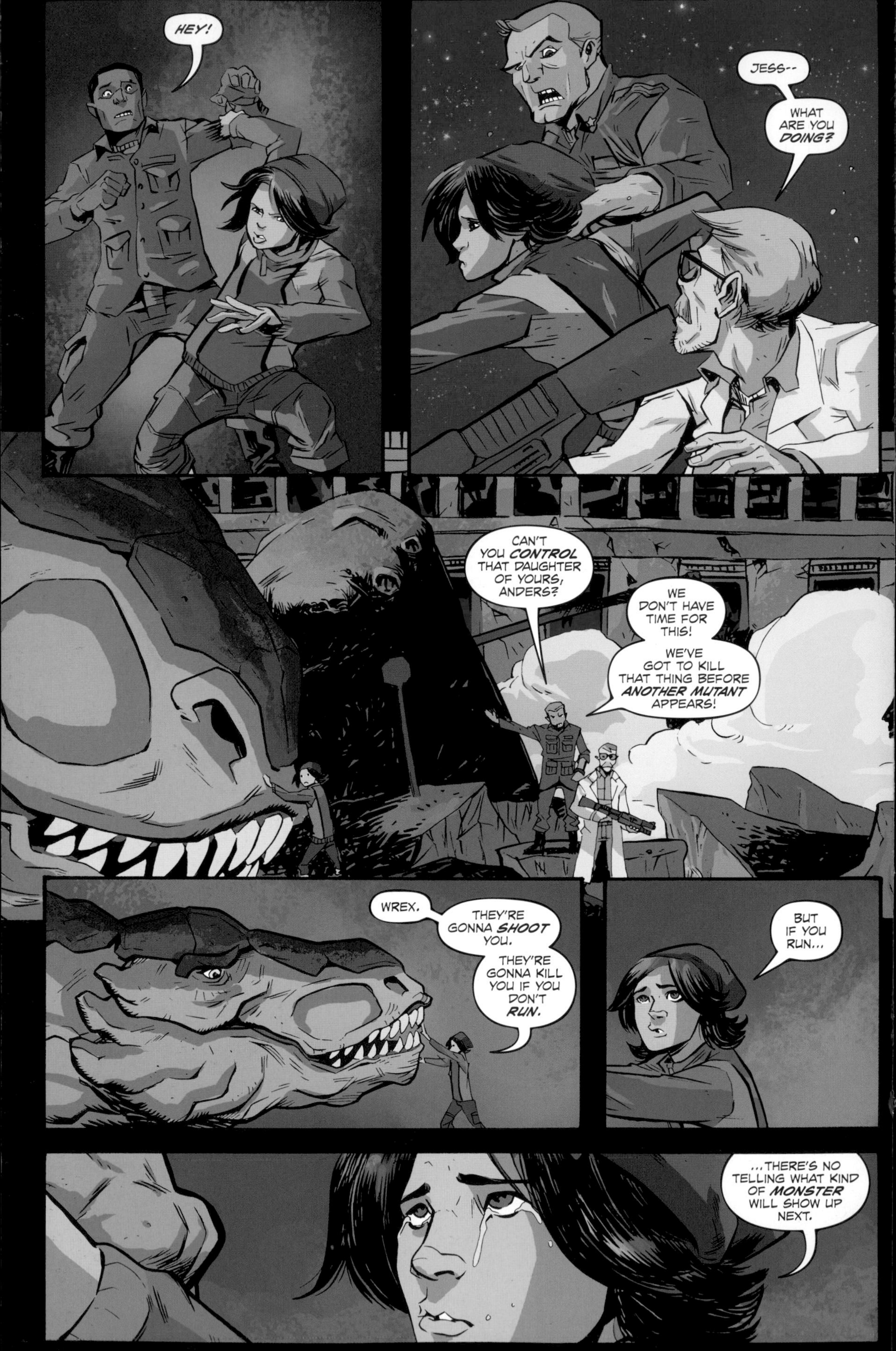
HEY!
JESS--
WHAT ARE YOU *DOING?*
CAN'T YOU **CONTROL** THAT DAUGHTER OF YOURS, ANDERS?
WE DON'T HAVE TIME FOR THIS!
WE'VE GOT TO KILL THAT THING BEFORE ***ANOTHER MUTANT*** APPEARS!
WREX.
THEY'RE GONNA ***SHOOT*** YOU.
THEY'RE GONNA KILL YOU IF YOU DON'T ***RUN.***
BUT IF YOU RUN...
...THERE'S NO TELLING WHAT KIND OF ***MONSTER*** WILL SHOW UP NEXT.

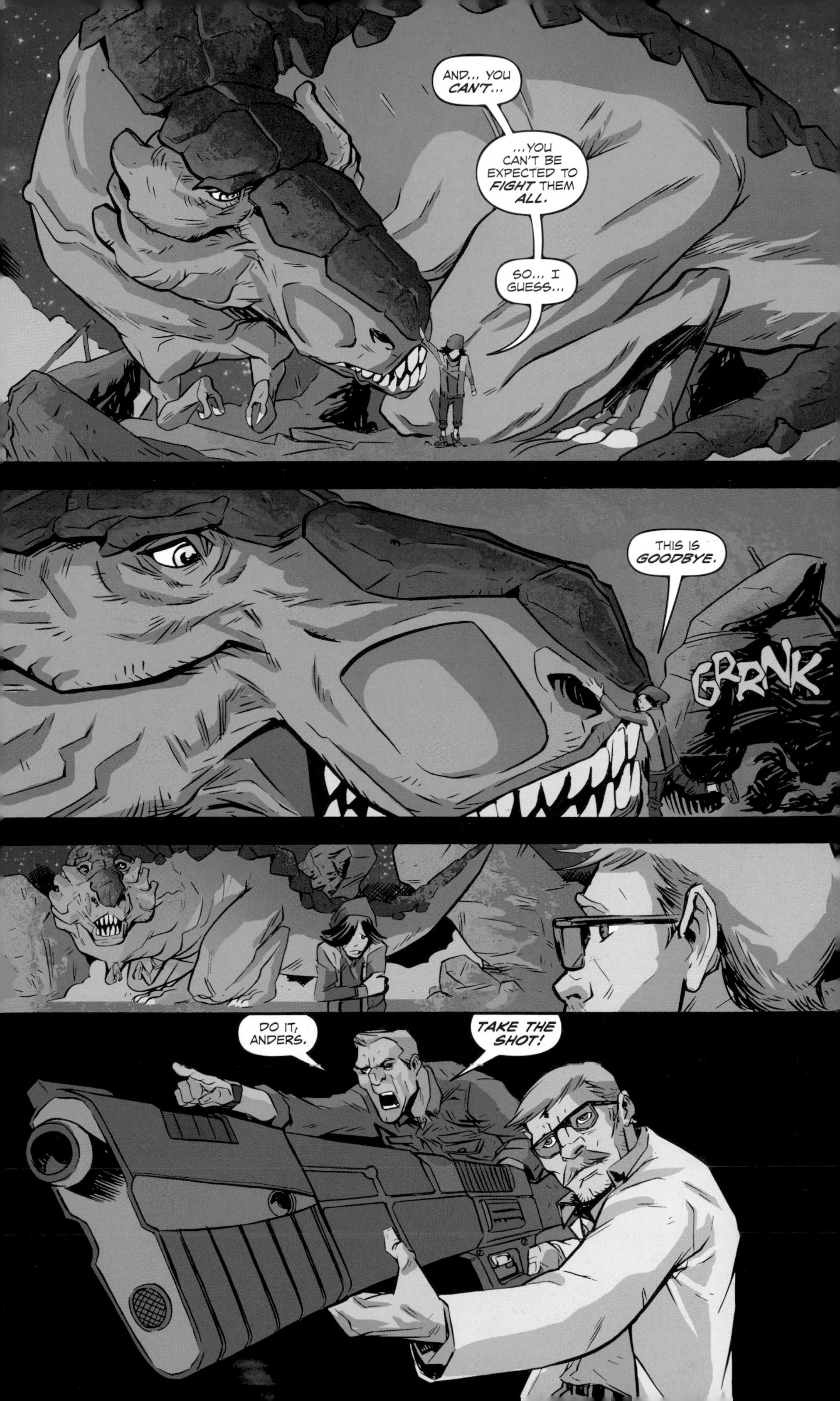
AND... YOU CAN'T...
...YOU CAN'T BE EXPECTED TO FIGHT THEM ALL.
SO... I GUESS...
THIS IS GOODBYE.
GRRNK
DO IT, ANDERS.
TAKE THE SHOT!

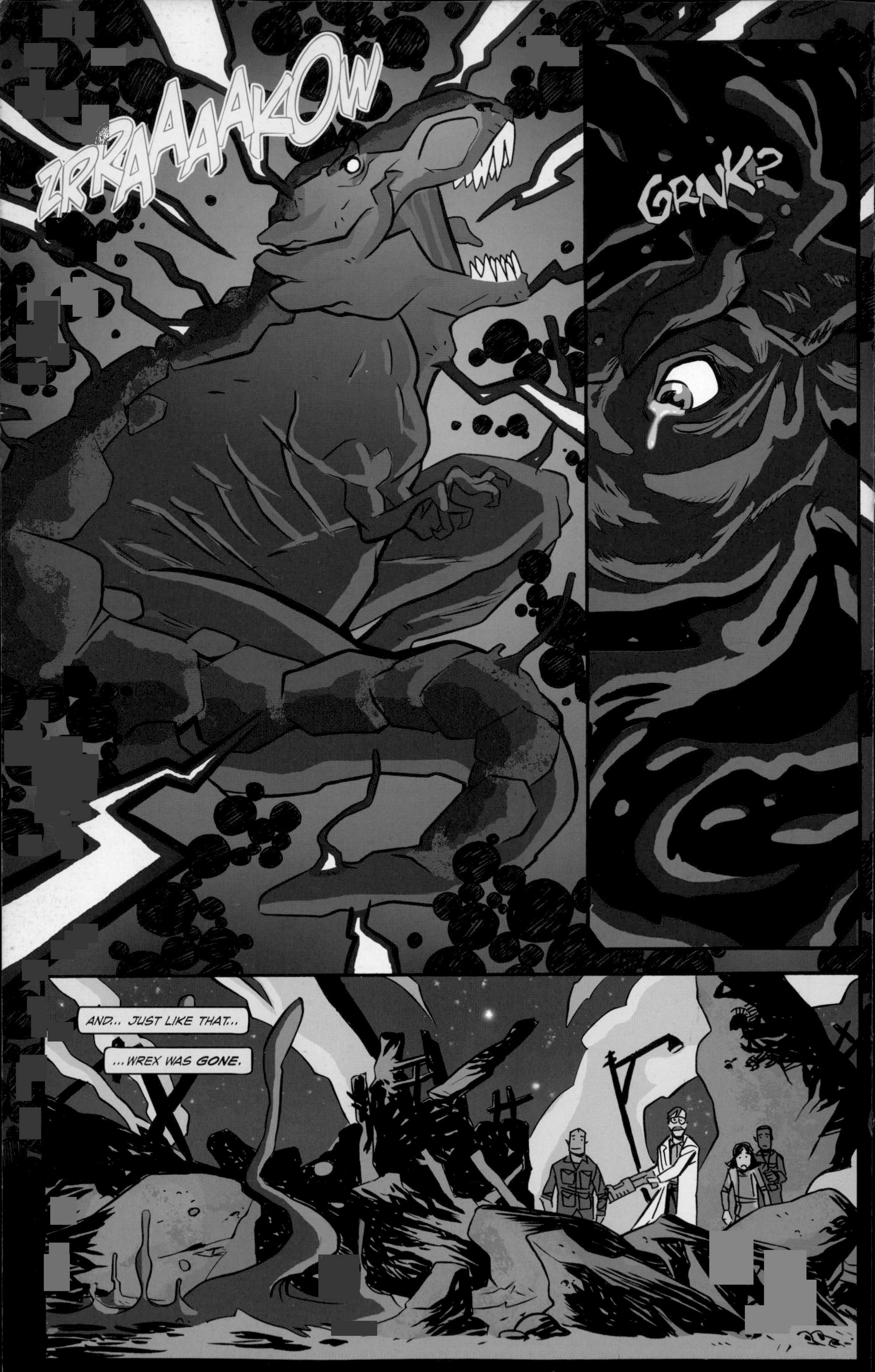
ZRRAAAAKOW
GRNK?
AND... JUST LIKE THAT...
...WREX WAS GONE.

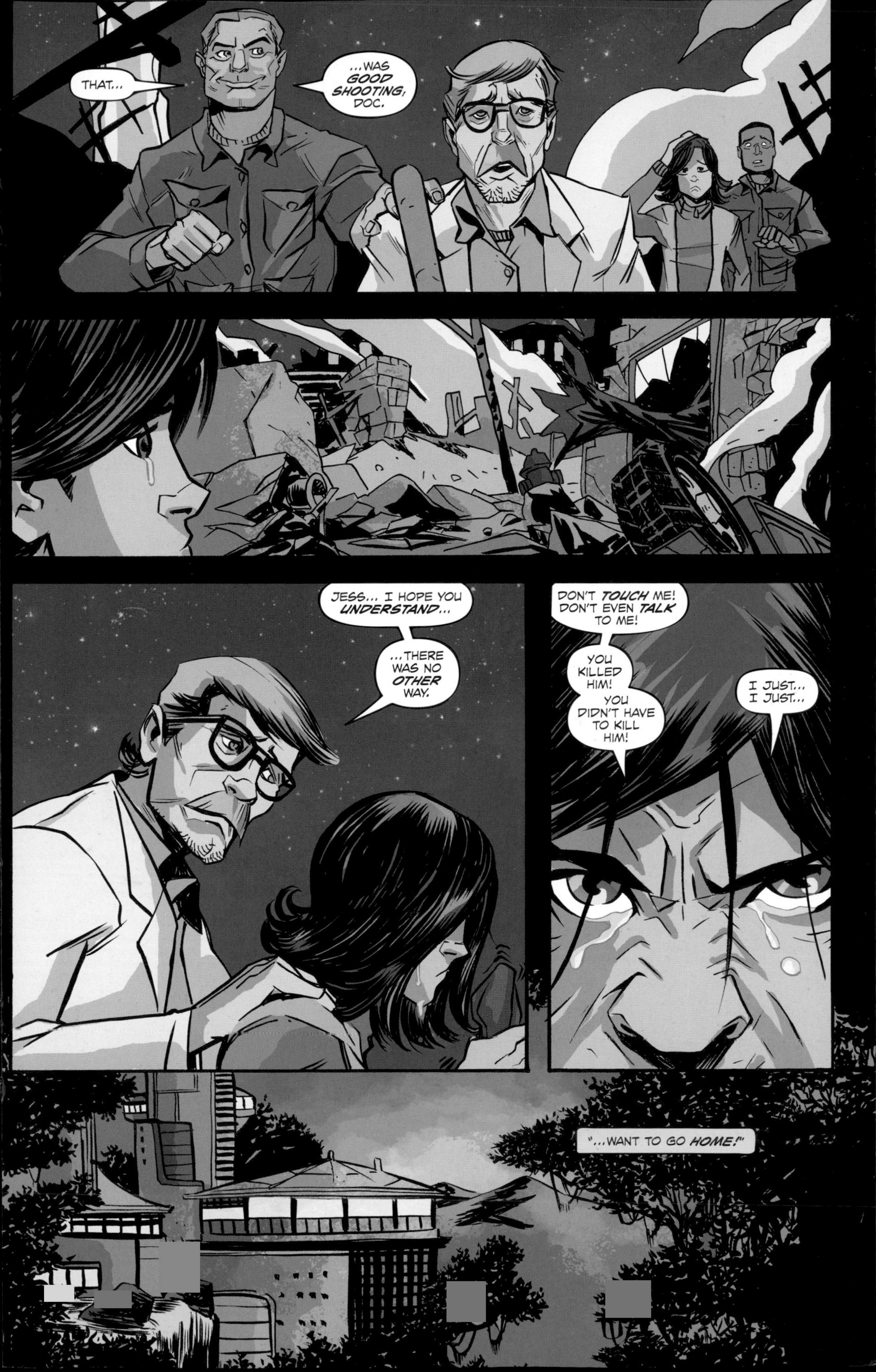
THAT...
...WAS GOOD SHOOTING, DOC.
JESS... I HOPE YOU UNDERSTAND...
...THERE WAS NO OTHER WAY.
DON'T TOUCH ME! DON'T EVEN TALK TO ME!
YOU KILLED HIM!
YOU DIDN'T HAVE TO KILL HIM!
I JUST... I JUST...
"...WANT TO GO HOME!"

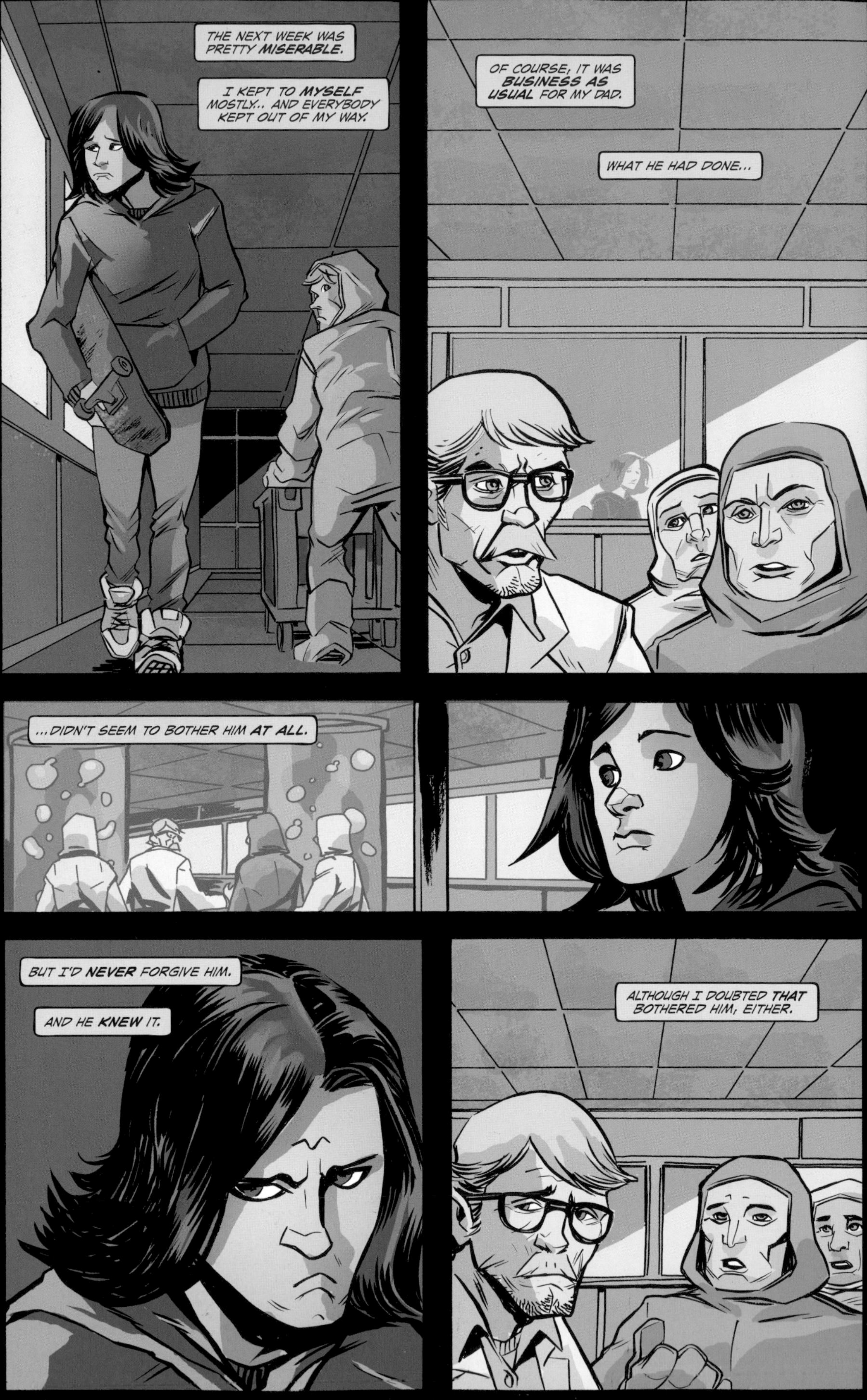
THE NEXT WEEK WAS PRETTY **MISERABLE**.
I KEPT TO **MYSELF** MOSTLY... AND EVERYBODY KEPT OUT OF MY WAY.
OF COURSE, IT WAS **BUSINESS AS USUAL** FOR MY DAD.
WHAT HE HAD DONE...
...DIDN'T SEEM TO BOTHER HIM **AT ALL**.
BUT I'D **NEVER** FORGIVE HIM.
AND HE **KNEW** IT.
ALTHOUGH I DOUBTED **THAT** BOTHERED HIM, EITHER.

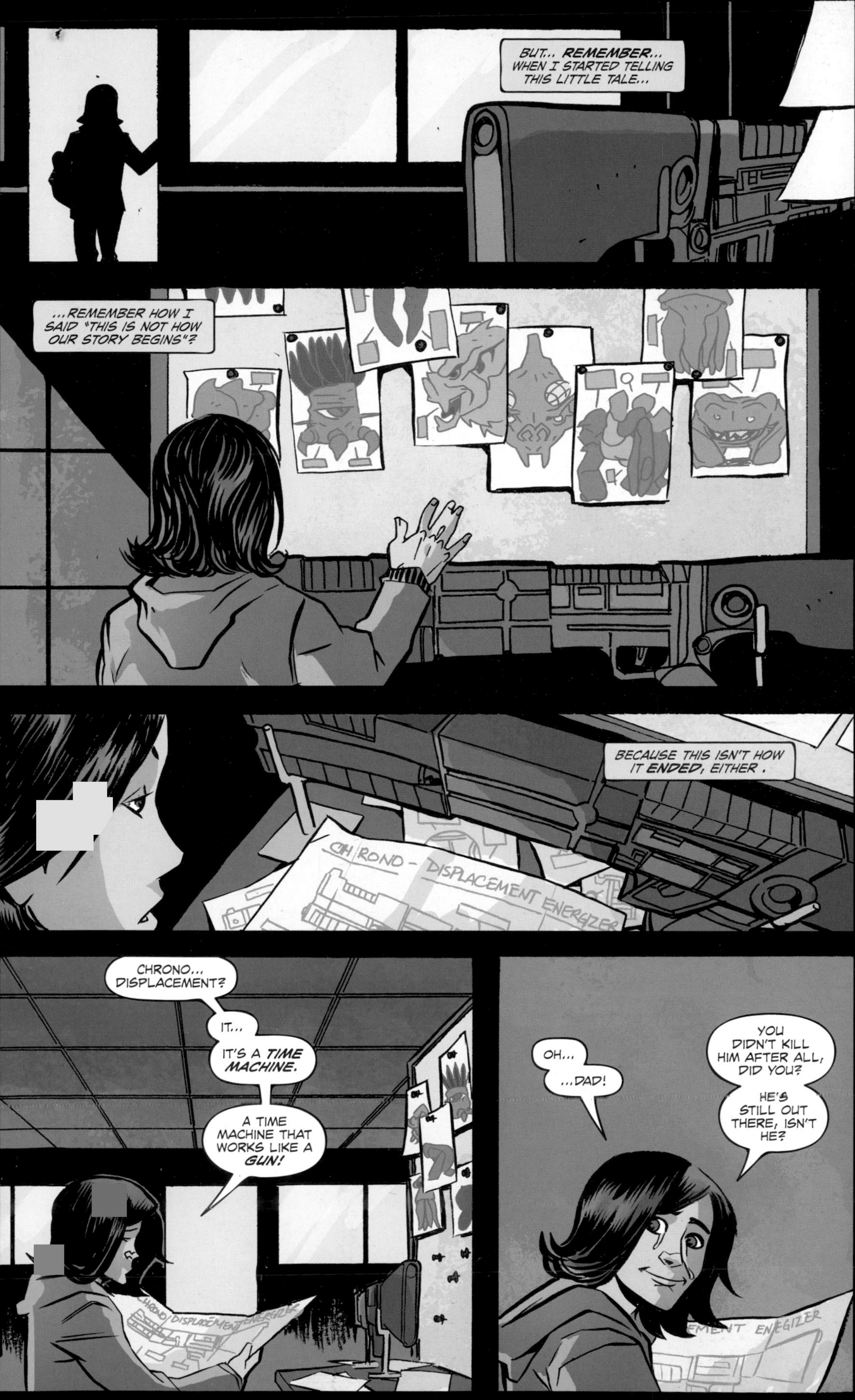
BUT... REMEMBER... WHEN I STARTED TELLING THIS LITTLE TALE...
...REMEMBER HOW I SAID "THIS IS NOT HOW OUR STORY BEGINS"?
BECAUSE THIS ISN'T HOW IT ENDED, EITHER.
CHRONO - DISPLACEMENT ENERGIZER
CHRONO... DISPLACEMENT?
IT...
IT'S A TIME MACHINE.
A TIME MACHINE THAT WORKS LIKE A GUN!
OH...
...DAD!
YOU DIDN'T KILL HIM AFTER ALL, DID YOU?
HE'S STILL OUT THERE, ISN'T HE?

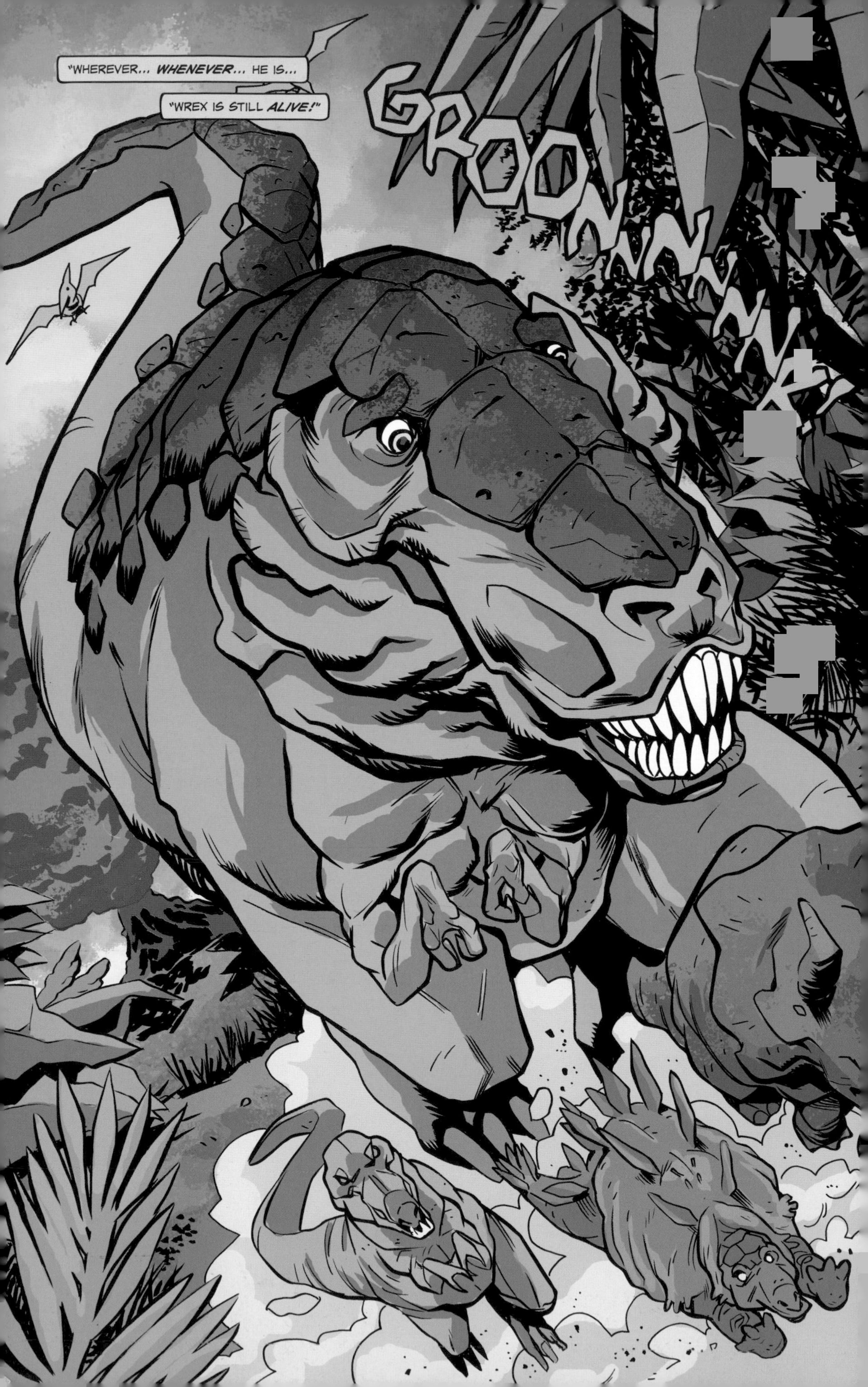
"WHEREVER... *WHENEVER*... HE IS...
"WREX IS STILL *ALIVE!*"

COVER GALLERY

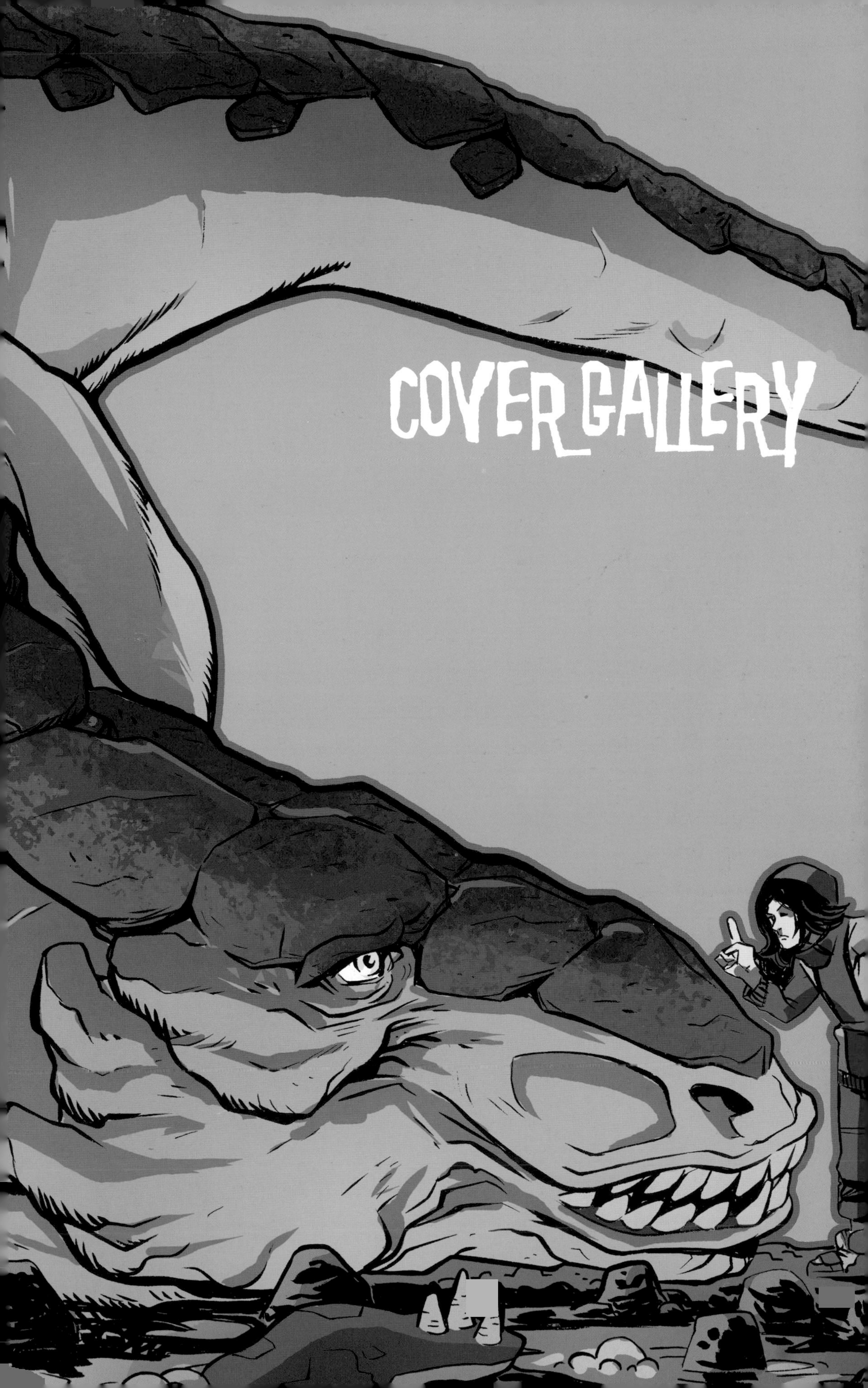

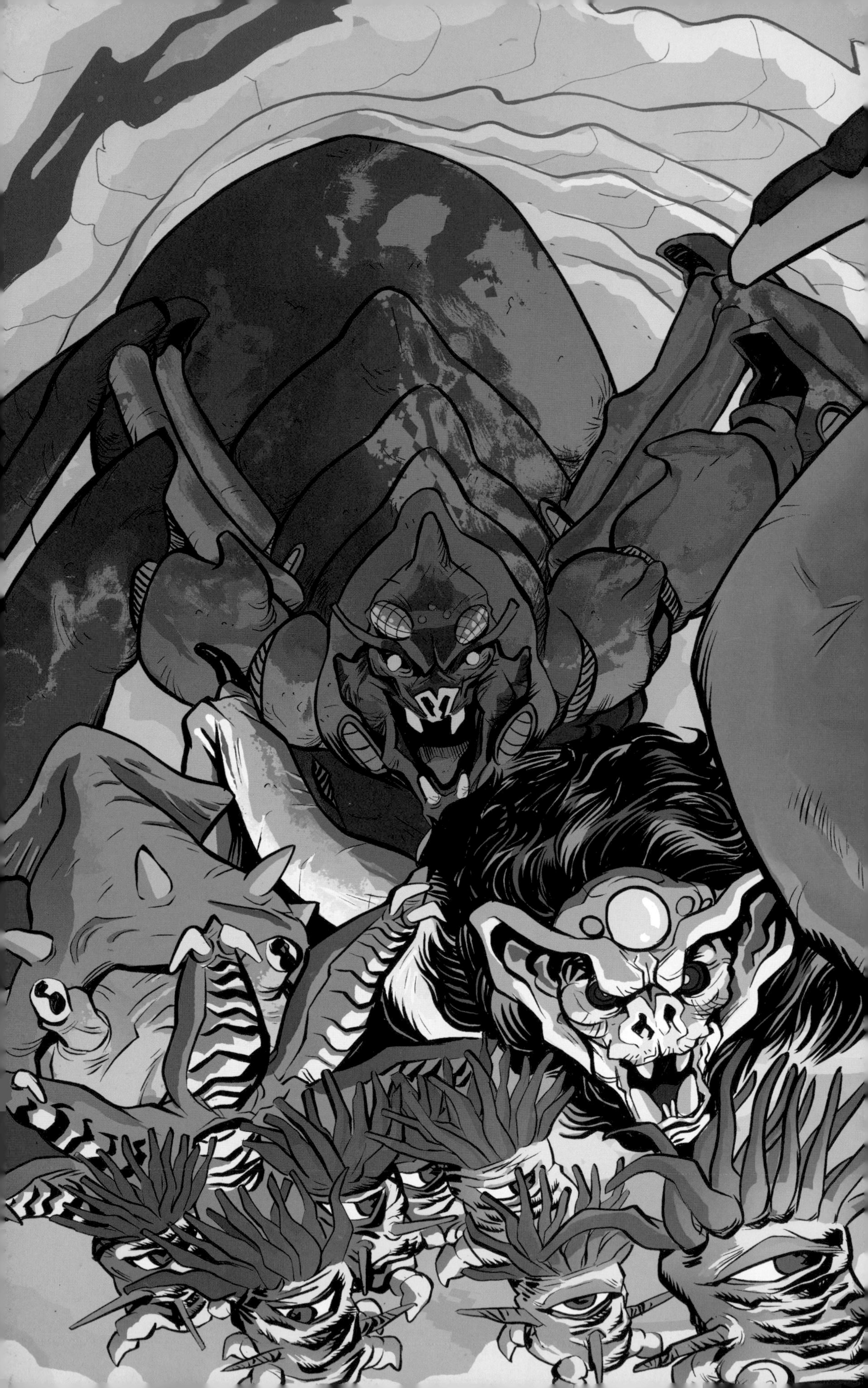

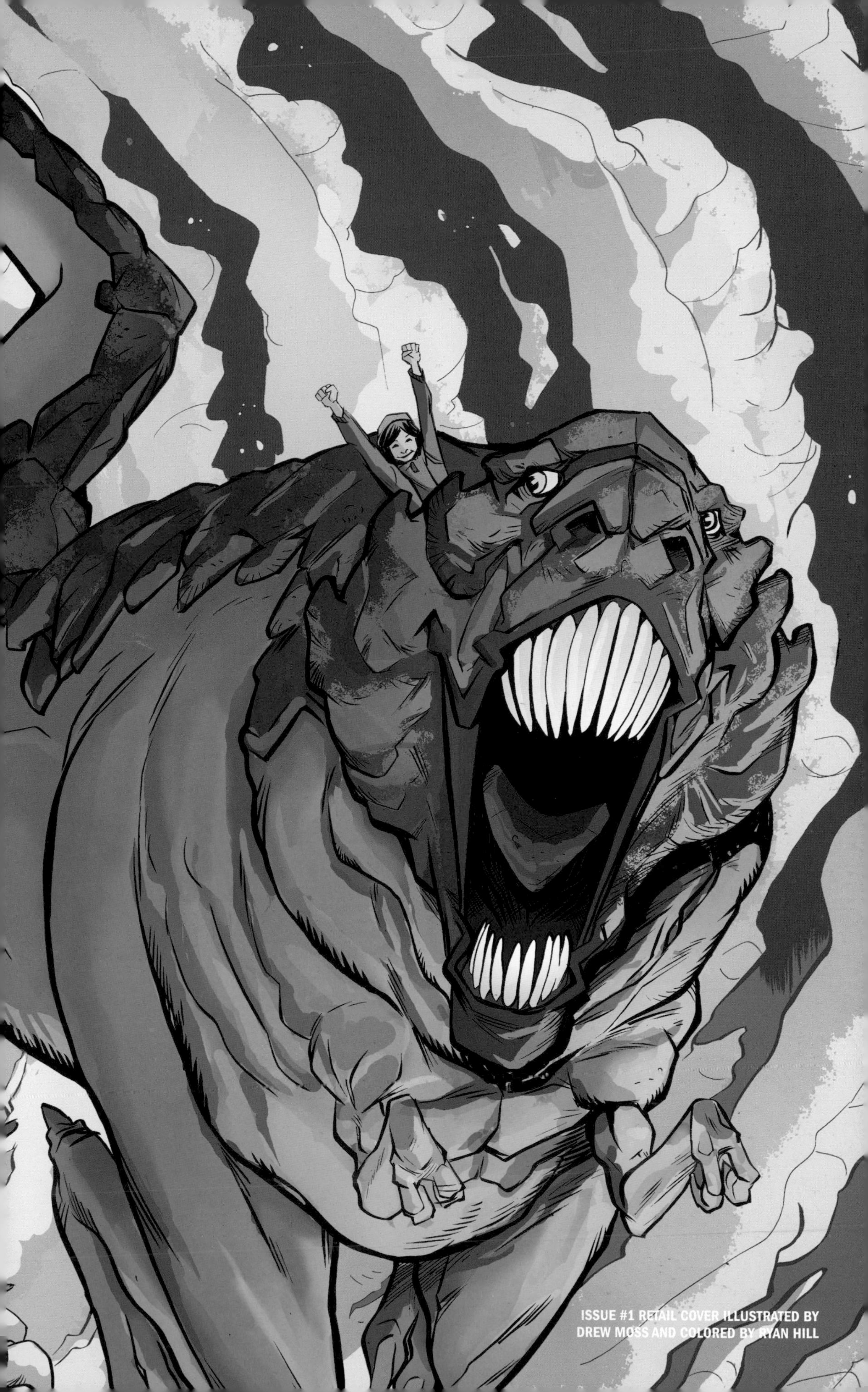

ISSUE #1 RETAIL COVER ILLUSTRATED BY
DREW MOSS AND COLORED BY RYAN HILL

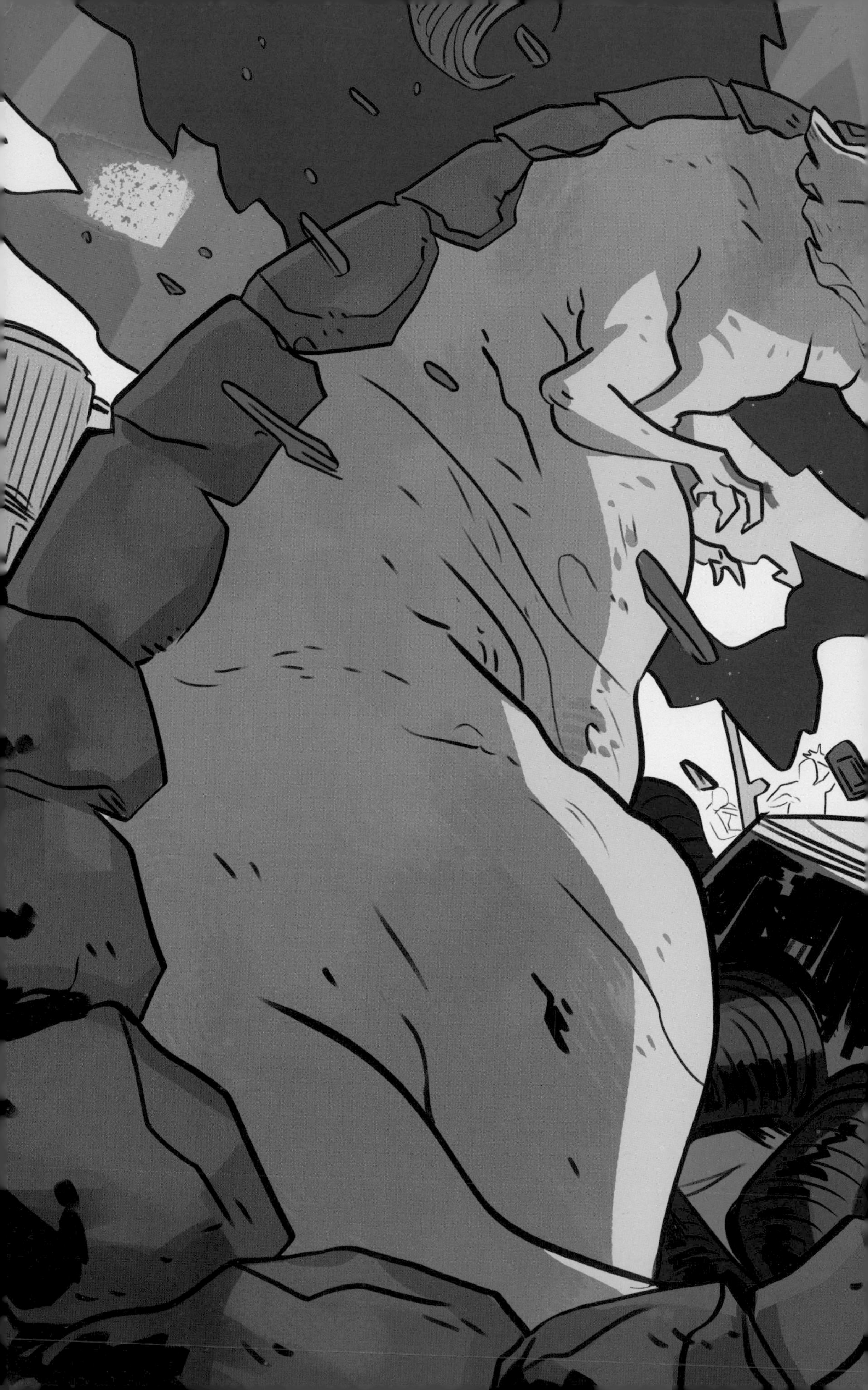

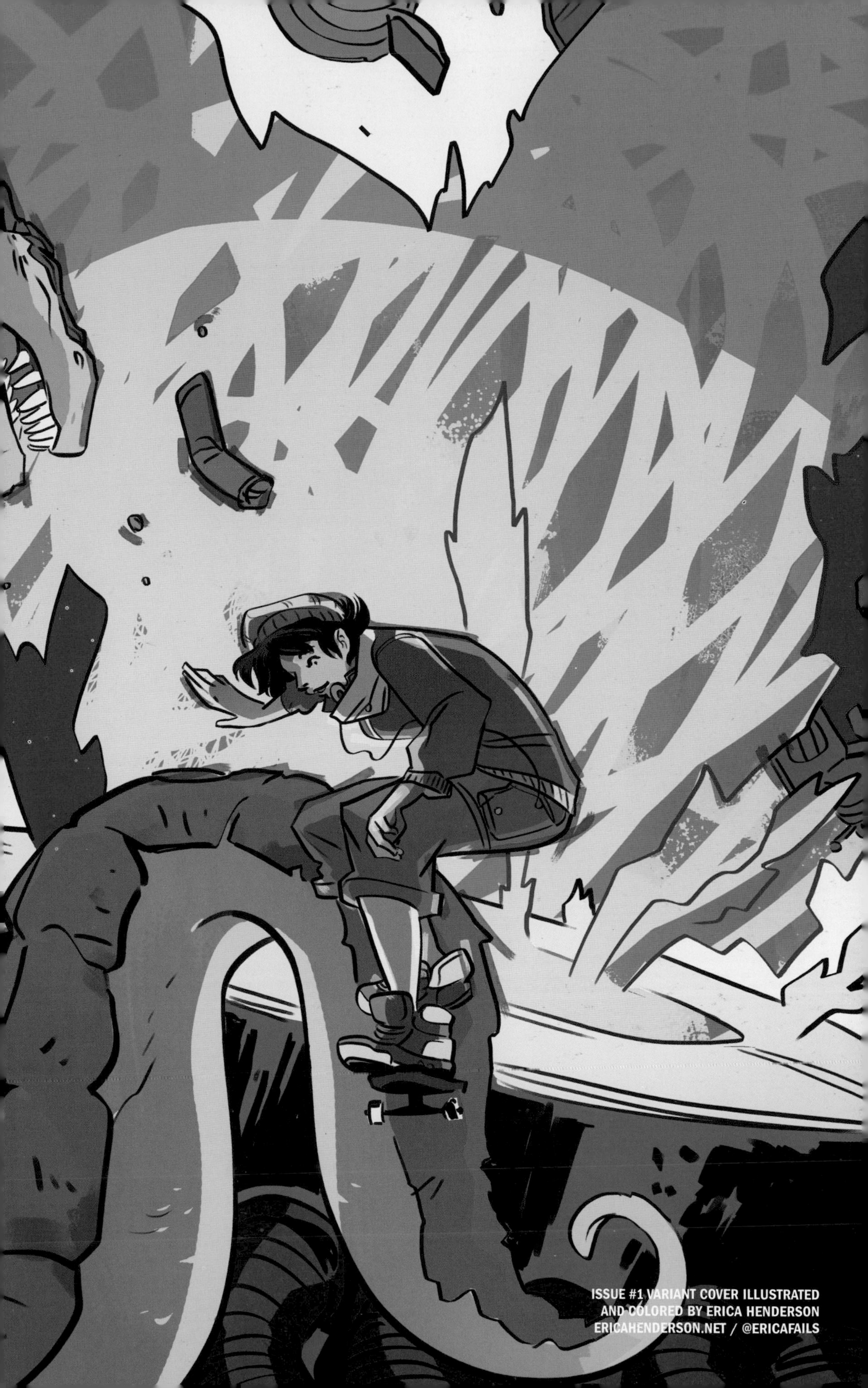

ISSUE #1 VARIANT COVER ILLUSTRATED
AND COLORED BY ERICA HENDERSON
ERICAHENDERSON.NET / @ERICAFAILS

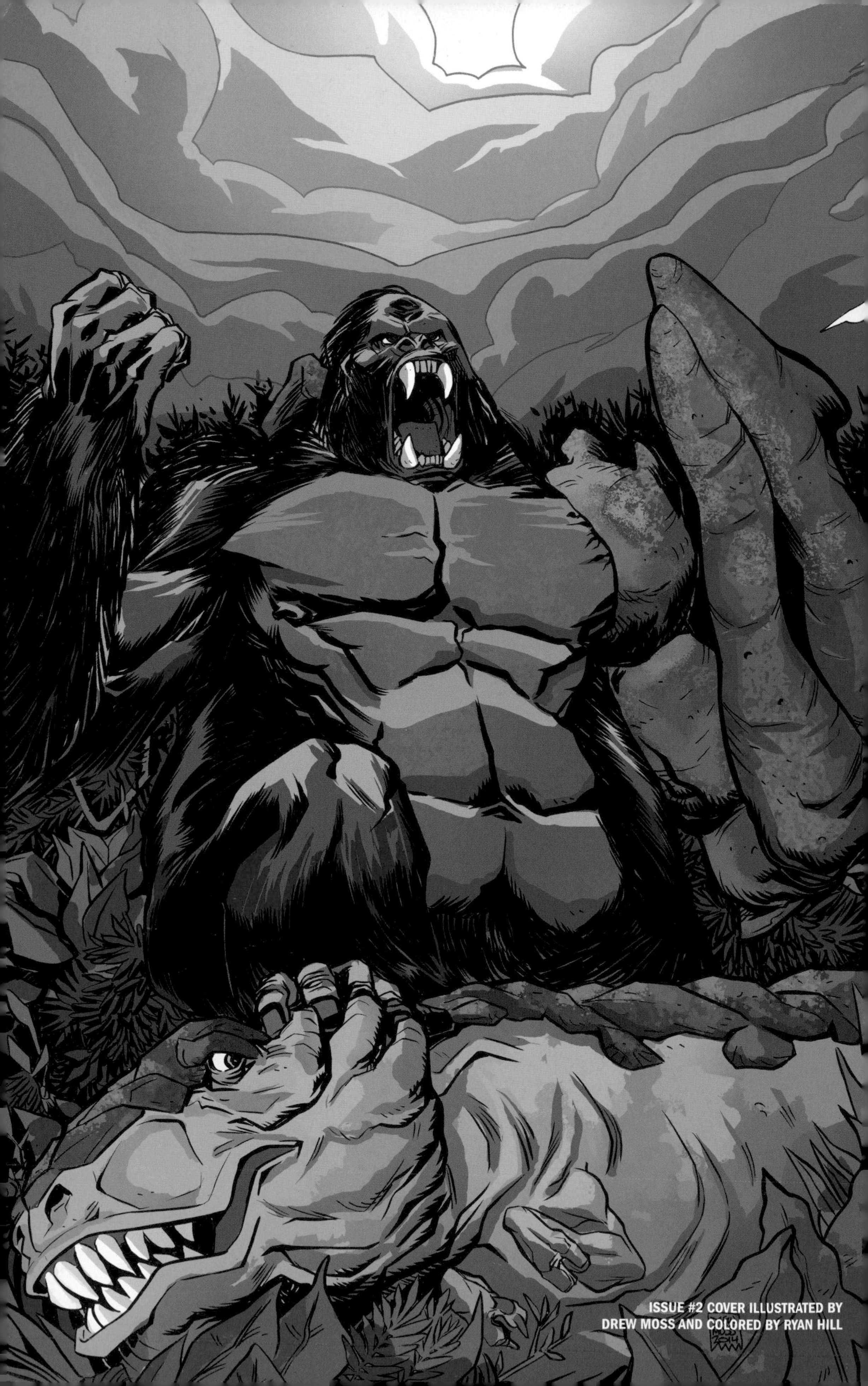

ISSUE #2 COVER ILLUSTRATED BY
DREW MOSS AND COLORED BY RYAN HILL

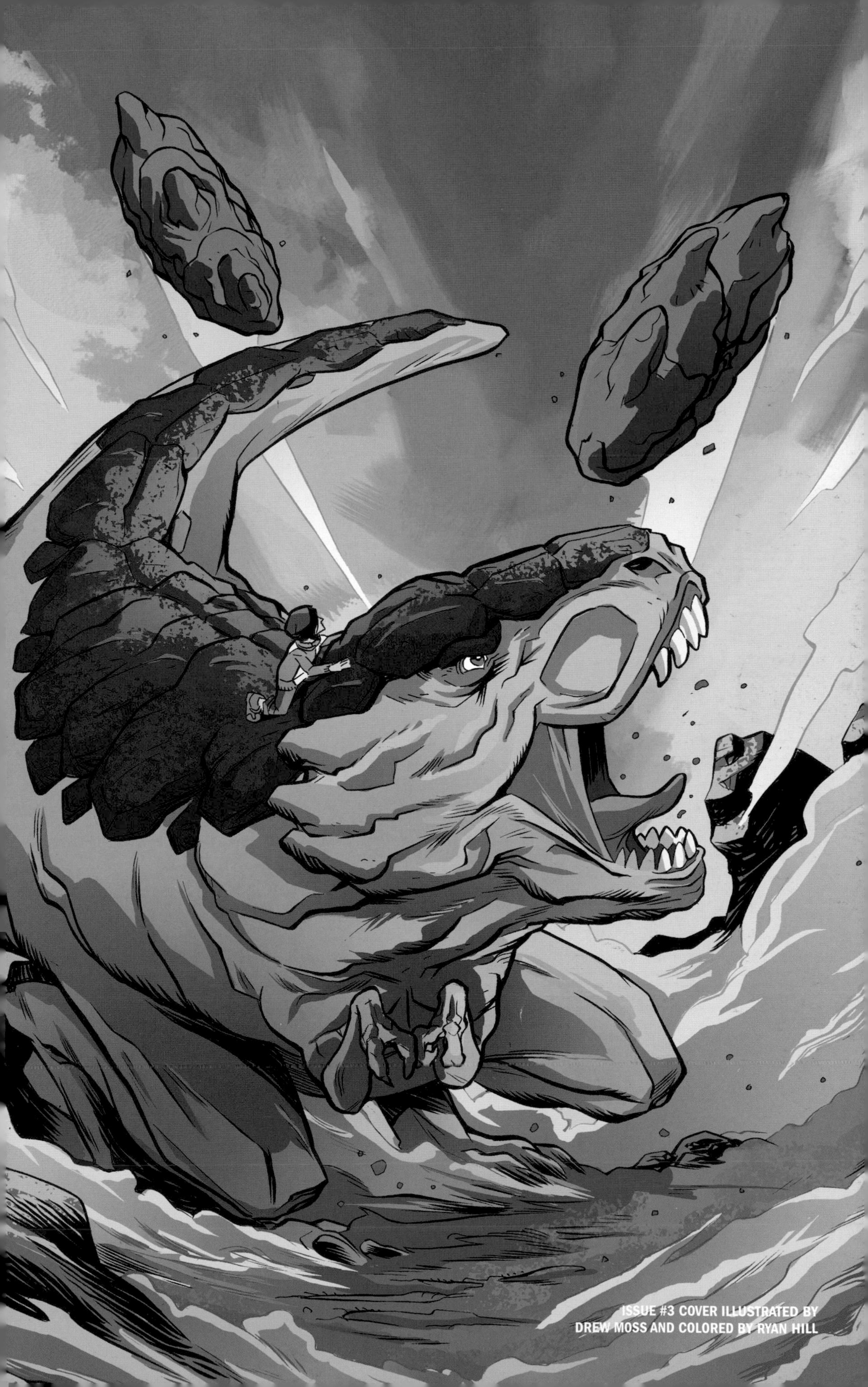

ISSUE #3 COVER ILLUSTRATED BY
DREW MOSS AND COLORED BY RYAN HILL

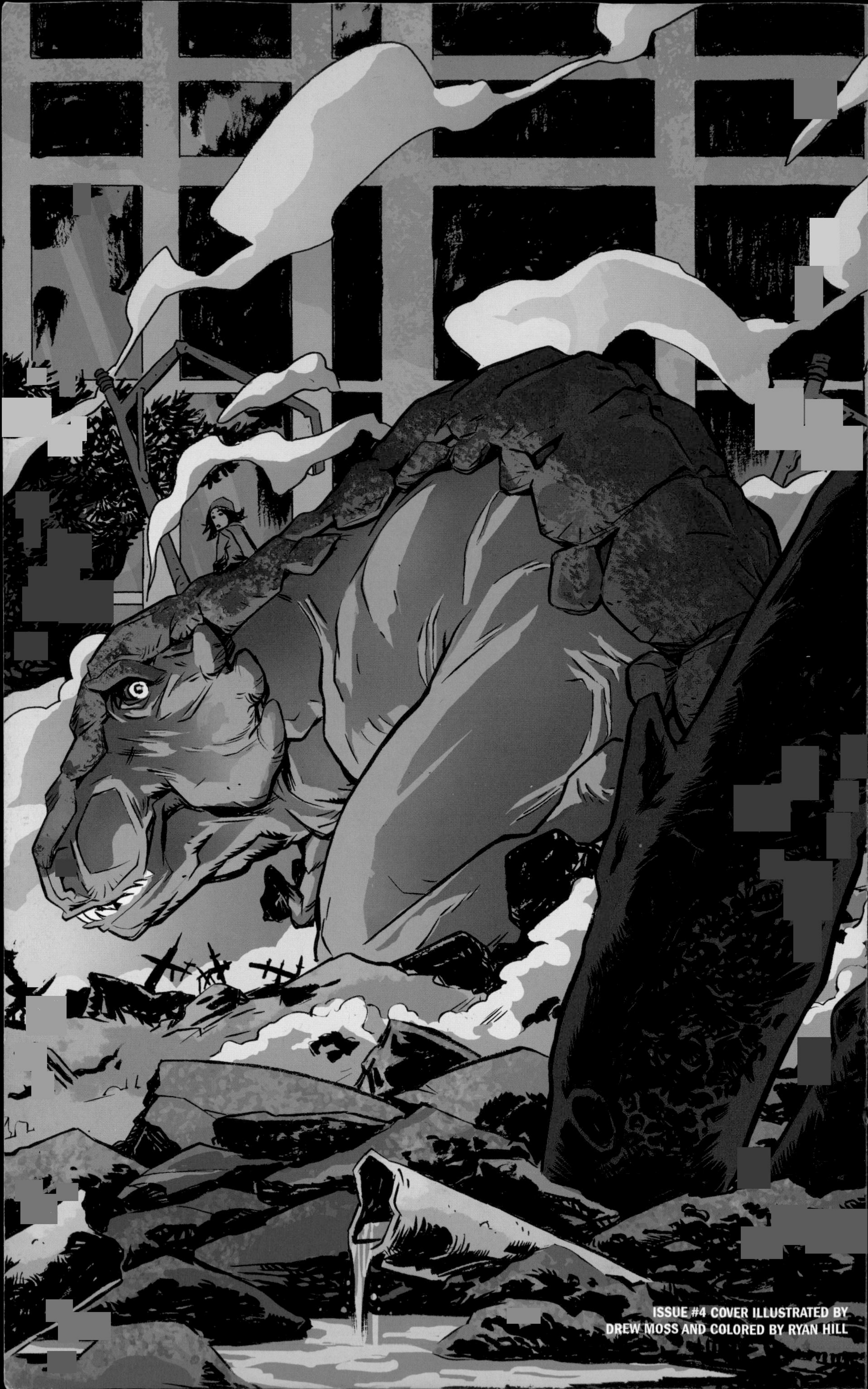

ISSUE #4 COVER ILLUSTRATED BY
DREW MOSS AND COLORED BY RYAN HILL

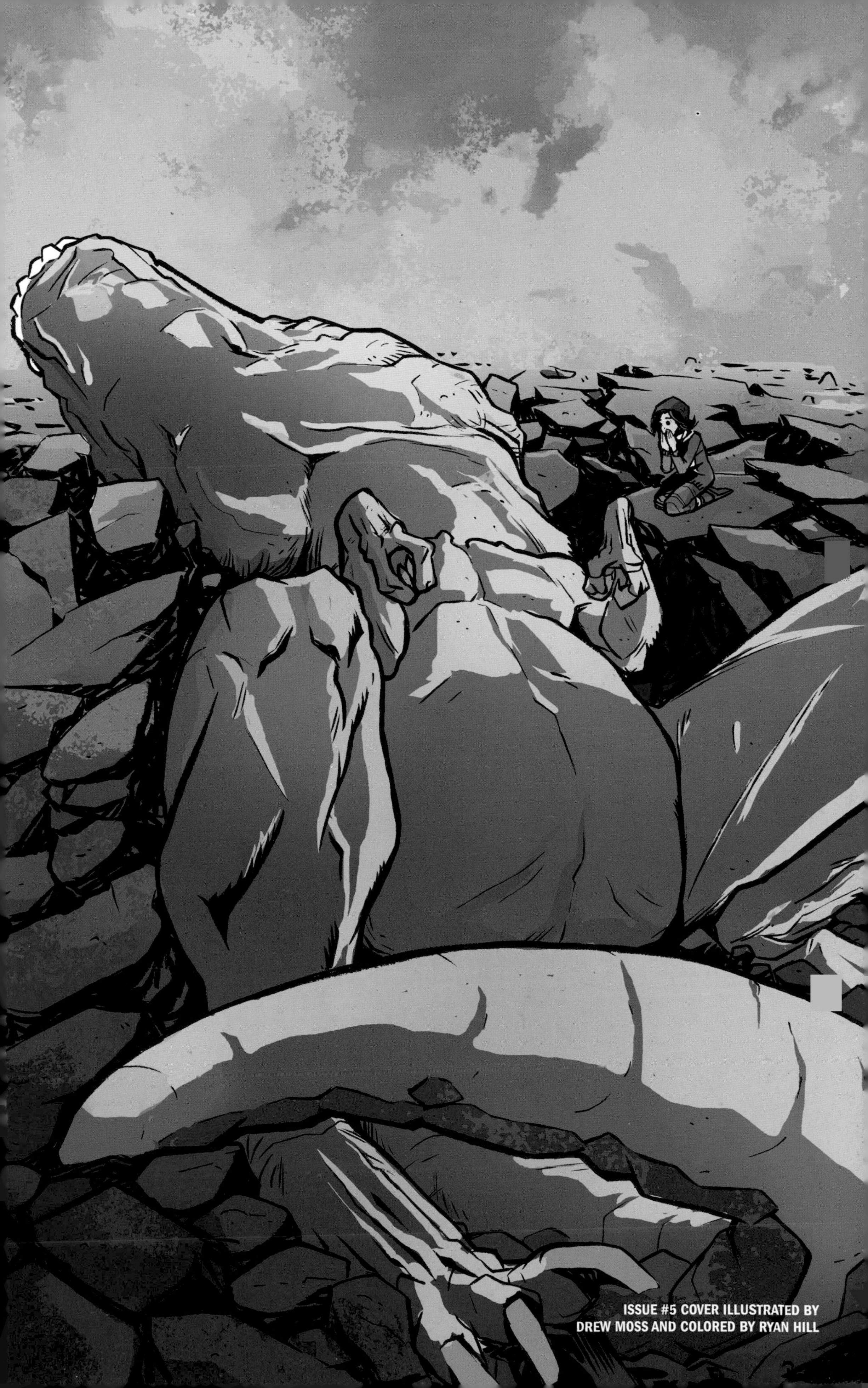

ISSUE #5 COVER ILLUSTRATED BY
DREW MOSS AND COLORED BY RYAN HILL

CULLEN BUNN is the writer of comic books such as *The Sixth Gun*, *Helheim*, *The Damned*, and *The Tooth* for Oni Press. He has also written titles including *Fearless Defenders*, *Venom*, *Deadpool Killustrated*, and *Wolverine* for Marvel Comics.

In addition, he is the author of the middle reader horror novel, *Crooked Hills*, and the collection of short fiction, *Creeping Stones and Other Stories*.

His prose work has appeared in numerous magazines and anthologies. Somewhere along the way, he founded Undaunted Press and edited the critically acclaimed horror zine *Whispers From the Shattered Forum*.

Cullen claims to have worked as an alien autopsy specialist, rodeo clown, pro wrestling manager, and sasquatch wrangler. He has fought for his life against mountain lions and performed on stage as the world's youngest hypnotist. Buy him a drink sometime, and he'll tell you all about it.

CULLENBUNN.COM
@CULLENBUNN

DREW MOSS is an illustrator that has worked for various comic publishers, with work including *Creepy* at Dark Horse, *The Crow: Pestilence and Zombies vs Robots* at IDW, and *Outlaw Territory* at Image.

He is a lover of monsters, superheroes, cigars, and fine baked goods. Drew resides in southeastern Virginia with his lovely wife, amazing kids, and Mowgli the Shar Pei.

FACEBOOK.COM/DREWERDMOSS
@DREW_MOSS

RYAN HILL lives in Portland, Oregon where he has worked within the comics industry for a little more than a decade. As an avid indoorsman, he has honed a desire to sit a computer all day and color comics. He's done this on books like *Stumptown*, *Judge Dredd: Mega City 2*, *Spongebob*, *Dark Matter*, *House of Night*, the upcoming *Effigy*, and *Age of Reptiles*. His mother keeps telling him the work looks nice and he's got real talent. He hopes she's right. She was right about "not eating desert all the time," so things are seeming pretty legit.

@JOSEPHRYANHILL

You might know **CHRIS CRANK**'s work from several recent Oni Press books like *The Sixth Gun*, *Brides of Helheim*, *Terrible Lizard*, and others. Or maybe you've seen his letters in *Revival*, *Hack/Slash*, *God Hates Astronauts*, or *Dark Engine* from Image. Or perhaps you've read *Lady Killer* or *Sundowners* from Dark Horse. Heck, you might even be reading the award winning *Battlepug* at battlepug.com right now!

If you're weird you could have heard him online at crankcast. net where he talks with Mike Norton, Tim Seeley, Sean Dove, and Jenny Frison weekly about things that are sometimes comics related.

If you're super-obscure you've heard him play music with the Vladimirs or Sono Morti at sonomorti.bandcamp.com.

You probably don't know who he is at all.

That's OK.

@CCRANK